BRAZEN

ALSO BY KATHERINE LONGSHORE

Gilt

Tarnish

BRAZEN

KATHERINE LONGSHORE

SIMON & SCHUSTER

First published in Great Britain by Simon & Schuster UK Ltd, 2014
A CBS COMPANY
First published in the USA in 2014 by Viking,
a member of Penguin Group (USA) Inc.

1 3 5 7 9 10 8 6 4 2

Simon & Schuster UK Ltd
1st Floor, 222 Gray's Inn Road
London WC1X 8HB

www.simonandschuster.co.uk

Simon & Schuster Australia, Sydney
Simon & Schuster India, New Delhi

A CIP catalogue record for this book is available
from the British Library

PB ISBN 978-1-4711-1698-8
E-Book ISBN 978-1-4711-1699-5

Printed and bound by CPI Group (UK) Ltd, Croydon, CR0 4YY

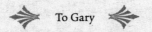 To Gary

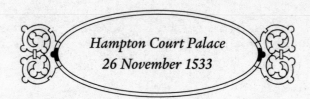

Hampton Court Palace
26 November 1533

MARRIAGE IS A WORD THAT TASTES LIKE METAL—THE STEEL OF armor, the gold of commerce, the iron bite of blood and prison bars.

But also bronze. A bell that rings clear and true and joyously. Like hope.

As my father guides me through the palace rooms to the chapel, I don't know which way the door to my cell will swing. It could ring loud, metal to metal, locking me into a life I never asked for. Or it could open wide, hinges creaking, into a life I never imagined.

I concentrate very hard on not tripping over my own train as we turn the final corner and proceed through the chapel doors. I will never hear the end of it from my mother if I blunder.

Henry FitzRoy is already there. Watching me.

My family has known him for years. When he was a child, Father helped organize his household, his tutors, his finances, his friends. My brother, Hal, was sent to Windsor to be his playmate.

But I don't know him. I don't know who he's become. All I remember is a little boy with golden-red hair and eyebrows that seemed to soar right off the top of his forehead. A little boy with no chin and an air of superiority.

It appears I'm marrying someone quite a bit more attractive.

His eyebrows still arc high into the fringe of hair ready to fall into his eyes at any moment. Eyes the color of a clear winter dawn. His nose is perhaps a little too big for the mouth below it, the full lower lip complementing the now well-defined chin.

The mouth tips into a smile. Of relief? Or of expectation?

As I watch, unmoving, one eyebrow curves even higher.

A question.

An invitation.

A challenge.

Father walks me to the altar. The shallow, barrel-vaulted ceiling looms heavy overhead. The magnificent stained-glass window in front of me filters the light of the wintry sky through depictions of the king and his first queen, Katherine. To either side of me stand witnesses dressed in gaudy blue and green and crimson. My eyes never leave the boy in front of me.

Father squeezes my arm and whispers, "Make me proud."

I say the only thing I can.

"I will."

We turn to face the priest and Father puts my hand in Henry FitzRoy's. His palm is rough beneath my fingers; his sleeve tickles my wrist. He is taller than I am, his presence beside me solid.

His breath comes easily, while mine is trammeled in my throat from fear.

And something else.

I search my heart. It can't be love. I don't even know this boy.

And it's not lust, despite his good looks. Besides, I don't really know what either of those is supposed to feel like.

I glance at my father out of the corner of my eye. See the glitter in his as he stares straight ahead, lips pressed against his teeth to suppress a grin. I recognize what I see there reflected in me.

Triumph.

A Howard marrying the son of the king.

"I take thee, Mary, to be my wedded wife."

FitzRoy sounds so assured, saying those words. As though making that promise is as easy as stepping into a role in a masque.

Which is really what we're doing. He wears the mask of husband. I represent wife. We will perform this showy little dance for the pleasure of king and courtiers, fathers and family.

Then we will exit the stage and go our separate ways.

I risk another glance from below my lashes.

FitzRoy catches me looking at him, and I turn quickly back to the priest. Watch the watery blue eyes floating in a sea of creases. Watch his mouth move, the words like vapors.

And then it's my turn.

"I take thee, Henry . . ."

I stumble once. *Till death us depart.* Death is so far away. We're only fourteen—*till death* is a long promise. It's a long time to be imprisoned by our *parents'* actions and not our own.

A breath of cold air brings gooseflesh to my arms and neck.

The priest takes my hand, his skin cool and papery, sliding like the discarded shell of a beetle. He places my right hand in that of my husband and binds us together with a white ribbon. Raises his hands in benediction.

Then it's over. All hands are dropped. FitzRoy and I turn together to face our collective families. My parents stand to my right, not touching, not speaking—in fact, each pretending the other doesn't exist. But together. In the same room. A miracle if there ever was one.

And suddenly, in the doorway, dressed in crimson and cloth of gold and shining like a newly fat sun, there is my husband's father. The king. And his wife, my cousin, Anne Boleyn. They must have been watching from the privy balcony, hidden above us.

The king calls me daughter and kisses me on the mouth. I fight the urge to wipe his spittle off as he claps his son on the shoulder.

"The bride and groom!" he shouts.

I look at my new husband again and find him already watching me. Bride and groom. Husband and wife. Strangers. I don't even know what to call him. Your Grace? Henry? Husband?

"Fitz!" My brother rescues me with a shout that rings off the windows. Hal kneels before the king and queen, then stands to throw his arms around my husband and pummels him.

"A married man, Fitz!" he shouts again, his joy contagious.

"Same as you, Hal."

My brother laughs, but with a little less mirth than before. I'm not sure he likes his wife.

Fear clutches at me and I look down at my hands.

"We're related now," Hal says, sounding overly gracious. "You can call me Surrey."

Mother and Father never called Hal anything but Surrey—making sure the earldom stuck for good. When the two Henrys met as children, they decided that calling each other by their first names was too confusing. And that Richmond and Surrey were too formal. Henry FitzRoy gave Hal his nickname. So Hal dubbed him Fitz in return.

Fitz laughs and wraps his arm around Hal's neck, nearly throwing him to the floor. The rest of the congregation charges forward, uplifting them both, so close there is no space between the bodies and I cannot breathe, my vision limited to the bright chevrons of green and blue on the sleeve in front of me.

I slide out between them all and swallow air like a landed fish.

"You blundered." My mother has dressed in black for the happy occasion, the velvet of her gown sucking the light from the chapel windows while the gold braid of her hood reflects it. Like a halo. The darkness of her eyes negating any semblance of divinity.

I try to still the trembling of my limbs.

"And slouched."

I stand up straight. Shoulders back. Neck elongated.

If my life is a prison, my mother is my jailer. Her words turn the locks of fourteen years of daughterhood, keeping them tightly closed.

The word *daughter* tastes of bitterness. At least in my mother's mouth, it does.

The group beside us bursts into raucous laughter, but we

are in our own little circle of misery. My mother's mouth turns down, the lines around it sharply defined.

I hold my breath. I know what that face precedes.

"A feast!" The king's voice breaks us apart and I take advantage of it to move closer to my father. He always takes my side.

That is why I will always take his. Even when it's the wrong one.

"And a celebration," Father says, his narrow face animated, "of the joining of families."

The king takes Queen Anne's arm and strides out the door into the cloister. My mother steps up behind them. She is the Duchess of Norfolk—second only to the king's kin and protective of her own precedence. She hesitates when my father doesn't move to join her. Glares her disapproval.

She opens her mouth and I cringe, waiting for the vitriol sure to spill forth.

"Your Grace." My new husband steps forward, nods his head in a quick bow.

Everyone stops—even the king and queen. They turn, eyeing the flow of people snagged in the doorway behind my mother.

"Your Grace," Fitz says again, quietly. Intimately. Yet his voice, rich and luxurious as velvet, deep and smooth, carries throughout the silent church. "Mother." He smiles, almost shyly. Engaging and embarrassed.

She hesitates.

And then she smiles back. I suppress a gasp.

"I feel I must remind you"—he pauses and leans closer to

her, his tall, supple frame curling slightly over her small, inflex-
ible form—"I am the Duke of Richmond and Somerset."

Mother goes pale.

"Your daughter is now my wife."

He cuts a quick sideways glance and a heart-stopping smile
my way.

"She is my duchess."

His.

His wife. His duchess. His prisoner, if he so chooses.

For the first time, I really look at him. Try to see the whole
and not just the parts. The eyes, brows, nose, mouth, chin
encompassed by a face still round with a boyhood completely
at odds with his bold self-confidence.

He raises an eyebrow into the flop of hair.

Definitely an invitation.

"She should have precedence." He unfurls his arm and holds
out his hand. To me.

I hesitate. I know that if I step in front of my mother, she
will never forgive me. But I do it anyway, my train whispering behind me. Or perhaps it is the hiss of Mother's breath as
she sucks it in through her teeth. I take Fitz's hand, warm and
tight and . . . comforting.

I allow my husband to escort me to the chapel door—behind
no one but the king and queen.

In the distance—beyond the great hall—I hear a bell ringing.

2

THE GREAT HALL CLAMORS WITH MUSIC, BOOT FALLS, AND THE collective voices of the hundred or so wedding guests. The mud carried in from the outside lies flat on the floor, leaving slick spots and the smell of earth. The food keeps coming, delivered first to the king and queen, then to my husband at the king's right.

And then to me, where I sit next to my father, just below the queen.

"What do you think of him?" Father asks.

I look down at the table, tracing the edge of it with a crumb of bread.

"He's handsome."

Father puts his fingers beneath my chin and lifts my face to his.

"It would serve you well to notice more than that." His voice is gentle, but carries a hidden steel. Like a dagger swathed in velvet. "He may be a bastard, but at least he's a boy. We expect great things. From both of you. You are the triumph of the Howards, Mary."

He releases me when he sees my mother approaching, and excuses himself quickly, leaving an empty chair and a half-full plate beside me.

My mother, still wearing black and an expression of deeply felt pain, kneels before the king, barely acknowledges the queen, and departs without giving me a first glance, much less a second.

Her absence should alleviate my discomfort, but I feel little relief. She is no longer watching me, but I am still on display.

"Congratulations, Cousin."

My thoughts made me forget that the queen sits beside me. I turn and bow my head, almost falling into her lap.

"Thank you, Your Majesty," I stutter.

She pulls me close and kisses me lightly on the cheek. She is only ten years older than I am, but the kiss is more motherly than anything I've ever received from the Duchess of Norfolk.

"May your marriage make you happy." The queen glances at the door my mother passed through. "And free."

"I don't know that I'll ever be free," I blurt, and immediately regret my words. It isn't my place to contradict the queen. But she laughs.

"You remind me of myself at your age," she says.

There are some people who make an impact as soon as you meet them. Lodge themselves in your mind. Embed themselves in your very soul.

Anne Boleyn is one of those people.

I am not. I can't even keep the attention of my new husband, who has not looked at me since we stepped into the hall.

Queen Anne is dark and poised and beautiful. I am clumsy enough to fall off a chair without moving, and my hair is the color of brass. She says exactly what is on her mind, while for all my love of words, I am afraid to use them at all.

"Thank you," I manage.

I want to smile. I remind her of herself?

The queen angles her body so she can speak to me more intimately. She wears a tight bodice that presses her breasts flat, tapering to a narrow waist. Her skirts are pleated at the hips to give an impression of curves. The peacock-blue damask only serves to make her coloring more striking.

"Your mother." Her voice is barely audible over the clamor of the wedding feast. "Is it true she opposed the match?"

When Mother found out that my father and Anne Boleyn had collaborated to marry me off to the king's son, she liberally employed the words *bastard* for my husband and *whore* for the queen.

She used worse for me when I acquiesced to Father's wishes.

"You will be sucked into the mire of Tudor refuse," she spat. "And if you deliberately defy me, I will be only too happy to watch you drown in your own muck."

I can barely meet the queen's eye.

"My mother . . . has firm opinions."

The queen laughs. "I can read equivocation as easily as I can understand Latin, Mary. Your mother opposes the match." Her dark eyes search my face. "What can she do about it?" She is truly looking for an answer this time. An honest one.

"Nothing, Your Majesty." The wedding is over.

"Nothing? She's the daughter of the Duke of Buckingham. The wife of the most powerful nobleman in the country."

"Forgive me, Your Majesty, but my grandfather is long dead, and my father hasn't spoken to my mother in years."

"A woman without male allies is a woman powerless, is that it?"

Her gaze penetrates me. She's daring me to speak my true mind.

The truth is that my mother has no allies. My brother avoids her. Father keeps a deliberate distance—even going so far as to lock her in her room. And yet the strength of her judgments unbalances us all.

"Power undetected is not the same as power*less*," I tell her.

"Well said, Cousin." The queen sits up again, our conversation open to the public.

"And what are your feelings, Mary?" she asks. "About your marriage."

I feel we have walked out onto a thin pane of ice over the Thames, the frigid blackness waiting to draw me under if I make a misstep. Above, all is blue sunshine and cheery laughter. But the water below moves swiftly.

"It is a great honor," I say finally. "For me and for my family."

"But you do not love him."

The little smile tugs at the corner of her mouth.

"I do not know him, Your Majesty."

That, at the very least, is the truth.

"Do you know who you are?" she asks. "Perhaps that is more important."

"I am a Howard," I say automatically.

"Not anymore," she says steadily. "You're a FitzRoy."

As if by the single swing of an ax, I am separated from the one truth that always held me secure. My father's name, my brother's name.

"You are more than a Howard or a FitzRoy or a wife or a daughter," the queen continues.

"My life is defined by those things."

"But *you* are not." The queen looks out over the crowd to where her brother, George, stands with Henry Norris and the poet Thomas Wyatt. The three men must be at least thirty years old—Norris is probably older—yet they maintain the air and attitude of adolescents. "I am a Boleyn. And the Boleyns always stick together." She turns back to me. "But I am also Anne. Able to make my own choices and speak my mind and fall in love, against all odds."

I glance at the king, his lips red from the wine, and back at my cousin, whose face has begun to show the seven years they spent fighting Queen Katherine, the country, and the pope for their right to marry. I wonder if love is worth the fight.

"What does love feel like, Your Majesty?" I ask.

"It's like music only plays when you're together," she says, not even pausing to think. "Like the very air tastes of strawberries. And like one touch—one look—could send you whirling like a seed on the wind. My brother's wife said that once, and I still believe it to be true."

I like the idea of *love* tasting like strawberries, but can't quite find it as I roll the word around on my tongue. So I nod, as if I understand. And wonder at the undercurrent of sadness in her voice.

She smiles at me and adds, "I hope we've stacked the odds in your favor. If Fitz is anything like his father, loving him will be a daily adventure."

Behind her, the king leans back, one hand on his belly, the other resting on the table beside hers. Their little fingers touching. He catches me staring and lifts her hand to kiss it.

I turn to look for Fitz. He has moved to sit with my brother, both of them leaning lazily against the wall, their feet up on stools, boot soles out. As if nothing in their lives has changed.

He doesn't look at me. My husband has not come within ten feet of me since we left the chapel. We've never even had a conversation.

The bridecup is passed. When it reaches me, it is slippery from the lips of all the others. The bridecake is consumed. And the evening starts to feel like fantasy—the atmosphere that comes with the overconsumption of celebration and wine and the underconsumption of reality.

Fitz wanders the room, greeting guests. I watch the way he walks, his movements completely uncalculated. The way he stands, his weight resting on one foot, cocked, as if ready to try anything next—running, dancing, riding.

I wonder if he's ready for this marriage.

"We must bed them!" George Boleyn stands by the fire, goblet raised, his dark eyes and narrow face alight with mischief and something not entirely innocent.

I can't move. A wedding—and banquet—is one thing. But the thought of getting into bed with a complete stranger makes me feel as if my skin is creeping with a thousand tiny feet.

Especially when the process is to be done in public.

I look for rescue. My father has already left. Hal is part of the cheering throng around Fitz.

The king frowns

"So be it."

There is no rescue.

3

I STAND UNSTEADILY, REACHING FOR THE TABLE. EITHER IT'S TIP-
ping or I am.

Fitz is in the corner, surrounded by men. He is by far the
youngest of them. Hal is nearly seventeen. Francis Weston—
also already married—is a few years older than that. George
Boleyn and Thomas Wyatt and Henry Norris are all thumping
on Fitz and whispering in his ear, and he's laughing and ges-
turing until he catches me watching.

He stops altogether and blushes like a redhead. Like a boy.
He's not ready for this, either. The other men roar.

I turn around quickly, pretending I'm going to my chamber to get ready. Pretending my heart isn't crawling out of my
throat.

I don't have to pretend relief when my friend Madge Shelton
throws her arms around me. She's two years older and half a
lifetime wiser than I am, but we've shared a bed in the maids'
chamber since Queen Anne's coronation, making her the closest friend I have at court in more ways than one. She, too, is
the queen's cousin—on the Boleyn side—so in a way, we're also
family.

"This is going to be fun!" Madge crows.

I can't return the smile. All those men. Watching.

"It's humiliating," I tell her, not looking at the raucous crowd behind me.

"It's just blessing the union," Madge says. "It's not like they're going to take you through it step by step." I can taste the laughter just under the surface of those words.

Rumor has it that Madge had an affair with Thomas Wyatt, who has been married for at least ten years and publicly separated from his wife for almost that long. All I know is that early on in our friendship, there were a handful of nights she didn't spend in our bed. When I finally asked, she said his heart wasn't in it. Whatever that means.

Queen Anne approaches and we curtsy.

"Your Majesty," Madge says, "your permission to attend the duchess in her chamber?"

The queen smiles broadly. "Of course, Mistress Shelton."

And she winks. The queen winks at us. Then she turns and leaves the hall.

Madge pulls me up the broad stairs and down a gallery.

"Where are we going?" I ask.

"To his apartments, of course." Madge negotiates a cluster of maids by the chapel. "There's a dressing chamber that leads into them. We'll get you ready there."

"How do you know all this?" I ask, trying to keep up in the rabbit warren.

Madge pauses and whispers in my ear. "I make it my business to know *everything* about the handsome men of the court." This time she laughs out loud. More like a cackle.

She slips into a plainly decorated room, pulls me in behind her, and closes the door. I back up to it, flattening my palms against the oak, and scan the room for another exit. There is a door, just opposite. I hear shuffling and laughter percolating through it.

"I don't think I can do this."

"Of course you can!" Madge says. "It's your duty." She shakes her head and waggles the little volume of Chaucer she always keeps hanging from the chain at her waist. "No, actually, it's *his*. The Wife of Bath says that man is a debtor, and must yield his wife his debt."

"A debt doesn't sound very romantic," I say. Madge is always going on about the romance of Chaucer, but I don't entirely see it. Of course, I'm not a poet. Not like my brother. All I do is play with words.

Reading Chaucer always makes me doubt myself.

"The debt isn't romantic," Madge says, unpinning my hood and gently unweaving my hair from its plait. "It's purely sexual."

The thought makes me want to cross my legs. I'm not ready for this. Not ready for marriage. Not ready to be a duchess.

I don't even know if I deserve to be.

I press myself harder against the door.

"I don't know how to do this," I admit.

Madge drops her hands to my shoulders and looks me in the eye.

"You don't have to know how," she says. "You just do."

"I don't know how to be married!" I cry, and then look

away from her. "And I don't know how to be a duchess."

"Learn by example."

I laugh hollowly. "The only two duchesses I've ever known are the king's sister—God rest her blackened soul—and my mother. The only marriage I've ever seen up close is my parents' disaster." Every interaction between them ended with my mother's fists and my father's abandonment.

"You can learn about marriage by watching the queen and king." Madge runs her fingers through my hair, pulling skeins of it over my shoulders. "You know, he said he'd rather beg alms from door to door than give her up. That's true love."

It was like a romantic ballad. What they went through—falling in love, being kept separate by rules and the Church of Rome. And what she became. My cousin, Anne Boleyn—a nobody. A queen. The woman with the most loving husband in England.

"They are perfect together."

"Yes," Madge says dreamily. "And when he looks at her—have you seen it?"

"It's like his gaze is a nod. As if he agrees not only with everything she says but with everything she is."

"We could all aspire to have someone love us that much."

"That kind of love can change your life."

Madge bites her lip and lets me go. Something in her stance—in the way she holds herself so tightly—keeps me in my place.

"What is it?" I ask.

"Now that you are a duchess, will you forget about me?" she asks. Her voice, normally full and resonant, is nothing but a thin whisper. I am so stunned, I can't even answer.

"You'll be dining with the queen and probably sleeping in her room, and all the women will want to be like you and all the men will want to be *with* you, and I'll be . . ." She looks dejectedly around the plain, empty room, the sickly light from the candle not enough to reach the corners.

"You'll be happy," she says. "And I'll still be me."

Her body feels like wood when I wrap my arms around her, but after a second, her shoulders relax a little and her hands release their fists.

"What would I do without you?" I ask. "I don't know what I'm doing! I don't even know how to kiss a boy, much less"—I swallow for effect—"anything else."

I hold her at arm's length and look into her eyes. "Whom else can I talk to?"

"I'm sure someone will be willing to be your friend," Madge grumbles, but I see a smile beginning on her face, and her voice is stronger. Louder. More Madge.

"I don't want another friend. I certainly don't need another *best* friend. I've got you."

Madge decided we would be friends when I first set foot in court and we were assigned to be bedmates. I decided we would be inseparable.

"What about your husband?"

I tell Madge the same thing I told the queen. "I don't even know him."

"In the biblical sense?" Madge smirks.

There's a loud thump from the next room, and Hal's shout

travels clearly through the door. "Take his boots off!"

I move back to the other exit.

"Surely it's not required . . ." I leave off the rest of my sentence. I didn't imagine we'd have to remove our clothing before the bedding ceremony.

"Wouldn't that shock them all?" Madge says. "Maybe you should, just to see their faces!"

"It's not *you* parading yourself in front of the most important men in the court."

"But I would!" she cries. "And we'll put a veil on me and he'll think I'm you! And it will incite him to lust after you for years and years and he'll never stray, just like the knight in the Wife of Bath's tale."

"I think you just want to get my brother's attention."

"I love his poetry," Madge says quickly.

I leave the safety of the door to tug at the hem of her hood, and she squeaks.

"It's true!" she cries, edging away from me in a crouch, giggling. "His shoulders are poetry. His legs are poetry. His face is poetry."

"Hold your tongue, Madge; he's my *brother*!"

"His ass is poetry!"

Madge turns to run and I chase her, tripping over the end of my train.

Our laughter is suddenly echoed from the bedchamber on the other side of the door by the kind of laughter that comes with ribald jokes. It rocks the walls and douses my giggles.

The door flies open and the glaze of candlelight blinds me.

"Like a startled deer!" a voice shouts.

"Like a lamb to slaughter," says another.

"Be gentle with her, FitzRoy." I recognize Wyatt's voice.

Madge pushes me into the chamber. "Go make him love you."

Even completely dressed, I feel naked beneath their stares. My skirts are huge. The pink brocade bodice binds me so tightly I can feel the pounding of my heart against it.

The men bow. All of them. Hal stands first and smiles. He's been through it all himself. Under similar circumstances.

Then I realize he is looking over my shoulder. At Madge.

A giant tester bed piled with damask and fur dominates the room. Gorgeous and barren.

Fitz is pummeled forward from the crowd. They've removed his boots and stockings, his bare feet vulnerable on the wooden floor.

"Enter and enjoy!" George Boleyn calls, and bows to the howl of laughter that follows.

His wife, Jane, brings a stool and places it at my feet. When she straightens, she whispers in my ear.

"Tonight is just for show," she tells me. "You have time to fall in love."

I think of how she told the queen that love tastes of strawberries and try to smile before taking her hand to climb into the bed, Fitz beside me.

We don't touch.

The priest flicks his holy water and bows his head. He mutters his Latin and gives us his blessing.

Then comes the moment when everyone should leave the room. When we should be left alone to do what married couples do. Fitz starts to climb back out of the bed.

"Give her a kiss, Your Grace!" Wyatt says. Ever the tempter and purveyor of young love.

Fitz turns to me, eyebrows raised in question. Not a challenge—a request for permission.

I nod. Just a tiny bit. Thinking of the suggestions the men made that I never heard. Thinking of his body so close to mine, both of us burdened with layers of velvet and damask and heavy gold braid. Both of us watched so closely—our audience half hoping to see us fall into each other's arms, while half afraid that we will.

And I am excruciatingly aware of my lips. Are they too dry? I daren't lick them. What do I do with my nose? How do I turn my head?

My husband leans into me, the mattress tipping us toward each other like the concave mouth of a vault. Our shoulders touch and we both startle back, laughing nervously. The crowd roars.

Fitz leans forward again and raises his left hand to my face, partially sheltering us from the gaze of the spectators. I close my eyes.

"You're beautiful."

My eyes fly open. He smiles and leans ever so slightly closer. His words taste like bridecake and hippocras fruit and cinnamon and sweet wine. I wonder if his mouth tastes of the same.

The mattress lurches, and my nose thumps his painfully. I

lean back, rubbing my nose, trying to blink away the tears that burn the corners of my eyes.

My brother worms his way between us, flinging himself back onto our pillows and putting his hands behind his head.

"Enough of that, children," he says with a grin. "There will be no kissing and cuddling in this bed tonight."

Fitz groans and falls back, mimicking Hal's posture, both of them looking up into the folds and drapes of the canopy. They look like brothers, so easy in each other's presence. Even their facial expressions mirror each other—Hal's wide eyes and long nose, Fitz with his soaring eyebrows and tiny mouth.

"By decree of your parents—and the king—you are forbidden to consummate this marriage," Hal declares to the canopy as the rest of the company in the room mutter and judge. "At least until such a time as you are deemed of an age to be emotionally, physically, and morally mature enough to do so only for the production of an heir and not for any fun whatsoever."

Despite the wedding, the banquet, and the bedding ceremony, we are not allowed to sleep together. Which is a relief.

Half the room bursts into guffaws and the other hisses. A hand reaches in to pull Hal from the bed.

"All of you out, now." The priest. Of course.

"You can resist everything but temptation," Hal declares, shaking off the hand and leaning in close to us. "But I can find a way to allow you to indulge it if you wish."

He waggles his eyebrows at Fitz, and I have to look away. My own brother.

"Because a marriage isn't really a marriage until it's

consummated." Hal's voice lowers even more. "I should know."

We're all too young. At the mercy of our parents. And the boys—the boys are too valuable.

"Think on it!" Hal cries as the priest pulls him bodily from the bed. He stumbles exaggeratedly, steadying only when he falls into Madge's arms.

Hal isn't allowed to sleep with his wife. But that doesn't stop him from sleeping with other girls.

I wonder if Fitz will be the same. I wonder if I care.

I don't even know him.

I risk a glance and catch Fitz staring at me. No. Not at me, at my lips.

I'm not sure I want to be married.

But I wanted that kiss.

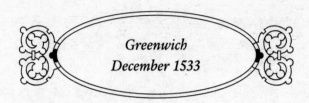

Greenwich
December 1533

4

Every morning throughout the four weeks of Advent, I expect to wake to the sounds of the girls in the maids' chamber. I expect to hear laughter and coughing and the gasp when bare feet hit the cold floor. I expect to be woken by Madge bouncing on the end of my bed.

But I am awakened by the silence of my own room. To the curtains of my own bed closed against the chill.

When I wake up, I am a duchess.

The word *duchess* is like cake. Crumbly. Gravelly with sugar and almond paste. Sweet and rich.

And empty.

The aloneness reminds me of my childhood. Of Kenninghall, battered by wind and bleached bone-dry by my mother's presence. In the bleak heath of Norfolk, it was impossible to get warm or to feel loved.

On Christmas Day, I huddle under furs and velvets, my toes and fingers stinging with cold the fire does little to dispel. I tuck everything in around me, leaving no gaps of air and pulling the fabric right up over my head, only my nose and hair exposed. I'm conserving all my heat in a little cocoon of middling warmth.

I wish I had another body to share it with. Anyone warmer than I am. I would go back to the maids' chambers and sleep with Madge, gladly tolerating her flailing limbs.

But I no longer belong there.

I am now one of the queen's ladies. I have more freedom. And less. I serve the queen, but I am not her servant. I am here by invitation, not by pledge. I can come and go as I please.

I just have nowhere else to go. It's not like I wish to visit my mother.

Suddenly the door bangs open, and I just have time to cower further into my covers when the curtains are drawn apart with a violent jerk.

"No rest for the wicked!" Madge crows, leaping onto the bed.

I groan and roll over. I missed her sleeping presence, but not her raucous awakenings.

"Up, lazy bird," she chirps, and smacks me once on the ass. She stands shakily, wobbling precariously close to my head. And then jumps—twice—for good measure.

She's wearing a gown of a deep, almost shimmery blue, and her kirtle and the plastron of her bodice are orangey-red.

"You look like a kingfisher," I mumble at her.

"And you're moaning like a goose."

She drops back to the floor and pulls the counterpane all the way off of me. I immediately start to shiver and roll toward the edge of the bed, gathering the furs around me again.

"Just because you're a *lady* now doesn't mean you can loll in bed all day."

"I don't feel old enough to be a lady." I should just be a maid of the court. Like I was a month ago. A little girl with flat hips and no cleavage. And yet suddenly I'm a woman.

"Certainly not old enough to sleep with your husband, according to the king."

"On the contrary," I argue. "*He* is not old enough to sleep with me."

"You're the same age! It's a ridiculous notion that it could kill a boy. It should make him stronger. Boost his confidence."

"The king claims it killed his brother."

"Don't believe it, Duchess." Madge opens up my clothes chest and digs through it. "So." She pulls out an azure-blue bodice and holds it up to her chest. "How is married life?"

"You would know as well as I," I grumble.

"But I'm not married." She puts it back and pulls out a pair of green sleeves.

"Exactly." I flop back onto my bed to let my head hang off the side of it, my hair trailing almost all the way to the rushes on the floor. Sometimes, it's easier to look at the world upside down. "I don't feel like I am, either."

I've seen Fitz, of course. At the banquets and dances. He doesn't dance. And generally he spends his time out of doors, when the weather is fine. Sometimes, even when it isn't.

It's almost like he's avoiding me.

Madge picks up my pink wedding bodice and dances it in front of her in what I'm sure she thinks is an enticing manner. I stick my tongue out at her.

"What do you mean?" she asks, throwing the bodice at me.

"Well, between Christmas and hawking and"—I wave my

31

arm at the window—"tilting or whatever they do out there, I feel like I don't even exist."

"Welcome to my world," Madge mutters.

"Oh, Madge," I sigh. "I don't mean to say I deserve your sympathy. I know I have it all. The position. The friendship of the queen. The . . . husband." I sigh again. "I just thought it would be different. I thought I would be . . . happier."

Madge puts on a suitably sympathetic expression.

"You know what you need?" she asks. She squats down to look me full in the face. Her features are upside down, her little bow mouth above her nostrils.

I don't much like looking into her nostrils.

"What?" I roll back over and sit up. I want the answer. The one thing that will rescue me. Make my life perfect. Finally.

"You need to make him fall in love with you."

"I don't think that can be dictated."

"Perhaps just fornication, then."

"Madge!" I swing my feet from the bed, dragging the furs after me.

"There's a prize offered for virginity!" she cries, waving her miniature Chaucer in my face.

I reach for her hood and she runs off, shrieking, back to the chest of clothes. She selects a skirt the color of midnight, embroidered in gold, and looks at me with her head cocked to the side.

I shake my head. "I don't think the Wife of Bath really has anything to say to me, Madge," I tell her. "No one has offered a prize for my virginity. I get to keep it."

Madge makes a *humph* sound and reaches back into the chest, this time pulling out a gown so orange it makes my eyes hurt. She holds it up to her chin. The color looks good on Madge, with her dark hair and deep-blue eyes. I really should give it to her.

"That one makes me look sickly," I say instead. My hair is practically orange in itself. And my eyes are pale. More gray than green.

Beautiful. That's what Fitz said.

He has to notice me eventually. Maybe I have to *make* him notice me.

"I'll wear this one," I say quickly, picking up the pink bodice. "And the pale-green sleeves."

"These?" Madge holds up a sleeve the color of spring grass.

"No." Suddenly feeling urgent, I go to the chest myself and start digging in it. I want the green sleeves and the wine-colored kirtle. They're different from the wedding garments. But they still look good against my skin, without showing off any freckles. I reach deeper, and our hands get tangled, so Madge steps back, laughing.

"I say, it's a good thing you have a maid," she says. "I don't see how anyone can keep track of your things. You have absolutely no regard for order."

Maybe that's why I can't write poetry.

"One of the perks of being a duchess," I say, and swing around from the chest with my treasures.

"Trying to impress someone?" Madge asks, helping me into the bodice.

Madge tightens the laces with a tug sharp enough to make me gasp. But it's easy not to answer her questions. She wants to think she's learning my secrets but is really more interested in telling her own.

"Are *you*?" I ask her.

"Maybe I'm trying to seduce your brother."

I don't respond immediately, but pull my skirts around me, pretending to fumble with the fastenings. It should seem natural. My friend and my brother. A few months ago, I would have been overjoyed. But it bothers me that poor Frances de Vere—Hal's wife—is out in Kenninghall with my mother. Waiting for a time when she can consummate her marriage. Is she waiting for Hal to fall in love with her? Just like I'm waiting for Fitz?

But Fitz doesn't know me. Has never spoken to me. Just as Hal has never known his wife. Fitz has never even kissed me. What if he's with someone else, and his marriage to me is just a legality?

"What?" Madge asks, standing back.

"He's married," I blurt.

"It's flirtation only, Mary. And flirting can do no harm." Madge widens her eyes and presses her lips together in a pout.

"Your innocent act will work wonders, I'm sure."

Madge cackles and heads to the door. But before she reaches it, she stops, her shoulders rising with tension. And she steps aside. To let me go first.

I'm not the only one still trying to get used to the fact that I'm a duchess.

Greenwich is much more tightly quartered than Hampton

Court. The lodgings are all on top of each other. I still don't warrant rooms as good as my father's, but at least I'm in the castle proper, and not out past the courtyards or down near the stables.

I don't have to get my feet wet in the rain.

As we traverse the little rooms and galleries and climb the stairs of the donjon, the other ladies and courtiers step aside. They bow and curtsy, and some of the servants even call blessings.

I feel like a fraud. Like I'm playing a game. Pretending to be regal. Pretending to be elevated. I'm just a little girl in nice clothes. Married, but not married. Daughter of a duke. Wife of a duke. But really . . . nothing.

Just like Mother said, the day I told her I'd agreed to marry the king's son.

"You will always be subject to the king's will," she said. "Not a Howard. Certainly not a Stafford. And in the end you will amount to nothing."

I've always had my mother to tell me who I am. Or at least how I should act. Stand up straighter. Walk more slowly. Keep your head still. Keep your head up. *Keep your damn head up!*

I snap my head up. I've been watching my feet, as I did as a child.

I wish I knew what I was doing.

I wish someone could tell me. Someone besides my mother. I can't ask my father—I can't risk him thinking that I'm stupid. That I'm not worthy of this honor. I can't tell Fitz. I almost laugh at the very idea.

I glance over my shoulder. Madge is frowning.

I can't ask her, either. She thinks all my problems are solved already. She may be my dearest friend, but this has already started to come between us. This and my brother.

Even before we reach the queen's watching chamber, I hear the buzz from her rooms. It fizzes down the stairs and hums on the landing. My footsteps slow of their own accord. I can picture the crowd already. The press of doublets and sleeves, feet tangled in skirts that aren't their own. The inability to escape stray elbows or rank breath.

Madge reaches forward and squeezes my hand. Only she knows that I'm not comfortable entering a crowded room. I gather up my courage and my skirts and walk through the open doors.

The room is a riot of color. Walls and windows and courtiers decked in greater finery than usual. In spite of my wedding bodice, I feel underdressed.

"Happy Christmas!" Henry Norris cries, and then announces my presence to the room. "The Duchess of Richmond and Somerset."

The entire assembly sinks to the floor.

Except the queen, of course.

My breath leaves me. "Mistress Shelton." Norris is bent in reverence over Madge's hand. Her face is lit like a candelabrum. She's truly beautiful in her kingfisher dress.

It's no wonder I get lost in a crowd.

"Come," Madge whispers in my ear. "Let's play that we're at court."

She sweeps me into a dance of her own devising, improvising to the flow of the music, with much swirling of skirts. Her movements are extravagant and spontaneous, and she doesn't care a whit what others are saying or thinking or judging. Or that they're laughing.

She whips me around and lets go, and in my dizziness I spin directly into a girl who has just walked in the door. She is very tall and thin, with a long, narrow nose and a swath of rich mahogany hair showing beneath her hood. Her gray eyes are sharp and her gaze penetrating.

I've met her before. She's Margaret Douglas, the king's niece. Daughter of his older sister and a Scottish earl.

She used to live in the household of Lady Mary—the king's daughter with Katherine of Aragon. I'd heard she might be moved to court, and here she is. In June, during Anne Boleyn's coronation, Margaret had worn an expression of detachment. I'd thought at the time that she didn't accept Anne as queen. Now I wonder if she is just proud.

A moment stretches into eternity as we gaze at each other. She does not curtsy.

Neither do I. I don't know if I'm supposed to.

Margaret is in the line of succession to the throne. I am the wife of the king's only son. By law, the king's children should inherit based on sex and birth order. But Fitz is the son of the king's mistress, not his wife. Lady Mary, the king's oldest daughter, was declared illegitimate and stricken from the succession when the king's marriage to Katherine of Aragon was annulled.

That leaves three-month-old Elizabeth, Anne's daughter.

And King Henry's nieces.

No one wants a queen to rule. Least of all a baby. Or a Scot, like Margaret.

If the king can change the legitimacy of his eldest daughter, could he change the legitimacy of his son? Am I a princess? A duchess? Or just a girl?

"I believe my royal blood takes precedence."

Margaret's voice is low and even. Confident. She knows who she is and where she belongs.

I start to bow, but am interrupted.

"In this court, Lady Margaret, you and the Duchess of Richmond are equal."

The room comes back in a rush—the press of bodies, the reek of sweat, the chains of gossip—and both of us turn together to curtsy to the queen.

I watch Margaret from the corner of my eye. Her back is straight and her head bowed, but she is still regal. Restrained. She has done this her entire life.

If we are equal, I still have a lot to learn. And I hope I've found the person I'll learn it from.

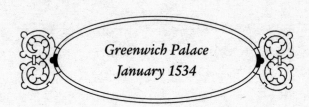

Greenwich Palace
January 1534

5

JANUARY COMES ON THE ICY FEET OF WINTER AND THE COURT IS awash in gifts. Everyone gives something to the king and queen—this is a requirement. With the hundreds of gifts they receive each year, you'd think it wouldn't matter if one person neglects her duty.

But it does.

My mother doesn't send a gift to Anne Boleyn. This shouldn't surprise me—the terms Mother used to describe my cousin were never fit to be repeated. But Mother has always sent gifts to the queen on January first.

This year, Mother sends oranges to Katherine of Aragon. She was called queen since before I was born but is now just Princess Dowager, as the king claims they were never legally married, despite a ceremony and twenty years of cohabitation. Mother's offering is duly noted by the court. And I hear whispers when I leave a room.

I give the queen a small book of poetry that I copied out myself. It isn't much, but at least it is personal. It's not my own poetry, of course. Just a couple of Hal's better pieces. And one or two by Thomas Wyatt. Madge insists I include Chaucer, reading over my shoulder as I write.

My father supervises my gift to the king. He says it must be expensive. And impersonal, in case the king decides to pass it on to someone else.

"It's the perception of the thing that matters," Father tells me. "The fact that you gave him something. That he received it."

So with much trepidation, I give the king a little gold tablet set with pearls. He kisses me wetly on the cheek and thanks me and gives me a ring in return, from his own stash of gifts.

I recognize the ring. Margaret Douglas gave it to him. After I thank him, I hide it in the pocket at my waist and hope she hasn't noticed.

I have a gift to give Fitz—a gold ring decorated with an enameled white lion, the symbol of the dukedom of Richmond. But I'm not sure how to give it to him. I don't understand the protocol. I see him at the far end of the great hall. But I cannot penetrate the wall of people to reach him.

The crowds threaten to smother me. I escape the castle to go to the empty orchard, the bare-branched trees running dark and bony up the hill toward Duke Humphrey's Tower. The grass is wet underfoot, but at least there are no bodies pressing into me. I'm not breathing in someone else's stale air.

"Duchess!"

Only one person calls me that. And she shouldn't. I turn to see Madge struggling up the hill in heavy skirts already soaked.

"This is for you," she says, thrusting a package at me, thumping me in the stomacher.

"For me?" I ask. "Why, Madge, you shouldn't have."

"It's not from me, Duchess," she replies. She raises an eyebrow and grins wickedly. "It's from your husband."

How did she get close to him when I couldn't?

I take the gift and slowly unwrap it. It's a book. Bound simply in leather, stamped with gold. The pages are thick, and creamy. And blank.

Not a single word written on them.

"Not even a love note?" Madge takes the book from me. Flips through it. Turns it upside down, holding it by its spine to shake it.

A piece of parchment flutters out. She swoops down on it like a falcon diving for prey and smooths it open.

"'For your words,'" she reads aloud.

I feel like I'm in a crowded room, hardly able to breathe. What does he know about my words? What does he know about me?

Madge turns the paper over. "That's *it*?"

"Well, what did he say?" I ask. "When . . . when he gave it to you?"

"*He* didn't give it to me," she says. "He gave it to someone else, who asked me to deliver it."

Of course it was Hal to whom Fitz gave it. And of course it would be Madge whom Fitz asked to deliver it.

I touch the letters stamped on the front cover.

"M. F."

"Your initials."

"M. H.," I remind her. "I'm a Howard."

"Mary *FitzRoy*. Ownership stamped in gold and bound in leather."

I run my finger along the two letters again. FitzRoy. Not Howard.

"Perhaps it's to write your own love letters in," Madge continues. "Or poetry."

Hal is the poet. I look away.

"Ahhhh," Madge croons, leaning close again. "Love poetry, perhaps? Something by your brother. Or Thomas Wyatt? Something swoonworthy and seductive." She pauses. "Or Chaucer!"

"I imagine I can write in it anything I please."

"It seems a very impersonal gift," Madge says, taking it from me and flipping through the blank pages. "The least he could have done was to leave a note."

But he did. And I've got it folded in the palm of my hand.

For your words.

He knows something about me. And I know nothing about him.

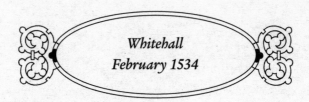

Whitehall
February 1534

6

It's so easy for him. He spends his days surrounded by friends. Sure of his position. At his father's side.

He doesn't have to think every moment about the way he walks, the way he holds his head, the way people look at him. He doesn't have to *be* a duke. He just *is* one.

I wake up every day feeling like me, and then I remember. I'm not me, anymore. I'm a duchess. And I need to act like one. So I spend the entire day as if on a stage. Always watched, but never listened to.

The entire court moves to York Place—or Whitehall, as it's called now. But everyone still calls it by its old name. From here, we are close to the City and Westminster, and most of the men find excuses to escape the palace boundaries.

My freedom is more restricted, but the combination of more space and fewer people gives me a chance to breathe. I find myself a little in love with Whitehall, with its interconnected rooms and the windowed galleries right along the Thames.

I seek out Margaret Douglas. She was born into this. Her mother was King Henry's sister, and queen of Scotland. But after the Scots king died, her mother's second marriage, to

Archibald Douglas, went horribly awry, and Margaret grew up under the protection of her uncle.

Margaret has true royal blood in her veins, not the murky depths the Howards cling to. Or the lineage of treason and betrayal that rocks the foundations of my mother's side of the family. Not that my mother would ever lose her balance.

I find Margaret in a bubble of quiet at the far side of a sparsely populated gallery. I thread my way between posturing courtiers to stand in front of her. But I have no idea how to begin.

"What?" She doesn't take her eyes off the book in her lap.

"What do you mean?" I'm embarrassed and pretend to gaze out the window. The fog has rolled in off the Thames and seems to swallow the palace whole.

"You're staring at me."

"I'm sorry."

Margaret sighs and looks up at me. I see a resemblance to Fitz, her cousin. Her hair is less red and her mouth wider, but she does have the slightly pouty lower lip and the long nose, and her eyebrows arch like question marks over her dark eyes. She's stunning.

"What do you want, Your Grace?" she asks. "You came here for a reason."

I can't just ask her to teach me how to be royal.

All I've succeeded at is making myself look stupid. And possibly a bit deranged.

"Peace and quiet?"

It seems like a reasonable request. Court is noisy. Crowded. There is no such thing as privacy.

"I'll leave you to it, then."

Margaret shakes out her sleeves, picks up her book, and stands. This is where Mother would point out everything I've done wrong. My manner is wrong; my state of dress is wrong. Probably wanting to befriend Margaret in the first place is wrong.

"I didn't mean—"

"To offend me?"

She rests her book on her hip, held in place by her hand. Her knuckles are larger than most women's, her fingers long and slender. Not like mine, which almost appear jointless, merely short, round sausages. She makes a noise deep in her throat and I look back up at her hard expression, the eyes giving nothing away.

"To take my place by the window?" she asks. "To displace me?"

"Displace you?" I ask.

"From my seat. From my place at court."

She means that I have risen suddenly from being the awkward daughter of a duke to claiming a status comparable to hers.

"I didn't ask for your seat or your place." I don't intend to ingratiate myself, but years of living with my mother have made my tone habitually subservient.

"Did you not hear the queen? We are *equal*. I am the king's niece, and who are you?"

No one. I refuse to repeat my mother's words. But I hear them. Feel them.

"I'm married to the king's son."

"And he will displace me in the succession," Margaret says. "Just you wait and see. Even Elizabeth could be surpassed by a boy—no matter that he's illegitimate. Especially if that boy has a son."

I almost choke. "Fitz is unlikely to have a son anytime soon. He won't even look at me."

Margaret blinks. And then laughs. "I've never met anyone so . . . honest before, Your Grace."

"My mother says it's my worst fault." I reconsider this. In my mother's eyes, all of my faults are heinous. And countless.

"Your mother comes from good, dishonest stock."

I frown. She means my grandfather, the Duke of Buckingham, executed twelve years ago for his pretensions to the throne.

"I think many of us hope to leave a better legacy than our parents," I tell her.

Margaret looks away, twists her long fingers around her book, and then regards me steadily. "Forgive me. I did not mean to disparage your family."

"And I did not mean to displace you," I say, hoping my tone conveys that I feel no offense. "I also did not mean to chase you from your window seat. I only sought a place to sit, and an amiable companion."

"So, not peace and quiet."

A wicked smile lifts her lips as she throws the half lie back at me. She has proven that honesty is not my greatest fault.

She sits and pats the window seat beside her. I acquiesce silently.

"You're a duchess," Margaret says, tilting her chin down and looking at me critically. "And you don't know how to be."

Her assessment hits me like a slammed door. I stare straight ahead, unseeing, into the gallery. And I say nothing. I don't belong anywhere else, either.

"Your mother is one," she says. "Follow her example."

"God forbid." The words spill out and I can't take them back. Treacherous tongue, slandering a Howard.

But Margaret laughs. It transforms her. Softens her. Just enough so I think I can tell her the truth.

"Margaret," I begin. "I was never going to amount to much. Hal was always an earl, and always going to be a duke. Mother even hoped the dukedom of Buckingham would be revived for him and he'd be two dukes in one, like Fitz. But me? At best, I aspired to marry an earl. Possibly only a knight with delusions of grandeur. That's what the Howards do with their girls."

Margaret sniffs. "True. Look at your aunt."

"Which one?"

Margaret chuckles. "You have a Howard aunt who married a grasping knight, and she is now mother to the queen. You never know where luck and good placement will take you." Her smile disappears in an instant. "Some of us are not so lucky. You should embrace it."

"Can you help me?" I ask suddenly. "I feel like a fraud. Especially when people call me 'Your Grace.' I have never had grace, and the very word sounds like a lie. Hal calls me 'Your Gracelessness.'"

Margaret laughs.

"No wonder Madge Shelton appears to like him so much," Margaret says, and I'm surprised by her perception. Or perhaps by the fact that Hal and Madge have been so indiscreet.

She levels a hard look at me.

"You have no choice," she says. "Your life has changed. You are now a duchess, whether you like it or not. Perhaps just the wife of a bastard prince. An almost-prince. But everyone will be watching him—and you."

"But what if I make a mistake?"

"You will make mistakes," she says. "But you will also set precedents."

"I don't know how to fit into this life, this family. I barely know where I fit into my own."

"*How* and *where* are different questions. The how is entirely up to you. The where depends entirely on the king."

"I just don't understand the rules," I say lamely.

"Your Grace," Margaret says, and places her hand over mine. "Mary."

I look up. She's staring at me intently. Not with irritation. Not with condescension. With the look of someone who needs her words to be heard and understood.

"Yes?"

"The first thing you have to learn is this: in Queen Anne Boleyn's court, there is only one rule."

"Only one?"

The wickedness returns with her smile, backed by determination.

"Yes. The only rule in your cousin's court is that there are no rules. She doesn't follow them. So why should we?"

7

"So." Madge won't look at me. "You're friends with the king's niece now?"

The queen has been ill—pregnancy doesn't treat her well—and we are on our way to her apartments to entertain her. I glance back at Madge as we make our way up a spiral staircase. She doesn't look very entertaining. She looks cross.

"Margaret's only just returned to court," I say. "I thought she could use a friend." I don't want to divulge my true reason for befriending her.

"Oh, so it's *Margaret* now, not Lady Margaret. I told you you'd forget about me, Duchess."

"I haven't forgotten you."

"You will when there are more important people around. Like Lady Margaret Douglas."

"I like her. I think you'd like her if you gave her a chance."

"She's cold." Madge frowns. "It's like she thinks she's better than everyone else."

She is.

"She's *amiable*," I retort. "Which is more than I can say about you right now."

"Did you tell her all your secrets?" Madge asks as we enter

the queen's watching chamber. "Did you tell her all of mine?"

"No!" Irritation surges into my throat. "I don't tell secrets."

"So how does she know about me and Hal?"

I turn to face her. So close we're almost nose to nose. "*I* don't even know about you and Hal."

"Is it jealousy, Duchess? You want what I have?"

"Don't be disgusting, Madge; he's my brother."

Suddenly, Madge's narrowed eyes open wide and she laughs so loudly the rest of the room goes silent. She whips me into a quick, spinning hug and—just like that—our animosity is forgotten. As it always is when we argue.

"So what *do* you want?" she asks, ignoring the crowd parting and bowing as we cross the room.

Maybe I really do want what Madge has. Confidence. "I want him to notice me," I say. "To look at me."

"Fitz." She doesn't have to ask; it's a statement of fact. She stops at the door to the queen's privy chamber and looks at me seriously. "But I think you want more than that." The corners of her mouth tilt up with malicious glee.

My skin gets hot and I drop my chin. Madge grabs it and lifts my head to she can see my face. Read me.

"Are you blushing?"

"No." I twitch my chin out of her grip.

"You are," she says. "Your skin has gone all blotchy just above the lace of your bodice."

I slap a hand across the top of my chest, and her laughter is so contagious I have to join in.

"I hear two little wrens giggling outside my rooms!"

55

The door to the queen's privy chamber has been opened for us to enter, and we find her sitting near the fire, listening to music. The lutenist is Mark Smeaton, a favorite of hers. He's a rather smarmy Flemish man, but he can play, that I grant him.

"Are you well, Your Majesty?" I curtsy. "Is there anything I can do for you?"

"Your laughter has inspired me to grant you your freedom," the queen says, her smile indulgent. "Drop your sewing. Have some fun. Find a tennis match to watch."

She pauses and glances from Madge to me and back again.

"I believe young Surrey and the Duke of Richmond have challenged each other to a duel of sorts."

I look to Madge, and she wears the exact expression I can feel on my own face. Deliverance. And expectation.

The queen laughs. "Go!" she cries. "I will stay here, indulging myself in all of Smeaton's skills."

Smeaton's fingers stutter on the strings, and she laughs again.

"Your musical skills, Master Smeaton."

We retreat, and Madge grins when the door closes behind us.

"She's a wicked one, that Anne Boleyn," she says, and looks at me with eager eyes. "And quite a matchmaker."

I grin back at her, suddenly feeling a little wicked myself. Ready for whatever might happen next. For whatever I can *make* happen. I grab Madge's hand and practically run through the watching chamber.

Madge keeps pace with me until we reach the stairs and she

drops my hand, so she can place both hands on the walls. I skitter down and wait at the bottom, watching her take each step as if her life depends on it.

"I hate heights," she murmurs to her feet. "And I hate spiral staircases even more. When will we ever live in a bloody castle that is all on one level?"

Impatience gets the better of me and I stamp my foot. I've decided to act and I want to act *now*, before I lose my courage.

Madge frowns and I feel a rush of guilt at not being more sympathetic. I reach up to help her, but she swats my hand away. As soon as her feet hit the ground at the bottom, her expression changes and she's Madge again. She lifts her nose like a pointer and sniffs the air.

"I know where they are," she says. "Follow me."

She strides across a courtyard into the shadow of the king's privy gallery.

"You can smell them?" I laugh.

"Of course." Madge stops so abruptly I almost run into her. She turns and looks at me expectantly. "Sweat, lust, and youthful energy. Can't you?"

She doesn't wait for an answer, but continues on her quest, pausing before she crosses the road and then barrels into the courtyards and galleries of the park-side recreation buildings. Madge hesitates almost imperceptibly before charging up a set of stairs, her fingers making hardly a noise as she drags them along the walls.

We look down into the largest of the tennis courts. The viewing platform is crowded with courtiers and the queen's ladies making bets on the outcome. I slow, looking at them all, my breath coming tight and sharp. The only person not seeming to enjoy herself is Jane Seymour, hiding in the corner behind her brother.

Madge whispers in my ear. "See that?" She nods her head in Jane's direction. "That's the way *not* to be. Boring. Colorless. Waiting for life to happen to you instead of going out to grab it by the horns." She pauses. "She's been at court *forever* and she's *still* not married, despite her handsome siblings."

Thomas Seymour catches me staring and winks, but Madge has already turned away. She pulls me through the crowd by the elbow, but never lets go. I don't breathe until we reach the barrier overlooking the game, next to Jane Boleyn, the queen's sister-in-law. She's leaning against a stanchion, and her eyes are on the spectators, not the match. She smiles at me, but then her gaze moves on.

Henry Norris is at the far end of the court ready to serve. Just below us stands the king. He has stripped down to his shirt, which sticks to the sweat of his broad back. He moves like a man who was once graceful, but now dives for the ball rather than running to it, his weight hitting the floor with a sound like thunder. I look at Madge out of the corner of my eye. She watches his every move. Like—well, like a tennis match of one.

"Your sense of smell has betrayed you, Madge."

Madge doesn't even look at me. "That's what you think."

Norris misses the return and the crowd cheers. Coins clink and clatter to the floor; laughter and the swish of skirts surround us like smoke. The king pauses below us, running one hand along the back of his neck, waiting for Norris to come and shake his hand.

"See that?" Madge says. "Make them come to you."

I watch the top of the king's head. His hair is the color of gold in firelight—a bright, shining red. Though the color has begun to dull around his temples. And there is a thin swirl at the crown of his head, where freckled skin has just begun to show. Vulnerable.

"The king is going bald," I whisper to Madge, sure that she'll laugh.

Instead, she turns to me with disappointment in her eyes.

"Oh, Mary," she says, her voice dripping with contempt. "You're so . . . *prosaic*."

For one who loves poetry the word stings like salt in a wound. But Madge doesn't know, so she cannot see the hurt she's caused. She just turns and creeps back down the stairs and moves on to the next tennis game.

We find Fitz and Hal in the last court. It is the smallest one and open to the bleak winter chill, so no one has stopped to watch. The boys don't seem to care, however, playing to win rather than playing for the audience. They have removed their doublets and jackets and draped them over the barrier rail of the viewing platform.

They have not yet seen us, so we remain in the shadows, watching. Hal is smaller. More wiry. His hair is the color of brass, like mine. Like Father's, his legs are slightly too short for his body.

Fitz is taller, despite being younger. His legs are longer. But they are both quick. And both strong. The pop of the tennis ball echoes in the little enclosure and their grunts sound animalistic. They don't speak at all, so neither do Madge and I.

Hal misses a wide shot and Fitz lowers his racket for a moment, presses both fists to his hips, and arches backward, looking up to the sky. There's a glimmer of sweat in the hollow above his collarbone.

"You're blotching again."

Madge's comment makes my skin even hotter, and she smirks.

Fitz turns. And for the first time in weeks, he sees me. Looks right at me. I struggle to smile as he bows, his eyes never leaving my face. Then Hal serves the ball straight into his ass and both of them laugh, returning to the game.

"Nothing can stop their play," Madge says, making it sound suggestive and somewhat salacious.

"They do seem to be enjoying it."

I can see Hal darting looks over at us almost every time he hits the ball. It's destroying his accuracy. But I can just imagine what he's thinking: *What are they talking about? Are they talking about me?*

He misses an easy volley, and Fitz laughs.

"Your mind is elsewhere, Hal."

"How can it not be, Fitz? With such lovely examples of womanhood watching our every move?"

Fitz ducks his head and peeks at me from the corner of his eye. Hardly discreet. But it gives me hope. He sees me.

"'O happy dames, that may embrace the fruit of your delight,'" Hal calls, and serves the ball again, so powerfully this time that I am sure Fitz will miss it, but he dives and sends it back with a roar. Hal stops spouting poetry and watching Madge and returns to the matter at hand.

"They look set to kill each other," I say.

"They look set to prove themselves," Madge replies. "And to the victor go the spoils."

"Then I had better hope Fitz wins."

I can't believe I've said something so audacious, but Madge just raises an eyebrow.

"Blotching," she says.

We don't speak again, just stand at the rail and watch. I watch Fitz's body move. The strength with which he strikes. The grace. How his eyes never leave the ball. The intensity of his expression.

He shines.

Fitz misses a shot and lopes over to it. Tosses it up in the air twice and catches it. Looks at me.

His gaze ignites every latent nerve in my body and sets a rush the strength of an ocean wave through me.

Fitz tosses the ball back to my brother, who grins. Hal sizes up the length of the court and the height of the net. When his calculating gaze settles on Madge, he winks at her.

Then he serves.

Fitz dives for it and misses it by a finger's breadth.

I wonder if he planned it that way.

Hal shouts in triumph and spins his racket in his hand.

Tosses it to his left to shake Fitz's and comes over to us at the rail.

"Sister." He bows slightly. Even Hal should call me Your Grace in public. He grins at me as if to say, "What?" and then turns to Madge.

"Mistress Shelton." He's practically purring.

"Congratulations," she purrs in return. "You win."

Without another word, they leave together. I feel my intrepidity leaking after them as I watch Madge's bright yellow skirts disappear.

"I think they're going to be all right." Fitz's voice is close. Just behind my shoulder.

"Hal can charm anyone," I agree.

I hear his breath. Feel his gaze on me. Catch the scent of warm linen and salt. He reaches around me and my eyes snap to his. The quickness of my movement makes him falter.

"My doublet," he says cautiously, and pulls it from the rail behind me, but the fabric snags on something and tumbles to the earthen floor. Fitz curses under his breath and I laugh at the way his ears turn pink. He steps around me, picks the doublet up and shakes it, then turns away to dress.

I know this is my moment. I glance once to the rest of the gallery. No one is here. No one watches. Everyone has gone inside to see and be seen. To speak to the king. To flirt with the queen. To ready themselves for the big show that will be supper this evening. I am here. Alone.

I salvage the remnants of my courage and reach out a hand to lay it on his shoulder. My fingers tighten on the muscle and bone through the damp linen of his shirt. I tug just slightly. To turn him to me.

I take my eyes away from the bare skin at his collarbone. At his throat. Confusion is written all over his expression, and the doublet hangs slack off of one arm. Before I can think or hesitate or ask the hundred questions in my mind, I step closer, drowning in the scent of skin and linen and air.

I stand on my toes, lift my face to his, and kiss him. When his mouth opens in surprise, I tug at his lower lip and feel his exhalation like a caress. I feel a rush of rightness and take one step closer, press my body to his. I twitch the doublet from his arm, wrap mine around his neck.

And realize that his hands remain at his sides. That his body has gone stiff. That he's not kissing me back.

I drop to my heels, my hands on his shoulders, and rest my forehead on his chest for just a second. I can hear his heart beating.

And I can hear my mother screaming at me. *Wanton. Shameless.*

Whore.

Fitz doesn't move.

I close my eyes and bite my lip, my shoulders tightening. I can't look at him.

His chest rises against my forehead. "Don't."

My entire body burns. I step back, crossing my arms high on my chest and turning away to hide the blotchiness.

I can't believe I just did that.

I can't believe I thought it would work.

I. Am. So. Stupid.

"Oh, God," I stutter.

"Don't."

I feel him take a step. His right hand lands on my left shoulder, turning me toward him again. But my humiliation and anger and insecurity conspire to make me feel small and trapped and infuriatingly vulnerable.

I swing round, quick as a wet cat, my right hand upraised. Fitz catches it with his left, and I can do nothing but stand there, our eyes locked. I try to block out the thought that overwhelms all the others: *I'm just like her*. Just like my mother. Faster with words and blows than with forgiveness.

I squeeze my eyes shut and wait. Father always hit back. Mother was quick with her hands, but Father was a warrior. A soldier. He could sense an attack coming a mile away. I'd see the two of them, snarling and wrapped in combat like dogs bred to tear out each other's throats.

But Fitz lets go and smooths the veil of my hood away from my face. His touch is gentle.

This is even worse.

"Sorry," I whisper hoarsely. I can hardly get the words out around the cluster of fear and shame in my throat. "I thought . . ." God. I can't tell him what I thought.

"Don't be sorry," he says.

But he doesn't follow me when I run.

8

THE WORD *KISS* TASTES LIKE SMOKE—SULTRY AND INTANGIBLE.
More air than substance.

I can't erase the flavor of it from my lips. Or the scent of him. Every time I see him—through the crowds in the great hall, or from a window of the queen's rooms, I think of that misdirected kiss and how much I wanted to hurt him when he didn't respond.

My parents cannot be in the same room without hurting each other.

I don't want that kind of marriage.

So I gather together the only two people at court I consider friends.

Madge is still wary of Margaret, whose apparent aloofness and reserve don't invite easy confidence. But I can't bear to tell my story twice, and I want both of their opinions.

I don't tell them everything. I don't tell them I tried to slap him. I can own up to being wanton. I can't admit to being like my mother.

"Well, *your* actions are perfectly understandable," Madge says, and lies back on my bed, staring up at the canopy. "After all, he really is quite enticing. He's young, he's handsome, he's powerful, he's connected. And I can just imagine what that body looks like under all those clothes." She slides a grin in my direction. "Or how much fun it would be to get them off him."

"What about Hal?" I ask, biting off the words between rigid lips.

"I didn't say *I* would pursue Fitz," she says. "Just that it wouldn't be a hardship to do so." She rolls onto her stomach, looking over to the fireplace where Margaret sits, straight-backed and, so far, silent. "Don't you agree, Margaret?"

It's almost a challenge.

Margaret flicks her gaze from me to Madge and back again. "It is against the king's wishes," she says.

Madge rolls her eyes and I turn away.

"At this point, I think it's against Fitz's, as well." I busy myself at my little writing desk in order to hide my face. But the book Fitz gave me lies there accusingly.

For your words.

"No man can resist a girl throwing herself at him," Madge says soothingly. "It's physically impossible."

I turn to her. "Have you not heard a word I said?"

"Maybe you surprised him. How long did you give him to respond?"

"Isn't he supposed to respond right away?"

Madge pauses. "Perhaps." She looks at me sadly and then sighs. "Maybe he's just slow."

I laugh. "Oh, that makes me feel better."

"A dullard of a husband is easier to manipulate."

"I don't want to manipulate him, Madge! I just want . . ."

"What *do* you want, Duchess? When you already have so much?" Madge's tone is bitter, and I can't respond.

Margaret does it for me.

"Love."

"Yes." I want to hug her. "That's exactly it."

Even Madge softens.

"What you really need to do," Margaret explains, "is not to make him fall in love with you, but to find out if you are in love with him."

"How do I do that?"

"Kiss him again," Madge says.

"Get to know him," Margaret replies at the same time.

"Both of those are highly unlikely as he's required to attend Parliament, and after Easter he's going back to his own estates."

"Or to Ireland," Margaret murmurs.

"Ireland?"

"Haven't you heard? The Duke of Richmond is set to lead the invading army and suppress the insurrection."

"Fitz?" Go to war? Fight in battles? I lived in Ireland when my father was lord lieutenant. I was two and ill almost the entire time. My mother still complains about Ireland. As if my father invented it himself just to make her miserable.

"It's said they might even make him king," Margaret adds.

Madge and I both gasp.

"Of Ireland." Margaret winks.

We're silent for a fragment of second before Madge starts to laugh and the corners of Margaret's mouth lift.

"You were right, Duchess," Madge says with a grin. "I do like her."

A little bit of tension releases from my shoulders. I have friends. I can't get my husband to kiss me. I barely have a marriage. But I've got these two girls.

"So how do you know?" I ask. "If you're in love?"

"You just know." Madge throws herself onto the stool by the fire and picks up a mug of small ale. As if that's enough of an answer.

"But *how*?" I ask.

I study each of them in turn, but Margaret looks as expectant of an answer as I feel. I think Madge is the only one amongst us who has ever been in love. I'm not even sure she has, despite having committed the physical act of it.

"Well"—Madge cocks her head to one side—"what are you looking for?"

We hesitate.

"In a man." Madge leans forward. "What's important to you?"

She gets up, thrusts her mug into my hands, and searches my desk. She pulls out a quill and some ink, and spies Fitz's book.

"Perfect," she says with a grin. "Let's make a list. Of the things that are necessary for love, and the things that would prevent it."

I exchange a glance with Margaret, who shrugs.

"Well?" Madge says, and turns to me. "What would your ideal husband absolutely have to have?"

"We'd never argue," I say quickly.

"I think that's asking a bit too much, Duchess."

"Then I'd have to like his family," I say, thinking of how Mother has always hated the Howards. Their pretensions and opinions and rules. And how Father has always considered her family traitors.

Madge tilts her head and looks at me quizzically. "What about the man himself?" she says. "What is the one most important thing about forever? You know, 'till death us depart.'"

"Poetry."

Madge hesitates and then laughs, turning back to the desk to write it down. "Fine."

"Fine features," Margaret says.

"So he has to be handsome." Madge hunches a little to form the letters.

"Maybe not classically," Margaret amends. "But he'd have to be appealing." She looks at both of us. "To me."

"It's true that one woman's meat is another woman's cheese." Madge grins wickedly. "Mary?"

"Other . . . physical attractions?"

"You're blotching again, Duchess," Madge points out cheerfully, and turns back to the book. "A nice ass? Broad shoulders? A big pizzle?"

"A healthy body." I close my eyes against the rush of images her words have produced.

"Excellent." Madge giggles.

"Ambition." Margaret's extraordinary contribution stops us all. Again she shrugs.

"I don't want a man who's content to do nothing," she says. "Who accepts his lot. Who has no goals and no power."

"Power is good." Madge nods and keeps scribbling, before adding, "A good kisser."

I hold my breath and the room goes silent. Madge's face is full of apology, but she tosses her head. "It's true, though. I can't fall in love with someone who kisses like a donkey with a drooling problem."

"Or who doesn't kiss back," Margaret says with an emphatic nod.

"A good dancer." Madge begins writing again.

"A pleasant voice."

"An interest in politics."

"He's got to be charming."

"With a good sense of humor."

"Quick-witted."

We gush ideas, and Madge scrambles to write them all down, holding up a hand to stem the tide.

"He has to like me," I say when she looks up.

"Of course he will like you," Madge says, and squeezes my hand, but she writes it down anyway. "Now, what must he never be?"

"Ugly."

"Smelly."

"Narcissistic."

"Vain."

"Married."

Madge drops the last word, and it ricochets in the silence that follows.

"I know I can't be with Hal forever," she says without looking up or pausing in her writing. "He has to make a Howard heir."

"I'm sorry, Madge," I whisper.

"I can live with being nothing but a dalliance." Madge shrugs, then crosses out the word *married*. "As a matter of fact, maybe I don't want forever."

She returns to her list and reads it silently.

"One more thing," she says, and writes it carefully and precisely at the bottom of the page, speaking all the while. "And this one is absolutely essential." She makes a final flourish with the pen before looking up to share it with us. "He must get along with my friends."

Hatfield Palace
Spring 1534

9

Despite my newfound objective, I'm very glad when the queen invites me to leave London and accompany her to Hatfield to visit her daughter. I'm happy to get away from the tangling, all-consuming thoughts of *him*.

When we arrive at the palace, the queen doesn't even give her ushers time to announce her. Her eyes are bright as she strides toward the house and the front doors open wide, revealing the dark maw of the entrance, in which stands Madge's mother. Lady Shelton is Anne Boleyn's aunt, responsible for the royal nursery.

The queen swoops to the top of the stairs and catches up the bundle of blue damask and gold embroidery that Lady Shelton carries. Her daughter, Elizabeth.

I follow silently as Lady Shelton shows us the entire palace. The queen carries Princess Elizabeth everywhere. Talking into her ear, holding her close, kissing her forehead and hands. I feel a bit guilty that I am here and not Madge. But her mother is distant. Removed. And I wonder if perhaps Madge wouldn't have wanted to come—even if she had been invited. Lady Shelton has the appearance of someone who is afraid that ghosts may come and haunt her.

The baby is beautiful. She has her father's red hair and her mother's dark eyes. And a serenity that comes—I imagine—from being loved.

A dark, misshapen demon rises slowly in my heart. I am jealous of Elizabeth. Of the joy in Queen Anne's face. The demon twists and seeks out other easy prey. It reminds me that I am not lovable. That my mother despises me and my husband won't even respond to a kiss.

I suppress the coiling envy as we inspect the beds and rooms, the cleanliness and the linens. The queen herself unpacks a small trunk she brought, full of new things she's had made for Elizabeth. Jackets embroidered with gold braid. Counterpanes of damask and velvet, to swaddle her cooing daughter in luxury.

When Elizabeth falls asleep in Queen Anne's arms, Lady Shelton puts the baby in a cradle beneath a canopy of the cloth of estate, and another woman sits down to rock it.

The queen invites me to walk in the formal gardens, and we step from the oak-beamed great hall into bright spring sunlight that does little to soften the bite of the north wind.

"How do you enjoy life as one of my companions rather than one of my maids?" the queen asks, walking just slightly ahead of me toward the aggressively structured hedges of the knot garden.

"It's very different, Your Majesty."

"How so?"

I have never been a good liar, but with the queen, I feel I need to be as truthful as possible. "I have more leisure time.

More freedom. Yet my own rules and thoughts and foibles keep me prisoner."

The queen laughs. "Yes, I think I understand."

She was a maid-in-waiting once. I think she does understand.

"And what do you do with your leisure time?"

Again, the truth just spews from me. "I play with words." It was the last thing I intended to say. And it sounds so stupid.

The queen catches the expression on my face and smiles, but doesn't laugh.

"You write poetry?"

"I suppose I should say I would *like* to write poetry." The queen watches me. Waiting for an explanation. I love poetry, I just don't have the confidence to write it. Or anything. Which is why Fitz's book lay blank for so long, until Madge finally picked it up.

"I love words," I tell the queen. "My brother and I used to have . . . contests. Word wars." Hal must have told Fitz. *For your words.* I don't want to think about Fitz, so I stumble on, saying anything that comes to mind. "Hal is the poet in the family. And I . . . admire Sir Thomas Wyatt."

"Well," she says quietly, "there is much to admire."

We pass beneath a tall hedge and the shadow of it falls across her face, making her cheekbones more prominent and the darkness of her eyes fathomless.

"He is very handsome," I say lamely. Before Madge's affair with him, I'd harbored a secret crush on Thomas Wyatt. I sometimes still find myself hoping his blue eyes will land on me. Or better yet, that he might write a poem for me and only I would know it.

"His poetry," I continued. "It seems to mean something. Or several somethings. More than it's actually saying."

I can't get my thoughts straight.

"I wish I could do that," I say finally. "I wish I could do more than just . . . tell the truth flat out. I wish I could tell the truth . . ."

We walk back into the sunlight and a gust of wind threatens to bowl me over.

"And have it seem like nothing but poetry?" the queen asks, steadying me by my elbow.

"Yes!" I cry. "That's exactly it."

"I feel that way with music," she says dreamily. "Like somehow, I could say what I think and see and feel, and no one would really understand but me. It would be like pulling the wool over the eyes of the entire world, while telling them the ultimate truth."

We remain silent all the way back to the house. She, lost in music; I, lost in words.

But just before we enter, the queen turns to me.

"Have you seen—" She stops. Takes a deep breath. "The king's other daughter?"

Lady Mary. No longer a princess. The king ruled that he and Katherine of Aragon were never married, and that Mary is no longer legitimate. She is the king's daughter, but no more in line to the throne than Fitz. Perhaps, in fact, less so. Because she is a girl.

Mary lives at Hatfield as a kind of servant to her baby half sister. Who *is* a princess.

This is the ghost that Lady Shelton has been afraid of. Because Mary and Queen Anne have not made any attempts to hide their animosity toward each other.

I shake my head. "No, Your Majesty."

"How old are you, Cousin?"

I'm surprised by the question. "Almost fifteen."

"The king's daughter is not much older than you are. What would *you* want from a stepmother? From a person who took your mother's place?"

I think of Bess Holland—the woman who replaced my mother in my father's affections. Or filled them, as the case may be, because I doubt my father ever felt affection for his wife. Bess is good and kind and well-intentioned. If a little dim. She tends to float through life. She is courteous to me, but does nothing to make me feel wanted. Or loved.

I think of Mary.

If I am jealous of Elizabeth, of Queen Anne, how must Mary Tudor feel?

"I should like someone to intercede for me," I tell the queen. "Someone to tell my father that I'm worthy of his attention."

"Of his love." The queen nods. She understands.

"I shall do this then," the queen whispers fiercely. "I shall offer to speak to the king. On her behalf. He will be furious. He thinks he should be allowed to treat his children any way he wishes."

"Some parents need a little help," I admit bleakly.

Again she nods. "That they do."

She squares her shoulders. "All right, Cousin. Will you do me this? Will you seek out the king's daughter and offer . . ." She pauses. "No, not a place at court. But if she honors me here as queen, I can plead for at least a return to his good graces."

This is not an order from my queen. Nor even a request. She is honestly asking me if I will do this. And I don't wish to. The Lady Mary is like a hornet—small and quick to sting.

But I look into the queen's eyes and nod anyway. She wants to make things right. If I can help in some small way, I will be doing them all a service.

As the queen is shown rooms in which she can dine and rest the night, I search all of Hatfield. No one will tell me where Lady Mary is. I wonder if this is because of my mother. The oranges she sent to Katherine of Aragon were reported to contain treasonous hidden messages. Perhaps Elizabeth's household thinks I'm a spy. Inciting a revolt.

I don't know Lady Mary well. I've only met her once. I think of Fitz, her half brother. How he is always on his way to the tiltyard or the tennis courts. How he rides out with his father early in the morning, returning on winded horses and waves of bonhomie.

The demon twists again. I am jealous of Fitz, too. Of his easiness with his father. I will never fit into that world.

I wonder if Lady Mary feels that way. She doesn't seem to be the sort to spend her day at archery or hawking. She always seemed a little sickly. A little too pious for physical pursuits.

I've heard that her mother wore hair shirts at the end of her reign. Both Katherine and Mary are staunch believers in the Roman religion.

I slip into the chapel as silently as I can. It's smaller than the chapels at Greenwich or Hampton Court, but larger than the one at Kenninghall. The walls have been washed white, though the ceiling is still crisscrossed with stars and gilded battens. The saints have been removed, but the altar remains—glowing with gold in the candlelight.

A figure in purple kneels before it. She is small and round—a velvet dumpling. Tinier, even, than the queen. When she stands and turns at the sound of my footsteps, I see that she probably only reaches my shoulder in height. But the energy that emanates from her is equal to that of her father. Frightening.

I kneel and bow my head.

"You married my brother," she says. Her voice is low—almost as low as a man's—and hoarse. It rumbles from deep below her rib cage.

I nod. "Yes . . ." I don't know how to address her. She is not a princess. She is not a duchess. But she is the daughter of my king. "Yes, Your Grace," I finish lamely.

"I hope you deserve him," she says. Her tone indicates she doesn't think I do. Deserve him.

Her skin is pale, and looks limp against her face. She may be only three years older than I am, but she appears to be much more. She has the same high-arched eyebrows as Fitz, the same vibrant hair. But Lady Mary has deep, bruise-like shadows beneath her eyes. If I didn't know better, I would believe the rumors that she is being slowly poisoned.

She stares at me for a long moment. Long enough that I grow uncomfortable. I get the feeling that Lady Mary has more to say. So I wait, helplessly, hoping she gets it over with quickly.

"Have you consummated it yet? Your marriage?"

I am shocked rigid by her bluntness and can't reply.

"Oh, no, of course you haven't. You're not allowed." Her words drip with mock sympathy.

I shake my head, but she hadn't intended for me to respond. She intended for me to listen.

"You're nothing but a pawn, Mary Howard. A simple, expendable female piece in a man's game. You were married to a king's son to placate your father for a short while. But you will be replaced when something better comes along."

"That's not true." I can't believe I have the strength to dispute her.

"No?" She whips the word like a lash. "If the rumors are valid and Henry FitzRoy is made king of Ireland, he will be able to do much better than *you*. Perhaps a French princess. Or the daughter of my cousin the Holy Roman emperor. He could do much better than a *Howard*."

She says my family name as one would the word *whore*. In her mouth, they almost sound the same.

"My mother never consummated her marriage to the king's brother, Arthur," she continues. "It wasn't a real marriage. Therefore it never really happened." She pauses and lifts her chin. "They are still married. My parents. No matter what Anne Boleyn says."

I regret taking up Queen Anne's cause. I regret seeking Lady

Mary out. I regret getting involved with this family at all.

"The king can change your life in an instant," she says coolly. "Just as he changed mine. Taking away my birthright and giving it to a mewling infant *bastard*." The word tastes like saltpeter. I wonder what she thinks of Fitz.

I wonder if she's right. If my status can be changed in an instant. If suddenly it will be declared that I'm not married at all. If I will go back to being nothing but Mary Howard. I feel the anger and humiliation simmering in my veins and I grip my hands into fists, hiding them behind my back.

But she hasn't finished yet.

"How would you feel, *Duchess*, to be shunned by your father? Ripped from your beloved mother, never allowed to see her again?"

"I would be overjoyed," I retort.

"Then you are a worse child than I thought. How ungrateful." She practically spits the words.

She reminds me overmuch of my mother, her words echoing those I try to keep from my mind. My limbs are desperate to attack. Or to retreat. To escape her vituperation. But I have a promise to fulfill.

"We all have two parents," I say, trying to keep my voice even. "And often it is difficult to keep both of them happy."

She stops. Frozen.

"I obeyed my father's wishes," I continue. "As the rules of court and the rules of God dictate."

"The rules of God say to honor thy father *and* thy mother," Lady Mary corrects. But she is hesitant.

I nod. Pretend to agree. Pretend that a person can actually honor both parents when they are as at odds as mine are. As hers are. Like me, she must choose one or the other.

The word *honor* is like an unripe berry dipped in cream. Rich with the expectation of sweetness, but tart with spite.

"This is why I sought you out," I say. "To offer the possibility of restoring you to the king's good graces."

I see hope blooming on her face, bringing a little color to her cheeks. Her eyes are bright blue. Not at all like Fitz's—or their father's.

That hope is painfully familiar. If I had the opportunity to make amends with my mother, I would do anything—anything—to achieve it.

"The queen has offered to intercede. If you go to her now—honor her—she will speak with the king. Soften his heart to you."

All signs of hope vanish from her expression, replaced by a stony resolve. And the blue eyes darken.

"I honor no queen but Katherine, daughter of Aragon," she says, her voice cold, the Thames breaking free of the ice.

I can't let this person see she has riled me. Every time I get angry, her energy rises. It's as if she feeds on it. So I release my fists. Struggle to find a diplomatic reply.

But Lady Mary is not finished.

"However, if the king's *mistress* would like to speak on my behalf"—she pauses—"I would be grateful."

The temper of her voice is anything but appreciative.

Lady Mary turns away from me and kneels again before the

altar. She doesn't acknowledge my status or even my presence, and I'm left hanging, caught between retort and retreat.

"Give my brother my best," she says to her hands, clenched before her. "If you see him."

She knows that I may not see him. Or that when he sees me, he may run away. And after a moment of trying to decide how to take my leave, I just go.

The next morning, as we prepare to go back to London, the queen asks about my mission, though Lady Mary's continued nonappearance is testament to my failure.

"Tell me what she said, *exactly*," Queen Anne insists.

I don't want to. But I do. At the word *mistress*, the queen's lips go white and her hands clench reflexively. She climbs silently into her litter and pulls the curtains closed.

I look up to the windows of Hatfield, all of them staring blankly out at me, mute and expressionless. And then I see Lady Mary's face at the center. Just for a moment. Alone.

I want to prove her wrong.

I am married.

But I can mentally strike through one of the things on our list of reasons to love a man.

I definitely don't like Fitz's sister.

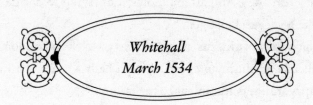

Whitehall
March 1534

10

Lent is always the gloomiest time at court. There are no revels, no celebrations, no banquets. The men spend all their time in Parliament, and the women sit and sew, and everyone is cross and on edge.

So the day the men return from Parliament slapping backs and jovially haranguing one another, the entire court ignites on the spark of their energy.

Everyone crowds into the public rooms, and I am trapped at the far wall, against the windows. The room has two doors. One leads to the queen's more private chambers. It's closed, and I wouldn't be allowed access. The other door is the one through which everyone is entering. A flood of them. Doublets and boasts and faces red with wine.

I feel the wedge of panic pressing into my lungs. I search for a familiar face. Madge. Margaret. Hal. I'd even be relieved to see Fitz. Anyone to keep me upright.

I stand on my tiptoes. I am so much smaller than all these men. I see only shoulders and velvet caps. Drooping feathers and gold braid. I try to suck in a deep breath, but it catches halfway and I cough.

Sharp, bony fingers grip my elbow, and my delirium

threatens to overtake me. The edges of my vision blur and go dark, and I can only see as if through a tunnel. As if I wear blinders.

I turn my head, wobbling like a drunk, and almost cry at the sight of Margaret's long nose and wide mouth.

"Let's leave this place," she says, and drags me away from the wall.

The two of us together cause a wave of bows and curtsies, parting the crowd like the prow of a ship. Margaret is the figurehead. The throng on the other side of the door is even more densely packed, and all my breath leaves me. But Margaret forces her way through and down the spiral stairs. We pick up Madge in our wake as we tumble out into a tiny courtyard.

Margaret releases me, and her hands flinch closed. She looks up to the sky, her face like a thunderstorm already broken.

"He's done it," she says.

"Done what?" I ask, my breath still short. I press a fist to my stomacher and finally fill my lungs.

"He's gone and taken control of everything."

"Who?"

"My uncle," she says.

The king.

We should stop talking now. I should go find Hal. Or Father. Or sew. Or write poetry. Madge should be serving the queen. And Margaret should let her anger subside before she speaks out against the king to the wrong person.

But none of us moves.

"They've just voted," Margaret says, more quietly, though

her anger hardly seems to have dissipated. "The king has rat-ified it."

"Ratified what?" Madge seems awed by Margaret's anger.

"An act of succession to the throne."

I hold my breath. As King Henry grows older, everyone worries about who will be next in line. Princess Elizabeth is barely crawling, much less walking or talking. And Lady Mary . . . I can't imagine what the country would be like if she came to power with her spite and her need for revenge.

Then there's Fitz. And Margaret, the king's niece.

It's treason to speak of—or even picture—the death of the king, making the succession a touchy subject to discuss.

"The act declares that King Henry's first marriage was invalid and therefore Princess—*Lady* Mary cannot inherit." Margaret looks at me pointedly. "Because she's a bastard."

She means Fitz will never inherit, either. Which is good for me. Or at least my marriage. No French princess would want to marry a bastard. They'd get in line to marry the next king of England.

"We knew that already," Madge says.

"*Some* people didn't," Margaret snaps. The people who sup-port Katherine of Aragon.

Like my mother.

Madge just shrugs.

"They're also saying that everyone will have to take an oath," Margaret continues, "that the succession is valid. That Queen Anne is the true queen."

"But she is," Madge says.

"Lady Mary doesn't think so," I tell her. But I am watching Margaret. She grew up with Lady Mary. And I wonder if she supports Lady Mary's right to inherit. Or does she support her own?

"Anyone who won't sign it is a traitor." Margaret pauses to let that sink in. "And can be executed accordingly. Even speaking out—against the oath, the king, Queen Anne—could lead to imprisonment."

I am glad no one ever listens to my mother. Except me. Because the things she says would send her straight to the Tower.

"He wants to control everything," Margaret murmurs. "Lives, love, faith, words. Probably even the afterlife."

"Shhh." If what Margaret says is true, she's putting us all in danger.

But Margaret doesn't listen. "Look at his daughter. She's been betrothed countless times. She has believed herself in love. Every. Single. Time."

"Don't be ridiculous, Margaret," Madge sniffs. "She was betrothed to the dauphin when she was two."

"And remained so for three years!" Margaret stands straight as a poker. She keeps her hands folded tightly together. But her body leans forward, her face screwed up in emotion, the passion behind her words breaking through the mask of royalty.

"And then the emperor." She loses her grasp on her hands and they fly up over her head in despair. "She thought he was the most handsome man she'd ever met. A six-year-old girl madly in love with a grown man."

Margaret frowns in disgust.

"And now she'll never marry at all. Or if she does, it will be the second half sibling of some minor backwater prince. It was once even proposed she marry FitzRoy. Did you know that? That the king would have married his bastard daughter to his bastard son?"

The very idea makes me feel sick.

"She may be the king's daughter," Margaret says, and her eyes hold pain and anger in equal measure, "but it has done her little good. Just as I have garnered no profit from being the king's niece. I am eighteen years old. And my life, my love, my marriage—my very survival—are all beholden to him. To be dispensed at the king's pleasure."

"He *is* the king," Madge says, as if this explains and resolves everything.

"He's not God," I say. "There have to be some things he doesn't control."

"He will not control me," Margaret says. "He may control my inheritance. He may control my past and my future. But he will not control my feelings. Not my mind. I am not his."

I feel an ache within me—one of recognition and complicity. The king may control my marriage, but am I not in command of my emotions?

Margaret goes very still, perhaps thinking she's said too much, but she doesn't ask us not to tell. In this court, asking such a thing is an assurance that everyone will know before we sit to supper.

We stand in an awkward silence until Madge tosses her head.

"Well," she says, "no one will control me, either."

"No one *can* control you, Madge," I tease.

Margaret laughs and I see a chink in the wall of her anger.

"May our thoughts and emotions—and, most importantly, how they guide us—always be our own," she says.

Madge cheers and does a little dance, and I grin when she swings me around. But I add my own caveat to Margaret's proclamation:

May our emotions always guide us to make the right choices.

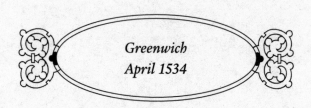

Greenwich
April 1534

11

We leave Whitehall and the City behind and return to the king's birthplace. The rooms feel more crowded; they're smaller, and the number of people in them seems to grow every day. But we are bounded by water on one side—which gives the illusion of space—and the gardens, orchards, and forests on the other. Where I can breathe.

We are here preceding the grass season—for hunting and riding and jousting—and to celebrate the end of Lent. The court has shaken off the mantle of winter and launched into spring with a vengeance. There are more parties. More flirting. And suddenly, the entire court is in love.

Except for me. I never see Fitz anymore. He has yet to come to Greenwich. He may be sent to Ireland in the summer, which approaches at an astonishing rate.

At the very least, I'd like to see him. And apologize. Something my mother never did.

So I go to find the one person who has always taken my side. To ask him to intercede. To arrange a meeting. Perhaps, even, to mediate.

Father is in the king's good graces at the moment, and has

rooms in the central donjon—the tower in the middle of the sprawling palace complex.

"I'd like to see His Grace," I tell the usher at the door to my father's apartments. And mentally kick myself. I should have said, "I *want* to see His Grace." Or, "I *must* see His Grace." There is a subtle but tremendous difference between asking permission and issuing a command.

"He is with the master secretary at the moment, Your Grace."

The king's newly appointed secretary, Thomas Cromwell, is reputedly a mercenary. Or used to be. The son of a blacksmith—or a brewer—he is quite possibly the cleverest man at court. Father despises him as an upstart—even worse than a "new man" like Thomas Boleyn, the queen's father, who at least had knights and earls in his ancestry albeit Irish ones.

Father also says Cromwell deserves watching.

But I'd rather not. His face is hard. Brutal, even—like a murderer's. He doesn't tolerate nonsense. He's known for getting things done, and getting them done properly. Without any mistakes. Without any argument.

Without any warning.

I'm a little afraid of him.

Father's usher goes to announce me, and I shake the feeling off. Through the slightly open door I can hear Father's voice rising.

"No, he will *not* be going, Master Secretary, not if there's anything I can do about it."

"And of course, you can do much." Cromwell's tone is flat, his words riding behind my father's like a slick on the river.

"I do what I can."

"Close relations with the queen certainly do no harm," Cromwell muses. "Though it is truly the king's wishes that matter."

"The king does not wish to be separated from his son."

"The king does not wish to be separated from his kingdom. You keep that boy too close."

There is a tense silence. It's not a friendly discussion. It's a battle for power. Over the king's decision. Over Fitz.

Suddenly the door is open and the usher is standing right in front of me, my nose practically pressed into the Howard livery emblazoned on his chest. I move away and he smirks, stepping aside to let me in.

"Your Grace." Cromwell gives me a quick, short bow—barely noticeable. Father glares at the back of his head.

"Master Secretary." I am about to incline my own head in deference to his title, when I remember Mother's words.

Keep your damn head up.

So I keep my eyes on Cromwell as he approaches. He pauses when he comes abreast of me and whispers in my ear.

"Always good to see you, *Princess*."

His words taste like charcoal.

"I'm not—"

But he is out the door before I can say three words.

I glance back at my father, who is deep in thought—hardly noticing my presence. When he looks up, he doesn't see me at all, but stares past me to the door.

"He will not win," he murmurs. Then he turns to me, a smile

on his face, and his eyes seem to hold no concern at all.

"My dear," he says, and grabs my hands to squeeze. He does not hug me. We are not that kind of family. Only Hal is that effusive in a greeting. We put it down to his poetic sensibilities.

Father turns back to his desk, and his shoulders slump. As though he can no longer keep up the court façade.

"Father?"

He straightens quickly, but doesn't turn. "I've been to Kenninghall."

Mother. I don't need him to describe their interaction. All I have to do is remember. Mother planting herself in front of him before he even gets in the door. Unloading all of her pent-up frustrations and accusations. Father, motionless, the color rising in his face. Until one of them explodes.

"Did you hear me, Mary?"

I look up. He's watching me. I can't answer. The images still flash at the edges of my vision.

"I said, I told her I want to formalize our separation."

I rock backward.

"A divorce?" I ask. *Divorce* tastes like a posset. Curdled and fermented and heavily spiced—a weak remedy for a serious affliction. And easily poisoned.

"A formal separation," Father corrects. "She refused."

I would expect nothing less from my mother.

"She flew into one of her rages, so I had to lock her up." Father says this casually, but his hands are shaking.

So am I. I am shaking with gratitude that I am here at court. That I have the protection of Anne Boleyn. That I have friends.

That I no longer have to witness destruction and imprisonment.

"And what will you do now?" I manage to ask.

"I will wait her out," Father says. "I have moved her to Redbourne. She is no longer welcome at Kenninghall. I have taken all of her jewels. I have reduced her staff. She does not control my life." He pauses, his shoulders rounding once again. "She doesn't even control her own."

But we both know that Mother has power over all of us. That she observes and judges all our thoughts and deeds, and she will act accordingly, sending us all into ruin. Or she will die trying.

Father thumps his desk once, startling me, and takes my hands again, an expectant smile on his face. "You came to see me."

Fitz.

The remembrance hits me like a clap of thunder.

"I never see Fitz," I say quickly, and catch the look on his face. "Henry FitzRoy. I never see my husband. I should like to."

"There's really no need," Father says smoothly. Soothingly. "It's more important right now for you to get to know the queen. And the rest of your new family."

He means the king. It is truly the king's wishes that matter.

The king who can decide in an instant to send Fitz to conquer Ireland. Or into marriage with a French princess.

"Besides," Father says, and strokes my cheek, "your husband is busy. With Parliament and the running of the country. I never saw your mother when we were first married. I never saw you."

I know. That's why I want to change things. To be different.

"I just . . ." I can't say that to my father. "I heard he will be going to Ireland. I wanted to see him"—*speak to him*—"before he goes." *Before he dies.*

"He won't be going to Ireland," Father says, and his tone is short. Defiant. "And there really is no need for you to see each other. You are only fourteen."

"Almost fifteen." My birthday is just a few weeks away.

The muscle at the back of Father's jaw twitches. I've contradicted him.

"The king has declared that you will not sleep together until it is deemed appropriate."

I can't tell him I tried to kiss Fitz. Father's wishes match the king's.

"I don't want to sleep with him," I blurt. "I just want to find out who he is."

He comes back to stand in front of me. Not touching. But demanding attention.

"He is the son of the king," he says, his voice such a low murmur that I have to strain to hear him. "That's all you need to know for now." He takes my face in his hands. "If we are very careful, and very lucky, you, my dear, may one day be queen."

Treason. Imagining the queen's death. Imagining the king's.

But my father has a way of making things happen. Of pushing things in the right direction. He is the Duke of Norfolk, and if not the most trusted nobleman in the country, he is certainly the most powerful.

I run the word *queen* around in my head and roll it on my tongue. The beginning is tart and brittle like the skin of an apple. But the long *e* is bright and sweet.

There is a flaw in this plan of his. One that can't be disregarded.

"Henry FitzRoy can't inherit the throne," I say.

"Laws can be changed with a press of the king's seal," he says. "FitzRoy may be a bastard, but at least he's a boy."

I can feel the power in his fingers as he holds my jaw prisoner, studying me. Appraising me.

I hope I can live up to his expectations. When I smile, I feel my skin tug at his fingers.

My father nods. Satisfied. And pats me once on the cheek. Then he goes back to his desk.

"Do not worry, little one," he says, using the pet name he gave me when I was young and would follow him as far as the gates of Kenninghall when he left for the north or for France or for court. Always going somewhere.

"Do not worry," he repeats. "You have all the time in the world."

12

"So I have to do as my father wishes," I tell Madge and Margaret in explanation of why I will no longer seek out Henry FitzRoy. "I'm still his daughter."

I don't tell them Father said I could become queen. The word becomes more unpalatable the more I think on it. As if worms have begun to dig in.

"His prisoner, more like," Margaret murmurs behind me.

"So we find you someone else," Madge says, slowing her steps as we go down the spiral staircase.

"I don't know if I want someone else." I don't even know if I want Fitz.

Madge reaches for her miniature Chaucer, swinging it in my face so I nearly fall as I stumble into the courtyard.

"What were the generative organs made for?" she asks dramatically. "They cannot have been made for naught!"

The palace is alive with the May Day festivities and with the men enjoying them—jousting and banqueting and making bawdy jokes—so Madge's exclamation gets a rumble of appreciative laughter.

"I can help you with that, Mistress Shelton," Francis Weston quips, his narrow face alight with mischief.

"I'll come to you if I get no better offers, Master Weston." Madge threads us through the knots of revelers and into the great hall.

The queen helped preside over the joust, but her growing belly has begun to slow her down. She insisted that she needed to rest, and sent us in search of other entertainment. Madge has taken it as a strict command. She links arms with both of us as we enter the hall. The men are dressed in their best and preen before the windows. All to the desired effect.

"All right," Madge says, pointing with her chin, none too discreetly, at the line of men. "Which one?"

I look away. Margaret shifts next to me. If possible, her back gets a little bit straighter.

"What do you mean?" I ask Madge.

"They're obviously lining up for harvest," Madge says. "So let's be the first to pick!"

I flick my eyes to the left. The men do look like horses at auction. Or prisoners lined up for judgment.

"See!" Madge crows. "You can't help looking!" She turns to face the group full on, elongating her neck and shifting her hips so her vivid yellow skirts swirl around her.

"I'm married," I remind her.

"And your father has told you not to see him," Madge says, looking at me over her shoulder. "So all the more reason to practice on someone else. Now pick." She levels her gaze at Margaret. "Both of you."

"I like the tall one," Margaret murmurs.

"You would have to," Madge says. "I don't think any of

the rest of them could match you in height, even if you were barefoot."

Margaret frowns, a tiny downturn of her mouth.

"Oh, Margaret." Madge says placatingly, "No one can fault you for being tall. It proves you're related to the king. It's something you should be proud of."

I stare at the tallest man in the group.

"I think I'm related to him," I say.

"You are?" Margaret turns to me. "Can you introduce me?"

"That smitten already, Margaret? Let's see. He's got nice enough features, seems in good shape, though the bloom of youth is starting to fade. . . ." Madge trails off. She looks a little jealous.

I squint at the man. His face is dominated by the Howard nose—long and straight, with a tiny hook at the end. Pointed chin. Minuscule beard—just a scrap really, like he's left something on his chin for later. I search through memories to see where he fits. Which family we visited and when.

The Dowager Duchess of Norfolk, my step-grandmother, approaches him. She's at court for the festivities. Or perhaps escaping from her disreputable charges at her house in Lambeth. She grabs his hands, and he kisses her on the cheek. And I remember.

She's his mother.

"He's my uncle," I say. "Thomas Howard."

"You're addled," Madge laughs. "Your *father* is Thomas Howard."

"Half uncle," I clarify. "The dowager duchess's son."

"Why must the nobility insist that everyone have the same name?" Madge cries. "Thomas. Henry. William. Mary." She pouts and scrunches up her face at me.

"You're a Mary," I point out.

"Why do you think I call myself Madge? Shout 'Mary!' in this room, and half the women will turn around. Call 'Thomas!' and it will be half the men."

"Or Henry," Margaret adds.

"Exactly!" Madge thumps me on the shoulder. "Look." She points unabashedly at the men by the window. "Thomas Wyatt."

Wyatt sees her pointing and raises an eyebrow. Once again, I find myself wishing his eyes would land on me, but when they do, I freeze.

Wyatt winks.

Madge frowns a little, but continues down the line.

"Thomas Howard. Thomas Seymour. Now *he's* good-looking."

"Like a fox is good-looking to a goose," Margaret says.

I laugh.

"Henry Howard."

Madge pauses in her running commentary. Bites her bottom lip to keep from smiling. Hal can't take his eyes off her, and the buzz resonating between them makes me jealous.

"Henry Norris."

"Oh, Madge, he *is* too old. He must be at least forty. Almost as old as the king."

"We never put an age limit on our list. Besides, I assume everything still functions properly."

Madge slips away from me as I try to yank on her hood. Margaret steadies me, and I hear a shuffle by the windows and know, without looking, that we are now the ones on display.

Madge brushes her skirts. Holds out her hand to me.

"Walk with me?"

"We'll all walk," Margaret says.

"You just want to be introduced to Mary's *uncle*."

"And you just want to make her brother mad with passion."

Madge sucks in a breath, but doesn't respond.

"Lady Margaret." Hal bows. "Your Grace." He grins at me, but the smile slides quickly to Madge. "Mistress Shelton."

I'm afraid to step between them for fear of getting burned by their intensity.

"Mary, you remember our uncle, Lord Thomas?" Hal asks, not looking at me.

Perfect.

I introduce Margaret and search for a getaway. Leave Hal and Madge to fend for themselves. Leave Margaret to my uncle. Just leave.

"Mary."

Hal stops me, one hand gentle on my arm. I look him in the face, and he raises an eyebrow.

Then his eyes flick to someone behind me. Hal is never uncomfortable in public, and yet here he is, barely able to speak.

He doesn't have to. I know who is behind me. My stomach churns with anxiety and I turn reluctantly.

The broad brow, the hair like gold reflecting sunset, the soaring eyebrows. And that mouth.

Fitz doesn't speak, but the color deepens across his entire face like a cloud.

"Another Henry," I hear Madge whisper as she drops into a curtsy. We all do, and the men all bow.

"Handsome," she says in my ear as the men greet one another. "And excellent physical attributes."

Then Fitz and I are facing each other. Again. Every excruciating detail of that day comes back to me. The stiffness in his limbs. The shock in his eyes. The taste of his mouth.

I lick my lips.

"Blotching, Duchess."

I pretend not to hear Madge's comment and pray that Fitz hasn't.

"Your Grace," I say stiffly. He nods.

Madge elbows me in the ribs. "Oh, excuse me, Duchess!" she says with exaggerated apology. "We were just going to go *dance*."

I watch helplessly as Madge drags Hal into the center of the room. Margaret and my uncle Thomas follow. They are leaving me. Abandoning me.

I can't even look at Fitz.

"Would you like to?"

The sound of his voice startles me. He's hardly said ten words to me since we married, but in the intervening months, his voice has deepened and mellowed. The way he speaks words makes my mouth water.

I don't want to say yes, but I do. I don't want to like the way his hand feels in mine. But I do.

I want to fall in love with him.

But I don't.

As we move to the center of the floor, I learn one thing I can mentally scratch off of the list written in the little book he gave me.

Good dancer.

He finally speaks the second time he misses a beat and I stumble. "I can see why Hal calls you Your Gracelessness."

I immediately cross off another: *He has to like me.*

"And what does he call you?" I retort. "For you have no rhythm."

I finally look up at him and catch the smile disappearing from his face.

"I have perfect balance when I ride, can beat Hal any day at archery, and always win at tennis."

A third item. *Is not vain.*

"You didn't the last time I saw you play."

He stops moving altogether, so I force him into the next turn and press my advantage. Feel my mother's tongue sharpening in my own mouth.

"What about academics? Latin? Astronomy? Diplomacy. Strategy. Poetry." I pause. "But no, you need rhythm to write poetry."

"I'm not at all like my father," he says. "No mind for facts and figures. They bore me. And I leave the poetry to your brother."

Another element off the list. I'm beginning to be glad he didn't kiss me back.

"So you excel at *other* things," I say. "Physical pursuits."

His hand tightens on mine reflexively and I realize what I've just implied—that he must be good in bed. My eyes snap to his. His eyebrows have disappeared beneath his hair.

"And you excel at words," he says.

I can no longer hold my tongue or make a clear judgment.

"At least I can dance."

"A little."

"With the right partner."

"And what about the wrong one?"

I glare at him. "Obviously not."

"When grace meets rhythm, the effect is beautiful."

That's certainly not us. I am suddenly exhausted. "Like the king and queen. They each have both. They are well matched."

"What about when gracelessness meets rhythmlessness?" he asks. "Can the effect not be beautiful? Because we, too, are well matched. Equal."

We are not equal. He has been royalty all his life, and I am nothing but a fabricated duchess.

I think to tell him this, but he pauses both the conversation and the dance, and my eyes lift to his of their own accord. He leans over me. Intimate. His eyes seek not information but permission.

"What has Hal told you?" I ask. It is the first thing on my mind. Actually the second, but I cannot ask, *What have you told Hal?*

"That you love words."

Silence stretches out between us. Long and silver like a thread pulled from a tapestry. Unraveling.

"Perhaps the writing of them more than the speaking," he says. His voice is low and sonorous. Confiding. But his eyes brighten with merriment. He's teasing me.

I find that I cannot reply.

A sweep of skirts flashes past us and I realize we are standing amongst the dancers, some of whom are giving us dirty looks. Fitz takes my arm and guides me gently to the end of the room. I wonder if he is looking for a place to deposit me so he can find someone more interesting.

He finally stops nearer the exit, along the path the servants follow to bring platters of food and take the carcasses and bones back to the dogs behind the kitchen.

Perfect.

But Fitz doesn't leave. He cradles me in his shadow.

"I'm afraid the last time we spoke—" He stops. Coughs. "Or didn't speak. I'm afraid my reaction—or lack of it—embarrassed you."

That embarrassment flares up in me again and I'm glad to be sheltered from the rest of the room. Madge would be able to see my blotchiness from the dance floor.

"I can't tell you how sorry I am," he says.

He's sorry? I can't speak, so I hold my breath. Wait for the *but* that begs to be tacked onto the phrase. There's always a *but. But I'm just not attracted to you. But I'm in love with someone else. But my father says I can't.*

"But . . ."

I groan and turn to the tapestry behind us, wanting to press my face into the woven Adriatic. Maybe I can drown in it.

He's silent. Forever.

"But what?" I ask finally, not looking up from the sea of threads.

"But it's different." He pauses. "It's . . . you're . . ."

Again the silence.

Belligerence turns me to face him. "I'm what?"

He flinches at the sharpness of my tone.

"You're my wife."

I clench my hands into fists. Pray that I don't use them. "And that makes me what? Undesirable? Untouchable? Ugly?"

"No!" The sharpness of his tone matches my own, but then it softens. "Just the opposite, actually."

He takes my hand and turns it palm up, strokes my fingers open, and rests his palm on mine.

"You are beautiful and desirable and singularly and utterly touchable." He's looking at my hand, tracing the lines there with his index finger. I watch his face for any sign of a tease or a joke. But there is none. I hold my breath.

He raises his eyes to mine.

"Then why . . . ?" I can't even ask him in words.

A smile tugs at his mouth.

"You surprised me."

I wait. But he's not forthcoming.

"You mean you didn't want me to kiss you first. You mean you think I'm . . . bold. Presumptuous. Immodest."

He looks back down at my hand. And nods.

My mother's assessment of me stands.

He takes a step. Closer to me. His knee presses mine through my skirts. He brushes the hair away from my face and runs his fingers down my neck, his forehead to my temple so he can whisper directly into my ear.

"Your kiss surprised me," he repeats. "But I liked it."

I can add one quality to the list.

Honesty.

Guildford
July 1534

13

"That's the perfect way to leave it," Madge says. Fitz left in May to preside over a gathering of the Order of the Garter at Windsor. From there he traveled on to his own estates in Dorset.

Now, despite the queen's growing girth, court has begun the summer progress. Hampton Court to The More to Cheyne to Woking. I start to lose track after a while, one house blurring into another as we pack and unpack, move and stay still.

In Guildford, the queen asks for rest, seeking quiet indoors while the king spends most days out hunting. We don't stay at the castle that dominates the town's highest hill. It has begun to decay, the walls crumbling a little. In the past, it was even used as a jail, and I shudder at the thought of prisoners watching us parading by in all our finery, though now the windows stare blankly out over the town.

Instead, some of us stay at Sutton Place—the residence of Francis Weston's family. It is square and grand and beautiful. My room is small and has a single window that looks over the hills and forests of Surrey. I envy Weston growing up here.

"I'm afraid Fitz will forget about me," I tell Madge. *Or meet someone else.*

"'Love's tide flows stronger toward absent lovers.'"

"We're not lovers."

"It doesn't matter." Madge pauses, her head tilted to one side. "I think I'm going to write that one down. Where's your book?"

With all the moving involved with the progress, I haven't been able to find anything in weeks. But I know where the book is.

I pull it out of my smallest traveling chest. I don't want to admit to Madge that I read our list from time to time. Trying to pin any of the attributes on Fitz. Or anyone else.

She takes it from me and snaps her fingers for a quill and ink.

"I'm not your serving wench."

She squints up at me. "Oh, that's right. You're a *duchess*." I feel completely wrong-footed as she unlatches my desk and writes the phrase in the book.

"Is that Chaucer?" I ask, hoping to make amends.

"Sextus Propertius."

I shake my head at the extent of Madge's knowledge. "Sometimes I think you're better read than the queen."

Madge tries to hide a grin, finishing with a flourish. She blows on the ink to dry it, then touches the last word with a finger.

"Mary," she says, and then stops. I wait, but she doesn't continue.

"What?"

She turns to face me. "If I knew something—something that

could upset someone, but also something that was none of my business—should I tell?"

"I guess it depends on what it is."

"What if I knew something about the king?"

I begin to feel a real sense of dread. So I repeat, much more slowly, "I guess it depends on what it is."

She looks down at her hands. "He's having an affair."

I think of the queen's growing belly. The king hasn't visited her rooms since she had morning sickness. To protect the baby. Perhaps absence does not increase love's tide after all.

"With whom?"

"Does it matter?"

I shake my head. But it does. The queen will want to know. Is it a friend? A rival? Or just a dalliance?

"So do I tell?"

The king will be furious. But my loyalty is to the queen. And so is Madge's.

I wonder if I would want to know. If Fitz had run off to Windsor or Dorset and met some other girl. If he kissed her. Bedded her. Would I begrudge him that? Since we are not allowed?

And then I wonder—would he want to know if I did the same?

"We should take this to someone closer to the queen. Someone she trusts," I say. "Lady Rochford will know whether or not to tell her." Jane Boleyn—Lady Rochford—is the queen's sister-in-law and oldest friend.

We make our way to the queen's rooms. Even her space is

limited here, and the size of the room seems to decrease as more people enter. I try to take full and regular breaths.

The queen sits by the fire, despite the warmth outside, and taps her foot in time to Mark Smeaton's playing, smiling at him lazily.

Then abruptly she stands, and turns to me.

"Cousin," she says, "dance with me."

The queen takes me by the hands and we move slowly into a pavane. I feel her belly bump against me and wonder at the life inside it. At what that child will see, growing up. I wonder what kind of king he'll be. And if he will change the shape of the world as his father did.

I see Madge make her way over to Jane Boleyn. Whisper in her ear. And I see Jane's face lose all its color. She nods once.

A few steps in, the queen pales and lets go of my left hand to cradle her belly. I reach for her, but she waves me away.

"Continue, Cousin. Dance with Madge there."

While the queen hoists herself back into her chair, and her ladies scramble to pry her slippers from her swollen feet, Madge and I shuffle through the dance together.

"You told?" I whisper.

Madge looks worried. "I hope it was the right thing."

We spin once, our skirts flaring, and I grin at her. "You're a much better dancer than Fitz."

"And you're not nearly as good as Hal."

I stick my tongue out at her.

"He's very light on his feet. He seems to have some kind of

inner sense of how to move. Almost . . . instinctual. Like an animal."

"Ma-adge," I whine. "He's my brother. I don't need to know that sort of thing."

"What are you two whispering about?"

The queen is sitting up against a dozen pillows, peering at us. Her eyes are puffy.

"Nothing, Your Majesty."

"Not nothing, Your Majesty," Madge corrects me. "We were talking of . . . Francis Weston. And his innate ability to find the music in his feet."

"Weston?" the queen asks. "He's a good dancer, is he?"

"Yes, Your Majesty." Madge sends a sly smile my way. "It makes me wonder if he's as good at other physical endeavors."

I look up to see the queen's eyebrow arch.

"You know," Madge continues. "Like . . . archery. Or tennis."

"Of course," the queen says. "Perhaps one day we should invite Master Weston to display his skills."

"Yes, Your Majesty," Madge says.

"For your sake only, Mistress Shelton." The queen leans back against her pillows, her belly rising with the shift of the down. She looks up into the stars embroidered on the canopy over her head and strokes the underside of her belly.

"I have all I want."

I feel guilty because I know she doesn't.

14

Two days later, I hear them fighting.

I've escaped the crowded hall for the wide stretch of wilderness beside it. Madge refused to come with me—Francis Weston had agreed to show her some of the secrets of the manor. So I go alone.

The forest is all beech and oak, the sun dappling through the leaves, so I head in that direction. The summer sun is warm on the back of my neck, and the snood of my hood weighs heavy. I look around me, wondering if I dare remove it.

The more formal gardens are dotted with a scattering of courtiers, intent on catching the ladies out for a stroll. But no one else is nearby.

Swiftly, I reach up to unpin my hood, quickening my steps so I can hide myself in the trees. I've just managed to shake my hair free, still in a thick twist, when I hear a shout.

Close.

Mother always said my timing was impeccable. That no matter how I broke the rules, I always chose the perfect moment to do so.

The moment I would be caught.

I try to stuff my hair back into its snood, but it uncoils like a snake and sticks to my already sweating fingers. Someone will see the Duchess of Richmond looking like a drab.

"You know nothing!"

I'd recognize the king's voice in my sleep. Full and resonant, but not as deep as one would expect. I freeze against the trunk of a copper beech, my loose hair plastering itself to the sweat of my neck.

"Then enlighten me. Prove me wrong. Prove Jane wrong. Or prove her right."

The queen. Her voice strong and steady.

"There is nothing you need to know."

"There is, Henry. I deserve the truth."

I slide down the tree trunk, fingers digging into the leaves beneath it, and bury my face in my skirts. I don't want to hear this. But I cannot move, or they will see me.

"You deserve?" The king is quieter. Even more dangerous.

"I am your *wife*. You pledged your troth. Your *body*. Forsaking all others. Or have you forgotten?"

When my mother found out about Father's mistress—Bess Holland—she said exactly the same thing. Using much the same language. She called Bess nothing but a whore.

It was the first time Father left us without having an excuse—court, diplomacy, war.

She came to me, her hair tangled about her, and told me to choose sides. She said Father was a savage.

I chose him anyway.

The king's voice softens. The forest is so quiet—not even the sound of a bird—I think I can hear them breathing. "I

119

remember where you have come from," he says "The daughter of a knight. Of no one."

"I am related to royalty."

"In your very distant dreams." His tone has not altered. It's the kind someone would use on a skittish horse. "You should be content with what I've done for you. And remember I made you what you are."

"I am myself!" The queen's voice is becoming desperate. "I am Anne Boleyn. You have not made me!"

The stillness that descends over the wood is as cold and thick and immovable as stone.

Until the king breaks it.

"I can make you nothing."

I don't know how long I sit against that tree. I hear the king leave, but I do not hear the queen weeping. Mother always cried. Every time Father left us.

That night, there's a flurry very late—one barely seen or recognized by those of us who don't sleep in the queen's chambers. She spends all the next day in bed—pale and wan, the hair hanging around her face like curtains.

No one says a word. But no secret at court is very well kept, so surely the news that the queen miscarried can't stay locked within these walls for long.

The king doesn't speak to her. He goes hunting, and comes back late.

But the next day, they sit beside each other at dinner, fingers touching.

And when we move to Woodstock, with its cramped cluster

of towers, their reconciliation is made painfully public when he visits her bedchamber.

The queen doesn't argue when her sister-in-law, Jane Boleyn, is exiled from court for her part in the debacle. And Madge doesn't say a word.

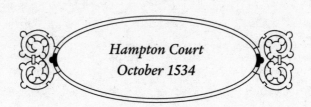

Hampton Court
October 1534

15

WHEN WE RETURN FROM THE PROGRESS, FITZ IS RECALLED TO court, and every day that goes by makes me more nervous. We haven't seen each other in months. We haven't spoken. Haven't written.

Will my list change? Will it matter that he can't dance?

Will he remember that he liked my kiss? Or will he, like his father, have found someone else? And if he has, will I be able to fight like Queen Anne did?

Will I want to?

At least it is a relief to pause at Hampton Court, despite the king's endless building works. After months of packing and traveling and cramped quarters, I almost dread our impending move to Greenwich. But a delegation of French diplomats is coming to visit the court in November, and the king wants to entertain them away from the presence of bricklayers and glaziers. I think he especially wants to impress Philippe de Chabot, the admiral of France and one of the highest-ranking officers of the French crown.

Even with the chaos, Hampton Court feels comfortable and sheltered, though winter seems to have arrived early and a bitter north wind pecks determinedly at the windows.

As we sew in the queen's rooms, I watch her. She sits with her head in one hand. Her eyes are trained toward the cloudy sky, but her thoughts are obviously elsewhere. The king's affair seems to be over, but it has taken its toll on her. Her cheeks are a little more hollow. Her eyes rest deeply in their sockets, the skin around them smudged like a bruise. As I watch, she closes her eyes, presses her lips together. I see her shoulders rise as she takes a deep breath.

She sits up, her back straight, puts her hands in her lap, tilts her head to one side, and gazes about the room. When she finds me watching her, she smiles. Just a tiny bit. I lower my head in deference. When I look up, her eyes have once again trailed to the window.

Behind me, I hear whispers. They sound like waves approaching the shore and retreating again. Buffeting. With each approach, they grow louder. I turn, and see women speaking behind their hands.

Whatever the rumor is, it feels malicious, like something crawling from beneath the floorboards and getting ready to pounce. I wonder how this rumor has started in a closed room, with only the servants entering and exiting. Perhaps it creeps through the chinks in the wall like fog.

The doors open and the usher stands aside to let a woman enter. She is of medium height and somewhat blonde, her brown eyes warm, but a little distant. Her skin is the color of poured cream, and though she is getting old, I can tell she was once very pretty.

She is the queen's sister, Mary Boleyn. Now Mary Carey.

As she walks, people turn away. She doesn't look left or right. Doesn't acknowledge the whispers that precede and follow her. Doesn't seem to care that everyone is staring.

Or what they are staring at.

Her approach is preceded by a belly so great she looks like a ship in full sail. Her husband died six years ago from the sweat.

"Oh my God," Margaret whispers beside me.

I glance at Madge, who is just behind her, wide-eyed.

I turn to the queen. There is no color to her cheeks, to her lips. Her eyes are like stones in snow.

Mistress Carey sinks into a curtsy. The pregnancy makes it awkward and difficult, but no one moves to help her. She is absolutely huge.

"It looks like she could drop the baby right here on the floor," Madge mutters.

Queen Anne says nothing. It is as if she has been turned to wax.

Mistress Carey keeps her head bowed. She lived at court for years and knows how things are done. Even though she must be uncomfortable, she waits without complaint. She doesn't shift or fidget. She seems perfectly content to stay there all day.

"You know, some people say she was the king's mistress, *before*."

Before Anne. When we called Katherine of Aragon queen.

The room breaks into waves of whispers.

"Everyone said she was beautiful," Madge says. "She's got

nice hair, I suppose, but do you really think she's pretty?"

"She's *pregnant*, Madge. It's not like we can comment on her figure," Margaret snipes.

"I wish to speak to Mistress—my *sister*."

The queen's voice cuts across the rumors. We all turn to go. No one wants to have to face the queen's sharp tongue. Mistress Carey trembles.

"Cousins, attend me."

I feel Madge startle beside me. The queen is looking at the two of us. She knows that we will keep her secrets. We've done it before. We stop, shoulder to shoulder, and wait as the room empties and the ushers close the doors from the outside.

"Stand."

"Nan." The word is a whisper, but we can hear it in the empty silence.

"Do *not* call me that."

The queen steps down from her dais so she and Mistress Carey are face-to-face, like cats about to attack. They are still, yet they give the appearance of circling.

"What are you thinking, showing up here like . . . like that?"

Mistress Carey bows her head, her fingers linked below her belly as if it is too heavy on its own.

"I wanted to tell you in person."

"Wanted to tell me *what*? That you have continued in the manner in which you acted at the French court? That you've come to me for assistance? For a position? For a person to take your baby on as ward? That you don't know who the father is?"

The queen's questions fall rapidly, like hailstones, and

Mistress Carey flinches with every one. Until the last. She looks up.

"I know exactly who the father is. He is my husband."

Again, the queen goes waxy and rigid as a candle. Then she raises one eyebrow.

"Your husband?"

The quiet question is somehow more frightening than the ones she shouted. But Mistress Carey doesn't flinch.

"Yes. We have been married secretly this past year. The child is his."

"Whose?"

"William Stafford."

The queen leans forward, tipping one ear toward her sister as if she's hard of hearing.

"Who?" she asks, her eyes snapping to the point of almost shooting sparks.

"William Stafford."

"And who, pray tell, is he?"

Again the queen's voice raises, and again Mistress Carey— Mistress *Stafford*—doesn't flinch.

"My husband. I met him when I journeyed with you to Calais."

I went, as well, at the age of twelve, when Anne was just Marquess of Pembroke. *Not* the king's mistress. She made very sure everyone knew that. She was just . . . there. I don't remember a William Stafford in the king's entourage, or in my mother's family. She is a Stafford—daughter of the Duke of Buckingham—and taught me the lineage like catechism.

"He was a soldier," Mistress Carey continues. "A yeoman. His people own land in Essex."

"A commoner," the queen spits. "A man of no birth, no gentry, no nothing! Is he at least to inherit?"

"No. He is the second son."

"You are the sister of the queen, Mary! How could you do that? Were you pregnant before? Is that why? Was he the closest thing you could get to security? You could have come to me. You know that. I would have found you something—someone—better."

A moment spins out between them, and it is as if the two sisters are the only people in the world. I can see their shared history in their eyes and in the way they stand near each other—close, but not touching.

"My child was conceived in wedlock. And I could do no better, Nan." Mistress Stafford looks up and her face is glowing. "I love him. There is nothing better than that."

It shows in her pregnancy, in her attitude, in her countenance. Like the sun breaking free of swift-moving clouds. I want to know what she knows. I want to stand in full sun.

"I shall have to send you away," the queen whispers. Madge inhales sharply, but the queen doesn't seem to remember we're in the room. "It cannot be tolerated. You're . . . you're the sister of the queen. You can't just go marry whomever you like. You can't marry without permission. Have babies . . . And showing up here . . . I can't beg the king to bring your husband into the Privy Chamber. It's just not possible."

"I know."

"Where will you go?" The queen's voice drops even further, and I struggle to hear without giving the appearance that I am. "Father will not have you. He will cut you off. Completely."

Mistress Stafford hangs her head. "I know."

"Then why did you do it, Mary?" The words sound lodged in the queen's throat. "Why did you marry him?"

Mistress Stafford looks her sister—her queen—in the eye.

"Because I love him. And I would rather beg alms from door to door with him than give that up."

The queen's face hardens and the pleading look dissolves.

Mistress Stafford straightens her shoulders, tips her chin up, and I see her chest rise and fall with a deep breath. When she speaks again, it is with absolute certainty.

"I would rather have him than be the greatest queen in Christendom."

Madge gasps, and the queen takes a quick step back. Clenches her hands into the pleats of her skirt.

"Then go," she says. "And never come here again."

16

"She banished her own sister," Madge tells Margaret as we thread our way through the crowded galleries and courtyards on our way back to my lodgings. Hampton Court is teeming with courtiers who didn't travel with us on the progress—all of them hoping to make themselves indispensable. I lose Madge as she slips between two fat barons before they close the gap. I go around.

Margaret never has to dodge. It is like a law of nature—water runs downhill, the sun rises in the east, and crowds make way for Margaret Douglas.

But Madge and Margaret don't mind the press of bodies. They don't shudder at the touch of strangers or feverishly count the heads between them and the next exit. All my fears slow me down, and my friends are already in my room by the time I catch up to them.

These days, my room is never empty. And I am no longer alone.

"She was so cold." Madge continues her train of thought as though she was never interrupted. "Like blood doesn't matter. Like rules are more important." She sits on her favorite stool by the fire and takes her slippers off.

"Margaret says there are no rules in Anne Boleyn's court."

"Maybe not in Anne's, but there are in the king's," Margaret says darkly.

"So if Mary here were to go and get herself impregnated by Fitz, she'd be expelled as well?"

A wash of nervous energy chills me. At the sound of his name. At the possibility of being thrown from court. At the thought of what needs to happen in order to be impregnated.

"They wouldn't . . ." I hesitate, fear filling my throat. "The queen wouldn't let that happen."

She treats me almost as an equal.

"It looks like she would," Madge says.

"I'm a duchess. The queen's sister hasn't even been at court these nine months."

Madge frowns. "Your mother is a duchess, too, Mary. And she's not here."

"My mother refused to serve in Anne Boleyn's court," I admit painfully.

"Your mother wasn't given the option," Margaret says.

"You mean she wasn't invited?" I ask.

When my mother refused to carry Anne's mantle at her investiture as Marquess of Pembroke, I took her place. Mother cursed at me. It never occurred to me that was her last opportunity to serve the queen.

Margaret shakes her head. "All it takes is one offense. Look at Jane Boleyn: her husband is here, an intimate of the queen. But she has not returned. We could be asked to leave at any moment. For any kind of indiscretion."

"For sleeping with my husband?" I ask. "For flirting?"

"The queen flirts all the time," Madge says.

"There's a distinction between talking and doing," Margaret says. "And when you make the doing obvious, as Mary Boleyn has, there will be consequences to face."

"The queen told me once that the Boleyns always stick together," I say. Like me and Hal. Always taking Father's side.

"It wasn't the queen who broke that bond," Margaret says. "It was her sister."

"How so?"

"If she really honored the Boleyns above all, she would have let the queen arrange her marriage. Or she would have kept it a secret."

"She said she would rather have love than be a queen," Madge says.

Margaret's eyes widen and she shakes her head. "That's like a slap in the face. She's saying there's no love in the queen's relationship. That despite her status and her jewels, Anne Boleyn is no better than the rest of us. Married for ambition and family alliances."

"But the king loves her."

Margaret looks at me disparagingly. "For now."

I turn away and busy myself with pouring us each a mug of small ale. "Do you think she really loves him?" I ask.

"The queen?" Madge says.

"Her sister."

"She must," Margaret says. "She knew what she was risking when she married him."

132

"I wonder if it's worth it," I muse.

"It's going against the king's direct wishes," Margaret says, and I get the feeling she's aiming her words at me specifically.

"And what about you, Margaret?" I ask. "What if you were to fall in love with my uncle Thomas?"

Margaret stands so close to me, I can see the pores in her skin and the flecks of black and gold in her eyes.

"If you're going to make a choice between love and survival, you have to be absolutely sure you're doing the right thing."

"And are you?" I ask. "Doing the right thing?"

A flicker of doubt crosses her face, but it's quickly closed down by her familiar reserve. Then she breaks into a smile.

"At the moment, it's more talking than doing."

Madge throws herself onto my bed and rolls back and forth. "This would be a nice place for more doing than talking."

Margaret and I exchange a look and run across the room and leap onto the bed to join her. Madge sits up with a start and we throw her back down again, Margaret pinning her arms so I can tickle her.

Madge squirms and kicks and gasps for breath.

"Talk or do, Madge?" I ask. "Talk or do?"

Madge gasps again. "Talk!" she wheezes.

Margaret and I let go and collapse onto either side of Madge, all of us looking up into the folds of the canopy.

"So when are the two of you going to *do* something?" Madge asks, sounding not at all as if she's just been tickled into submission.

"I haven't even kissed him yet," I tell the canopy.

"Yes, you have."

"Fine. He just didn't kiss me back. So I'm unlikely to be doing anything else."

"Chaucer says a woman wants sovereignty over her husband and over her love. It's up to you. You can't sit around waiting. You're already married. It's not like he can change that just because you flirt a little."

"I suppose," I say, unsure.

"In fact, most men like it when the woman takes the lead," Madge continues. "Why do you think they all flock to the queen? The whole idea of this game of courtly love is that *both* sides indulge in it. Shouldn't it be the same for real love?" She pauses, eyeing me up and down. "Or at least the physical act of it?"

I feel the heat rise in my chest, and she laughs.

"You're going blotchy again, Duchess." Then her tone softens. "There's no harm in being curious."

"What about the harm in acting on that curiosity, Madge?"

We stare at each other for a good, long moment.

"I suppose it depends on whom you ask."

I wait.

"Think about it," she says. "If you ask the priest, he'll tell you it's a sin." She pauses, and then adds, "Unless he's the one who wants you to commit it."

"Ew."

"If you ask the king, he'll tell you it's against his rules."

I wait, one eyebrow raised.

"If you ask most of the men at court, they'll suggest they take you up on it instead of Fitz. Believe me."

"I don't want to ask most of the men at court."

Madge jumps up and starts rummaging through my desk.

"You wouldn't ask *most* of the men at court, but that doesn't mean you wouldn't ask *some* of them." She pulls out the leather-bound book. "Another list!"

Margaret frowns. "Of what?"

"Of the most kissable men at court."

"Don't be silly, Madge," I say. "Anyone could find it."

"No one's found it yet, Duchess. I imagine you sleep with your little book."

I try to imagine kissing someone else. All I can really imagine is what it would have felt like if Fitz had actually kissed me.

Madge opens the book to an empty page. "We won't title it. Even if someone finds it, it will be nothing but a list of names. So." She pauses with her pen hovering over the page. "Who's in?"

"Fitz," I blurt, at the same time Margaret says, "Thomas Howard."

Madge snorts and starts scribbling.

"Thomas Seymour," she says.

I frown. "I don't like him."

"I don't trust him," Margaret agrees.

"Doesn't mean he's not kissable," Madge says. "Who else?"

"Thomas Wyatt?" Thomas Wyatt, with those amazing eyes and that sensuous mouth.

"Good choice, Duchess."

"George Boleyn."

I turn to look at Margaret. "The queen's brother?"

"What?" She shrugs. "There's something about those dark eyes of his."

"Henry Norris," Madge adds. "At least he's single."

"Francis Weston," I say.

"He flirts outrageously with the queen," Madge says.

"Maybe that's why I find him appealing."

Madge grins. Then her eyes open wide and her smile even wider. She scribbles down one more word, and Margaret and I lean over to see what she's written.

"The *king*?" I cry. He's getting fat and bald, and that temper reminds me of my mother. "He's my father-in-law."

"He's my uncle," Margaret adds. "You have to cross him off, Madge."

"No." Madge closes the book. "You two don't have to think he's kissable. But remember our other list. Ambition. Power. Good dancer."

She slides the book back into my desk.

"Now," Madge continues, "by the end of the week, my friends, I expect that each of us will have kissed *one* of the people on this list." She grins. "If not more."

"What about the rules?" I ask, thinking she can't possibly hold us to this pledge. "What about it being a sin?"

Madge sits very still. When she looks up at me again, she smiles.

"Sometimes, I think it's a sin," she says carefully. "And I

know it's against the rules. But with some men, I just can't help but offer."

A wave of sadness passes across her face, and though her smile returns, the sadness remains in her eyes.

"Which would you choose?"

"A prince." Madge takes our hands so we form a circle. "A prince in word and deed," she proclaims. "For all of us. Because we deserve to be treated like princesses."

I'm bathed in the warmth of gratitude. My mother always said I deserved a man who treated me like my father treated her. Viciously.

"Let us go forth and conquer." Madge strides to the door and opens it, standing to one side to let Margaret and me precede her.

It is only when the door closes behind us all that I realize Madge didn't put Hal on the list.

17

When we step outside, the wind cuts through the damask of my bodice and brings a rash of gooseflesh. I wrap my arms around myself and rub them hard.

"Where are we going, Madge?"

"To the fields of course," Madge says, leading the way across the base court. "To see the men. And the boys. And to sort the one from the other."

"You expect us just to walk up and kiss someone?" Margaret asks. She keeps up easily with Madge's trot, her long legs covering more ground in one stride than mine do in three.

"Of course not," Madge replies. "But I do expect us all to get a little attention. They can't want to kiss us if they don't know we're here."

Madge pulls us through the massive two-story gate and across the bridge over the moat. The outer courtyard is busy with workers and messengers and servants and piled with bricks and lengths of timber.

"They're all out attacking each other and the quintain or whatever it is they do because they can't do it to the French delegation when they arrive."

Madge pauses in the final gate and we peer around her. King

Henry has plans to build a tiltyard in the empty fields between the outer court and the great orchard, but for now it's a wide expanse of flattened earth.

The archery butts have been set up at the far end of the field, and the men seem to be betting on who is the best shot. I pause to watch Fitz—his red hair obvious in the sea of brown and blond—take aim. The *thwack* of the arrow driving home reaches my ears while the arrow still quivers from the impact.

"They are supposed to watch *you*," Madge says, grabbing my wrist, "not the other way around."

Madge pushes me out onto the field and disappears into a half-built structure obviously used for storage. She comes back with three wooden broadswords, the kind boys use to practice war games. She grabs one by the "blade," turning the handle toward me, and throws.

"Catch!"

The sword sails through the air—surprisingly swiftly and surprisingly far, considering how tiny and delicate Madge looks. I reach out my left hand, and the hilt cracks my knuckles.

"Ouch!"

The sword clatters at my feet as I put my fist up to my mouth, trying to suck out the sting.

"Pick it up, Mary." Madge hands another sword to Margaret, who takes it as one might a dead animal.

"Is this really necessary, Mistress Shelton?" she asks.

"Watch," Madge tells her, and turns back to me, holding her broadsword in both hands, her stance wide.

I look down at the wooden sword. There are stains on the blade of it. I hope they're mud.

"We could get hurt doing this, Madge."

"We could get hurt going down the spiral stairs, Mary. We could get hurt eating a capon. We could get hurt falling in love. But we do it anyway. Pick it up."

She almost spits the last words.

"Are you teaching me, Madge? Or fighting me?"

She softens a little. "Just trying to get you riled up. Unbalance your complacency."

"Are you challenging me to a duel?" I ask, picking up the weapon. It's heavier than it looks, the long blade tipping the weight of it back toward the ground. My wrists bend unnaturally and I struggle to straighten them.

Madge lunges forward, swinging her sword like a tennis racket, knocking mine sharply to the right. I follow it, so she slaps me on my backside with the flat of her blade and laughs.

"That's not fair!" I drop my weapon and rub the offended area.

"All is fair in love and war, my friend!" she sings, turning circles with her sword held out in front of her, the weight of it carrying her around in a dizzy spin. I step back. Directly into Thomas Wyatt.

"It looks like you could use some instruction," he says, steadying me before flourishing a bow. "Your Grace."

I ignore Madge's ridiculously delighted giggle and struggle to keep my gaze on his eyes.

Not his lips.

"Would you like some pointers, Your Grace? Between us, I think we can beat your whirlwind over there."

"We were just playing," I say.

"You shouldn't play at love or war, Your Grace." I wonder for a moment if he's flirting with me, but his tone is serious.

He retrieves the sword, abandoned in the mud.

"Would you like to learn?"

"Love or war?" I blurt, and, thankfully, he laughs—a rolling rumble that comes from deep in his chest.

"I told you," he says, stepping behind me to place the hilt of the sword in my hand, and I can feel his words along the curve of my ear. "You shouldn't play at either."

Is Thomas Wyatt flirting with me? I think frantically. *And am I flirting back?*

"I don't intend to play," I say.

Wyatt laughs again. "You will certainly break some hearts, Your Grace."

"Somehow I doubt that." I heft the sword with both hands.

"You will without knowing it, Your Grace, for your beauty is unsurpassed."

I almost drop the weapon again, fumbling the handle slick with mud. I jerk back on it to keep my grip and elbow Wyatt in the stomach. His breath comes out in a laughing gasp.

"I'm afraid I'm as clumsy at flirtation as I am with this sword, Master Wyatt," I say, and try to lighten things by adding, "I don't suppose you have anything to teach me there?"

Wyatt's expression completely closes down.

"No, Your Grace."

Wyatt steps away from me. I have made another complete blunder. I glance at Madge, who is leaning on her sword and looking at me bemusedly. Behind her, I see Hal and Fitz together, walking toward us.

Madge tosses her head. "I need some instruction, Master Wyatt!" she calls. "In love *and* war." She lowers her voice seductively. "And I never play games."

"Everything is a game to you, Mistress Shelton," Hal says as he reaches us. "You help my sister, Wyatt. I've got this one under control."

"You could never control me, Surrey," Madge quips, and starts to spin again, but he grabs her from behind and wraps both arms around her, gripping the broadsword. He whispers something into her ear, and one corner of her mouth rises.

I dare not look at Thomas Wyatt, for fear I'll see that same expression of desperation I saw on Fitz's when I tried to kiss him. The same one Fitz wears now, standing at a distance. Watching.

"Do you think he needs rescuing?" Wyatt asks. He sounds sympathetic. Or perhaps he's just sorry for Fitz, with such a clumsy wife. Gracelessness.

"Don't we all?" I reply.

"Your Grace!" Wyatt calls. "I dare not abandon this fair maid except to one more qualified than I."

I freeze, and Fitz turns pink. I feel more than hear Wyatt's chuckle as he turns to Margaret. "My Lady Douglas," he says. "Would you accept the humble instruction of one such as I?"

Madge crows. "Remember the list!"

Margaret raises her sword with little effort, looking like Boadicea out for vengeance.

I look down at my own sword, the tip still settled in the mud. And then I feel the length of Fitz's body as he reaches both arms around me and places his hands over mine on the sword's grip. His are so warm. I resist the urge to turn my face to his as he guides me through a sweeping gesture with the sword.

He has grown in the last five months. At least an inch taller. And definitely broader. He's more man than boy—his nearness makes that conspicuously clear.

I look up to where Madge and Hal are practically bonded together, laughing so hard they can't control her sword.

"I think Mistress Shelton can take care of herself," Fitz says. He raises my arms and angles my body to show me how to slash with the sword.

"It's not Madge I'm worried about," I say. I am overly conscious of my heartbeat. Of the taste of his words. Of the pressure of his chest on my back and the touch of his skin on mine.

Fitz releases me. "Oh, I don't think you have to worry about Hal, either."

I attempt to slash with the sword on my own, and he ducks away, laughing. But my momentum pulls me sideways, my train tangling my ankles.

Fitz rescues me in one swift, graceful move that catches me before I crumble and takes my breath away. For an instant, I hang suspended in his arms, and everything else disappears. I can do nothing but stare into his eyes as he effortlessly sets me back on my feet.

"Thank you," I say and add, stupidly, "That was impressive."

"As you once said, I do excel at some . . . physical pursuits."

I try to suppress my blotchy blush.

"It is time to choose, my friends!" The yard comes back in a rush at Madge's shout. She has stepped away from Hal and holds her sword up above her head.

"Love or war?" she asks.

I look up at Fitz, only to discover him smiling at me, so subtly it makes my insides wobble.

"I know which one I choose," he says.

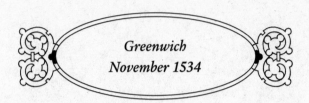

Greenwich
November 1534

18

THE FRENCH ARRIVE, AND WITH THEM ALL THE FESTIVITIES OF the holidays. Everyone delights in the revelry and the debauchery. In the innuendos and the insinuations against the French. The court is a whirl of fine fabrics and subtext, of one thing covering another.

After the greatest of the banquets thus far, the king and queen sit with Chabot—the French admiral. He has curly hair and an even curlier beard, both cut so straight that his head looks rectangular. He has the round cheeks of someone jovial, but eyes that are suspicious of everyone.

I study the king and queen from a distance. They married for love. Went through hell for love. Faced censure and name-calling and ill will and even excommunication for love. If anyone sets an example for me of how to love or what it means, it should be them.

Yet I cannot forget their argument I overheard at Sutton Place. The abuse. The venom. The ease with which the king said that he could make her nothing.

I believe he could do it, too. The Act of Supremacy has made King Henry the head of the church in England. He has made the pope—once universally thought to be God's representative on earth—into nothing. King Henry could do the same to the queen. People who refuse to acknowledge the king's supremacy—who refuse to take the oath imposed by the Act—are imprisoned. Margaret's prediction has come true. He has taken control of our faith.

But through the Act of Succession, it is also treason to speak against the queen. People are being imprisoned (and possibly worse) for saying Anne should be burned. One was imprisoned for calling Archbishop Cranmer a pimp, thus implying that Queen Anne is a whore. Daily, I wonder when it will be my mother who is sent to the Tower.

The king does it for Queen Anne. He protects her virtue, champions her name. He believes in her. In their love.

Doesn't he?

The queen's sister didn't seem to think so.

The king and queen seem happy today, if a little tense. The presence of Admiral Chabot could excuse that. Word is that we need French support. That Katherine of Aragon's nephew—the Holy Roman emperor—is likely to declare war to defend her honor.

Our king is using Princess Elizabeth as a bargaining chip. Offering her in marriage to a French prince, the Duke of Orléans. She's barely a year old. He's eleven. The French know how desperate King Henry is. So he plies them with wine and promises and calls for dancing.

I see Margaret dancing with one of the French delegation. Doing her duty for the English cause. My uncle Thomas stands to one side, his gaze never leaving her.

"Any progress?" Madge asks, appearing at my elbow.

"Not for me," I muse. "But I think perhaps Margaret has come closer than we expected."

Madge narrows her eyes, watching Thomas as a cat would a mouse.

"He's definitely smitten."

Margaret's own eyes are lowered as the Frenchman leads her into a turn.

"Do you think she is?" Madge asks.

"It's hard to tell," I say. "She's so reserved. She certainly doesn't divulge any secrets."

"Then she's the right kind of friend to have."

"True. But it's hard to know what she's thinking. Not like you and Hal. Everyone on the tiltyard knew what you were up to."

Madge smiles. "I'm not married. I'm not related to the king. I have little reputation and few prospects. I've got nothing to lose."

"What about your heart?"

"Come," she says by way of reply. "Let's dance."

"Together?"

"We dance together all the time in the queen's rooms. It's not like we don't know how. We can set a precedent! Things don't change unless people are willing to change them."

The dance is a pavane, so at least there is no lifting involved. Madge dances well—especially when she knows she's being observed. All I have to do is follow.

"Get a little more lively, Duchess!" Madge whispers as we circle around each other.

She does a little twist that flares her skirts and shows off the sensual movement of her hips.

"Try that. Your husband is watching."

I don't look up, but I try Madge's move. I like the feel of my skirts as they brush against my hips and twist around my ankles. So I do it again.

"Ha!" Madge crows. "I knew you could!"

We laugh and ignore the prescribed steps of the dance as we turn the circle, each trying to outdo the other. Madge shakes her sleeves, putting her hands up over her head, wrists exposed, hands turned out. I attempt one of her signature twirls, which gets us laughing again.

I try another and stumble. The hand that catches me isn't Madge's. It glitters with rings, tight to the fingers. And the gold embroidery at the cuff of the sleeve is delicately traced with roses.

I am suddenly ashamed and hide my blush in my skirts when I curtsy.

"Your Majesty."

"As lovely as you ladies look dancing together, I had to interrupt, and take the pleasure myself."

The king's voice rolls like honey, syrupy and viscid. As the king cannot be refused, I look up to accept, but he has already taken Madge's hand and is escorting her into the next steps of the dance. She doesn't take her eyes off his face.

I step backward, ready to lose myself in the crowd, and come up hard against another velvet doublet behind me.

"You seem to have lost your partner to the king," Fitz says

150

into my ear. "Allow me to rescue you and finish the dance."

"I don't really need rescuing." I sound hoarse. I press my lips together and look at him over my shoulder.

"You danced so . . . bewitchingly, I had hoped you would want to continue. Even if it means dancing with me."

I can't help myself. "Sounds dangerous."

Fitz laughs. "Perhaps we shouldn't. If only for the safety of the other dancers."

We stand there for a moment, just looking at each other.

"Come with me?" he asks, holding out a hand.

I take it but hesitate when he leads me toward the crowded watching chamber.

He turns, his eyebrows raised in a question.

"I . . ." I can't tell him about my fear of crowds. He will think me irrational. Absurd. "I shouldn't leave the queen."

He guides me to a quieter spot near the dais. The queen sits alone with the admiral, but she seems a bit inattentive.

"Did you know we've been married for a year?" Fitz asks.

I shake my head and smile. My whole world changed. Yet it seems like it's been this way forever.

"You've forgotten?" He almost looks hurt.

"No!" I remember how tight my bodice felt. The challenge in his eyes when I entered the chapel. I remember stepping in front of my mother. Being in bed with him when he almost kissed me. "I just didn't think . . . I didn't know it was today."

"The day after tomorrow, actually." He rolls his eyes. "But who's counting?"

I laugh. He seems much more of a boy again. Silly, almost. Like Madge.

Then he adds, all in a rush. "We've been married a year, and I feel I don't even know you."

"There isn't much to know. I'm the daughter of the Duke of Norfolk. Sister of the Earl of Surrey. And now the wife of the Duke of Richmond and Somerset. End of story."

"I should think there's much more than that. I've been a duke for as long as I remember. But that's not who I am."

The queen said much the same thing to me. A long time ago. And yet, I still haven't changed my answer.

"So who are you?" I challenge.

Fitz tips his head slightly and smiles at me.

"I'm still working on that. Aren't we all?"

"Well, what do you want? Out of life?"

"To be happy."

I laugh. It's such a frivolous desire. Not to serve God or the people. Not to help the poor or defeat France or promote religious reform.

"Happy."

"Yes. Like the queen. *The most happy.*"

The queen's motto. I glance at her. She's half listening to Philippe de Chabot, half watching the dancers.

"And what makes you happy?" I ask.

"Being who I am."

"You speak in circles, Henry FitzRoy." I can't help but laugh again. Until I turn back to him and see the intensity of his gaze.

"Please call me Fitz. It's part of who I am." He suddenly seems far too close. I can feel his warmth and breath and heart-beat, even through the distance between us. "And I'd like to get to know you."

I can hardly breathe, but manage to squeak, "We're not allowed to know each other."

"We're not allowed to sleep together," he says bluntly. "But at this point, I'd rather know you as a person. I think it"—he coughs—"helps."

My face flashes hot and I turn to hide it, but end up pressed against his chest. He's telling me he's slept with another girl. He's admitting it to my face. I suppose I wished for honesty. I certainly got it.

"It was in France," he says quickly. I lift my eyes and watch his lips moving, barely able to follow his words. "And I fancied myself in love. It was before—before we were married. Before I met you."

Fancied himself in love.

"But you haven't . . . since?" I can't ask the question outright. If he's bedded anyone. Or fallen in love again.

He shakes his head. "I take my vows seriously."

"That makes you unique in this court," I say.

"It's not just the vow, Mary. It's this." He moves his hand back and forth through the narrow distance between us.

What about this? I want to ask. I want to ask if he likes me, but it seems hopelessly juvenile. So instead, I count back the months to his time in France. He was only fourteen.

"Weren't you awfully young?"

"Probably too young," he agrees. "Certainly too young to know if I was in love."

"And your father has forbidden you to . . ."

"The king doesn't know."

"Obviously."

Fitz sighs. "Sometimes, I think the king is too protective of me, Mary. And sometimes, I think he asks too much."

"You are his only son."

"A son who can never be king."

I wonder if he's right. Father seems to think differently. But the sadness in Fitz's eyes tells another story.

"That doesn't stop him from loving you."

He stares hard at the dancers. Margaret is dancing with my uncle. They are matched in height, and look into each other's eyes.

The king has Madge in an embrace that approaches the boundary of impropriety. I think about our lists. *Good dancer. Pleasant voice.*

Power.

"Is it love?" Fitz asks quietly. "Or is it self-interest?"

We watch silently as Madge leaves the room. Seconds later, the entire assembly drops their heads—bows and curtsies rippling like waves—because the king exits through the same door.

I think about our other list. The one Hal isn't on. But the king is.

A noise behind me turns me back to the head table. Queen Anne's shoulders are shaking, her mouth open. The sound coming out of it is more of a howl than a laugh. Next to her,

Philippe de Chabot sits stiff and unmoving, his face as craggy and cold as roughly cut marble.

"Is she laughing at him?" Fitz asks, and I hear an edge of fear in his voice. "She could destroy our relationship with France."

"She's not laughing at him." I can't take my eyes off her. She sheds no tears, but her eyes gleam like glass.

The admiral stands and bows.

"How now, madam," he says. "Are you amusing yourself at my expense?"

Queen Anne stands with elegance, but with great speed, wiping her already dry eyes.

"Sir," she says, and her voice rings out across the nearly silent room. Everyone is watching. Everyone is listening. "I mean no offense. My husband had gone to bring another guest for me to entertain." She begins to chuckle. "Someone important. But on the way . . ." She begins to laugh. "He met a lady. And the errand has gone straight out of his head!"

This time the tears stream down her face. Chabot looks horrified, and the English courtiers begin to buzz—fervid with gossip.

The question *who was she?* sparks through the room like the crackle of fireworks.

I look at Fitz, whose mouth is in a straight line. He knows, just as I do. But he doesn't say a word.

I can add another item to our list of things to love.

Can keep a secret.

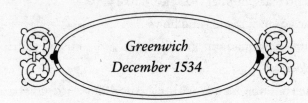

Greenwich
December 1534

19

I WATCH MADGE UNTIL SHE BARKS AT ME TO LEAVE HER ALONE. I think of asking Margaret to do it for me, but I hardly see her. Perhaps this thing with my uncle is bigger than we expected.

I watch the queen, who seems to grow paler and more frail by the day.

I watch the king. When he leaves the room, I always look for Madge.

I watch the French, who do not seem to have been greatly offended, but it's difficult to know with the French. Offense comes so easily to them.

I look for Fitz. To see if he is facilitating the king's affairs—both personal and political. To see if he is telling the queen about Madge. To see if he looks for me. But he has been deputized to entertain our guests—including hosting the Saint Andrew's Day feast—until they leave. I don't see him, no matter how hard I look.

The day the French depart, the halls of Greenwich are like the mudflats after a storm. Detritus everywhere. A few scavengers picking at bones. And a strange calm. As I climb the stairs to the queen's apartments, I pass a few courtiers, and then a huddle of maids. They're whispering and almost fall in their haste to reach the floor below.

I hear the king's voice as soon as I enter the presence chamber. They must be in her bedroom, but his enormous chest is like a sounding box, projecting every word through solid oak.

Everyone in the presence chamber looks terrified.

"Madam, I think you do not know to whom you speak."

"I know exactly to whom I speak. I speak to my husband." The queen's voice is higher. Lighter. Angrier.

"You speak to your king, madam. And I would counsel you to shut your eyes and endure as your betters have done before you."

The presence chamber is in a bubble of silence. No one moves. This is why that gaggle of maids was in such a hurry. This is why the chambers are so empty. Except for the few of us too terrified to flee. All of us staring at our feet or the window or the ceiling, afraid to see our own horror reflected in the faces of others.

"My *betters*?" The sarcasm rips the air. "But I am queen."

"I should seek to remind you that I raised you in a moment."

"A king can marry a commoner." The queen is speaking, but I can taste the bitterness in my own throat.

"And I could humble you in the same amount of time."

This growl carries an unmistakable warning.

The queen doesn't seem to hear it. Or she doesn't care. "There is more than one way around the problem, is that it?"

"And there is always hope." Ridicule spills and puddles

around the words. Ridicule. Disdain. And threat. *Hope* is such a pretty, fruity word, and he has made it taste like smut.

The silence in the presence chamber is like a held breath. Then we all fall to our knees reflexively when the door opens. I do not look up. The thump of heavy boot heels tells me it is the king who strides across the room and out the other door without pausing.

I remain in my curtsy, recovering my breath, aware only of the faint rustling of the others around me. It seems everyone is following the path of the king. Leaving the queen, as he has done.

"Walk with me, Cousin." The queen has stopped in front of me, the toes of her gold damask slippers just peeking out from under the hem of emerald-green skirts. The threads on one slipper have started to fray.

I stand, and as we leave the room together, I can feel the eyes of the palace watching us. We walk down the spiral stairs and through the courtyard. Instead of heading along the wall and into the orchard, the queen turns the opposite direction, toward the river.

I look at her—a small woman, dressed in the height of fashion. Her black hair swept back into the glittering coronet of her French hood. Her eyes dark. And knowing.

"So, Cousin," she says quietly. She glances at me, and I see what might be a smile. "How do you fare with young FitzRoy?"

I don't have the courage to tell her I don't know.

"We are . . . cordial, Your Majesty."

She laughs, a similar bark to the one she made the other

night with Philippe de Chabot. "Which is more than can be said of many marriages."

I think of the argument I have just overheard. I think of my parents. Were they ever cordial? They had five children, and I can't imagine how that was ever achieved, since they can't stand to be in the same room together.

"Yes, Your Majesty."

"And your friends?"

Frigid anxiety squeezes my heart.

"What about them, Your Majesty?"

"Have they all fallen in love?"

Her voice sounds casual, but I feel the sharp point of it.

"Lady Margaret is very reserved."

The queen snorts a little through her nose. "That is an understatement, Mary."

I relax a little at the use of my given name.

"And what of Madge Shelton?" Again, she sounds too casual. The cold fear sends its tendrils through my lungs as well.

I attempt deflection. "At one time I heard her name linked with Thomas Wyatt's."

She turns her head so sharply that the gold edging of her hood catches the rays of the sun, a quick flash and then dullness. She has not turned toward me, but away, looking up the hill. Toward the orchard. When she speaks again, her tone is distant, and almost disinterested.

"And you, at one time, admired him."

I think of Wyatt's eyes and the shape of his mouth. I think of the taste of his poetry. Of how he stepped aside for Fitz.

"Madge told me his heart is elsewhere."

She says nothing, so I speak again, to fill the gap.

"I also think Madge has her sights set on my brother."

"I wonder if Madge doesn't have her sights set on everyone." The bitterness of her laugh is as brittle as the scree of ice on a pond. "She wants something, that one. I just don't know what."

I shrug and attempt to adopt her casual tone. "I think perhaps Madge just likes the challenge. The adventure."

"Well, tell her to stay away from Thomas Wyatt," the queen says. "That's more adventure than she ought to bargain for."

I nod. I think the queen and I are both really talking about someone else.

"What are the rumors in the maids' chambers, Lady Richmond?" she asks. The formality chills me.

"The court is always full of unfounded rumors, Your Majesty."

"Yes." I sense irritation in her now. "But the maids' chambers more than the rest. Don't forget, I know of what I speak."

She doesn't have to remind me that's where she started at court. A commoner. The king made that point.

I tell her about the rumor that she wishes to have the king's daughter poisoned, and she laughs. A genuine laugh.

"Me? A poisoner? Don't be ridiculous." She drops back to seriousness so quickly I feel dizzy. "And what of the king? What hear you of him?"

I weigh my answer carefully, thinking of the way he looked at Madge. Of the argument I just heard. I study the queen. Her face is a little drawn. Her eyes are no longer disinterested.

Looking into them is a bit like staring directly into the sun.

"I heard that he said he would rather beg alms from door to door than lose you."

Sadness beats from her like heat.

"He loves you," I add. Wanting to believe it.

"Is it love?"

"Of course." I speak with more conviction than I feel. I don't even know what love is, so how can I say?

"What would you do . . . ?" The queen turns suddenly and begins striding up toward the orchard gate. I have to trot to keep up with her.

"What would you do if you were given the chance to take my place?" she says as we enter the orchard. The setting sun tops the bare branches with fire.

She stops just inside the gate and stares at them.

"I couldn't . . . " I say, terrified that somehow my father's intemperate words have passed through the walls of the palace like air. Like all the gossip that follows the queen. "I wouldn't. . . ."

"Of course not." She shrugs. "But some opportunities you have to take when they're offered." Her voice trails off until she almost seems to be speaking to herself. "They don't come again."

We stand together—me just behind her, out of deference— watching the light fade from the treetops.

"You will tell me," she says. Her statement is more of a question. The wind that blows between us catches the veil of her hood and it flaps against her cheek until she shakes it away from her face. "If you hear anything. About the king."

I want to bite my tongue. I don't want to hurt her. But I can't be an informant against my friend. Can I?

"Please," she adds.

So I nod. Because wouldn't I want to know? If I loved someone as much as she loves the king?

"Jealousy is a brutal and depleting emotion, Mary." The queen turns to walk back to the castle. "It smacks of ownership and appropriation, and I had hoped I would never feel it. I never thought I would give in to it."

She pauses, her thoughts far away.

"It's . . . difficult." I have no idea what I'm talking about, but want to offer comfort. "When you love someone."

She refocuses on me. Sharply.

"It's not love," she says. "It's survival."

20

Margaret comes unwillingly when I insist we follow Madge outside the next day. I can't confront Madge alone. The grass crunches with frost beneath our feet when we turn through the gate and into the orchard.

"What are you doing?" I call.

Madge turns and plants her fists on her hips.

"Trying to find some peace and quiet," she says bluntly. "I was walking up to Duke Humphrey's Tower."

"By yourself?" I blurt. Everyone knows Humphrey's Tower is where the king meets his mistresses.

Madge laughs. "Wouldn't that just be the evidence the court needs?"

"So it's true?" I ask quietly when we reach her.

Madge stops laughing and drops her hands to her sides.

"Gossip is rarely true," she says. "But I suppose it's what's believed that matters."

"Madge." I reach for her hand, but she pulls away from me and starts up the hill again. "Madge, you can't do this. He's the king."

"I'm not doing anything," she says. "I just danced with him."

"He left with you. The queen almost caused an international incident because of it."

"He wanted to show me the stars." Madge's voice breaks, and she stops to look up at the sky. It's the kind of icy blue that only happens in December. Her chest heaves, but I'm guessing it's not from the near run up the hill.

"He talked about the stars," Madge says. "The constellations. He told me the stories of Perseus, right up there in the sky." She points upward as if she can still see it.

"What about the queen?" I ask, barely willing to break the spell Madge has woven around herself.

"She doesn't care for astronomy."

Madge reaches up to pull a tiny withered apple—too small ever to be edible—from the nearest tree. She rolls it between her fingers.

"But do you care for her?"

Madge shrugs. "She's my mistress. It's my job to tend to her. But it's not my job to put her happiness before mine."

"What about the list?" I ask. "He's *married*."

"I crossed that one off, remember?" Madge offers a ghost of her wicked grin. "He can dance. He has a very pleasant voice."

"It's a little high-pitched," I say, thinking of Fitz's rumble, and how close it was to me.

"He is quick-witted. Intelligent. Charming. Handsome. Has a good body."

The king is about twice Madge's size. When he and the queen spar with each other, it's like a bear and an ermine. "He's going bald in the back." *He's old.*

Madge tosses her head.

"He likes me," she says. "Which is more than *you* can say about his son."

The words hurt. Because I'm afraid they're true. Or might be. Fitz said I'm beautiful and even desirable, but he never tried to kiss me again. I swathe the pain in a tissue of pretended indifference and refuse to reply.

"What about his wife?" Margaret asks. "They liked each other once. Even loved each other. Can that be so easily discarded?"

"What if he wants us both?" Madge asks, her head cocked to one side, her expression pleading. She wants to believe this. Wants to think she's not hurting anyone.

That she won't be hurt.

"What if he doesn't know what he wants?" I mutter.

"We just looked at the stars." Madge sounds exasperated. "It probably doesn't mean anything. He flirts with all the girls. Just like the queen flirts with all the handsome men."

She wants it to mean something. I can see it as plain as the sunlight on her face. My heart threatens to tear itself in two— between loyalty to my friend and duty to my queen.

"Madge," Margaret says, and looks at me for affirmation. "We just think you should be careful. Because if he's given an ultimatum . . . whom do you think he'll choose?"

"Why can't a woman be an active participant in love?" Madge turns around and sets her shoulders belligerently. As if Margaret is the person she's trying to convince. "Why can't she choose? Not be the silent object. Not the languid, beautiful face and soft, beguiling arms. Not the frozen figure waiting for a kiss to bring her to life. But a living, breathing person."

"Don't spit at me, Madge Shelton," Margaret huffs, and draws her skirts around her. "I'm on your side."

"We're just saying we don't want to see you hurt by a man who's in love with someone else."

"He doesn't love her!" Madge shouts, and then more quietly, "Don't you get that?"

"How do you know?" I ask.

Madge tosses her head. "I don't see how he can be in love with her and at the same time be sleeping with me."

We have walked far enough into the orchard for the silence to rain around us like the sunlight through the barren branches.

"No need to be so shocked," Madge says, but doesn't move except to stretch her arms down to her sides. "With something like this, it's . . . inevitable."

"You mean you were destined to commit adultery?"

Margaret's tone rests on the edge of sarcasm.

"I mean," Madge begins, and then swallows, as if against a surge of tears. "I mean that we're meant to be together. No matter that he's married."

"Or twenty years older than you."

"Or that he's the king!" Madge cries. "None of that matters, don't you see?"

"No," I say quietly, thinking of how I would feel if someone were saying that about Fitz. If someone had already claimed him before I had a chance to discover if love is possible. "I don't see. All I see is how it hurts the queen. How it undermines the court. How it makes you . . ."

"A whore." Madge finishes for me. "Why are you ganging up on me? Why are you judging me?"

"I wasn't judging you."

"You called me a whore."

"I didn't!" I cry, feeling helpless. "I just don't want anyone else to! Maybe you need to take it slowly."

"Well, thanks for your concern, Duchess. But I'm not willing to wait around."

"Stop being so obtuse," I say. "Sometimes you have to wait."

"Some of us just aren't as accepting of waiting as you are, Duchess. Some of us think that we should take things when they're offered."

"You've never waited for anything in your life," I say, feeling the anger rise in me. "Or considered anyone else's feelings. You just go and grab what you want when you want it, regardless of the consequences."

"When have I ever got what I wanted?" she cries.

"You always get what you want!" Thomas Wyatt, my brother, the *king*.

"You've got a duke," Madge spits, her face red and pinched. "A gorgeous young man and a nice one at that, and you don't even realize how good you have it. Oh, he's not *poetic* enough, you don't see him enough, he won't kiss you. Always whining about whether or not you're in love. Maybe you'll find out what love is when you stop questioning and start *living*."

The truth in her words makes me tremble, and the years of bitterness behind them hollow me out. I look her directly in the eye.

"So that's what you're doing, is it?" I ask. "Living?"

"More than you are."

"And you say *you* feel judged."

I almost think I see a flicker of regret on her face before she tosses her head again.

"Mary." I'd almost forgotten Margaret was there. Forgotten she existed. "Madge," she pleads. "You're friends."

"Are we?" I ask, and turn my wrath on Margaret. It's easier, almost. "And where do you stand on this, Margaret?"

"I take no sides."

"Well, you'd better," I say. "Because once the queen finds out, there will be only one place safe to stand."

Madge's face goes white.

"You won't tell her," she says. "You can't."

"It's the *king*, Madge!" I don't admit my promise to the queen.

"And you remember what happened to the last of the queen's ladies who dared to interfere with his mistress," Madge says.

Jane Boleyn. Thrown from court.

"I'm married to his son." My argument has no force behind it. If I'm thrown from court, I'll have to go live with my mother.

"I don't think that will matter," Madge says. "And don't you know? Until the marriage is consummated, it isn't a real marriage at all."

We stare at each other, Margaret still between us.

"Perhaps it's time you started living your own life, Duchess," Madge says. "And keeping your fingers out of mine."

21

I WILL.

Tonight. Tonight I will do something that will change me. I will prove that I am living and not waiting. I stand on one side of the room. Madge is on the other. We haven't spoken. I can hardly look at her. Margaret won't speak to either of us. She's holding true on her pledge not to take sides.

It gets dark so early in December. The queen's chambers flicker with candles, but the darkness outside is a vacuum, just waiting to suck us up into the void.

As always, there are men in this presence chamber. Mark Smeaton has spent what seems like hours tuning his lute. The noise is beginning to make me want to throttle him. The queen's brother, George, sits next to her, at her feet. They look like two children from a fairy story. Lost.

She puts her hand on his shoulder and he takes it in his. Kisses it. And then leans his cheek against it on her skirts. Absently, she strokes his hair.

She won't look at Madge, either.

I don't know how I'm going to manage this. Do I tell her? Dare I keep it to myself? And how can I prove to Madge that I know how to live, too? That I can take control of my own life—that I'm not just waiting?

The usher at the door announces the arrival of the king, who strides into the room so quickly that the candles flicker.

"Music!" he shouts, and for an instant, we all stand still.

He glances about.

"Have you all gone deaf?" he asks jovially. "Have you been turned to stone? What am I, the son of Medusa?" He laughs, and several of the courtiers laugh with him.

"Music!" he shouts again, and this time his tone brooks no refusal.

Mark Smeaton strums his lute and then begins a complicated trill, his fingers moving so swiftly they seem to blur.

"For dancing, you bloody cockscomb," the king growls, and Smeaton looks up, aghast. He hesitates for a fraction of an instant. Then he starts a *volta*, and the king grins.

"Mistress Shelton," he says, and Madge joins him in the center of the room. As if the entire scene were as choreographed as the dance itself. His hands touch her waist, her hip, her hand, lingering longer than they should. Her eyes never leave his.

The silence from the rest of the room is deafening.

He should have danced with the queen first. Or at the very least, Margaret. Precedence is power. He's just turned it all upside down.

The queen stands, and everyone freezes except the king and Madge. And Smeaton. He is too lost in the music.

Lucky man.

"Master Wyatt." The queen doesn't raise her voice, but the entire room hears her. I think, perhaps, the king hesitates in his dance. Not enough to stumble. But enough to interrupt the smooth rhythm of their footsteps.

It is the look in Thomas Wyatt's eyes that makes me hesitate. They are usually full of humor. Occasionally scorn. They are eyes that never take anything seriously, least of all women.

Right now, they are full of pain.

Quickly he rubs both hands over his face and reaches them out to her, his single dimple appearing.

"A pleasure, Your Majesty," he murmurs.

When they move together, it is beautiful. Rhythm and grace. It reminds me of Fitz. What did he say? We're equal. In clumsiness.

"Your Grace."

I don't realize I'm staring at the floor until I focus on the two brown leather shoes in front of me and look up into the earnest face of Francis Weston. He is handsome, if a bit sharp-featured, with his blond hair curling beneath his cap, his neatly trimmed mustache, and as yet unfinished beard.

"Forgive my presumption," he stutters. "But it would be an honor to dance with you."

I want to say no. I can hear the misery beating from the queen's breaking heart. The king has come to her rooms to humiliate her. And I want no part of it. That's not love. That is nothing but spite.

When I look up to refuse, Francis Weston is watching Madge, swept up in the arms of the king.

"I can see I'm not your first choice," I say bitterly, but he hardly seems to notice.

"Why should he be so lucky?" he blurts, and blushes so severely it's a wonder he isn't reduced to a pile of ash.

"To be married to the queen," he rushes to add.

"You're married, Master Weston," I remind him. And he shrugs.

"My wife is not here, Your Grace," he says, and bows. "And neither is your husband. So it would be my great honor to escort you in the dance."

He's barely six years older than I am and yet he has already learned the lying and pretext necessary for success at court. He is no longer blushing, but smiling a charming, affable smile. One not meant for me, but for all the others in the room.

How can I refuse him?

Because Fitz isn't here—he's gone to London on some errand, something for his father. Because I want to show solidarity with the queen. Because Weston likes Madge and I'm feeling spiteful myself.

Weston can dance. He knows he does it well. He never has to check his footing, or the others around him, but gazes directly into my eyes the entire time. His eyes are a penetrating blue. Not stormy, like Fitz's. Not vivid like Thomas Wyatt's. But like an arrow well aimed.

"You dance well, Your Grace," he says as the music slows to the final bars.

"You flatter well, Master Weston."

He grins at me, his narrow face illuminated as if from

within. He's handsome. Charming. Ambitious. He has a pleasant voice and is a good dancer.

He's on our list of kissable men.

If I kissed him, would he kiss me back?

Neither of us has anything invested in the other. He cares for Madge and is married to someone else. I'm married to Fitz and don't know how I feel about anyone. It's a perfect situation.

"Come with me," I say. I leave the room without looking to see if Weston is following me.

The gallery is crowded and I have to weave in between people, holding my breath. Ignoring them when they bow or call me Your Grace.

When I get to the courtyard, I'm sweating. I can feel a wisp of hair sticking to my face. But I can't stop now. Can't think about what people are seeing. Can't imagine what Weston is thinking. I have to do this thing. I have to be and act and not care.

I have to stop questioning and start living.

Start *feeling.*

I step into a disused room and breathe in relief to find it empty. When Weston hesitates in the doorway, I pull him in and shut the door behind him.

No one can refuse a kiss, right?

Fitz could.

I hesitate. There is a look of perplexity on Weston's face. Coupled with a knowing. A subtle arrogance.

I stand on the toes of my slippers and close my eyes, start to lose my balance, and reach out to stop myself from falling. My

174

hand grips velvet and gold braid, and I almost lose my nerve.

When his mouth clamps down on mine, my first reaction is surprise. I didn't expect him to meet me halfway. I expected him to be like Fitz. Stunned. Immobile.

But Weston puts an arm around me and pulls me closer. His narrow mustache chafes my upper lip when he opens his mouth hungrily, and his tongue dives deep, flicking relentlessly against mine.

I try to enjoy it. The length of his body. The taste of pepper and mint on his tongue. He was obviously expecting to kiss someone tonight. A voice at the back of my mind observes that it probably wasn't me.

His right arm releases its grip on me and I think I can come up for a breath, but he bites my lower lip and his left hand slides between us to cup my breast and his thumb strokes the skin exposed by the cut of my bodice.

No.

I'm not enjoying this at all.

I push against him, fingernails digging into the nap of his velvet doublet. As I pull my head back, his lips follow mine until I turn my head away.

"I can't," I gasp. It sounds like passion, but I think it has more to do with the fact that I was holding my breath.

His thumb attempts one more stroke.

"No one will ever know," he whispers.

I push again, and his hand breaks contact with my breast.

"I will," I tell him.

I do.

Weston steps back and pulls down on his doublet to straighten it. I try not to notice when he adjusts his codpiece. He stands still for a moment, his only movement a flexion of his fingers. He looks confused. Unsure of what happens next.

Oh, God. Kissing someone who is not my husband. It makes me no better than the king.

"I'm sorry," I add.

"Don't be," he says. A hint of his arrogance returns. "I'm not."

He grins at me and winks. He's young. Attractive. Passionate. A good dancer.

And I feel nothing for him.

"Not sorry you kissed me?" I ask, cocking my head to the side. "Or not sorry we stopped?"

The grin disappears until he realizes I'm teasing him, and then he laughs.

"Neither one," he says with a quick bow. "Because I always enjoy a good kiss, Your Grace. And because I hope I always know when to stop."

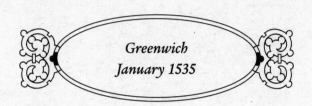

Greenwich
January 1535

22

Shame tastes like ashes, and *guilt* like soured ale, and both hang heavy on my tongue.

The gaudiness of the Christmas celebrations makes me impatient. The bowing and scraping of the court, the jostling of position as people choose, discard, and interchange their friends and enemies. I'm barely keeping my mind together, every thought eroded by self-reproach and impending panic.

The crowds are suffocating. Fitz returned from London the day before the celebrations commenced, along with seemingly every other person of noble birth or aspiration in the country. He does not come to find me. Doesn't speak to me. The anticipation makes me edgy.

The court works itself into a frenzy over the gifts to be given on January first. The queen usurps all of the silversmiths and even Master Holbein to create her surprise gift for the king—a magnificent silver-gilt table fountain that recirculates rose water for guests to rinse their hands. It is beautiful and elegant and breathtakingly expensive, and the king kisses her lightly on the lips in front of us all when he receives it.

I don't see Madge's reaction.

The thrifty and the clever unearth last year's gifts for

regifting. Silver salts and little gilt coffers, acres of plate and oceans of jewels. Like Midas, everything the king touches turns to gold, and piles around him in a great, glimmering mirage.

I sew. Because the more I sew, the less I see.

I don't see Madge fashioning a velvet collar embroidered in gold and I don't see it on the king on January second. I don't see Fitz thanking the queen for the silver-gilt jar she gives him. I don't see him send it on to his half sister, Lady Mary. I don't see my brother return to court for the festivities.

Without his wife.

And then it is Twelfth Night. The night when nothing is as it seems.

The great hall is swathed in holly and blood-red velvet. Attendants stoke the fires with fir boughs to scent the air and fill the queen's silver fountain with wine rather than rose water, each courtier filling his cup as often as he likes.

The king and queen sit together on a dais, holding hands on the table. They are served on bended knee by the highest nobles of the land, including my father, who is decked in gold and green, his narrow, pointed beard giving the impression of Saturn himself.

Food floods out of the kitchens. It is a wonder they can produce it all. The centerpiece is a swan—all befeathered in gold leaf and holly—stuffed with a goose, which is in turn stuffed with a duck, a quail, and a swallow. There are boar and venison, fish and more fowl, all washed down by quantities of wine not even the fountain can provide.

I sit near the queen, and Margaret sits next to me. Ladies of precedence together.

I can easily watch my husband on the other side of the king. When I do, I cannot eat. The bean cake is passed around, and I just pick at it. The spices and dried fruit remind me of the bridecake at my wedding. And I have no desire to find the hidden bean and be ruler of the feast. I don't want that kind of responsibility.

"What's bothering you?" Margaret asks. She's so calm all the time. Responsible. She doesn't take sides. Never does anything without considering it first.

I want to tell her everything. That I want to apologize to Madge, but don't know how. I want to tell Margaret about Weston, but I'm afraid of what she will think. Because she would never do such a thing. So I find the simplest, most innocuous way to explain my anxiety.

"Fitz hasn't come to find me yet."

Saying it out loud makes the fact crawl uncomfortably through my stomach. Why *hasn't* he come to see me? Does he already know about Weston?

"Have you gone to find him?"

Margaret smiles when I snap my gaze to hers. She tilts her head to one side and raises her eyebrows questioningly.

"No," I say slowly. "But I live here. And he's visiting. And . . . and he's the man." Boy. Boy-man.

"You have far too many rules in your mind, Duchess."

I startle at Margaret using Madge's nickname for me. Did

she just pick it up naturally? Or is she trying to tell me to act like one?

"We live at court," I say. "There are social rules for every-thing." I take a bite of the bean cake. Spice and orange. But no bean. I will not be queen.

"And there are rules that are made to be broken."

"But breaking the rules hurts people," I say, thinking of Madge. If only she had been able to stay away from the king. Breaking those rules hurt the queen. It hurt our friendship. It hurt me.

I think about my own indiscretion. How Fitz said he takes his vows seriously, and yet I haven't. He lives up to his father's expectations. Though I suppose I live up to my mother's—I haven't amounted to much yet.

"Every action has consequences," Margaret says. "It's up to you to decide whether or not it's worth it."

"How do you know when it will be?"

For a moment, Margaret stares at her hands, folded together, resting on the edge of the table.

"I think . . ." She looks up at me, her eyes searching my face. For once, she doesn't seem complacent. Or reserved. She looks agitated. Concerned. Impassioned. "Don't hate me, Mary, but I think Madge was right. You know it's worth it when you stop questioning. When you just . . . know."

I look away from her and pinch the soft, inner part of my lower lip between my teeth. Far across the room, Hal is stand-ing in front of Madge, the fingers of his right hand resting at the base of her goblet.

She picks it up and drinks from it, eyes on him. And shrugs. Hal turns away.

"I don't mean to offend you." Margaret puts a hand on mine, her long, narrow fingers ringless except for a single enameled thistle. Her tie to Scotland.

"I'm not offended," I manage to reply. "I just don't know that I'll ever stop questioning." It always kept me one step ahead of my mother. By evaluating every angle of a situation before taking action, I avoided her wrath. Though sometimes, my deliberation was the very thing that brought out her cruelty at its worst. I run a crumb of cake along the table with my finger.

"You will," Margaret says. She glances once about the room. Leans in closer. "I have."

Her eyes are full of light and mischief. She sits up straight as ever, but not with stiffness. No, she's more alert. As if every nerve is tuned and ready to sing. And I know—without asking— that she's in love with Thomas Howard.

A shout goes up from the far end of the table. Thomas Seymour is the bean king. The lord of misrule. He stands, already a little unsteady, but his voice is loud and clear.

"How now," Margaret whispers to me. "What mischief will this man cause?"

My father stands behind the king at the dais, looking thoroughly put out. His place has been supplanted, for the evening, by this honey-haired junior courtier who plays at matchmaking. Thomas Seymour takes far too much joy in dragging men from their seats and encouraging them to dance with partners specifically chosen from among the queen's maids.

"Your Majesty," he says, approaching the king. "May I?"

The king smiles indulgently and nods.

"I should like to introduce you to my sister, Jane."

Beside me, Margaret laughs through her nose.

"If he thinks he's going to elevate his family through that connection, he's going to be severely disappointed," she says, as the king allows himself to be led down the table.

Jane Seymour is blonde and round-faced and has not a trace of the guile that both of her brothers exude from their pores. I don't think she's ever said more than two words to me. Or to anyone.

Seymour places Jane's hand in the king's with a flourish and a bow, and she rises without once looking the king in the eye.

"And the king's son," Seymour cries, clearly relishing his role.

I look up, startled, to see Fitz's expression mirror my own, but he allows himself to be led around the room. A parade of two. Seymour pauses behind Madge's chair; she can't take her eyes off of Fitz, one corner of her mouth raised. I feel the bean cake rising in my throat. But Seymour walks on and stops behind Margaret's chair. She sits stiffly again, and will not look at him at all.

"It's a night for breaking rules, little lovebirds," Seymour says, his body just a little too close to mine. He takes my hand and Fitz's and ceremoniously joins them together. It reminds me of our wedding. Except I realize as I turn and look up into Fitz's face that I no longer fear the prison of this marriage.

Seymour turns to Margaret and offers his hand to her.

"Or perhaps for making new ones," he says.

23

"THAT MAN HAS MORE AMBITION THAN THE ENTIRE HOWARD family put together," I say, watching Seymour lead a reluctant Margaret toward the crush of dancers.

Fitz laughs, and instead of taking me to join them, he sits in the place she just vacated.

"You aren't going to dance with me?" I ask.

"I figure we're safer here."

Out in the middle of the room, Jane Seymour almost looks happy, but as I watch I see the king sneak a glance at Madge. She's dancing with Hal, their movements methodical. Almost mechanical. Poor Margaret looks like she's suffering.

"I don't think all of Thomas Seymour's matchmaking efforts are effective," Fitz says.

"I think Margaret would prefer to dance with my uncle."

I'm ready to bite my tongue off as soon as the words escape. Margaret is so private, she would hate to know I'm telling anyone. Especially the king's son.

"Which one?" Fitz asks with a sly smile.

"The Howards *are* notoriously fertile," I respond. And then wish to bite my tongue again. I've just told him I can potentially provide him with lots of babies. How can someone who loves words so much misuse them so blatantly?

"Shall I guess?"

I nod, mutely, not trusting myself to speak.

"Your uncle Edmund."

"Ed*mund* or Ed*ward*?"

"You choose."

"Well, uncle Edmund is a bit of a reprobate. And he's older than your father. Married three times already and can't even take care of his own children." I'm thinking of my cousin Catherine, dumped on the doorstep of my step-grandmother the dowager duchess.

"And Edward?"

"Is dead."

"Which takes him out of the running."

"True."

"So that leaves?"

"John. Henry. Charles. Richard. William." I neglect to mention Thomas. Or the fact that half of them are dead, too.

"I relent!" he cries, putting his hands up over his head in mock surrender.

I smile and pretend to watch the dancers again, but I'm really watching Fitz. He leans forward on the table, resting his elbows on it, his chin on one hand, eyes following the movements of the dance. After a moment, his smile fades.

"His heart is broken."

I know immediately he's talking about Hal. Little stabs of guilt pelt me.

"I haven't spoken with him."

"I know."

I groan and drop my forehead to the table. *So ungracious a daughter and so unnatural*, my mother called me. I can add that to my sisterly traits, as well.

I think I hear Fitz chuckle. "He's been avoiding you."

I turn my head so I can squint at him through my right eye.

"He's afraid you'll take Madge's side."

"I'm not in any position to take sides," I say. "'He that has a head of glass should not cast stones.'"

Fitz tips his head to the side and grins at me. "Chaucer?"

I find I can actually laugh. "Of course. From *Troilus and Criseyde*. Madge has been quoting him to me since we met. It was bound to sink in eventually."

He pauses, watching me. "And why do you feel you're made of glass?"

Guilt.

Suddenly, I am far too aware of the press of other people around me. Most have left the table and are now standing near it. Behind us. Talking. Drinking. Laughing. There is little room between the table and the wall. Not enough room. The edge of a doublet brushes my shoulder. I look up to a tower of bodies surrounding us, and my throat constricts.

"Mary?" Fitz's voice reaches me through the tunnel—echoey and warped.

I try to breathe and manage to gasp in a tiny bubble of air. All I hear is the roar of waves—carrying with them a bark of laughter, the bang of a plate on the table, the hollow sound of swallowing.

Something seizes me by the armpits and hefts me from my seat. An arm wraps around my waist and my feet barely touch the ground on the way to the door. Percussive laughter like fireworks follows us and I think I catch a lewd remark, but don't have the capacity to interpret it.

The courtyard outside the great hall is nearly as crowded but much cooler, and I am able to get almost an entire lungful of air. But Fitz doesn't let go. And he doesn't stop moving. His arm stays around my waist—almost carrying me—until we are through the lodging gate and almost at the river.

The frigid air suppresses the usual riverside stink, and the water is black and glassy. On the surface of it, the stars seem to move and swirl, as if the sky were a whirl of activity. When I look up, they are still and peaceful.

I can breathe again.

"Was it something I said?"

I can see Fitz clearly, despite the darkness at the water's edge. There is a narrow V pinched between his eyebrows.

"The crowd," I manage to say. I can't explain. I don't even understand it myself.

"Too many people?"

I nod.

"So *that's* what makes you vulnerable."

His question. About why I said I couldn't take sides. Not because it's between Hal and Madge. But because I have no right to judge.

Change the subject.

"Do you know which is Perseus?" I ask, looking back up at the stars.

I feel Fitz shift beside me, his shoulder almost touching mine as he tilts his head back to look.

"The king taught me the constellations the year I turned twelve."

The stars look to me like nothing but a smattering of freckles across the sky. No rhyme or reason to them. Certainly not images of mythological warriors.

"That one." Fitz wraps an arm around my shoulder and puts his face close to mine so we are looking at the same angle. He points with his other hand. "See the three bright stars in a row?"

I squint a little. "They're just in a line?"

"Yes. At an angle."

"That's Perseus?"

"No, it's Orion, the Hunter. It's the only one I can remember."

I remember everything my father taught me. I shift a little to get a look at Fitz, and he moves slightly away from me.

"Which god was Orion?" I ask.

"He wasn't a god, he was a hero. Maybe. Some say he was the son of the sea god, and that he could walk on water. Some say he rivaled Artemis, the goddess of the hunt. Many say he violated Merope and was blinded because of it."

He turns to face me. "My favorite story tells that he was the lover of Eos, the golden goddess of the dawn."

I can't look away.

"Why is that your favorite story?" I ask.

"Because the dawn is my favorite time of day."

He says this so simply, so sincerely, that it stops my heart. Then my stupidity kicks in.

"I should think it's difficult to see, considering the hours the court keeps." Late nights and even later mornings.

"It's worth the lack of sleep." He moves closer to me. "I should like to show it to you. See it with you." He looks back over the water. "From the river, perhaps."

I can't keep it in any longer. The more I hold it back, the harder the truth is to tell. Secrets have a way of festering, becoming septic.

"I kissed Francis Weston," I blurt.

Fitz doesn't move, looking out to where the earth meets the sky.

"I have to tell you the truth. I kissed *him*, not the other way around."

Fitz rests his hands on the stone boundary wall in front of us. I am suddenly numb with cold.

"Why?" he asks, his voice toneless.

Why did I? I hardly remember my reasons now.

"Because I wanted to see what it felt like. To kiss someone." God, that sounds horrible. Like an accusation.

Fitz finally looks at me. "And what did you think?"

I want to squirm. He's so calm. So distant. My mother had to be physically restrained when she discovered my father had a mistress.

"It was . . . awkward."

His eyes rise again to look at the river.

"As awkward as our first kiss?"

"No."

Fitz nods and looks down at his shoes. "Did he return the favor?"

"Yes," I whisper.

He turns away from the river and leans back against the barrier, burying his head in his hands.

He hates me. He's going to go to the king and annul the marriage. We're incompatible. And we haven't consummated it. Lord, we haven't even kissed each other. He can find some French girl, like that one he slept with when he was fourteen. I'm so stupid.

"I'm such a fool."

Fitz's words echo my thoughts so precisely, I wonder if I spoke them, the panic from the crowd addling my mind.

He stands up quickly, slapping his palms against the wall, his face raised to the sky, neck arched all the way back.

"I didn't—" I start to tell him I didn't enjoy it, but he turns around so swiftly, I don't have time to breathe before he puts one hand on either side of my face and lowers his mouth to mine.

At first, the kiss isn't magical. It's not a great rush of passion or like butterflies and flowers or whatever else the poets say. It's a little awkward—though not as awkward as the last one.

His lips are soft. Hesitant. Then he puts his arms around me and I move mine to his waist. I tip my head so our noses aren't pressed against each other and he bends my body backward just a little, the wall and river behind me.

This kiss is an exploration of how we fit together. How far to open our mouths and when our tongues can touch. What the velvet of his doublet feels like beneath my fingers as my hands slide up his back. How close I can press myself to him. And then how much closer when he moves his hand to the base of my spine.

Fitz kisses the corner of my mouth and then moves his lips to my ear, his breath hot on my winter-chilled skin.

"I'm sorry," he whispers.

I pull away just a little, so I can look him in the eye.

"For what?"

He smiles. "I'm sorry I didn't do that before."

24

WE SEE EACH OTHER EVERYWHERE. IN THE QUEEN'S ROOMS, where everyone gathers to flirt. In the great hall, where the men stamp and grumble in anticipation of moving back to Whitehall. In the courtyards.

We smile. Once, in passing, we touch. But we don't manage to speak—or kiss—again. I begin to wonder if I dreamed it.

I long to talk to Madge. To confess how desperate I am to touch him again. I want to ask her what happens next. If this is love. But we're still not speaking.

I want to know if she feels the same. If she feels this rush of emotion when she's with the king. If this is only the beginning—this cramping of my ribs when I think of him, how I feel weightless when I see him—then I can't imagine what it's like to be with someone, truly. To be in love. Feeling that way, I, too, might break the rules. I hope I wouldn't break a heart or betray someone's loyalty. But I can begin to understand the desire to do so.

I cannot sleep, so I wrap my velvet counterpane and a fur around myself and find the little book that Fitz gave me. I trace the initials on the cover with my finger. M.F.

I am not a Howard. I am a FitzRoy. And there are only two of us in the entire world.

The thought warms me, but also sends a chill down my spine.

Quickly, I light a candle. But when I open the book to write down something—anything—about Fitz, I discover I cannot find the words.

I flip the pages backward, studying Madge's scrawling hand. Her lists. I want desperately to scratch the king off. To add Hal to the bottom.

To apologize.

To accept an apology.

So instead of writing about Fitz or about love, I copy a remembered poem. One of Thomas Wyatt's. *I abide and abide and better abide*, I write. It doesn't say what I want to say. I hope Madge can discern its meaning.

That I'm here. That I'm waiting. That "much were it better for to be plain" as Wyatt wrote, and I hope that she will do the same.

I drop the book into her lap as I walk into the queen's rooms. I don't look at her. I don't watch her reading it. Later that day, the book reappears beneath my pillow.

At first, I think she hasn't responded. Then I come across four lines scrawled across a random page in the middle of the book.

All I have at other lost
Not as my own I do protest.
But when I have got that I have missed,
I shall rejoice among the rest.

She's missed me as much as I've missed her.

My maid knocks and enters so quickly that I don't have time to hide the book, and I am relieved to see Margaret enter.

"Reading something good?" she asks when my maid closes the door.

"I sent Madge a sort of peace offering."

"I know. She told me."

"You've been talking to her?"

"I've been talking to both of you, Mary. I told you I wouldn't take sides."

I show her Madge's response and she smiles. She starts to take the book from me and pauses.

"May I?"

I almost laugh. Though it has my initials stamped on it, from the beginning, the book has belonged to all three of us. I hand it to her and she begins to write.

"Do you think he's told her that he loves her?" I ask. "Madge, I mean."

Margaret hesitates, pen hovering over the page. She doesn't want to get involved.

"Yes," she says finally. "He probably has. It would be the only reason she'd believe him."

"Do you think he does?"

"No," she says with assurance. "I don't believe he loves anyone but himself."

I allow this to penetrate through the curtains of my presumption that the relationship between the king and queen is the perfect illustration of love.

"He loves the queen," I manage to whisper.

"You just keep pretending that, Mary." The contempt in Margaret's voice is plain.

"Don't you think love is possible?" I ask. "Don't you think anyone can aspire to it?"

Her face softens. "I do," she says.

I feel a gush of relief.

"Then don't you think we ought to talk to Madge? Convince her that . . . that he doesn't love her?" That she deserves someone better.

Hal comes to mind. But he's married, too. He and Madge can never have anything but an illicit romance.

"We'll never convince her," Margaret answers. "Because even if he doesn't love her, I believe she loves him."

"But she can't!"

"Maybe we don't get to choose who we love."

"Then who chooses?"

"Fate? God? Or maybe just plain physical attraction."

"Is physical attraction enough?" I think of how that kiss with Fitz makes me feel like my skin wants to wrap itself around him. Is that enough?

"For some."

"Do you think it is for Madge?" I just manage to keep my lip from curling at the idea of being attracted to the king. His barrel chest. His bald spot. His jowly face.

His eyes. So like Fitz's.

They have the same eyes. The same eyebrows. The same little mouth. The king's has learned cruelty over the years.

Could that happen to Fitz, too?

"I think Madge likes the power," Margaret says. "The conquest."

"Of him?" I ask, not wanting an answer. "Or of her?"

"She always said no one will ever control her."

"I imagine the king would say the same thing."

I think of the ongoing battle between my parents. Neither one will ever give in. Or give way. Neither will admit defeat.

Margaret turns a page and continues writing on the next one, her handwriting getting more hurried and loopy as she curls over it, writing faster.

"I think you have to give up a little when you fall in love," Margaret says, still scribbling. "There's a part of everyone that wants to be conquered. That wants to resign responsibility. Let someone else be the master. It's part of being in love."

I think of my mother. Never willing to give up anything.

I think of the queen. *I am myself! I am Anne Boleyn. You have not made me!*

And the king's response. *I can make you nothing.*

"I don't want to be conquered," I tell her. "No matter how badly I want to be loved."

25

I AM WOKEN INTO FRIGID DARKNESS ONE MORNING BY A RUSH OF even colder air coming in through my open door. The blackness in the room is equal to the one behind my eyes and I lie still, listening for any sound that may tell me what—or who—has come into my room. I hear a slip-stride like feet trying to tiptoe and not collide with unseen objects. A quiet footfall. A woman?

Or a very light-footed man?

I try to see around the curl of velvet that covers me, but all I see are shades of charcoal. Black only occasionally alleviated by a ghost of dark gray.

Until the dark-gray ghost moves and I gasp.

"Duchess? Are you awake?"

I sit up and shiver as my shoulders are bared to the air of the room.

"Madge?" I hiss. We still haven't spoken to each other since our argument. "What are you doing here? You nearly scared the life out of me."

"It's a surprise. I'm here to get you dressed."

"In the middle of the night?"

"It's not the middle, anymore. It's nearly dawn. Fitz says we have to hurry."

Dawn. Fitz's favorite time of day.

"Fitz?"

Madge chuckles. "He's very persuasive, Mary. I'm afraid I can't refuse your husband anything."

I swing my legs from the bed and wince when my feet touch the floor. The cold is as sharp as a blade.

"And when did you see him?" Suspicion sours my voice and all my words taste like vinegar.

"I haven't." Madge's tone is as cold as the room. "The message was sent through someone else."

A torrent of shame douses my jealousy. Madge and I are still on wrong feet with each other. She shouldn't have made such a tactless joke. And I shouldn't have taken it seriously. We're like two people dancing to dissonant tunes.

"Where are we going?" I ask, trying to return to neutral ground. A pause in the dance.

"I told you, it's a surprise."

Madge lights a candle and starts rummaging through my clothes, pulling out the pale-pink bodice that replaced my wedding gown when it got too small and tattered. She helps me dress quickly and then pauses, looking at me. We cannot speak apologies yet, but at least we're in the same room.

I turn toward the door, but she stops me, silently dabs rose water behind my ears, then douses the candle.

"Can't have anyone see us," she whispers, and promptly

shuts the door on my hand before I'm all the way out of the room.

"How dare I think secrecy less important than keeping all my fingers," I mutter.

In the darkness, Madge goes down the spiral stairs without hesitation. I'm the one feeling for the edge of each riser before reaching my foot out into the abyss. At every step, I'm relieved to find solid stone beneath my slipper, and even more so when I leave the stairwell and enter the courtyard.

"Hurry up!"

Madge's breath comes in puffs, like she's breathing fire. She glances once at the sky and grabs my hand to drag me at a run toward the river.

Only then do I realize I can see. See her breath. I can almost see the cobbles beneath my feet and the silent wraiths and servants ignoring our indecent haste. It may not be morning yet, but it is no longer night.

On the river walk, the cold breath of the Thames hollows out my lungs and shrieks inside my nose. My eyes close involuntarily and icy-hot tears sting the corners. I wish Madge had thought to make me bring a cloak. Her hand is the only warmth I feel. I squint through the darkness for something familiar. For some hint of Madge's "secret."

A shadow breaks away from the wall of the palace and approaches us. Tall, slender, with sweeping skirts.

"Margaret?" I whisper. "You're in on this, too?"

"Secret note," she replies. "All very mysterious."

A splash on the river turns us all to stone. For a moment.

"There," Madge says, and points. Looming out of the deep gray mist on the deeper gray water is a black boat propelled by shadows.

"What's going on?" I ask.

Madge walks down to the little water gate where the barges land to take the king to London. One of the shadows leaps from the boat and swoops down on her, spinning her around once before depositing her on the boat and running up to where Margaret and I stand together.

"Sister." Hal's face emerges from the blurry darkness, and all the tension leaves me. I throw my arms around him and he whispers in my ear, "The game is not yet won, Mary. But at least I have a moment to play my hand."

Then he turns. "Lady Margaret. Allow me to escort you."

He takes each of us by the arm and leads us down the steeply sloped bank to the waiting boat. On closer inspection, I can see that the dark canopy is a deep green or blue, and that it is fringed with something light and shimmery. Gold.

When I am close enough to step into the boat, I see that Fitz stands at the side of it, arm upraised to help me down.

This time when we touch, my fingers tingle. And it's not from the cold.

"Let me get you warm," he whispers in my ear as he tucks me under his right arm, so he must lift his left to help Margaret into the boat.

"I fear I'm the gooseberry here," she says, her feet not making a sound as she drops lightly to the deck.

"Not at all," Fitz says, and points to another figure, at the far end of the boat, both hands on a long pole that keeps the vessel from drifting away from the dock and prevents boarders from being dumped unceremoniously into the reeking waters at the river's edge

The sky must be getting lighter, because I can see that it's Thomas. He nods and murmurs, "Your Grace," but is at least as reserved as Margaret. They don't touch.

I raise an eyebrow at Fitz and he grins. "It turns out I'm a good guesser," he says, and wraps a fur around my shoulders. It's not nearly as warm as his arm.

"And a matchmaker," I whisper, nodding to where Hal is getting Madge settled. Her shoulders look stiff beneath her cloak.

Fitz glances at the sky and turns to the others. "We have to go soon." He puts a hand on my shoulder. "You should sit down."

The boat lurches a little as Thomas pushes us away from the dock, so I take Fitz's advice. The bench feels damp—a little sticky—beneath my fingers. I wrap the fur more tightly and watch our escorts scurry about, attaching oars and arranging furs.

When I look back, Greenwich is yards away, the stone just beginning to gleam against the black hill beyond it.

"Where are we going?" Margaret calls out.

"I told you, it's a secret." Madge stands and wobbles showily, then collapses next to me. "Aren't you glad you came?"

"Very." Despite the cold.

For a while, all I hear is the slosh of the water on the sides of the boat and the oars that steer it. I feel the current when it takes hold near the center of the river and we start to move more quickly toward the sea. I worry that the three boys won't be able to keep us from washing all the way out into the Channel, but they seem in control.

For the most part.

The sky above us melts from black to gray, the fog lifting from the river and obscuring the stars. Fitz says something to the others, and they scramble to steer the boat closer to shore. Then I hear the scrape of grass on the hull and a squelch as Thomas's pole is sucked into the mud beneath us.

The marsh rises all around us.

"Don't get us stuck!" Fitz calls, and sets the boat rocking as he runs to Thomas to help push us away from a particularly thick clump of grass.

The boat slides into an inlet, the still water around us completely surrounded by fen. The mist is tinged pink by the sky beyond it.

Fitz comes to sit beside me, but we don't touch. Hal sits facing Madge and takes her hands in his. She won't look at him. Just hangs her head. Thomas guides Margaret beneath the canopy and they disappear from view.

For a moment, we are all silent. The only sounds the whisper of the marsh grass on the boat and the lap of the river beyond. Then a distant moo.

"Where are we?"

"The Isle of Dogs. The embankment was breached almost fifty years ago and it reverted to marsh and wetland. The kingfishers love it here."

"And the cows?"

Fitz smiles. "Graze on drier ground."

"You promised to show me the dawn," I whisper.

"It's coming." Fitz turns his face to me. We are so close.

"Tell me your words, Mary," he says softly.

"My words?"

"Your poetry."

"I'm not a poet, Fitz. I don't have the rhythm for it."

"Like I don't have the rhythm for dancing. But that doesn't mean I don't love music. That I can't feel it. What do you love about words?"

I think for a moment. "I love the way they sound. The way they sing. The way they taste."

"Words have a taste?"

"Most of them do. Have you never thought about it? *Dawn* tastes like cool air and freshly cut grass."

He nods, and his eyes leave mine to look at my lips. As if he wishes to taste the dawn on them.

A thin, reedy double note turns his head and he cocks it to listen until the note comes again.

"Kingfisher."

I tilt my head to mimic him—closer to him—listening. The song is nothing special, but when we hear it, we both smile.

I turn a little farther, so we are almost nose to nose. His eyes are the color of the sky behind him, just turning from gray to blue. I hope he'll kiss me again

"Look."

Fitz points past me, and I turn away. A tiny bird sits precariously at the top of a reed, the feathers of its bright blue head and red-orange breast glinting in the rays of the sun. All around it, the tips of the grasses have kindled to gold.

Fitz lays his face next to mine, the warmth of his skin reminding me how cold the air is. He wraps his arms around me from behind and tucks the fur down over my hands. Gently, he rests his chin on my shoulder.

"This is my poetry, Mary," he says. "These are my words."

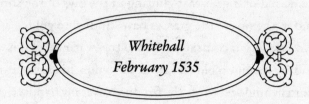

Whitehall
February 1535

26

We leave Greenwich the next day, and I keep that dawn in the coffer of my memory when Fitz moves to a separate residence on the Strand and then is required to go straight to Collyweston. I won't see him again unless he is recalled to court or the City out of duty to the king.

Madge hasn't spoken much since our boat ride. She's distant and uncomfortable. I don't think things went well with Hal. I'm fairly certain he arranged for Madge to be Fitz's messenger, knowing she wouldn't refuse the opportunity to facilitate a clandestine tryst. I suspect that Madge believes I'm implicated, as well.

Margaret divides her time between us, and I feel a ridiculous, childish jealousy. She was my friend first. Every connection is faulty. It is as if the three of us only function when we are together. With a piece missing, the mechanism of friendship fails.

The only way we communicate is through the book. We use margin notes and regurgitated verse to convey meaning. But half-finished thoughts aren't the same as conversation. I'd like to hear Madge's voice and judge by her tone. I'd like to see Margaret's facial expressions—so subtle, but so telling.

All I find is the book under my pillow or in my sewing basket.

I write what feels like nonsense and pass it on.

And I sew. The queen requires it of all of her ladies. We sew clothing for the poor so she can distribute it on this summer's progress. Endless hems and simple stitching. The repetition—the rhythm—are soothing, but offer little solace.

Hal finds me in the great hall one dreary afternoon and perches on the bench beside me.

"This seems an odd place to sit and sew, Mary."

I glance up at him. His eyes are laughing at me.

"There's a little more space here," I tell him, "than in the queen's rooms."

"You mean it's not as crowded."

"That's exactly what I mean."

"And you can get away from Madge."

"Madge and I are not unfriendly."

"That's not what it looks like to me." Hal stands and starts to pace back and forth. His eyes deepen below his brow, the heavy fringe of his hair almost covering them.

"We had an argument," I manage to say.

"About *him*?"

I don't need to ask who *he* is.

"Amongst other things."

Hal sits back down beside me and speaks so quickly and quietly his words hiss.

"I hate him," he whispers. "He controls everything. He controls us all. It's like the entire court is a chessboard and he can maneuver us however he wishes. And sacrifice us as it pleases him."

"Hush. You can't say such things." I stay as calm as I can, but my hands shake. My stitches grow uneven.

"I can't be *heard* saying such things," Hal says. "But you won't repeat them."

I shake my head. Of course I won't.

"It's not only me, Mary. It's not just Madge." His voice cracks a little. "It's this bloody Oath of Supremacy. Forcing people to acknowledge he's head of the church. He's put Thomas bloody More in the Tower, for Chrissake. Those Carthusian monks are on trial for their faith. He's made it treason to speak your mind—to have your own beliefs and thoughts! It's treason to question his marriage. A midwife in Oxford was jailed for calling Anne a whore."

"It proves he loves her," I say automatically, but Hal just laughs.

"Even you can't be that naive! He's fucking someone else."

I flinch at his choice of word. It tastes like spoiled meat.

"So have you been," I snap.

"Proving my very point! I don't love my wife."

"Have you tried?" I turn to him, thinking of Fitz wanting to get to know me. Thinking of him showing me the dawn.

"I have no idea how to talk to her."

"Because she's your wife?" My voice is sharp.

Hal turns to face the near-empty hall. "I'm sure you are well aware that we didn't have very good examples growing up."

A day from our childhood rises to my memory unbidden. Mother's ladies pinning her down by her arms. And still she shrieked and struggled until one of them sat on her chest. But my father wouldn't run. He waited until she was exhausted and broken and then told her exactly what he thought of her.

That was the night he left with Bess Holland. I don't think my parents have spoken aloud to each other since. But their letters fly back and forth and through their friends at court, their animosity leaving a haze like smoke.

"I believe we can assume you shouldn't physically restrain Frances."

Hal smiles. "And if Fitz does that to you, I will kill him personally."

"You'd choose me over your best friend, Hal?"

"I'm completely fair, Mary." Hal is still teasing, but I can hear an edge of truth in his voice. "I can promise to do the same to you if you treat Fitz as our mother treats her family."

I nod.

"Then I would deserve it."

Hal throws an arm around me.

"Mary, you are so unlike our mother, it seems improbable that you're related."

I can't quite say the same about Hal and Father. They have the same ambition. The same . . . entitlement.

"High praise, Brother."

I relax beneath his arm. Hal sits back, leaning against the

wall, one hand still on my shoulder and his boots outstretched. He seems to be over his rage at the king.

"She wrote to me." Hal's hand flinches and drops to the bench beside him.

"Your wife?"

"Mother. She said I'm unnatural."

"She said as much to me."

"But it's her, Mary. She's the one who's unnatural. Trying to pit her son against his own father. Everything is a contest of preference and precedence."

I think of Fitz taking my hand on our wedding day. Of stepping out in front of her and leaving her behind. "Just like the court," I say. "A dog pile at the command of the king."

"I should like to escape the king's control as well," Hal mutters.

His gaze is on his hands in his lap. He still holds the casual pose, but the knuckles of his fingers are white with tension. I know his anger stems from the king's relationship with Madge. But I also know it shouldn't affect his allegiance.

"You are his subject and therefore subject to his command."

"Subject to his whims, more like."

I can't make this any easier for him. But I can't allow Hal to speak treason. "If that is so, then so be it."

He looks up at me, his eyes pleading. "Will you speak to Madge? Just let her know how I feel."

"Of course," I say, hoping I get a chance to speak to her at all. "But you have to do something for me."

Hal's face hardens for a moment, but he manages to force the ghost of a smile. "Anything, Sister."

"Speak to your wife," I say. "Find out who she is."

"Are you saying there's no hope for me and Madge?" I can hear his heart breaking.

"I'm saying there might be hope for you and Frances. You'll be living with her soon, and you never know what might happen. I think . . . I think it's possible to love someone even when you're forced to be together."

Hal truly smiles and leans forward to whisper in my ear. "That's what Fitz says."

I drop my chin to hide the flush of delight that blooms on my chest, and Hal laughs. He flings himself up and stamps his feet twice as if trying to secure his place in the world. I think he'll walk away, but he hesitates for so long that I finally look up at him.

"Father thinks he'll be king one day," he says, so quietly I almost think I've imagined it. "Fitz."

I nod. Father said as much to me. I dare not speak it.

"I think he'll be a good one. He's nothing like his father."

Before I can reply, Hal turns on his heel and leaves the hall.

I pack up my sewing and return to my room, pulling the little book from its place between my mattress and the bed frame. I find a blank page and begin to write, hoping Madge will remember the day we caught Hal and Fitz playing tennis. It seems a lifetime ago, though it's only just a year.

Hal's poem is in the voice of a woman whose lover has gone

off to sea. But I know she'll recognize it as his. I just hope she recognizes why I write it down.

> O happy dames! that may embrace
> The fruit of your delight . . .

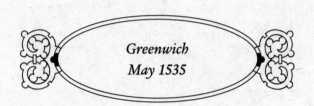

Greenwich
May 1535

27

THERE IS NO REPLY. I CHECK EVERY PAGE WHEN I FIND THE BOOK in my sewing basket. All I discover is a correction that Margaret has made in her usual, detail-oriented way.

—*Now he comes! Will Alas, no, no.*

In my haste to scribble the last line, I omitted some key words that Margaret squeezes into the space above.

—*Now he comes! Will he come? Alas, no no.*

Alas, for weeks, neither does Madge. But then, soon after May Day, she flops down into the seat next to me in the queen's chambers as if nothing has altered at all. As if we still shared a bed. As if the past five months have never happened.

"How would you feel if someone was thrown into prison for speaking against you?" she asks under her breath.

"I guess it would depend on what they said."

"Well," she says shortly. "I suppose if they said they were going to kill me, I'd want them locked up. But for calling me goggly-eyed?"

"You forget, Madge. That midwife called her a *whore*. Not just goggly-eyed."

"You called me that, and I don't think you should be hanged, drawn, and quartered for it."

"I did not call you that. The word *whore* tastes like bile and I wouldn't spew it at anyone. Least of all you. I said that others would."

Madge is quiet for so long, I wonder if she's controlling her anger. Wanting to argue. Then I see a tear slide the length of her nose.

"Madge—"

"I know, Duchess. I know you warned me."

"I just . . ."

"You didn't want to see me get hurt. You didn't want to see me hurt Hal. But don't you see, Duchess? You can't control everything."

"I wasn't trying to control you."

"You were trying to control the outcome," Madge says, taking my hand in hers and patting it. "But I—" She stops, two fingers resting lightly on the back of my hand. "He made me feel so alive."

I want to gush with relief. *Made*. Past tense.

"I think I understand," I tell her. "I didn't then. But maybe I'm beginning to."

Fitz. His touch makes me feel more alive.

"And you didn't feel that way about Hal?" I ask finally.

"I love his ass," Madge says with a brief return to her typical sense of humor. "I loved the way he kissed me. But no. I didn't love him." She waits a beat. Shrugs. And looks up at me plaintively. "I don't even know what love is. Obviously."

I want to ask her if things are over with the king. I want to ask who ended it. But we've just started speaking to each other again.

Madge turns to watch the queen. She is pale and drawn and seems so frail she might blow away. She's been edgy and snappish, hardly eating and not sleeping well. In the past, she has asked me to sleep in her room, a typical request of her ladies. But recently, all she wants is privacy, and no one attends her.

"She's pregnant again," Madge says, her voice as flat as low tide.

"Oh." I guess that answers my question.

"He says it's his duty." She looks back down at her hands. "That he doesn't enjoy it."

That answers my question more fully than I care to know. I don't want to hear this.

I stand. Madge leaps to her feet and grabs both of my hands in hers.

"I think sometimes he can't even . . . you know. Even be aroused. With her."

"Madge!" I hiss. "Stop!" I can no longer think of her feelings. All I can think of is escape. The queen's rooms are near empty since she hasn't been well, but I feel the very walls pressing in around me.

"I have to tell someone, Mary!" Madge is pleading with me. "I can't—"

"Lady Richmond!" The queen's voice cuts across Madge, and we both turn to stone, staring at each other.

It takes more energy to turn and curtsy than it ever has to wake in the cold of my room.

"I would have you come and speak with me."

I give Madge's hand a squeeze, and she grips mine for longer than is seemly. It's like she wants to pull a promise from me. One I can't give.

I kneel before the queen and she indicates a little stool near her feet. I sit and look up at her. She's wearing gold and a lapis blue that looks like the sky just escaping the bindings of winter. There are gray smudges beneath her eyes, but otherwise she looks serene. A single ring set with a pearl adorns the hand that rests on her belly.

"Cousin, are you happy here?"

The question shocks me for a moment. "Of course, Your Majesty."

"There is no matter of course with happiness, Mary," she says tightly. "You either are or you aren't."

"I am, Your Majesty."

"Mostly."

She has finished my sentence for me. Better than I could myself. I never would have said it out loud.

"I enjoy my work, Your Majesty."

"But do you enjoy your *life*, Mary? That is what matters, after all."

"I don't know what I'm supposed to do with it, Your Majesty."

"With your life?" She sounds exasperated. "You're supposed to use your God-given talents, Cousin. You're supposed to be the person you are, faithfully and truly, because that's how you were made."

I allow the words to settle in my heart, but I don't know what to do with them. Her eyes seem to look through me. Into me. Searching for answers I can't provide. So I look back into her eyes and hope she finds me.

"Do you think you're in love, Mary?" she asks. "Are you happy with your husband?"

"I am not with my husband."

"Yes." She says this musingly, as if she's not really thinking about me at all. "And what of your young friend, Mistress Shelton?"

I force myself not to turn and look at Madge.

"She's not married, Your Majesty."

"Perhaps it's time she was."

"I'm sure she would appreciate your interest, Your Majesty."

"I'm not so sure," the queen says bitterly, then pastes on a smile. "Your diplomacy and your equivocation will serve you well in this court, Cousin. But several months ago, I asked you to tell me nothing but the truth. You gave me your promise."

Now is the time I must choose. I must choose either to betray my friend or betray my promise to the queen. My throat fills with all the possible words. I taste them at the back of my mouth, but I cannot sort one from the other. And I cannot find any that will be sweet.

Finally, I swallow.

"Madge is old enough to marry," I finally whisper. "And I think she grows tired of waiting."

The queen nods, her eyes unfocused, lips pressed into a tight line. Her chin tips upward when she takes a deep breath through her nose, and when she releases it, she turns her gaze back to me.

"And Lady Margaret Douglas?"

"She . . ." I can't keep up with the queen's thoughts. All I can hear is the howl of betrayal in my own ears. Madge finally came to me. To speak to me. To renew our friendship. And I've ruined it.

I can't tell the queen about Thomas Howard. Margaret could be thrown from court for establishing an attachment on her own. Just like the queen's sister. Only worse. Because Margaret has royal blood, any relationship formed without the king's blessing could be considered treason.

"She, too, grows tired of waiting." The queen speaks for me.

Truly, the queen knows all.

28

I'M ON FIRE BY THE TIME I BURST INTO MY ROOM, STARTLING MY maid. I want to shed my own skin. No matter how unwillingly, I've betrayed my friends. I've betrayed my queen, because I couldn't stop Madge.

I don't even know if I should have tried. He made Madge feel alive. Who am I to take that away?

I growl in frustration. My maid bobbles a curtsy, and I scowl at her.

It doesn't make me feel any better.

She turns back to the fire, pokes it once, and then turns around again. I pretend not to look at her. I pretend I'm alone. I pretend not to notice that she's staring at me. I must look ghoulish, the frustration and shame etched all over my features.

"Your Grace," she whispers.

"What is it?" I snap. I've scared her. I never yell. I'm always gracious.

I'm sick of being gracious. I want to be like my mother.

"It's His Grace, Your Grace."

Just what I need. My father.

"Well?" I wait.

"His man came," she says. "His Grace is at court."

"Does he want to see me?" I ask wearily. The ebbing tide of anger has left me exhausted.

"I don't know, Your Grace. Just that he's back from Collyweston and London."

My head snaps up.

"His Grace the Duke of *Richmond*," I clarify. Not Father at all. Fitz.

"Yes, Your Grace."

I don't even thank her or say good-bye. *Stop questioning and start living.* I can't do either if I'm not with him.

Fitz's rooms are very near the king's privy apartments. I cringe at the idea of running into the king. Or Madge. I pass through the hall and up the stairs without seeing anyone.

A man in blue-and-yellow livery stands at the door.

"I wish to see His Grace, the Duke of Richmond and Somerset," I say in a loud, clear voice. Ridiculous that I have to request permission to see my husband.

"He is not available at present."

We eye each other warily.

"I was told he is in the palace."

"He is. But at the moment, he is"—the usher coughs—"indisposed."

Oh, God. He has another girl in there. Someone he met before. Someone he's met since. I feel the ugly blotching blush creeping up my breastbone and take a step backward, stammering.

The door swings open, freezing me.

"A basin of warm water, if you please, Lawson." Fitz stops and stares at me. His doublet is unbuttoned. His hair is wretched and shambly, as if he's been running his hands through it repeatedly.

There are haunts and nightmares behind his eyes.

"And a jug of wine," he finishes.

The usher bows and strides away. Fitz opens the door wider. I walk through and stand near the wall. His bed is unmade. The fire in the corner is barely spitting. He closes the door behind him and walks to the center of the room.

Then he stops, covers his face with his hands, and slowly sinks to his knees.

"Are you all right?" I ask. I don't know if I should go to him or not. I can't seem to move.

He doesn't say a word. His shoulders don't shake. He doesn't heave with sobs. But the misery emanating from him is more palpable than the cold.

"Fitz?"

He gasps in a long breath, and my feet move of their own accord. I kneel beside him and put a hand on his shoulder. He nearly knocks me sideways, with the strength with which he buries his face in my chest. It is not at all sexual, and not entirely pleasant.

Tentatively, I stroke his hair.

There's a knock at the door and he stands with one swift movement, a movement so perfect and graceful it makes me want to cry.

Two ushers enter, taking no notice—making no comment—of

my position on the floor. They set up the basin of water near the fire, and place a tray with a jug of wine and two goblets on a little table. Fitz waits until the men leave before he goes and splashes water on his face.

"It was horrible," he says. He picks up a goblet and drains it quickly. He sets the empty down on the tray and brings the other one to me.

"What was?" I ask.

He sits next to me on the floor, arms around his knees, and stares into the fire.

"I've been to London today. To Tyburn."

"That's where . . ."

"They executed the Carthusian monks," he finishes for me. "The king wanted me there. To represent him."

"Oh."

"I stood with George Boleyn and Henry Norris. They were both drunk. I wish I had been."

Fitz's expression is empty

"The monks were dragged to the square on hurdles, the willow canes snapping beneath their weight. When they stood, their pricks were cut off and burned in front of them."

I don't want to hear, but he needs to tell. I take a sip of wine.

"Did you know a man can still speak, after his heart is removed? Did you know the human body can be broken at the joints? Like a duck. Or a boar. And the pieces carted away like so much refuse."

I shudder and my stomach heaves.

"Did you know," he whispers, "that anyone could be capable of such barbarism? Such inhumanity?"

"They were traitors."

"Were they?" He turns on me. "Or did they just die for their beliefs? When did it become treason to disagree?"

I shake my head, because I don't know.

"He is becoming something I don't understand."

"Who?"

"The king."

"He's your father."

"He's the *king*. That's all that matters to him. Certainly no one else does."

It strikes me that Fitz never says *my father*. It's always *the king*.

"I'm sure it's difficult. Being the king's son."

"No, Mary," he says, bitterness lacing the edges of his words. "It's difficult being the king's *bastard* son. So much is expected of me, and yet I can expect nothing."

"I didn't think you did expect anything."

"That's what everybody thinks. I can't expect anything, so I should be grateful for all the little scraps I'm given."

I sit back and level my gaze at him. For I truly know what it is to be the least person in the household. The one in the corner. The one forgotten.

"I wouldn't say being the Duke of Richmond and Somerset is a *scrap*, Henry FitzRoy."

"Now you sound like the king."

"Have you ever *asked* him for anything?"

Fitz skewers me with his gaze.

"I've asked for you. More than once. And he keeps treating me as if I'm a child. A piece of furniture that can be moved and displayed and used, but never needs to be cared for."

"He does care for you, Fitz. He says he loves you."

"Like I said, words mean nothing. It's the truth that counts. Action and truth."

"Words mean everything."

I think of my own father. I can't remember ever having heard him say he loves me. But he took my side in my marriage. Battled my mother, who was disgusted by the very ground I walked on. Paid for my gowns and my slippers and my place at court.

"What about your status?" I ask. "The gifts he gives you. The way he welcomes you every time you come near. My mother can't stand the sight of me."

"Gifts can't take the place of love. What counts is . . . listening. Giving a person what he wants. Don't you see? I want him to see me. To respect me. To *respond* to me."

He puts a hand on each of my shoulders and looks directly into my eyes, making sure I understand exactly what he's saying.

"I want him to let me be *me*. Not a piece of furniture."

"So how do you do that?" I ask. "How do you make someone see you for who you are?"

Fitz laughs bitterly.

"With the king, I don't know if that's even possible. He's like a horse, blinkered, looking straight ahead, trained not to hear the crash of weapons and the fall of bodies as he charges on toward his own purpose."

"Madge thinks he's in love with her," I blurt.

"More fool she."

I take a gulp of wine, realizing that I had hoped she was right. I had hoped, for her sake, that she could find love. Or at least that she knew what it looked like.

But not with that. Not with a man who would order such cruelty. Not with a man who would force his own son to watch.

"Fitz," I say, and reach for his hand. "I'm sorry."

He turns to me finally, and I see the storm in his eyes, more gray now than blue.

"For what?" he asks. "What do you have to be sorry for? You are the one good thing in my life. That one stroke of dawn in a world that grows darker every day."

He takes my face in his hands again. This kiss is different. Like we're drowning in each other. Every one of my senses is tuned to him, overwhelmed by him. His arms are around me and I can feel the caress of velvet and the tickle of gold braid on the skin exposed by my low neckline. I can smell the City on him, but also his own scent—cool and clean like the first breath of wind after a hot day.

I twine the fingers of my left hand in his hair and slide the fingers of my right beneath his open collar. His skin is inexpressibly smooth, like it's been dusted with gold powder. I want to taste it and angle my mouth away from his, nuzzling his jawline. I feel drunk. Dizzy. Wild.

His skin is glowing where his collarbone meets his throat. I have the sudden, hysterical desire to lick it.

So I do. When my tongue touches him, he moans.

227

So I do it again. He tastes of salt and musk and linen and sugar.

Fitz buries his face in my neck, sending gooseflesh prickling down my arm. He kisses me right where my throat meets my jaw, and instinctively—unthinkingly—I arch into him, his hand on my lower back sliding even lower.

I want this so badly. Want to lose myself in him. Want to forget the queen and Madge and my mistakes. I want to make him forget the executions and his father.

I want to stop questioning. And start living.

I put a hand behind me on the floor and lower myself backward. Fitz follows, elongating himself beside me, one hand cradling my head, deepening his kisses.

His other hand travels down my body, my skin tingling despite the layers of clothes between it and his fingers.

When he pulls up my skirts, the questions start up again.

What am I doing?

I sit up so quickly, I butt him in the chin and he flinches backward. I reach out to steady myself and knock over my wine, spilling a string of ruby droplets across the floor.

"Ow," he says from behind a hand. "I guess I deserved that."

"Oh, God, I'm sorry."

I reach for him, but he grabs my hand.

"That, you can be sorry for," he says, and laughs.

I can't believe I've done it again. Ruined a romantic moment before it even started.

He stops laughing.

"On second thought, don't be sorry," he says. "Call it fate

telling us to take it slowly. Call it instinct, telling you it's not the right time."

It's as if he knows what I'm thinking. What I'm feeling. What I'm questioning.

"I can't lie and say it didn't hurt." He rubs his chin. "I won't ever lie to you, Mary."

He strokes my hairline with a single finger, and all my awareness follows its path.

"And please, always tell me the truth," he says. "If there's one thing I've learned from being the king's son, it's that the truth matters to me. It matters more than anything."

I look at him, at the horror and sadness still behind his eyes. I still want to kiss it away. Make him forget. Feel that heady rush that makes me want to forget myself.

"Will you?" His face is still only inches from mine, his eyes beseeching.

Tell him the truth. "Yes."

"What are you thinking?" he asks.

The skin at my throat starts to burn, and I know I'm blotching. I promised to tell him the truth.

"I was thinking . . . how you make me feel."

A slow smile starts in his eyes, and the corners of his mouth turn upward.

"And what's that?"

I swallow. "Lustful." The flare of heat travels up into my face and down into my fingers.

Fitz chokes on a cough, his eyes wide with surprise.

"I want to love you," I admit. "I feel *something* for you.

Something strong. Something wonderful. I don't know what love feels like. I know how my body feels."

"You want to know what love feels like?" Fitz asks, and his voice is now low and sweet, twining darkness and sugar.

I can't answer out loud, so I just nod.

"It feels like when you're separated, you can't think of anyone else."

I keep my eyes on the space between us. But I think of how Fitz—and seeing him again—remained in the forefront of my mind throughout the entire spring.

"It feels like you're a child again. And every new day is a discovery."

He leans forward. I see the jeweled buttons of his doublet, the gold braid at the hem of his jacket. I think of the kingfisher. The sunrise. The taste of his skin.

"It feels warm."

He puts his hands on my shoulders, and strokes them down to my wrists. The heat that follows his touch feels like it could never be extinguished.

"It feels"—he lowers his forehead onto mine—"right."

I tilt my face upward just a little, our foreheads still touching.

"How do you know?" I ask, my lips so close to brushing his.

His answer is a kiss.

This kiss is like the dawn. Slow and graceful and gilded. It is right and warm and a childlike discovery, and it answers all of my questions and erases all of my doubts.

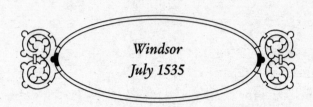

Windsor
July 1535

29

Fitz goes back to London and then to his lands in Sheffield—the farthest we've ever been apart. I revel in it. Because missing him—his touch, his voice, his warmth—is a sure sign that I am in love with him. That I no longer need to question or doubt or struggle. That I can just *be*. In love.

The court moves to Windsor, where we prepare to change locations every three or four days—looking toward Abingdon, Sudeley, Gloucester, and ultimately Winchester. And even though I carry Fitz with me in my heart, my life at court is lonely. Madge won't speak to me, and Margaret is more reticent than ever.

The queen is over her morning sickness, and has begun to let out the laces of her bodice to accommodate her increasing girth. She no longer looks gaunt and agitated. I remember her sweeping Princess Elizabeth up into her arms—the joy in both of their faces. I try to deny the twinge of jealousy I feel for this baby, who will have a mother to love him.

Then, on a Tuesday, Thomas More is executed. The news comes, and the entire court holds still, like a hive of bees stunned by smoke. The king looks blacker than I've ever seen him. Thomas More was the king's friend. His confidant. But More refused to take the Oath of Supremacy.

And refusal to take the oath is treason.

I remember Margaret, spitting mad about the Act of Succession. How she predicted that King Henry wanted to control "lives, love, faith, words." Even the afterlife. I remember she said he would never control her.

I spot her in the upper ward, walking alone along the southern side of the round tower and hurry from my lodgings to catch up with her..

"You've taken the oath, haven't you?" I ask, nearly breathless. I'm sure she wouldn't even be here if she hadn't. But I have to hear it from her. Lady Mary—the king's daughter—refuses.

"Of course."

I sag a little with relief as we turn together toward the castle proper.

"What will happen to Lady Mary?" I whisper.

"By law, she has committed treason. Just like Thomas More. And the Carthusian monks. She refuses to accept the king as the head of the church."

Lady Mary should be in prison. Awaiting execution.

"But what if . . ." I pause. "What will the king do?"

"That's the question, isn't it?" Margaret replies. "If he pardons her, how can he prosecute others? What makes it worse is that she also rejects the Act of Succession and the annulment of King Henry's marriage to her mother. In effect, she's claiming that Queen Anne is nothing but a concubine."

I flinch a little at the word. It's not as bad as *whore*. The round *u* and long *i* make it taste almost fruity. But the hard *c*'s are like seeds, puckering the mouth.

"He wouldn't kill his own child, would he?"

"I wouldn't put anything past him," Margaret mutters. "It's the only reason I took the oath."

"You think he would imprison you?" I ask, incredulous. "Put you to death?"

"Look what he's done already."

She is so blithe. Accepting.

When I look more closely, I see no acceptance in her eyes. I see anger. Hurt. Betrayal.

Defiance.

"You always said he would never control you," I say, pushing on the boundaries of this defiance. "You said you'd make up your own mind. Have your own feelings."

"Don't be naive, Mary. Don't you know it's possible to say one thing and mean another? The king does it all the time. I simply follow his example."

I think about Fitz and his promise never to lie to me. That he has learned to value the truth by living in King Henry's court. And I see the value in it, too.

I also see the misfortune waiting to happen. The *pop* of a ball in the nearby tennis court echoes, lonesome, in the silence that surrounds us.

I have to tell Margaret the truth.

"I told the queen—" I start to say, but then stop. What did I tell the queen?

"About Madge?" Margaret smiles bitterly. "I know."

"I didn't mean to! She guessed. Margaret, she guesses every-thing. It's like her mind is two steps ahead of mine. She asked me about you, too, and—"

Margaret's face goes as white as a bleached skull.

"You didn't tell her. You couldn't." She stops walking and reaches out for something to hold on to. A wall. A branch. But there's nothing there, and she wobbles.

I grab her, and her fingers wrap all the way around my wrist, biting into the bone.

"I didn't. I didn't say anything about Thomas. I never would. But she knows . . . she knows you're tired of waiting for the king's blessing."

The color slowly returns to Margaret's face.

"I don't want to be married off to some minor princeling," she murmurs. Her gaze is focused far away, past the tennis court and the stone battlement walls. Past the trees beyond, already starting to fade in the dry summer heat.

"I know," I say. "But things can change. I . . ." I've never said it out loud before. Not even to him. "I'm in love with Fitz."

She turns back to me, her gaze penetrating.

"I can't love someone because I'm forced to."

She looks at me accusingly. Like I've failed somehow.

"I haven't been forced," I say coldly.

"But it certainly wasn't your choice."

I didn't choose to marry Fitz, but I choose to be in love with him. Don't I?

No. It just happened.

"I don't think falling in love is ever a choice," I tell her.

She smiles at me then. "No, I suppose you're right. Or I'd be in love with a minor princeling, and Madge would fall for someone unmarried."

I feel my shoulders relax a little. I am still on even footing with Margaret.

There's a shout from across the courtyard and then a cry. We turn to see a flurry of courtiers and a flash of yellow skirts.

Madge runs toward us. There are spots of color high on her cheeks, and her eyes are wild—I can see the whites all the way around them.

"It's the queen," she says, bending over her knees and sucking in breaths impeded by her tightly laced bodice. Margaret puts a hand on her back and I crouch down in front of her.

"What is it, Madge?" I ask, trying to keep the edge of fear out of my voice. "What's wrong with her?"

"I was reading," Madge says, and gasps again. "I was in the chapel and I had my prayer book with me. I was just trying to find a place to . . . sit. Some place cool. Out of the sun."

Margaret and I exchange a look. We both think Madge was there to meet the king. But neither of us says so.

"The queen?" I prompt.

"She came in and found me there. She asked what I was reading." Madge takes another breath. "I felt very virtuous. I showed her my prayer book. I thought, *There's no way she can fault that.*"

Madge pauses.

"She's been finding fault with everything lately," she says, and flashes a dark look in my direction.

Then she turns a little gray.

"She took my book. She saw a little poem I'd scribbled in the margin." Madge looks up at us, pleading. "It was nothing, really. Nothing at all. From Chaucer." She gulps. "The one about at the king's court, each man for himself."

"Oh, Madge," Margaret says.

"She screamed at me. Said I'd desecrated the book with my 'idle poesies.' How dare I." Madge's voice trails into a whisper and then into nothing but breath.

"I'm sorry," I manage. Sorry for knowing. Sorry for telling the queen. Sorry that Madge ever laid eyes on the monarch.

"She threw the book across the room." Madge doesn't even seem to hear me.

"And then she cried out. Clutched at her belly. Her men—her ushers—they grabbed her. They're not supposed to touch the queen's person, but she was falling. They held her up. Got her out."

"Is she all right?" I ask. But Madge's face tells me all I need to know.

"There was blood on the floor," she says. "Too much blood."

The castle around us has gone silent. Even the tennis game has stopped. It's as if the news leached through the very walls.

"It's my fault," Madge says, her hands limp at her sides.

"No, it's not, Madge," Margaret says firmly. "It's his."

Langley
July 1535

30

Rumors flow out of the queen's chambers in torrents. The court is a tempest of gossip and lies. That the baby wasn't the king's. That he blames her for the loss of an heir. That he blames her for the murder of Thomas More. That he blames her for his infidelities.

And despite the queen's discomfort, the summer progress moves on. Trudging from Reading to Abingdon across a parched and rutted landscape.

The morning we are to leave Langley, I am called to my father's rooms. He has been in France with George Boleyn to help secure the French prince as a spouse for Princess Elizabeth and they have joined the progress in order to report to the king. Father will be returning to Kenninghall soon.

Mother is still in Redbourn. Safely out of the way.

Father is pacing when I'm allowed entrance. The drapes are pulled against the sunlight that comes in through the east-facing windows, creating a shadowy netherworld of which he seems to be king. He has cut his hair short over the ears, and it is graying at the temples. His beard has been trimmed to a fine point like the flat edge of a spade.

"Shut the door," he says.

And it is done, the usher disappearing behind it.

The quiet room suddenly seems more crowded than the queen's. With the curtains drawn and the door closed, the walls feel ominous. As does my father's expression.

"What I am about to tell you will never leave this room."

A chill settles over me, despite the stuffy heat coming through the curtains. I swallow.

"Do you agree?" he says impatiently.

"Yes." I hadn't realized he was waiting for an answer.

He starts pacing again, the rushes whispering beneath his boots. As he crosses the path of the single arc of sunlight coming between the velvet sheaths on the window, the gold in his doublet flashes bright.

He pauses and turns to me, a shadow of a smile on his face. "My darling girl."

And I am.

Throughout my childhood, my father was never around. Always in France or at court or leading a campaign. An old warhorse, only comfortable on the road. Or so it seemed.

When I got older, I realized it probably had as much to do with staying away from my mother as it did serving his king and country. Then I came to court and realized it had more to do with serving the family than everything else put together.

He only ever wanted the best for me. That's why he never saw me.

When I was about thirteen, he *did* see me. He asked after me. He got me away from my mother and made sure I had pride of place in Anne's household. I carried her train when she went to Easter mass. I carried the chrisom cloth at Elizabeth's christening.

I married the king's son.

Father coughs once. Staring at me.

I force myself not to squirm.

"Have you slept with him yet?"

Fitz. I immediately picture it. His body on mine, my hands in his hair, the taste of linen and the smell of salt.

My embarrassment could ignite me on the spot. That my father would think to ask me such a question.

There is no way I can tell him how much I want it.

It's a miracle we don't both go up in flames.

"No?" I squeak.

Father walks to the window and lifts one hand to part the curtains, the blade of sunlight blinding.

"Is that a question or a statement?" He sounds so detached. So businesslike.

"A statement." I can't tell if he believes me or not. Now I do squirm. I can't believe I'm having this conversation with my father.

"You have not consummated your marriage to Henry FitzRoy."

I shake my head. I don't even know if I could have this conversation with Madge. What I feel for Fitz—and what we almost did together—seems too precious to share.

"I thought I wasn't allowed," I say finally.

He drops the curtain, and his face is again shrouded in shadow.

"The queen has had another miscarriage."

"Yes." The doctors think it may have been a boy. They buried it without ceremony and without name. "I believe the queen is heartbroken."

Father looks at me, and I think I see suspicion in his eyes.

"The king is a bit vexed."

I frown. "It wasn't her fault."

"That isn't what the king thinks."

I don't care what the king thinks. Blaming the woman for the loss of a child is like blaming the soldier for the loss of his life in battle. But I can't tell my father that.

"There are rumors that she is unlikely ever to carry another baby to term," Father continues. "Much like her predecessor."

The former Queen Katherine. Languishing in some castle in the north. Dying of what my mother says is a broken heart.

"No one can know that," I say.

Father stops. The shaft of light glares off of the ring on his right hand. It winks.

"The king no longer goes to her bed."

I look away, wanting to be anywhere but in this room. "I don't think that's something I need to know."

Father takes two quick steps and is right in front of me. I hadn't realized before how short he is, but now that I'm more used to being this close to Fitz, I see that my father is diminutive in comparison. Small, lithe, and comprised of sharp points.

"Don't be clever with me, girl. I am still your father, and your attitude shows a brazen disrespect."

I look down at his boots. The toes are scuffed.

"Yes, Father."

"The king is apparently enjoying the bed of one of the members of the queen's household."

I look up sharply. *Madge.* How much does he know?

He gazes blandly back at me, one eyebrow lazily raised.

He knows everything.

He makes me wait. A heartbeat. Two. Then he reaches out and puts a hand on each of my shoulders.

"The king is getting tired of her, Mary."

"Madge?"

Father rolls his eyes. "The queen."

Oh. That's worse. That's much, much worse.

"She cares as little about him as he does about her," he continues.

But Queen Anne knows what love feels like. *Like music only plays when you're together. Like the very air tastes of strawberries. And like one touch—one look—could send you whirling like a seed on the wind.*

"That woman"—he throws an empty hand toward the queen's apartments—"her days as queen are numbered. And we don't know how many days the king has left either."

"Father!" I cry. Because he has just spoken the words that could get him thrown in the Tower. Attainted.

Executed.

"Remember, Mary, whatever is said here does not leave this room." Something like real fear flashes in my father's eyes. It's the first time I've ever seen him anything but absolutely confident, and this scares me even more. I no longer know him.

He squeezes my shoulders, his fingers biting into my flesh.

"One way or another, he has to have a male heir," he says. "If she never has a boy—there will be no future king."

"The Act of Succession states that Princess Elizabeth is the king's only legitimate heir."

Father goes very still. It's unnerving, how he seems to stop breathing. As if he is gathering all the meaning of what he is about to say and it takes every ounce of his being to do so. I know his next words will be the most important ones he will speak in this conversation. It's the way he operates.

"No one wants a girl on the throne."

My mind flies to all the possible retorts to this statement. That girls are as smart as boys. What matters is royalty, not gender. But I know he is right. Not that she doesn't *deserve* the throne. Just that no one wants her there. A woman can be queen because her husband is king.

Just like a girl can be duchess because her husband is duke.

She does not carry the title in her own right.

It isn't inherited. It's legitimized.

"Especially a child," Father says, breaking my train of thought. "England falls apart when rival factions claim regency over a minority reign. The second King Richard was only ten. The rival factions during his reign nearly destroyed the kingdom."

He sounds like he's trying to convince me of something.

Father's eyes go distant. Almost black. "The sixth King Henry was still with a wet nurse when he came to the throne." Father's grandfather was killed in the wars during Henry VI's reign. His father was imprisoned. Those wars were almost the ruin of the Howards, the dukedom of Norfolk, and the family in general.

Father looks up, and his eyes have lost their vacancy. In its place is a serene intensity.

"It is not unprecedented for a king to legitimize a bastard son," he says. "Your husband has less than two years until he reaches his majority. Don't you think the country would prefer a man on the throne?"

Father once said I would be queen. But the way he's talking sounds unnervingly like treason.

"The queen will have a boy," I say with more confidence than I feel.

"She hasn't yet." Father's tone softens and he comes nearer to me, putting an arm around my shoulder. It is the closest either parent has come to embracing me in a very long time. "All the people of the realm would feel more at ease with a king who already has a son and heir. And as the king is"—Father coughs—"getting older, it would be easier to take if the son had a son and heir as well."

I turn my head to look at him. At his hooked nose, his dark eyes, the beard that has only just begun to turn gray, despite his sixty-one years. His skin is thick, textured by wind and sun and war.

"What are you saying?" I ask, my voice a whisper.

"Give the king a grandson." He sucks in a breath and steps backward, away from me. "The consummation of your marriage may be the security this kingdom needs."

Dunstable
Summer 1535

31

I can do as my father wishes. I always do. We have always been allies—united against my mother's vitriol. I have always taken his side because he has always taken mine.

I want to consummate my marriage. Very much. It would be easy. Fitz wanted it, too. I know he did. I felt it in his kiss, in the way his hand moved on my back, on my hip, my thigh.

However, doing it because my *father* wants me to makes me squeamish. It's like inviting him into the room with us. Like the bedding ceremony, only worse.

But Fitz is in Sheffield, and I am required to move with the court. For the first time in my life, I am relieved to see my father depart. I don't want him to reiterate his request. Or check up on my progress.

As the court moves and shifts and turns to travel west, it begins shedding followers. Thomas Seymour moves on to prepare the Seymour stronghold, Wulfhall, for our visit. Francis Weston returns to Guildford. Thomas Boleyn retreats to Hever Castle. Margaret accepts an invitation to Kent.

Hal returns to Kenninghall to live with his wife.

The courtiers around the king are like a murmuration of starlings, swirling haphazardly, first following one faction and then another, hoping by some happenstance to get closer to the king. The Boleyns then Henry Norris's contingent, the Howards and then the Seymours. No one seems to know where their loyalties should lie.

Those who know of Madge's involvement with the king are paying her more attention. It's all very subtle. Nothing overt. I can see it. I see her struggle with it.

I think of what Margaret meant when she said Madge might be in love with the power. But Madge will not talk to me. She serves the queen with careful deference, but that is all.

We are recovering from our third move in six days when I think I hear my mother's voice.

"It is my right!" the voice cries.

I am in the queen's rooms, sewing for the poor. She sits listlessly by the window. Gaunt. Gray. The shout barely rouses her. Just a flicker as her gaze travels from the window to the door and back to the sky.

I cannot hear a response, but the shout comes again. Louder and more shrill.

"I am the Duchess of Norfolk, and I demand to see the king!"

My needle pauses over my work. The shirt is a coarse linen, scratchy beneath my fingers.

She did not come to see me. I can avoid her. I poke the needle into the fabric repetitively, creating a tiny hole.

The rooms around us go quiet. My mother has either achieved her aim or has been dragged bodily from the house.

I look up to see the queen watching me. She looks like she wants to say something. I wish she would. But she turns back to the window in silence.

The hole is beginning to fray beneath my finger. I go back to the hem of this shirt, carefully rolling the edge and binding it with tight, tiny stitches.

The door opens and an usher in the queen's livery enters, closing the door behind him and standing against it as if trying to keep closed the gates of hell.

"The Duchess of Norfolk, Your Majesty," he says, bowing to the queen just enough to show deference, but not enough to withdraw his hold on the door.

"I do not wish company," the queen says to the window.

"She asks for the Duchess of Richmond and Somerset, Your Majesty." The usher flicks a glance at me. There is terror in his eyes. And sympathy.

I push my fingertip into the hole in the shirt. Willing myself to be utterly indispensable to the queen. She needs me. Sewing. In her room. She cannot spare me.

"Take her to your room, Mary," the queen says.

I stand and leave my sewing on my stool, the hole well hidden beneath the rest of the fabric. I brush my skirts, wishing I had worn the green bodice instead of the blue. The blue has a stain, just to the left of my breastbone. The green I wore the last time I saw Fitz. Sometimes I even imagine I can still smell him on it.

When the usher opens the door, she is there. Waiting.

My mother is dressed all in a deep rust-colored red, the edging on her bodice and hem a black satin appliqué. I see her skirts, her sleeves, the edge of her hood.

But I cannot look her in the face.

The usher closes the door and stands before it. Happy to have saved the queen from this dragon.

I wish someone would do the same for me.

"Well." I flinch at the single syllable. Mother pauses, letting me live with that. "Your *Grace*," she says. "Shall we? I cannot lead, because, as you know, you have *precedence*."

I cannot move, precedence or not. The last time I stepped in front of my mother, I had Fitz.

The thought of him gives me courage. I have Fitz. My mother has no one.

I look up into her face, and see that the last two years have not served her well. Her mouth has grown smaller. Puckered like a hem badly stitched. Her eyes have fallen deeper into the sockets of her skull. She is thinner. Smaller.

But not diminished.

I imagine I am again on Fitz's arm. That his hand is steady beneath mine. I move forward, but she doesn't get out of my way, so I have to walk around her. She turns with me—not even a step behind. I increase my pace, but she does not fall back.

When we reach my room, she strides in proprietorially, and I can see every criticism of my quarters on her face. It's too small. There is no fireplace. The window is too high up. The velvet bed curtains are growing bald where they brush the frame.

If she had been assigned this room, she would have

demanded something better. She would have brought her own linens. I'm not good enough to be a duchess.

"Your father isn't here."

It takes me a moment to realize that she hasn't actually said any of the words that have flown through my mind. I don't respond. I do not speak to my mother unless she asks a direct question. She doesn't tolerate it.

"I see you still refuse to carry yourself like a duchess."

I hold myself a little straighter. Try to elongate my neck.

"And that bodice has a stain."

Unwillingly, I put a finger on the stain. I should have feigned surprise. But I cannot seem to act any other way around my mother than the way I did when I was ten. Silence.

And humiliation.

"I came to see the king," she says. "To importune him to get your father to handle me better." She says *your father* as if he is something I created just to vex her.

"Redbourn is uninhabitable," she continues. "Especially for one born and brought up daintily."

Redbourn is a fine house.

"Your father locked me up," she says, "He took away my jewels and clothes. It's no better than a prison."

She starts walking around the room, lifting things up and putting them down. She brushes the sill of the window for dust, picks at the loose threads on the bed hangings, toes the rushes on the floor, wrinkling her nose because they aren't terribly fresh. She pauses at my writing desk, one finger on the lid of the inkpot.

My book lies right next to her hand. My book with the poems I've written back and forth to Madge. With the list of attributes a man would need in order for us to love him.

With the list of men we'd want to kiss.

I watch as her eyes and finger touch the pen, my prayer book, the ring I removed because it kept twisting around my finger.

The book.

"And what did the king say?" I blurt, and then bite my lower lip so hard I taste blood.

Mother turns like a falcon spotting prey and I feel the fear of a small animal about to be eviscerated.

At least the book is safe.

"I told him everything. I told him how your father treats me. How he beat me nearly senseless before I gave birth to *you*."

This is an old tale and one long told. I do not know if I believe it. Father has always denied that he hit her when she was pregnant with me. Yet she claims that he threw her to the floor and kicked her in the belly and that is why my character is so deformed.

"I said I would rather be locked in the Tower of London than be handled so cruelly by that man," she continues. "After all, I am used to imprisonment."

She adopts a practiced air of martyrdom, her face turned just to the side, gaze fixed on the middle distance. She uses it to incite sympathy in her audience. I have none to spare.

Mother scowls at my lack of response.

"The king told me outright that as a Christian, I owe obedience and submission to Norfolk."

Mother never calls him Thomas. He's always *your father*. Or Norfolk.

"He said I should submit to ill-treatment. To imprisonment. Because it is my duty as a wife."

The king said this. Submit. Be a prisoner.

It's what he expects from a wife.

From any woman.

We are silent for a moment. Like a held breath.

"This is the family you have married into," Mother says finally. "It is what you've brought upon yourself. You and that father of yours."

She warms to her topic, stepping closer, her chest and shoulders thrusting forward like the prow of a ship through choppy seas.

"Has he included you in his machinations?" she hisses. "First he marries you off to the bastard. And then he designs for you to have the bastard's son, since the king can't seem to get one of his own."

The words strike so closely to the truth that I flinch.

My mother sees it and, for an instant, her eyes are wary. Almost sad.

Then she smiles. A slow and sour smile, full of rancor.

"You had better do as he says," she murmurs, the sound sonorous as distant waves and just as dangerous. "Get yourself into FitzRoy's bed. Produce a grandchild. A king. It is the only way you can prove your worth to him."

She turns to the door. Pauses with her hand on the latch.

"It's the only way you can prove your worth to any of them.

Your father, your husband. Your king. So you had better do it soon. Or you may find yourself with no marriage at all."

She leaves silently, the only sound the click of the latch as the door closes behind her.

But my thoughts are loud and fierce and violent as a storm at sea. The things I should have said to her. The arguments I could have made. I could have told her I love Fitz. I *should* have told her that marriage is a collaboration. A bond.

I should have shouted that my marriage will make me free. Of her. Of the muzzle that suppresses my ability to speak whenever I am around her. Except it hasn't. Because I spoke all of six words to her. Blurted in a moment of desperation.

I stand in the center of my room, fists clenched, lips pressed tight, teeth grinding against withheld words. Until finally, I say the ones I should have shouted before she shut the door.

"At least I am worth more than you."

My voice is weak and hollow and bears no weight, the words vanishing upon creation.

I swallow the rest of them. Hold my head up straight. Elongate my neck. Keep my shoulders square.

I walk back to the queen's rooms, pick up my sewing, and I darn the hole I made with stitches so smooth and tight, the ragged edges vanish beneath the mend.

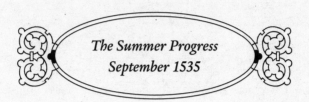

The Summer Progress
September 1535

32

THE PROGRESS IS SLUGGISH AND SOMBER. WE MOVE FROM Gloucester to Thornbury, Acton Court to Bromham. The queen hardly speaks, and when she does, it's to her chaplains. The king spends all his free time hunting or hawking, barely acknowledging his subjects when they come for justice or sanction or to receive his touch for some horrifying disease.

In September, we stop at the Seymour manor of Wulfhall in Wiltshire. It is just on the edge of the Savernake Forest, an ancestral woodland of oak and beech, the great, saddle-backed ancients sheltered by the sprawling coppices of spidery saplings. The chalk plateau is patched and pocked with flint that strikes sparks from the horses' hooves as we thread our way through the trees to the wide valley where the manor stands.

When we reach the manor, I remain on my horse, on a slight rise overlooking the barely controlled chaos of our arrival.

The house is timber framed, with a single stone tower dominating the corner of one of the courtyards. The horses and carts and courtiers spill around the house like multicolored grain tipped from a silo. Everyone pushes in, trying to be seen, trying to be helpful, trying to be *necessary*. Old man Seymour nods and smiles and sends the servants hither and yon while his daughter Jane stands beside him, pretending to be the lady of the house.

I suddenly want to turn around and abandon it all. Ride my horse all the way to Sheffield. To wherever Fitz is. To find another moment with him like that morning in the boat—quiet, tranquil, and golden.

"Marvelous, isn't it?"

I turn to see Thomas Seymour beside me. He rode out to meet us four miles away, trotting up and down the cavalcade and welcoming each person in order of precedence. I should be offended that he has come to me so late, but I was rather relieved to avoid conversation with him.

The contrast between Jane and Thomas is like night and day. Jane is small and a little round, her face so average that it is nearly featureless. Whereas Thomas has presence. Sinewy and swift, like a greyhound. His features are sharp and dark, and when he directs his gaze at something, it's as if there's nothing else in the world. His hair falls in waves over his ears and his chin is clean-shaven. No spade-like facial hair for him.

The girls fall all over him. It's as if he breathes carnality from his pores, and they swarm to it like ants to honey.

He sees me assessing him and leans forward over his pommel with a rapacious grin.

"I could give you a tour," he says. "I know Wulfhall's most . . . *intimate* secrets and hiding places."

He tips his head to the side. It's as if he's waiting for me to look away first.

I don't.

"Thank you," I say with more graciousness than I feel. "My duty is to the queen."

"And mine is to make sure the *desires* of all of my guests are met."

We ride together, no longer speaking, to the melee of the stable yard, and when he hands me down from my horse, he holds on to me a little too long.

"Remember, just come to me if you need any . . . privacy while you are here."

When I don't answer, he blows me a kiss.

That's when I turn away. I don't look at him again.

I don't need to experiment anymore. Certainly not with the likes of Thomas Seymour.

Something alters while we are in Wiltshire. When we leave to travel back toward Windsor, through Winchester and Farnham and Easthampstead, the king is more jovial. It's as if the Seymours with their exuberant hospitality have somehow made everyone happier, more content, more fulfilled.

We make our slow way winding through countryside set to harvest.

What little there is. The weather has turned against the farmers, and they stand, still and stonelike beside their plows, watching the parade go by with little acclaim and less revelry.

Rumors abound that they blame the queen. That they think this is the result of the break with Rome. That it is all her fault.

She seems to shrink into herself, the closer we get to Windsor. She is no longer the mythical Helen, beautiful enough to incite men to war. She no longer calls her own to her, like the light to which moths fly. She looks lost.

And when we arrive at Windsor, the most astute members of the court begin to pay suit to Jane Seymour.

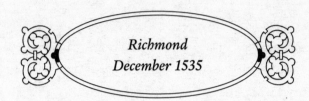

Richmond
December 1535

33

In November, Father and Fitz traveled together to the Welsh Marches, despite the impending winter, to assert English authority. I worry they won't be back before Christmas. I worry about what Father might be suggesting Fitz do with me.

The court moves to Richmond, slogging on roads choked with mud and detritus. The weather has been horrific—sheets of rain sliding from the sky and threatening to drown the unwary for simply stepping outside.

Everyone is pressed into closed rooms and narrow galleries—it's impossible to move without rubbing shoulders and stepping on toes. And when I'm alone, I carry in my nostrils the stink of wet and mold and the must of unwashed bodies.

I am surprised when my maid opens the door for a visitor late one evening. There are no parties planned. The queen chose to dine in her privy chambers, the king in his. Everyone separated.

I look up to see Madge standing in my doorway.

She is thinner. And probably more beautiful. But some of the shine has left her, as if the rain has washed it away.

I stand and we face each other.

"So," she says. That is all.

"So."

The maid stands helplessly behind Madge, obviously unsure of whether to go or stay. I finally put her out of her misery by asking for bread and cheese.

"And maybe some wine," Madge adds, with a flicker of her old bravado. But it disappears in an instant and she turns to me, forlorn. "If that's all right."

"Of course," I say. "Come in. Mistress Shelton."

Madge presses the knuckles of her right hand to her mouth, looking about to cry, and shakes her head.

I wait.

"So," Madge says again, hesitates, and then tosses her head. She flops down on my bed and speaks to the canopy. "When is the big night?"

"Big night?" I ask. I'm unsettled by her presence. By her attempt to take things back to the way they were. As if the last six months haven't even happened.

"Yes," she says. Then more slowly. "To start living."

I just sit down and pick up my sewing. I don't want to go back to that discussion.

"Fitz—the Duke of Richmond—is coming back for the Christmas holidays, is he not?" Madge props herself up on her elbows to look at me.

I hope so. I nod and lift the thread to my mouth to bite it off.

"Oooh." Madge reaches for the linen. "Very nice work, Duchess. What is this and who might it be for?"

I pull it away from her.

"Never you mind."

"I reckon it's a shirt for your husband. And I reckon that you—naughty girl that you are—would rather see him out of it than in."

I drop the shirt to my lap. It is for Fitz. Of course it is. I have thought of how something I've touched—hands, fingers, lips—will soon be touching his skin. And something gnaws deeply inside me when I imagine it. But I'll be damned if I admit it to Madge right now.

"What do you want?" I ask her.

"I want to see you happy."

"You mean you want to be happy."

She climbs down from the bed and kneels in front of me, taking my hands in hers. "Your happiness makes me happy, Duchess."

I can't help but smile. Madge is self-serving and indiscreet, but I have been so lonely without her.

"Are you happy, Madge?"

She stands abruptly and brushes off her skirts. She walks to the fire and pokes at it with the iron rod that sits nearby. The coals flare red and then go black. She looks at me over her shoulder.

"I am now that you're calling me Madge again."

She lays down the rod, and this time when she walks to me, I stand. She hugs me with a fierceness that brings tears to my eyes.

When I look at her, she wipes her own.

"I don't know what he sees in her."

I know who she's talking about, but I don't respond.

"Frowsy old Jane Seymour. The simpering sow-faced cow. She has no beauty and no spark. That woman wouldn't say boo to a goose. And she'd never tell anyone no."

"Maybe that's the appeal." No one would ever say that about Madge. Or the queen.

"There is no chance that woman is a virgin. She's almost twenty-eight years old. It's impossible to stay a virgin for so long. Especially at this court. Didn't she serve Queen Katherine?"

"There are ways to retain virginity, Madge."

She lowers her head and looks at me from beneath her brow. "And there are ways to lose it, Duchess. I'm sure Fitz wouldn't mind relieving you of yours."

I swat at her and she ducks.

"You're blotching."

I charge at her and nearly knock over the maid opening the door with her hip, carrying a tray laden with wine and bread. The tray totters precariously and we all watch as the jug slides to the floor with a thump and a shower of red.

Madge throws her head back and howls with laughter while I kneel with the maid, who is attempting to wipe some of it up with her skirts.

"Please, Your Grace," the maid says.

"Yes, Your Grace," Madge says in the same tone. "Let's rectify this situation by going to find wine on our own."

I thank the maid, who hardly looks at me, and Madge laughs again.

We make our way through the lodgings to the outer court.

The royal lodgings are stacked on top of one another, beyond the courtyards and the hall and moat.

Madge loops an arm through mine. "So," she whispers. "The queen. Is she well?"

"She seems melancholy," I say slowly.

"I've heard she's ill. But she still won't let me into her privy chamber."

I glance at her. "It could be morning sickness."

Madge wrings her hands. "My mother thinks it's poisoning. The lady Mary—the king's daughter—said she *hopes* it's poisoning. Do you think—would anyone do that?"

The queen has many enemies. I suppose poisoning could be a real possibility. The queen's face is drawn and colorless. She is so thin. She looks so old. But there is something in her eyes.

Something a little like hope.

"No," I say firmly. "I think she's pregnant again."

"We stopped sleeping together three months ago," Madge says. "And I don't think Jane Seymour will sleep with him."

As if that's the only reason to sleep with your wife. Because your mistress won't let you in her bed. Irritation bubbles in my lungs.

"So you care about her now that you are no longer rivals?"

Madge stops short. "I always cared about her."

I turn, unable to avoid the confrontation. "That's why you slept with her husband."

Madge hangs her head, and I can see the droplets of rain peppering the hair exposed by her hood. "I thought he loved me. I thought fate had brought us together. Like Margaret and Thomas." She looks up. "Like you and Fitz."

I feel not only guilt but pity. Because what would I do if Fitz were unattainable? What would I feel if he were already married or too old or too young or a priest? What if he were a prisoner, destined to be executed?

Wouldn't I break the rules?

For love.

But there has to be a line drawn somewhere. A boundary that shouldn't be crossed.

Or do I just feel superior because I'm married to the man I love?

"I don't know if I believe in fate," I say finally.

Madge stops at the courtyard gate. Through it can be seen the inner court and the storied donjon. The rain has stopped and the light from the windows glints on the wet cobblestones.

"Do you believe in love?" she says. It's not a question. It's a challenge. "Even Margaret, the queen of reserve, seems more besotted. Are you in love with the delectable duke?"

My chest gets tight and my first desire is to tell her—not sparing any details—how I feel. How my body is like a divining rod, specially tuned to his presence. How I feel like something's missing when he isn't nearby.

Her challenge stops me. If she had asked as a friend, I would bend my head near hers and whisper everything into her ear. As it is now, my confession of love would be a defense. And that seems like a cheap waste of truth.

Madge waits for a moment. Then two. She narrows her eyes, and then her wicked grin starts to tug at her mouth. "Or are you simply in lust?"

My thoughts flash back to that afternoon in Fitz's room. How my body reacted when Fitz's lips touched the skin where my throat meets my jaw. How his hand felt pressing me against him. How much it scared me.

"It's lust." Madge claps her hands. "I can tell just by looking at you."

"Aren't they all part of the same thing?"

"Absolutely not. You can lust after someone and not love him at all."

"You think you can want to be with someone physically if you don't like them personally?"

"I didn't say you could lust after someone you loathe," Madge corrects me. "Though I think it's possible. I was just saying that you can want someone's body and not necessarily be interested in his mind."

"Or his heart?" I ask. "Because don't you want to be with someone who at least cares about you?"

"I don't need to be taken care of."

"That's not what I said." But I wonder if it's what I want. My mother never took care of me. I'd like to feel protected.

"I think you and I look at the world very differently," Madge says.

As we stand at the courtyard boundary, each waiting for the other to say the next line, the rain begins to fall again, a veily shimmer between us. Neither of us moves.

"Well," I say finally, not letting my gaze drift from hers. "That must be why we are friends."

Madge blinks. Once. Twice. And then rapidly. "True," she says, lifting her face to the rain. "I guess we've made it this far." She starts to turn, her arms stretched down at her sides, fingers spread wide. "We can't stop now!"

She whirls once more and then grabs my hands to pull me in a circle around her. We both lean back, faces upward, the walls of the courtyard spinning past, the clouds above like a whirlpool, ready to suck me up and away.

A flash of blue and yellow catches the corner of my eye. The colors of the livery Fitz's ushers wear. If his servants are here, Fitz will be, too. I stop and Madge twirls into me, knocking our spin out of kilter, and we clutch at each other to keep from falling onto the wet and mucky cobblestones.

Francis Weston comes to our rescue. He is perhaps too careful not to touch me. And perhaps too attentive keeping Madge's body from coming to any harm.

"Why, thank you, Master Weston." Madge actually bats her eyelashes, and Weston actually blushes.

"Your Grace," Weston says to me, and bows. He doesn't let go of Madge, but greets her with an arm still around her waist. "Mistress Shelton."

Another married man.

But we have just rediscovered the footing of our friendship, so I hold my tongue and renew my determination to live my *own* life.

I turn to the courtyard gate to look again for the man in his livery, and there stands someone else. Dressed in gaudy black and white, his crimson cloak trimmed in fur, and sporting a new-grown brassy scruff of beard.

My brother.

He's staring at Madge in Weston's arms. She hasn't seen Hal yet. She's still giggling at Weston, one hand flat on his chest.

"Hal!" I cry. It's like watching the jug of wine earlier—an accident happening as time slows to a standstill.

Madge's eyes widen and she falters, Weston's arms tightening around her even more. Then Madge tosses her head and looks at him again. As if Hal doesn't exist.

I catch a glimpse of him as he disappears again around the corner of the gate.

"Hal!" I stumble once in my rush across the cobbles, but catch him before he gets too far. I grab his hand from behind and he starts to jerk it out of my grip, but then turns and hugs me ferociously.

"I thought I would be fine," he says with a bark of a laugh. "I mean, I haven't seen her in six months. I've been living with my wife. I should be fine."

He looks at me. He is not fine.

"We don't always do what we should," I tell him gently.

"Spoken like a true rule breaker," Hal says, and kisses my cheek.

"And you do like your wife. Don't you?"

Hal leans in to whisper to me. "I made her pregnant."

I step back and he tips his head to one side and shrugs minutely. Blushing.

I hug him again. "Congratulations." I look up into his face. "You must like her a little then."

Hal looks back over his shoulder to the gateway. All we can see from here is the inside of the stone arch—none of the court-yard at all.

"I like her," he says. "She's sweet and pretty, but . . ." He doesn't finish his thought and turns back to me with an unde-niable intensity. "You are so fortunate, Mary. Never forget that. Fitz loves you. He hasn't stopped talking about you since we left Kenninghall."

"Fitz is here?" My mouth has gone dry and my fingers flutter against my skirts. "You rode together?"

I look over Hal's shoulder, as if Fitz might be standing there.

Hal laughs. "He had to present himself to his father first. And then . . ." Something behind me catches his attention, and his smile grows even wider. "Talk of the devil."

My heart thrums into my throat.

And I turn.

34

He's taller. Fuller.

More than I remember. His shoulders have broadened, his legs lengthened; his face is more angular and there's a shadow of beard along the jawline. There is no boy left in that body, in that face.

But his hair is still golden-red like the dawn. His eyebrows winged and soaring. His mouth tipped into a smile of expectation. Challenge. Invitation. And those gray-blue eyes watching me with *hopefeardoubtjoylove*.

It is as if we are the only two people there. Everything else drains away—the courtyard, the rain, the queen, the gossip, Madge. I think I hear Hal laugh.

I walk forward, my feet not even beginning to beat time with the racing of my heart. Fitz meets me halfway and we stop a foot apart. I have to tilt my head back to look him in the eye, exposing my throat—all gooseflesh with remembered kisses.

"Your Grace." I drop my eyes and curtsy.

"Your Grace."

His voice sounds distant and detached. Nothing like that murmur in my ear the last time we saw each other. When he kissed me.

I can no longer look him in the eye. What if he has out-grown me? Just as his body has grown and mine hasn't. My forehead is now level with his chin. I see the reddish stubble on the point of it.

And the hint of a smile on his lips.

He coughs, and I am excruciatingly aware that we are in public. The ever-moving court flows around us like we are a rock at the center of a stream, but occasionally, someone gets caught in an eddy and filters past us several times.

Eavesdropping.

Fitz speaks so quietly I'm not sure I hear him. "So formal, Mary?"

His use of my given name makes me melt.

"Just . . . wanting to do what's expected." I try not to move my lips. Turn my face to the side so I don't look at him directly. Because if I do, everyone around us will see how much I want him.

"Expectations aren't all they're cracked up to be."

"Oh?" I smile, still pretending to study the far wall of the garden. "And what are the alternatives?"

"I am the king's son but not expected to be like him. I am expected to be a scholar, but I am a better athlete. In the end, it doesn't matter. My intellect will not change the world, and I will never be king, no matter how badly your father wants it."

He knows of my father's desire to have a Howard heir on the throne. *My* son. I finally look up into the face of the man who would help me make that happen, and a deluge of ice flows through me followed by the ignition of a fireball, thinking of what needs to *precede* the arrival of said heir.

"At the end of the day, my accomplishments, my striving to do what everyone else wants, don't matter," Fitz continues. "So I might as well just do what *I* want."

"What if you want to break the rules?"

He no longer blushes like a boy. He looks me right in the eye, one corner of his mouth turned up.

"I suppose it would depend on which rules I'm breaking."

I take a step closer, the tips of our shoes almost touching, and raise my face to his. I can smell the leather of his riding breeches, still horsey and green from the road; the wet, woolen odor of his cloak; the bright, sunny warmth of his linen shirt.

I can almost taste him.

His gaze moves to my lips, his head bowed.

We are in a public place.

"We shouldn't be here," I whisper. But I don't move.

"I am right where I want to be," he says. "It doesn't matter if there is anyone else around. It doesn't matter if I can touch you or kiss you or"—he coughs—"put my hands in your hair or on your breast or just hold your hand in mine. It doesn't matter if the space between us is an inch or the length of the room or nonexistent. I belong with you. Wherever you are, I'm complete."

And at that moment, I don't care who is watching. I stand on my toes and kiss him lightly on the lips. Just a taste.

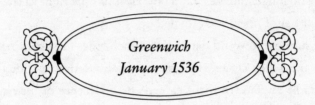

Greenwich
January 1536

35

FITZ COMES DOWN WITH A COLD AND A FEVER FROM HIS TIME ON the road and spends Christmas Day in bed while I spend it wishing I was with him. He has one of his ushers bring me a little gold box with an enameled kingfisher inlaid on the lid, and though it is my favorite gift by far, it doesn't make up for his absence. But by the first of January, he is nearly back to normal, if a little pale.

Every time I enter a room, I look for him. One party or banquet whirls into another and we dance poorly and laugh loudly and never again kiss in public, even though I want to. All. The. Time.

Margaret returns to court, and Madge is speaking to me again, and everything is back almost to the way it was before it fell apart, before the king came between us. We are all three friends again. I am buoyed by the knowledge that all is well in the world. I return to my room one day to discover my book beneath my pillow, a quotation from Chaucer on the end page.

Wax fruitful and multiply.

I return it to Madge with a reminder.

There's a price offered for virginity.

The next day, I find a note scrawled in the margin in Margaret's hand.

> *Leave virginity to those who have nothing else to offer.*
> *Our gifts are too numerous to be wasted.*

Two days after Epiphany, we return to Greenwich, and it seems the court is reluctant to stop celebrating. The great hall is festooned with the branches of fir trees and reeks of soot and resin. The trestle tables wobble under the weight of plate and wine. The head table, where the king and queen sit, glitters with Venetian glass. When they drink, it looks as if they lift the eye of God to their lips.

I run my finger along the lip of my own gilt goblet. I sit high at table, just below Margaret, far away from Madge. Fitz sits closer to the king. I watch him play with his food.

The king appears to be regaling him with war stories. Fitz laughs at something the king says, and the light dances on the sleek shock of hair that curtains his forehead. The laugh turns into a cough and he turns to the side; the king slaps him jovially on the back. When Fitz turns around again, his cheeks are red, his eyes still laughing.

He stretches his legs out beneath the table, his entire body appearing loose and unencumbered by doubt or fear or nerves or questions. But I know him now. I know he is not as easy as he looks. I have seen his distrust of his father. Of the *king*.

And I have felt the intensity of his emotions.

The sharpness in his gaze when he meets mine bathes me from head to foot with a warmth that ultimately settles low in my abdomen and makes me wish there weren't so many people in the room.

The subtleness of his smile is so slow and casual that I hardly know he's doing it until he nods and lifts his goblet in a mute toast. I raise mine in return.

"Flirting at table?" Margaret murmurs from beside me.

I notice her own eyes twitching quickly to my half uncle Thomas.

"What of it?" I ask, sipping my wine.

"The Countess of Worcester would take you to task," Margaret says with a grin. Elizabeth Somerset, the Countess of Worcester, has recently become the self-appointed warden of all the maids' chastity.

"Well, then someone should tell the countess that if the queen flirts, why shouldn't we?"

We both turn and raise our goblets to Madge, who sticks out her tongue. It is stained red by the claret. Margaret laughs her deep, throaty laugh, sounding so much older and so much more naughty than she actually is.

"I think the countess's real problem is that she is no longer beautiful enough to attract the eye of any man, much less the king."

I look at her questioningly.

"It's said she was once his mistress," Margaret explains. "Long, long ago, of course."

I look to where the countess hovers, halfway between the high table and the lowest ones. Her hair has begun to dull, and her skin to grow slack. But what mars her beauty are the pinched lines around her mouth, the narrow channel of displeasure between her eyebrows. It's possible she was once beautiful—in the traditional, English way, just as Mary Boleyn was. So different from the queen.

So different from Jane Seymour, pale enough to be invisible, though the king can't take his eyes off her. She sits with her brothers. Edward has been appointed to the Privy Council and has moved into Cromwell's rooms right next to the king. Thomas Seymour watches Margaret and me with furtive intent. As yet, he has not reaped the benefit of the king's interest in Jane.

"Making eyes at Thomas Seymour?" Madge plants one hand on each of our shoulders and cackles when we both jump. I didn't even see her get up from the table. "Remember what I said about practicing with someone experienced? He could give you a ride for your money."

"Ugh, Madge," I say under my breath. "He's a little ... creepy."

"He's deliciously creepy," Madge says. "That's why I think he'd be good for you. He could show you the ways of the world, my dear."

"Ugh," I say again, and shrug her off.

Madge laughs. "I'll take that as a no, then. So you don't mind if I have a shot at him?"

I look over to where Thomas Seymour sits with his back to the wall. He's watching everyone. Tirelessly.

"Just be careful, Madge," I say. "That man wants something."

"Don't they all?" Madge casts a not-so-subtle glance at the king. Even with the queen at his side—even with her pregnancy—his attention is all on Jane Seymour.

Madge squeezes her way between us on the bench. Our shoulders press against each other, but I don't mind being crowded against my friends.

"Don't worry, darling Duchess," she says, pinching a piece of marzipan from the plate in front of me and licking the sugar off her fingers. "I'm making eyes at someone else tonight."

Hal sits with Francis Weston. Both of them are looking at Madge.

"I think you've got your pick," I murmur. "Who might you be choosing?"

"Guess."

I hate guessing games. I always feel so useless at them. Especially when I'm trying to guess one amongst thousands.

"Give me a hint." I try to play along.

"He's handsome."

"Fitz is the only man who comes to mind." I flick a glance at him and suppress a smile.

Margaret leans in from the other side. "Give us another hint, Madge."

"He's a good dancer."

"Definitely not Fitz, then." I grin. He's looking at me with one eyebrow raised. He knows I'm talking about him.

Madge has stiffened and is looking down at her hands, clenched to the edge of the table.

"I wouldn't do that to you, Mary."

"I know." I lay a hand over hers, but it doesn't relax. I suspected her once. But as much as I disagree with some of her choices, I know she's a better friend than that.

And I trust Fitz.

I lean in close.

"It's not Thomas Seymour, is it?" I glance back at him. He smiles in a way I'm sure he thinks is seductive. Most women say he's irresistible.

I'm sure I can resist.

"I wouldn't say no." Madge grins. "But no."

"You haven't given us much to work with," Margaret says. "Good dancer and handsome." She looks around the crowded room. "That could apply to half the men here."

"Obviously you have lower standards than I do, Margaret," I tease.

Madge smirks. "His name starts with an *H*."

A tightness grips me. "Howard?" I ask. Hal has not yet recovered from the last time.

"No, you dolt, his first name starts with an *H*."

This doesn't help. "Henry?"

"You could say I have a thing for Henrys," Madge says. Margaret and I exchange a look and both lean closer, surrounding Madge like a little wall. Then we just stare. She won't escape until she tells us.

Madge glances from one face to the other, eyes wide.

I say, "Henry . . ." waiting for her to add the surname.

"Norris."

I sit back. "Henry Norris?"

"You needn't sound so surprised. Or so *pleased*." The sarcasm is unmistakable.

"I'm very happy for you, Madge."

She turns on me, and her blue eyes glitter darkly. "He's going to marry me. It's being arranged."

"Congratulations." I put my hand on her wrist, but she stands and shakes me off.

"Don't bother with your limp felicitations, Duchess."

"I just think you can do better."

"Better than what?" Madge's whisper is fierce, but we are the only two who can hear it. "I've had the king."

I'm almost afraid to touch her. To reach her with words or fingers. She seems so fragile. When she turns to me, her eyes look haunted.

"I wanted to be noticed. I wanted to be acknowledged. I walk through the rooms and galleries of every palace and no one even knows I'm there. Thomas Seymour falls all over himself to get to you, Margaret. Everyone defers to you, Duchess. Hell, everyone defers to Jane fucking Seymour! What's different about her? What changed?"

I hear the unasked question: *Why didn't that happen to me?*

I can't utter the answer that comes immediately to mind. *Because Jane Seymour hasn't slept with him yet.* Jane is so unlike Madge. So unlike the queen. Where Madge and the queen are dark and brash, Jane is meek and blonde and quiet.

"I don't know." It's all I can say.

Jealousy tastes like salted fish—pungent, slick, and at the point of spoiling. I can almost smell it on her breath.

"We're both very happy for you," Margaret says. "Henry Norris is a fine man."

Madge smiles weakly. "At least he's not already married."

The king stands abruptly and the hall roars as we all get to our feet. Then we fall into a ringing silence. A messenger—still covered in filth from the road and hanging his head in exhaustion—stands behind the king.

"God be praised, we are free from all suspicion of war!" the king says, and raises his goblet to the room.

Everyone follows suit. The queen's expression is blank with relief, but there are tears in her eyes.

Beside me, Margaret watches the king with something akin to loathing in her eyes.

"Katherine—the princess dowager—is dead," she says. "And he thinks it's a cause for celebration."

Katherine of Aragon. The king's first wife. Or not-wife, as he attests. The Holy Roman emperor is her nephew and has been threatening to defend her claim to queenship by invading.

Now it no longer matters.

"I think it's peace they're celebrating, not death," I say. The queen has steadied herself. She stands up straight, shoulders back, neck elongated. She brushes both palms on her skirts, then places a hand on her husband's arm. For the first time in months, he lifts her hand to his lips to kiss it.

"Believe what you like, *Duchess*," Margaret spits. "But he is celebrating the fact that there are no longer two queens in this country."

I try to maneuver myself over the bench, but Madge is too close, and the entire court seems to be packed into the space behind me. The dissonance of competing voices and laughter threatens to asphyxiate me, and I trip over strands of conversation.

"She died cold and alone. . . ."

"Maybe now we'll get some Spanish wine again. . . ."

"He'll be happy for her money. . . ."

"I hope her daughter soon keeps her company—"

I stumble and fall headlong into the last speaker, George Boleyn. He steadies me firmly, a roguish grin on his face.

"I'm so happy, I could kiss you, Your Grace," he says, "but I must bestow that honor on my sister first."

He turns and rushes through the rest of the crowd, snatching Queen Anne from the king's embrace. He kisses her on the mouth, spinning her around.

She throws her head back and laughs.

I turn back to Margaret. "It's the first time I've seen the queen look truly happy in weeks," I say to her. "And they're not fighting anymore. Isn't that worth something?"

I look to the Seymours. The two brothers are frowning.

But Jane has something that could be the start of a smile on her lips.

Margaret shakes her head. "You have built your beliefs on sand, Mary FitzRoy, and the tide will soon wash your feet right out from under you."

36

THE CELEBRATIONS CONTINUE THE NEXT DAY. THE KING AND queen both wear yellow, and even I question their judgment. The king enters the queen's rooms carrying little Elizabeth, who giggles uncontrollably when he lifts her up into the air in an impromptu dance. He schedules feasts and games and finally a joust.

He seems almost himself again. Or at least the king I imagined I knew when I first came to court. Happy and in love. A good husband. A good father.

Part of me says I know better than to be completely deceived. That he will treat Elizabeth no better than he's treated Fitz. She's a pawn.

My mother sends me a vitriolic diatribe. She claims that Anne Boleyn had Katherine of Aragon poisoned. That she will poison Fitz as well if we're not careful. She claims the king is now free to marry anyone at any time he likes because he no longer has to justify his abandonment of his first queen. I burn the letter immediately after reading it, wishing I had burned it before.

No one needs to know the extent of Mother's treason.

By the day of the joust, the queen is feeling ill again. She sends most of her ladies to the tiltyard, claiming she is well enough to entertain herself. Madge goes to watch Henry Norris, who always excels in the lists. I stay behind in the queen's privy chamber. Dreaming of Fitz.

"You may go if you like, Cousin," the queen says wearily. She's sitting in a window seat that overlooks the river. The light washes her face with a green tinge. She looks old. Older. There are hollows below her eyes, and her cheeks have lost all their color. Even her eyes are dull, and there is a crease of worry between her brows.

"Actually, Your Majesty, I have no taste for the sight of men battering each other," I say, wanting to offer comfort. "I don't like the sound of the lance when it cracks. I hate the thud of bodies as they hit the ground."

Though I'd love to be able to sit next to Fitz. Perhaps hold his hand.

The queen nods. "Your point is taken. Though I do enjoy the pageantry. The cryptic emblems sewn cleverly into doublets. The parade of colors matching men to a cause. Or a woman."

"It's a bit like poetry," I muse. "Saying something without really saying it at all. Telling your loyalties, your sympathies to the world, but really just to those who already know."

"How is your poetry, Mary?"

"Very poor at the moment." I don't write. My time with Fitz feels like poetry enough.

The queen sits up uncomfortably and cringes a little, one hand on her belly.

"Never say that, Mary. Never take yourself down. There are

plenty of other people in this world who are more than willing to do it for you. Because you're a woman. Because you are married to someone so close to the king. The only person you can depend on in this life is yourself, Duchess. It would serve you well to remember that."

I nod, mutely. And then remember myself.

"Yes, Your Majesty."

"Don't 'Your Majesty' me, Mary. I'm telling you this as your cousin. As your friend. Believe in yourself. In your voice. It's the only way you'll survive. If you only do as others say, be who they want you to be, you will lose yourself. And that will be the greatest loss of all."

I remember the day I heard her argument with the king. How he told her to do as her betters had done before her. Close her eyes. Look the other way. Queen Anne will never do that. Even if it kills her.

"Thank you, Your—" I hesitate. "Cousin."

The queen smiles, and it transforms her. She looks softer. Steadier. And I suddenly want to confide everything.

"I—" Again I hesitate. "I have learned much being here. About what I want." *Fitz.* "And how to be myself." *Without my mother's influence.* "You set a wonderful example."

The smile disappears from her face and she lowers her eyes. "You don't want to be like me, Mary."

Before I can respond, there is a noise—a clamor—in the presence chamber. Voices. Footsteps. A shout. My father.

"I don't care if she's in dishabille, she will see me and she will see me *now*!"

The door flies open with a bang and he marches into the room with his military stride, followed by two ushers and a very uptight-looking yeoman.

"She's my niece, for the love of God—it's not like I'll do her any harm. And she's my queen! Stand back!"

He continues to shout as he strides across the room. The queen stands to her full height. I hear her pull a breath in through her nose. It makes her a little taller. A little bigger.

Father barely bows before looking her in the eye. Even his military bearing can't hide the fact that he is quite small for a man. It's hard to believe that he has fought so many wars, brought down so many men. Until you see his face, with its scars and tyrannous nose. And you believe that this man could be capable of anything.

"Your husband is not dead."

The queen reaches for my arm and her hand tightens around the bone. Her face remains still, her body upright. She takes a deep breath and surreptitiously brushes the other hand on her skirts.

"He was unhorsed in the joust," Father continues.

The queen nods. This has happened before. Jousting is not a safe sport. I hear in my mind the sound of the cracking lance. The thud of a body come to earth. Almost as if my words predicted it.

"He didn't move and could not be awakened."

The queen's hand tightens further around my wrist, and my fingers begin to tingle. Still her face betrays nothing.

"But after two hours, he woke and stood."

"Why was I not told sooner?" The queen's voice is steady, but she does not release her grip.

"We did not wish to worry you in your . . . condition."

"You did not think I would want to be by my husband's side? To pray for him?"

Everything about her is still except for the hand on my arm. It pumps with each question, pressing down, squeezing. I hold my arm as steady as I can, wanting to help create the illusion that she isn't falling apart.

My father studies her. I know what he sees. Her steadiness. Her lack of tears.

He doesn't see her fingers whitening on my arm. Or how much deeper the shadows beneath her eyes have gotten.

"He was well cared for," he says stiffly.

"By whom?" The meaning in her question is apparent. Jane Seymour is out there somewhere.

"By his council."

Edward Seymour is now part of the council. I picture him praying over the king's unmoving form. Hoping for the king to live long enough to shower a few more titles on the Seymours.

"With your permission," Father says, "I will go and check on the king's progress."

The queen nods and sinks down to her chair, always gripping my arm. Father bows out the door.

I pat the queen's hand, gently loosening her fingers.

"Let me go and find out what I can," I whisper to her. She doesn't seem to hear me. Her eyes are vacant, her other hand resting on her belly.

I rush through the rooms, which seem pitifully unpeopled. I wonder if they are all at the joust? At the king's side? Or have they already begun to pay court to the king's new mistress?

Father may be short, but he's quick, and I only catch up as he reaches the bottom of the stairs.

"Father."

He turns around quick as a snake.

"You'd better hope that she loses that baby."

I stop short, stung as sharp as if he'd slapped me.

"Come with me. Now."

My father grabs my elbow and steers me into the courtyard. He doesn't loosen his hold, and I almost stumble three times as he pushes me past the gaping idlers.

"Shameless, goggle-eyed whore," he mutters under his breath.

I nearly fall again.

"Stop, Father," I whisper, desperately afraid that he'll be sent to the Tower. "You can't say those things."

"Can't I?" he rages. "She's said worse to me. Standing there completely unmoved, the bitch."

"Father, stop!"

I wrench away from him and turn to him in the courtyard. I'm near tears and can't catch my breath.

"I can't lose you!" I cry. "I can't . . ." My father is a hard man, but he's the only thing that could temper the damage done by my mother.

"You're not going to lose me, you foolish girl." Father's anger softens a little.

"You could be imprisoned for those words," I whisper at him. "Or worse."

Father's face hardens.

"I don't think so. In fact, at this point, I think the king just might agree with me."

I shake my head, remembering my mother's letter. I can't believe my mother and father are in agreement, albeit unknowingly. Father stills me with both hands. They are cold as gravestones.

"Do not fret, my dear," he says, and suddenly smiles, despite his anger and the king's fall. "This may be the making of us." He lets go, but will not let go my gaze. "You will be my triumph—you and that husband of yours. Forget your mistress and remember what I told you before."

The queen told me if I only do as others say, I will lose myself. I will certainly lose my self-respect if I supplant her for my father's sake.

"It's her place to make a king, not mine. It's her life."

"It's *your* life, Mary." Father steps closer, nearly standing on my toes. "You married into it. It's your life and it's your responsibility."

"Not just mine, Father. There are two people in this marriage. It depends on Fitz, too."

"Marriage is a contract, not a collaboration. Consummate your marriage before the king decides his only son and possible heir would be better off married to a foreign princess. Bind him to you before you find the contract broken."

Father says this with such finality that I know I've been

dismissed. But I'm now too frightened to let it go.

"If it's a contract, how can it be dispensed with so easily?" I push. "Aren't contracts binding?"

Father doesn't answer, so I push harder.

"And what if someone decides Fitz and I are not truly married? That we were never married in the first place? That it hasn't been consummated? What then, Father? What will you do with me then?"

"If you do as I say, you won't have to worry about that." Father pats me on the cheek. Almost a slap. "Make me proud."

I don't want to be with Fitz to give my father a royal grandson. I want to be with Fitz. Period. So the words stick in my throat. I cannot say I will make Father proud. Because doing what I want is becoming more important than what he wants of me.

Father takes my silence as acquiescence and walks back out toward the tiltyard, his short little legs snapping together like scissors.

37

EVERYONE WORRIES ABOUT THE SUCCESSION. ABOUT THE KING, and how close he came to death. About the queen and the child she carries. Lines are being drawn in the sand, and everyone is taking sides.

I hear all the whispers. About Jane Seymour. About Fitz. About me.

The day of the funeral the king wears black. For his "dear sister." Even now, he won't acknowledge that he lived with her for almost twenty years. All he will admit to is that she was his brother's wife first.

I try to stay close to the queen. She looks fragile. And despite the fact that she's carrying his child, the king seems to have turned his back on her. Left her stranded, her eyes searching the wide, flat sea of her empty rooms.

I know who she's searching for.

"Cousin, would you please go and find my husband for me? I wish to know where he is."

Neither of us have seen Jane Seymour. We both fear where she might be.

"Yes, Your Majesty," I whisper. I don't want to be the bearer of bad tidings.

I go, anyway. I slip through the great hall and into the chapel, hoping against hope that the king is in there, praying for the soul of the other woman he betrayed.

He's not, of course.

I drag my feet. Go as slowly as I can. Wander through empty rooms and crowded ones. Consider going to the stables. To the bowling green, despite the rain. I consider going anywhere but back to the king's rooms.

I know I'll end up there, eventually.

When I do, there is laughter coming from the watching chamber. The regular courtiers cluster in knots. Thomas Wyatt and George Boleyn almost seem to stand guard. Henry Norris and Francis Weston eye each other warily. There is gambling and posing and posturing. And laughter.

The king sits at the far end of the room. Jane Seymour is by his side. He laughs at something Thomas Seymour says, grabs Jane by the hand, and pulls her toward him. She stumbles a little. Or wishes to appear to. The king catches her before she falls, but she still slides to his knee.

His knee. His hands are on her waist. She's sitting in his lap. Laughing. They're both laughing.

I turn to leave the room, and the queen is there in the doorway. She couldn't wait for me to find him. To tell her. She had to find out for herself. Her face is bright white, like alabaster. It stands out against her dark hair. Like she's about to faint.

She doesn't see me right in front of her as she strides through the room. Straight for him. Straight for her.

With surprising strength, the queen pulls Jane Seymour off

the king's lap and slaps her. The sound drops into the room like an explosion, leaving us all deaf and dumb.

The king breaks the silence with a roar, and courtiers scatter like tenpins, falling all over one another to leave.

Even in his rage, the king is aware of the gossips in the room and pulls the queen from it. She hisses and spits like a wet cat caught in a trap. They go through his privy chamber and into the bedroom beyond, the great oak door slamming with a reverberating bang.

Then the screaming starts.

I can't be here anymore. I can't listen to them argue. I can't listen to the whispered rumors while they do.

"How dare you!"

That is the king's shout. Not the queen's. As if he is the injured party. Just like my father when my mother roared about his mistress, Bess Holland. Memories of their fights flash like fireworks. Of my mother scratching him. Screeching. Throwing all of Bess's clothes out into the muddy courtyard. Barricading herself in her room.

This can't be what love is. This can't be what marriage means. Anger and fear and hatred and misery. Jealousy and bile. Infidelity and desperation.

There has to be something else.

There has to be love and touch and being.

There is only one place where I might find it.

I run through the rooms of Greenwich this time. I don't look at the people around me, drawn to the king's apartments like the crowds creeping toward an execution.

No one is by the doors of Fitz's apartments except his gentlemen-ushers. One reaches out a hand to stop me, but snaps back. He knows his place. I open the door and have closed it behind me before I—or the ushers—even realize what I'm doing.

Fitz stands at the window that overlooks the orchard and the tiltyards. His hands are pressed against the glass, his head hanging down. He wasn't expecting me. Probably thought the opening door was one of his men come to dress him. He wears only his shirt and breeches, the embroidered hem of the shirt just reaching his thighs.

He looks so vulnerable, I almost want to try again. Knock.

"Your Grace?" My trepidation makes me formal.

He turns abruptly at the sound of my voice. The collar of his shirt is open, exposing the skin. His expression of joy refashions quickly to unease.

"What's wrong?" He doesn't move, so neither do I.

"Everything is such a mess," I say. "I don't want to be here when it all falls apart. I don't want to see Queen Anne displaced." I struggle for breath. "They're fighting."

"They've always fought."

"But the rumors—"

"Rumors said I would be groomed for king at the age of six. They said I'd be king of Ireland when I was eight. They wanted me married off to French royalty. Or dead. All of it came to nothing, Mary. Rumors are nothing but words. And so are arguments."

He never saw my parents argue.

I cross the room quickly, before he can move, before I can think. It's like going back to that first kiss all over again. Now I know how he'll respond. Now I know he loves me.

I press him back against the window with my body and stand on my toes to reach his mouth. One movement—a step away or a push—would throw me toppling to the floor. I'm completely unbalanced and he is my only anchor.

He wraps his arms around me, lifting me even farther from the floor. I feel weightless. Sheltered. I twine my fingers into his hair, run my left hand down his back. I can feel every muscle through the thin lawn of his shirt. The bones of his spine. The hard, flat plane of his shoulder blade.

I can't speak. Can't think. All I can do is want. Want this. His lips on mine, on my throat, on the swell of my breast. I want him to kiss me. Hold me. Touch me. I want it to build a shell around us that nothing else can penetrate.

And a tiny, mutinous part of my mind tells me I want to make my marriage valid. I want to make the bond unbreakable.

I want to do what my father says.

His arms encircle my waist and I arch into him when he traces my collarbone with his tongue.

"Lavender and linen," he murmurs, and I can feel his voice beneath my fingers and through my chest.

He takes a step—*toward the bed, please let it be toward the bed*— and I do lose my balance. My toes—already barely touching the floor—can't stay under me, and he isn't prepared to take all of my weight. It unbalances him and he almost topples. But he doesn't let me go. Doesn't even loosen his grip.

My feet aren't beneath me, but his arms are around me, and he's laughing.

"I wanted you supine," he says, "but that would have been a little dramatic."

"And perhaps a little uncomfortable." I'm laughing, too.

"Not for me." Fitz pulls his head back to look me in the eye. "My fall would have been broken by something soft and luscious. Perhaps I should try it."

He drops me so quickly, I screech before he catches me again, burying his face in my neck, below my hood.

"I'll never let you go, Mary," he whispers, and a shiver sizzles all the way down to my toes.

There's a bang at the door and we barely have time to separate before it flies open, revealing a man in Fitz's livery as well as one in the king's.

Shit.

"You must come at once," the king's man says. "His Majesty is asking for you."

"Thank you. Just let me . . ."

Fitz suddenly pales, and my mind finishes the sentence for him. *Just let me get dressed.* We may be married, but standing alone and half naked together is not part of the deal we made with the king.

"Now, Your Grace," the usher says. He appears to have taken no notice of Fitz's disarray.

He glances at me, turns back to Fitz, and speaks impassively.

"The queen has miscarried a son."

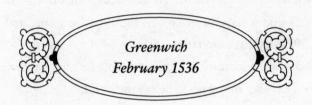

Greenwich
February 1536

38

"Rumor has it you were caught in a compromising position," Madge says, plunking herself down beside me in the queen's rooms a week later.

I pinch the sewing in my lap between my fingers. Force myself not to look up.

"Rumors are more relentless than the rain," I manage to say.

I haven't seen Fitz since that afternoon. His father has needed him by his side. Needed him on the hunt. Needed him in London to open Parliament.

The queen and her ladies are left behind in Greenwich. It is like prison.

"That's certainly true." Madge pulls the sewing from my hands and studies the shirt collar critically. She doesn't turn her head to whisper out of the corner of her mouth. "Did you hear that the baby was deformed?"

"I heard it was a demon," I tell her, snatching the shirt back. "I heard its heart was outside its body. I heard it had six fingers on its right hand." I look her in the eye. "But I've heard that about the queen as well, and we know that isn't true."

For a moment, neither of us speak.

Then Madge nods. "You're right," she says, and looks down

at her hands in her lap. "And I'm the last person who should be spreading gossip."

"I think we should all be more careful what we say," I finally tell her.

Madge looks up. "I just wanted to know," she says, "if everything is going . . ." She can't help her wicked smile. "If everything is going well with Fitz."

I know my smile mirrors hers when she outright cackles. "That well? So you *were* caught!"

"Not entirely. And it was the day . . . the day the queen lost the baby."

"So you think maybe they've forgotten it?"

I hate thinking that way. Hate hoping that somehow someone else's pain has saved me from my own.

Hoping that the uproar has bought me time alone with Fitz again.

"We haven't seen each other since," I finally say. "The king keeps him busy."

"It sounds like someone else has heard the rumors, then," Madge says. "But we'll find a way." She pats my hand. "Don't you worry. As the Wife of Bath says, we are made for procreation."

Margaret slips onto the bench—practically onto my lap— and leans over me to talk to Madge. "What have you done to Mary?"

"She's done nothing to me!" I squeak.

"We're cooking up a way for her to be alone with the delectable duke," Madge says, then whispers to me, "I'm glad to see he can invoke a little passion in you."

"We haven't actually done anything yet."

"But half the fun is in the flirtation," Madge says. "Look at the queen."

I do. She's having one of her good days, flirting outrageously with every man in the room.

On her bad days, she locks herself in her bedchamber and won't come out.

"Though the other half of the fun comes *after* flirtation." Madge grins.

"I don't know if I'm ready to *sleep* with him," I say. Because I'm not. Not sure what the right time would be. Not sure if it's what I want or what my father wants. I sigh. "I just want to *see* him."

Madge wraps an arm around me. "You *are* in love, aren't you, Mary?"

When I nod, she whoops and the entire assemblage turns to stare. Madge just inclines her head demurely until most of them go back to their own conversations. Then she leans drunkenly into me.

"Then we *must* find a way for them to be together, mustn't we, Margaret? Who are we to stand in the way of true love?"

"Who, indeed?" Margaret says drily, but I see the smile behind her eyes.

"You have made us realize that the room is far too quiet, Mistress Shelton," the queen calls. The three of us freeze. I'm sure we're all wondering the same thing: *Has everyone in the room heard our conversation?*

But she turns away from us. "Play us a tune, Master Smeaton.

305

Something . . . seductive." She laughs a throaty laugh, lounging back in her chair. There is a bright-red stain high on each of her cheeks, and her eyes are too bright. Feverish.

Perhaps she has heard. Perhaps she is also protecting me. I watch her gaze at Smeaton languidly. Then her eyes light on me and she smiles. Just a little.

"We must be more careful in our speech," I mutter.

"We must communicate all our secrets in the book," Madge agrees, her eyes shining.

Smeaton starts playing a Spanish tune, and everyone holds their breath, waiting for the queen to lash out at him—strangle him with his own lute strings. We all know she still resents the influence of Katherine of Aragon—a Spanish princess. But the queen just closes her eyes.

"I was convinced Smeaton would be racked for that," Margaret says.

"Maybe she likes having him around too much," I offer.

"I don't know what she sees in him." Madge picks up my sewing again and starts rolling the hem for me.

"Smeaton?" I lick the end of a piece of thread and jab it at the eye of my needle.

"Sure, he's a good musician," Madge says, "but he's so arrogant. And that stringy, greasy hair." She shudders melodramatically.

"I don't think she's bedding him, Madge." I take the shirt away from her and start stitching the hem she's created. "She's always been musical. I don't think it matters to her where beautiful music comes from, or what the package looks like."

"Where does he get the money for liveried servants?" Madge is still staring at Smeaton, and the man who stands behind him. "He's just a musician!"

"Why, Madge," I say, feigning innocence, "anyone would think you fancy him!"

She throws a scrap of fabric at me, but it flutters to my feet and I laugh.

"He has horses, too," Margaret says, and we stop playing to look at her. She's perfectly serious, her eyes narrowed. "He must have a patron. Someone wealthy and influential."

Just to the other side of Smeaton, Jane Seymour is playing with a locket. It's filigreed and gilt, glinting in the firelight. She opens and closes it with precision and intent. Open. Close.

Open. Close.

There's a little smile on her face. Like she's far away. But she is aware of everyone in the room. Her eyes flick once our way. She knows we're watching.

Open. Close.

With a flash like a diving falcon, the queen swoops to the fireside and snatches the locket. For an instant, she and Jane look at each other. Jane's hands have dropped. The smile is gone. There is real fear in her eyes.

The queen is a tiny tower of rage. Coiled and dangerous.

"May I see what's in your locket, Mistress Seymour?" she asks, and without waiting for an answer, pulls the chain so Jane's neck arches forward. The queen opens the locket and reveals something inside that glows crimson and gold in the firelight. For an interminable moment, the two of them stare into each other's eyes.

Then with a swift jerk, the queen wrenches the chain. Jane screams as it catches in her hair, straining at the skin of her throat. Then it gives way and she tumbles from her stool, clutching at her neck.

The queen stumbles backward and throws the locket at the fire. She turns, her face as cold and white as a snowstorm, her hands clutched to her breastbone as if in prayer. Then I see the red seeping from her fist.

Without thinking, I go to her, wrap her hand in mine. The chain bit into the knuckles of three of her fingers, laying the skin open. One of the maids brings a cloth, and I bind her hand. The little finger is crooked, with a little knob of bone bulging at the side, as if it had broken and hadn't properly reset.

The queen slips her hand out of mine.

"Thank you, Duchess," she says coldly. "I can tend to myself now."

She goes into her bedchamber without another word and closes the door behind her. Jane reaches for her necklace, and I see that the hinge on the locket has broken, the metal flapping open.

Inside is a miniature portrait of the king.

Jane's smile reminds me of her brother's. Handsome, but foxlike in its cunning. It disappears quickly and she walks away, clutching the miniature in her soft, white hand.

Madge steps up behind me. "Why is she so special?"

I can see the queen's solid door behind her, closed to all of us.

"Jealousy is a brutal and depleting emotion, Madge," I tell her.

I glance once more at the queen's closed door, wondering if what she felt was jealousy or a fight for survival.

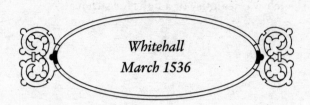

Whitehall
March 1536

39

We split into two courts—the king's and the queen's—and settle into a bitter truce. The king moves between Greenwich and London, taking courtiers and Fitz with him wherever he goes.

My father breaks ranks one day and comes to me, his face animated with joy rather than cunning, and for a starburst of a moment, I think it's because Fitz and I will finally be allowed to be together.

"A grandson," Father says, one hand on each of my shoulders in an almost-embrace. I feel the blotch starting to rise. "A future Duke of Norfolk."

My mind stutters and regains its footing.

"Hal," I say. I can feel the joy exuding from my father's pores. "Hal has a son."

"Thomas," Father confirms, glowing. He drops his hands and steps back to study me, the smile growing broader. "And soon you will, too."

"The queen—" I try to argue, but he cuts me off.

"Will never get pregnant again. And no matter how many trinkets or jewels or bags of money he sends her, Jane Seymour will not go to the king's bed."

"She refused the money." Everyone commented on how virtuous she must be.

"Because she wants something more."

I remember the look in Jane's eyes as her hand closed around her locket, and I know there is something more there than the façade of bland respectability she presents to the world.

"A divorce will take time," Father continues, and silences my protest with a glance. "If it can be accomplished at all. Meanwhile, I will recall your brother to court, and together we will remind the king of the value of his son."

Hope germinates deep within me, finding fertile soil in my heart. But I am ashamed that it is once again dependent on the suffering of the queen.

We move to Whitehall and I can *feel* Fitz nearby. In London. Perhaps in the palace itself. Near.

I am just leaving the queen's rooms with Madge when Margaret passes us on her way in. She bumps against me, and I feel something press against my hand. My book. I hadn't even realized she'd had it. I take it from her, and she enters the apartments without a word.

Madge and I walk together back toward my lodgings. I keep the book tight in my hand until we pass a knot of courtiers and then I open it, flipping through the familiar lists and poems until I find a newly written marginal comment in Margaret's careful hand.

In the tennis court.

I show it to Madge, who grins at me. I remember the day we found Hal and Fitz playing. How Madge found them.

"Can you smell them?" I ask, raising an eyebrow.

"I'm sure you can," she crows, and starts pulling me through the narrow courtyard and into the great hall.

We skirt the king's privy gallery carefully. I think neither one of us wants to encounter him. There is no one in the cockpit, but I can hear the king's birds that are kept beneath the seating. One in particular seems not to realize that dawn was hours ago.

The first two tennis courts are empty, but as we approach the smallest one, we hear the shouting. The sound carries out over the tops of the walls and echoes along the open gallery between the bowling green and the pheasant yard.

This is not the typical sound of a tennis match—not the grunts and banter and cries of anguish when one player misses the ball by a hair. This shouting is hard and angry. It suits the rhythm of the game, but it isn't play. It sounds more like war.

Madge hesitates and looks at me.

I'd know both of the voices anywhere, even raised in anger.

"Fitz?" Madge asks.

"And Hal."

Madge bites her lip. I don't know when she last talked to him.

"He's a father now," I tell her. "My nephew, Thomas, was born just over a week ago."

"And he's back at court already?"

I try to explain how our family works. "My father spent

most of my childhood on diplomatic missions or at war."

"But you've said he hated your mother."

"I think the feeling was mutual."

"I can see why," Madge says. "Perhaps your mother's anger stemmed from her resentment at being abandoned."

"Perhaps my father abandoned her because she's impossible to live with."

"Why has Hal abandoned his wife, then?"

Because he's still in love with you.

I can't tell Madge his secret. For her sake as much as for his. She's betrothed to Henry Norris. She and Hal both have the chance to be happy. To fall in love with someone else.

There's another roar from the tennis court followed by a string of curses that makes even Madge blush.

"You don't have to come with me," I tell her.

She takes my hand. "I'll stay." She smiles. "In case you need a minder."

When we enter the viewing gallery, it is empty. This game of tennis is not at all like the last time Madge and I caught them playing. Yes, they have removed their doublets, but their linen shirts stick to the sweat of their backs; their hair is plastered over their foreheads. They are completely focused on each other, on the ball. Hal does not look up and spout poetry. Fitz does not see me at all.

"He's your father," Hal growls, braced and ready for Fitz's serve.

Fitz roars, and the ball hurtles over the net.

"When was the last time you argued with yours?" Fitz shouts.

"Yesterday." Hal manages one of his characteristic grins before diving for the ball with a grunt.

"And when was the last time you argued with your king?" Fitz says, and slams himself backward to return a swift, low shot.

Hal doesn't answer, and they continue to pound the ball until one goes astray and sweeps to a stop at my skirts.

Then all is silence.

Both of them bow quickly, Fitz's eyes never leaving mine. His are a maelstrom of emotions—pain, fury, grief, *love*.

"We are sorry to interrupt your game," I say.

"Not much of a game." Hal turns away and starts putting on his doublet.

"It looked like quite a battle," Madge says, bending to pick up the ball. She squeezes it, watching Hal. He won't look at her.

I walk to Fitz, who is standing with one hand on the wall. His face is red from the exertion and he looks like he's struggling for breath. Madge is right. It must have been quite a battle.

"What were you arguing about?" I ask.

"Fitz's *father* is exiling us to the back of beyond." Hal has moved behind me, fastening his doublet. He's glaring at Fitz, the anger still emanating off of him. Like Father after an argument with Mother.

"The *king* wishes to send us to Scotland as insurance," Fitz says. "The Scots want security for their own king when the two of them meet in York next month."

"Insurance," Hal snorts. "We're going to be hostages, Mary."

"Scotland?" I find I can't speak above a whisper. I turn to Fitz. "Do you think this is because . . ." *Because he wants to separate us?*

"I think it's because I'm the closest thing he has to a son. And at present, more valuable than my bastardized half-sister."

I think of Father's promise. To remind the king of the value of his son. His ploy seems to have worked, but has had the opposite effect from that expected.

"You're not even in the line of succession," Hal says harshly.

"Why wouldn't he send Margaret?" Madge asks. "She's half Scottish. Her mother was queen."

"That's why," Fitz says. "King James is her half brother. The king thinks she might want to stay." He looks at me. "No point having a hostage who doesn't want to come home to his family."

Family. I have always thought of Fitz as my husband. As something separate. But we are bound to each other as surely as I am to Hal or my father. We are family.

"Or at least back to his life," Hal adds. He's looking at Madge. Not in a lovesick poet way. Sadly, out of the corner of his eye. He knows she's not in his life anymore. But his family isn't the reason he wants to be in England.

I turn back to Fitz. The damp hair has begun to curl at his temples. I reach out to stroke it.

"Any chance he'll let me go with you?" I'm barely daring enough to ask the question.

Fitz shakes his head and turns to where his doublet is neatly folded on a bench.

I look at Hal. "What about Father? Maybe he could convince the king?"

"Cromwell is still saying it's Father's fault Fitz didn't go to Ireland. It's been said that Father already controls too much of Fitz's life."

"I want to control my own life!" Fitz shouts, his doublet dangling from his hand. "I'll be seventeen in June. The *king* ruled the country when he was seventeen, and I'm not even allowed to rule myself." He stands in front of me, so close I can feel the heat and humidity coming from his chest. "I want you, Mary. I want to live with you. Be with you. He keeps postponing it. Finding things to come between us."

Right now the only thing between us is air. And his anger. I want to kiss it away.

Hal clears his throat. "As a respectable man who always does as the king wishes," he says, the sarcasm dripping from his voice, "I shouldn't leave the two of you alone." He stops and looks at me sadly. "But I think it only right to give you a chance to say your good-byes. Heaven knows when you'll be alone together again."

He turns to Madge and holds out his arm. "May I, Mistress Shelton?"

She takes it lightly, and they exit together, only her fingers touching his arm and nothing else.

"Do you think the king doesn't *want* us to be together?"

Fitz takes a breath that catches deep in his chest. "I'm beginning to wonder if he doesn't want us to be married."

"Why?"

Fitz starts picking at his doublet, pulling strands of gold from the embroidery. "Because I might be more useful married to a princess of France or Burgundy or Spain."

"Is he thinking of . . . ?" I can't say it.

"Making me legitimate?" Fitz says it for me. "Putting me in line to the throne?" He throws the doublet back on the bench. "I don't know, Mary. All my life he's played with me. Played with the idea of making me king of Ireland or marrying me to a foreign princess or even to my own half sister." He shudders in disgust. "I don't know what he wants of me or how he feels about me as a person. Maybe because I feel I've never really been a person in his eyes. Just a thing."

"He can't do that." I grab his wrist. "He can't *use* people. And he can't pretend we're not married. He was *there*."

"If a marriage isn't consummated, it can be broken." He looks deep inside me and his gaze doesn't waver.

I could throw myself on him. The clean, salty smell of his sweat and the warmth of his skin beg for me to taste him, touch him. I could use his anger and turn it to passion. Make him take me right here. I can see it in his eyes. Feel it in my own body. This knowledge makes me feel powerful.

But I can't do it.

"I don't want to sleep with you to fulfill a contract, Fitz."

He hangs his head and turns slightly away. "No. Of course you don't."

I slide my left hand along his back and reach around with my right to touch his stomach. I want to pull his shirt up. Take back what I just said. I stand on my toes to whisper in his ear.

"I don't want it to be a business negotiation. I want it to be for love. I want it to be at the right time."

He turns and kisses me full on the mouth. Hungrily. Desperately.

"I do, too," he says, lips brushing mine. "I'm willing to wait for that."

"I hope we don't have to wait long," I whisper into the next kiss.

"Come to Scotland," he murmurs. "After we're settled. The Scots king is a hard man, but we've always been cordial."

I pull away to look him in the eye. "You want me to travel to Scotland on my own?"

He grins. "You could dress up like a boy. Ride through night and day and have grand adventures."

"I can see it now." I laugh. "I can befriend the highwaymen and seek the protection of Robin Hood's band."

Fitz doesn't even smile. "I'm serious. When you get to Scotland, we'll tell them we're married. They'll never know the king's wishes. We'll live in the same room. Sleep in the same bed."

"We'd have to," I say, shivering. "I hear it's bitterly cold in Scotland."

"I'd keep you warm."

He wraps his arms around me and he does. He is warm and strong and solid, and when I lay my cheek against his chest, I can hear his heartbeat and the breath still ragged in his lungs.

It's a perfect dream. Running away to be together. Just the two of us.

"I can't," I whisper.

His answer hums in his chest. "I know."

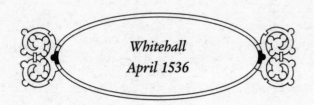

Whitehall
April 1536

40

I REGRET MY PRINCIPLES IMMEDIATELY.

Fitz moves to St. James's Palace, and I can't go out into the streets of London alone. The appeal of dressing up like a boy is enormous—the freedom of movement, of access, of legitimacy. But it's the stuff of fiction. No one would ever believe such a disguise.

Lent always seems long and arduous, with its added restrictions and dietary dictates. This year it passes quickly because the meeting with King James is scheduled for after Easter.

I take to walking along the garden wall at King Street, wishing some magic would bring it down so I could run out into London. Unsupervised. Unsuspected. I gaze up at the windows of the gate. The king's private study is up there. I wonder what he's planning. What he's signing. With whom he's making alliances.

It's just beginning to drizzle one day in April when Margaret catches up with me.

"May I walk with you?" she asks.

"I was just about to go in. Before I get wet."

Margaret stops. Waits a beat. "I'd like to speak with you. Privately."

Margaret always sounds serious, but today she seems even more so.

"I suppose I'm not made of sugar paste. I won't melt."

She takes my arm and turns me away from the windows of the king's gate. We nearly walk the length of the garden before she speaks again.

"I need your help."

"You're my friend, Margaret. You know I'd do anything for you."

"Would you?" she asks. "Even if it meant breaking the rules?"

"What are you planning, Margaret?"

"You have always been the good girl, Mary. You do as the queen asks. As your father asks."

"Not always because I *want* to." I haven't done what my father asked. But I can't tell Margaret that.

"You are also the most loyal and trustworthy person I've met at court. I know that you didn't tell the queen about Madge. She already knew. She would have heard it from somewhere else."

She speaks quickly. As if she's trying to convince herself as much as me.

"And I know how hard it is for you and Fitz," she continues. "Not to be together. So I know you'll understand."

I stop. "Understand what?"

"I need to go into London." Margaret presses me forward and glances again at the king's gate. "We may be watched. And I don't want anyone to suspect."

"Suspect that we are about to climb the garden wall and run giggling into the City?"

"I have a barge waiting."

She turns me toward the queen's lodgings and the river gallery.

"You've planned in advance."

"I've had to."

I look at her out of the corner of my eye. Her head and neck are straight and she gazes ahead as if nothing were troubling her. The perfect picture of royalty. The duchess my mother thinks I'll never be.

But her fingers dance nervously on my sleeves, plucking at the fabric and rubbing it between thumb and forefinger.

"Can you tell me where you're going?"

"To a wedding."

"Whose? I haven't heard of any. And why would you have to sneak out to do it? Surely the king would give his permission."

"No, he wouldn't." Margaret quickens her pace. "Because it's mine."

Margaret isn't allowed to marry without the king's knowledge and express permission. She is of royal blood, and that blood can be worth more than gold. The king will be positively apoplectic with rage when he finds out.

I almost stop right there. Margaret feels me hesitate and lets go of my sleeve, her face draining of color. The king would pay handsomely for being able to stop this marriage before it happens.

For an instant, I think of telling him. Using it as a bargaining chip to keep Fitz in England. To let us live together. *See how responsible I can be? How can you repay my trust?*

My trust would not be worth having.

I pull Margaret's hand back around my arm, pat it once, and keep walking.

"It would be an honor."

For once Margaret's perfect poise droops.

"Thank you."

We cross through the queen's gallery and into the river gallery. It's quiet, the sound of the rain on the water thrumming. Keeping the court inside its lodgings.

"May I ask who the groom is?" I grin at her. "Or is that going to be a surprise?"

"I think it will be no surprise when I tell you it is your uncle Thomas."

I think of how eager Margaret was to meet him. How they sat so quietly together in the boat when Fitz took us to see the dawn. How they have not been caught half-naked in each other's rooms or writing poems in prayer books.

"You've been planning this for quite a while."

"I've known I loved him since you introduced us."

I'm quiet for a moment, as we walk the shadowy depths of the gallery. She's known since the day they met.

"Is that how you can tell?" I ask. "That your love is real?"

Margaret stops.

"I don't think it matters when you know," she says. "Just that you do. And when you do know, you hold on to it. You don't break it for anyone."

Margaret leads me to the far end of the gallery where the light from the water barely penetrates the gloom. She leans over what looks like a bundle of rags and shakes out a long, roughly woven cloak and hands it to me.

"Keep the hood up until we're out of sight."

She slips into another cloak, and I wonder how she will get us to the privy stair where the barges land, but she turns the other way and takes us into the palace kitchens.

We cross through a dirty courtyard and into a room that can only be the bakery, rich with the scent of bread and the heat of the ovens. Only two men look up when we pass them by, and I hope they cannot recognize us. A door at the far end leads onto a narrow dock, where a little boat is waiting, shrouded in drizzle. The man at the oars doesn't even look at us, just silently pulls out into the current as soon as we sit down.

Margaret has been planning this for a while.

She pays the waterman handsomely when he moors at an unremarkable dock on the far western edge of the city. I can't even see London Bridge.

She leads the way down a muddy street, avoiding the shallow gutters full of effluent.

"How did you find this place?" I ask.

"Thomas did. It's out of the way, and the priest was willing to marry us discreetly during Lent."

I think of the proverb *Marry in Lent, live to repent* and pray that Margaret knows what she's doing.

When I see Thomas in front of the little stone church—when I see the utter joy on his face and the tenderness with which he takes her hand—I realize that Margaret knows exactly what she's doing. She is marrying the man she loves. I am a little bit jealous because I did it the other way around, marrying the man I was meant to fall in love with.

As I listen to them murmur through the hushed, hurried vows, I realize we are all lucky. Their quick, longing kiss is as binding as the blessing conferred upon them by the priest. This bond is unbreakable. Margaret and Thomas are united. Just as Fitz and I are.

Just like my parents, who cannot escape no matter how badly Father wishes it.

Just like the king and queen.

After the ceremony is concluded, Margaret and I hurry back to the waiting barge. As the ferryman pushes us away from shore, Margaret speaks into the gathering gloom of the river. "You don't regret coming with me, do you?"

We have broken the rules. Gone against the king's wishes—against the express dictates of the court. I am an accomplice. If anyone finds out, I will be as culpable as she.

And Fitz and I will never be together.

I reach out for her hand, long and thin and cold. There is no wedding ring on it to commemorate the day.

"Not at all," I tell her.

"You're very brave," she says. "It takes a lot of courage to risk my uncle's wrath."

"I think it would take even more courage to say no to love when it looks you in the face."

"You're right." Margaret watches the river ahead of us, where the lights of Whitehall flicker on the water. "We have to believe that love is more important."

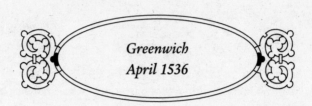

Greenwich
April 1536

41

THE COURT GETS BACK TO THE BUSINESS OF BEING NORMAL. At least, it appears normal on the surface. It's like looking at the world through glass—sight is impaired by waves and distortions and the other senses so utterly stifled that every experience is suspect.

Margaret manages to seem more ordinary than ever. She is quiet, reserved, charming, and the very picture of grace. No one suspects her, and yet I can't seem to go anywhere without being watched.

As the weather clears, I take more time outside. Spending more time with Fitz's "words." Fitz is still in London, though I hear he will be in Greenwich for the meeting of the Order of the Garter. So I may have a chance to see him before the journey north.

I hope.

I go to the orchard, which smells of cut grass and blossoms. I watch the birds that come to light on the apple trees and hop to the ground, flicking their tails. Wrens. Plain, brown, and ordinary. But their song tastes of freedom.

I close my eyes to listen more carefully. It's nothing like the thin whistle of the kingfisher. This sound is like spring. Clear and green and carrying a promise.

"Your Grace."

The voice startles me so much I almost fall over. A thick, strong hand clamps on to my arm, the fingers laced with scars. I look up into the face.

Thomas Cromwell. It's strange to see him here. He is always with the king or in London on business. He never associates with the queen's ladies. The last time I was this close to him was the day he argued with my father.

The day he called me *princess*.

"Master Secretary."

"I apologize for surprising you, Your Grace." His voice is gravelly. Like he's swallowed sand. His heavy forehead and conspicuous nose give him an air of menace; the pits and scars are what make him look like a murderer.

But his grip on my arm is gentle. More like he wants to keep me steady than prevent me from running away.

"I'm afraid I was lost in my own thoughts," I say, and he drops his hand.

"I'd like to ask you some questions."

What kind of questions? I think. He watches me carefully. I wonder what he knows. Some say he knows everything. Does he know how close I came with Fitz?

"I will answer you as best I can," I tell him.

"You have been at court for a long time." His eyes remind me of my father's.

"Not as long as some."

He smiles. It's hard to tell—just a thinning of the lips, and a little curve to the mouth. The smile is not one of humor, but one of recognition.

"You may speak freely with me, Your Grace."

His voice, like the scrape of sugar at the bottom of the bowl, invites confidences. He looks dangerous, but he sounds . . . friendly.

However, I can't trust anyone with my secrets.

"None of us can speak freely, Master Secretary. Society shuns those who reveal too many of their emotions. The church condemns those who utter heresy. It is treason to speak against the king or queen."

He nods gravely.

"Of course. But things are changing."

They are. Some things already have. Cromwell is known for being a staunch Reformist and has already advocated the dissolution of the monasteries, though he clashed with the queen over where the monastic riches should go. She argued the money should go to charity. Cromwell is using it to fill the king's coffers.

"I must do my duty," I say, "and follow the rules that have been laid down for me."

Let him assume I'm pious. And obedient. Let him believe that I would never sleep with Fitz without permission. That I would never speak out against anyone. That I wouldn't allow anyone else to break the rules, either.

"And no one in the court has ever gone against the rules?" he asks, looking casually out at the trees. Watching the wrens.

My own sense of peace vanishes. Because recently a significant rule was broken by a prominent member of the court.

Does he know about Margaret?

"I'm sure there are those who do." I try to keep my voice neutral.

"Have you ever seen them?" The concern that lowers his brow now shades his eyes.

It's Margaret. He wants to know about Margaret. About her marriage. I lay my hands against my skirts to stop them from shaking.

"Have you ever seen anyone in the queen's household behaving inappropriately?" When he tips his head again, the illusion of those dark sockets is gone and his eyes spark with curiosity. "Perhaps forming a relationship she shouldn't?"

I want to trust him. I recognize in him the hard edge of my father combined with the grave concern for my well-being. But I couldn't even tell Father about what Margaret has done.

The word *fear* carries the iron tang of blood.

"A flirtation, perhaps," Cromwell pursues.

"Everyone flirts," I manage to reply.

Now the light in his eyes is brighter. As if I've just given him a gift he's always wanted. He smiles. Almost fatherly.

"Everyone?" he says. "Even you, Your Grace?"

A torrent of questions and self-recriminations go through my mind. He's joined forces with Father to get me to conceive a royal grandson. He's working with the king to make sure Fitz and I follow the rules. To find reasons to annul our marriage so Fitz can marry a proper princess.

"Even the queen." The words taste empty in my mouth—like biting into a hollow puff of pastry.

He looks at me closely. "Are you well, Your Grace?" Again, he puts his hand on my elbow as if to steady me. And it does. Just like when Father would stand with me against my mother's harangues.

"I am." I attempt a smile. Father always said not to show Mother weakness.

"You'll tell me if you see anything . . . inappropriate? Or if flirtation goes too far?"

"Of course," I lie. Does he know it's a lie?

"Thank you, Your Grace." When he lets go of my arm, I falter. But he doesn't see because he has already turned to walk away.

I lean back against the orchard wall, the blossoms of the espaliered trees fluttering around me like the wings of ghosts. Cromwell has taken all my strength. All my mettle. Like my mother does.

I close my eyes, the sunlight glowing red through the lids, and struggle through the tangle in my mind. Was he asking about me? Or Margaret? Either of our actions could earn the king's disfavor. Margaret's marriage could have repercussions for all of us.

If only I could see Fitz. If only I could talk with him. If only he could rescue me from this entire mess. Spirit me away to Scotland, where we'd live amongst the savages in the Highlands, eating haggis and wearing animal skins, like in all the stories told to frighten children. Though the Scots sound less frightening than Thomas Cromwell, who somehow makes me feel safe and sabotaged all at once.

I can't talk to Margaret about it in the public rooms. I'm afraid I would give something away. Or frighten her enough that she would.

I return to my room and find my book. The only thing I can think to write is a snippet of a poem by Thomas Wyatt.

Take heed betime lest ye be spied. . . .

I don't even finish. I close the book before the ink has dried and search for Margaret in the queen's rooms. The queen is in one of her states of frenzied euphoria. She instructs Smeaton to play and blows him a kiss, then she laughs and insists that Henry Norris dance with her.

I drop the book into Margaret's lap and take a turn around the room so as not to appear too obviously eager to leave. All eyes are on the queen, who has now moved on to Francis Weston.

As I head to the door, Madge takes my arm.

"Get me out of here," she says, glancing over her shoulder at where the queen is laughing. "I don't think I can stand it anymore."

"You should dance with Henry Norris," I suggest, knowing that Margaret doesn't want even Madge to know about her wedding.

"The queen's castoffs?" Madge practically pulls me out the door. "No, thank you."

I have no choice but to walk with her all the way to my room, where she promptly puts herself in the middle of my bed, pulling my embroidery basket into her lap. I send my maid out and sit on the stool by the fire. Even on a sunny April day, my room is as cold as a crypt.

"So what are you secretly communicating with Margaret Douglas about?" she asks with studied indifference, and starts separating my embroidery silks, grouping them by color.

"What do you mean?"

"I saw you give her the book." There's a knock on the door. Madge doesn't even look up. "See? There she is now."

My maid steps in, followed by Margaret, who is careful not to show surprise. I think I see censure in her eyes.

I dismiss my maid and wait a moment to make sure she's out of earshot. When I tell Madge and Margaret about Cromwell, I endeavor to express fear only for my own marriage.

"Oh, yes, he asked me questions, too," Madge says, studying her arrangement of colors on my counterpane. Light to dark, red to violet, like a rainbow.

"You?" Margaret asks, and we exchange a look over the top of Madge's head.

"Yes. Questions about inappropriate behavior and what I'd seen happening amongst the queen's ladies."

"What did you say?" Margaret asks.

Madge shrugs. "Pretty much what the duchess here did." She winds red silk around her finger. "Everyone flirts. Especially the queen. Even with my betrothed."

"But it doesn't mean anything," I assure her.

"That's what I said. I was trying to illustrate my point. It's like a dance around the maypole. The queen flirts with Norris. Norris flirts with me. I flirt with Weston. Weston flirts with you. You flirt with Fitz. Fitz flirts with me. It's all just fun."

"Fitz flirted with you?"

"I told you I have a thing for Henrys." Madge winks, and that fiery itch rises again in my chest. Madge narrows her eyes. "I'm teasing you, Duchess. Fitz has never once looked at me sideways. That boy only has eyes for you." She glances up. "Kind of like Margaret here, who doesn't flirt with anybody."

"You told him that?" Margaret's question is a breath of relief.

"Of course! He was delighted with me. I answered everything he asked until he was as tangled up as the maypole itself." She looks at each of us in turn. "I do know how to take care of myself, you know. And I do know how to take care of my friends."

Madge's face hardens a little and she tosses her head stiffly. "Especially when they tell me the truth."

Margaret and I exchange another glance and Madge pushes me, almost off the bed. I stand up quickly, scattering multicolored threads.

"You think I can't be trusted?" Madge stands, too, and we're nose to nose. "You think I'll tell everyone you've gone off to fuck your own husband, even though you're not supposed to? Give me some credit, Duchess."

"I didn't . . . It wasn't . . ."

"Spare me the details and the apologies," Madge says,

gathering up the silks that stayed on the bed and throwing them—tangled—into my basket.

I look at Margaret, whose mouth is a straight line. She gives a single shake of her head.

It's not my secret to tell.

I can do nothing but watch helplessly as Madge turns back to me, the confidence replaced by doubt.

"I didn't say a word, Duchess, no matter how much I suspect. I deflected every one of Cromwell's questions. And I didn't accept his bribes."

"He tried to bribe you?" Margaret asks, and she's gone, if possible, even more pale.

He's serious about catching them. About prosecuting them. If he can build a case before he tells the king, there will be no denying their guilt.

"If he's asking questions, he doesn't know anything yet," I say to calm her.

"That man knows *something*," Margaret says. "Or he wouldn't be asking questions."

Madge takes a step back, the palm of one hand diagonally across her mouth.

"It was you," she says through it, looking at Margaret. "He's not trying to catch the Duchess in someone else's bed, he's trying to catch *you*." She drops her hand. "Margaret. What have you done?"

"The less you know, the safer you are," Margaret says.

"Oh, no, you don't," Madge says, her eyes hard. "You don't get to protect me, Margaret. You don't get to be noble and principled—the better friend. We are all in this together. We always have been."

Margaret licks her lips and tugs at the hem of her sleeve. She is less at ease than I have ever seen her.

"I'm married," she says finally, and her posture straightens again; her hands drop to her sides. "I married Thomas Howard."

A smile dawns on Madge's face. "You devil," she says, and then leaps at Margaret full force, seizing her in a bone-cracking hug. "Congratulations," she whispers, and spins her once before letting her go.

"You can't tell anyone."

"What do you take me for, a simpleton?" Madge scoffs, tossing her head. "Besides, Cromwell is finished with me. Or, more accurately—I'm finished with him."

Margaret laughs and Madge hugs us both, but I can't help but wonder at the dichotomy of Cromwell's personality. How either side of it could lure the unsuspecting into a trap.

42

A NEW POEM APPEARS IN MY BOOK, HIDDEN BENEATH MY PILLOW. I hadn't even realized the book was missing.

It's in Margaret's hand, and ends, *Thou should me find, I am your faithful friend assuredly.*

Across the top, Madge has written, *There is no cure for care of mind, but to forget that which cannot be.*

The rumors increase, including the one that there's nothing Cromwell's spies won't offer the ladies of the queen's bedchamber to tell all the secrets they know.

I hide my book deep within an old cedar chest, wrapped in the pink bodice I wore on my wedding day. The bodice doesn't fit—in fact, the girl who wore it wouldn't recognize the person I am now. My body has shape—curves and roundness and fewer planes and angles. As I tuck book and bodice away, I wonder if Fitz sees me differently. And how he felt about the awkward girl in bed with him that first night.

He's back in Greenwich for the meeting of the Order of the Garter. And we have seen each other—across a room, sitting at table. He looks thinner, and there are faint shadows beneath his eyes. I think he knows of the questions and spies. That we can't do anything that will inspire scrutiny. I don't want the rumors that slide through the rooms like noxious smoke to gather us up and suffocate us.

Nicholas Carew—a distant relation to the Boleyns, but a friend of the Seymours—is voted into the Order. Not George Boleyn, the queen's brother. Which causes a stream of gossip to be diverted that way for a while. Everyone seems to have forgotten about Margaret. I start to breathe again.

The king convenes the Privy Council, and they hole themselves up in the king's apartments, calling for wine and venison and beer and small ale. Every time the door opens, a thick fug emanates from it. The smell of men crowded into a small space. The smell of nerves and weighty decisions.

"We need fresh air," the queen announces. "Leave the men to their business."

She calls the dogs to her, and they come in a jumble: two wolfhounds and three lapdogs, who fit together like a mismatched family, bounding over one another and nearly knocking her down. As we near the forest, one of the wolfhounds—a brute named Urian—takes the head of a little spaniel in his mouth, growling.

Jane Seymour shrieks.

The queen laughs. "It's play. All of it a joke. The truth is that Urian loves the others. He just needs to show everyone who is in charge."

Urian drops the spaniel, who immediately jumps up and starts nipping at Urian's heels. They race each other up into the park until Urian trips over the spaniel's backside and they come to a jumbling halt, starting up again when we reach them.

Spring has finally arrived at Greenwich, and we walk out into the parkland. The bluebells have just begun to show, the blankets beneath the trees dark and creased, the green standing bright in the filtered sunlight, broken here and there by a single early bloom. The dogs throw themselves into the forest, dashing in and out of shadows, biting, barking, scaring off everything in all directions. The queen stops in the wood, takes a deep breath, closes her eyes.

"Are you all right, Your Majesty?" I ask quietly.

"What is your greatest fear, Mary?" she asks in reply, opening her eyes again and boring holes into mine with her gaze.

"Loss." The word answers for me. I'm afraid of losing Fitz. Of losing my friends. Of losing my position.

"Mine is regret." She looks up into the trees, where the sky is just visible through leaves as green as sunlight. "Not for things that I've done. But for things that I haven't, because I was afraid." As always, I immediately think of Fitz. Think of the missed opportunities. The moments I could have seen him in the past week, but didn't.

Because I was afraid. *Regret* is as acerbic as the dregs of wine.

The queen brushes her skirts with her hands and then clasps them together as if they've done something improper. She turns and walks down the hill, avoiding the orchard.

"Never be afraid to follow your heart, Mary," she calls over her shoulder. "And never be afraid to speak out. To make yourself heard."

I barely manage to keep up with her. Her pace is brisk, her

skirts flapping around her ankles and back in the breeze. A few wisps of hair come out of her hood, and she wipes them from her face. The dogs run straight to the kennels, knowing the master there will treat them with scraps of bread from breakfast. The queen turns through the gate and into the inner court.

Several courtiers mill around on the cobblestones, and all conversation stops when we enter. The narrow mouth of the crowded hall is packed with people who squeeze up against the walls to bow and curtsy to her as she passes through and up the stairs. On our left, the queen's apartments echo with emptiness, but the king's watching chamber on our right is unnavigable, there are so many bodies. All startled into silence.

Whatever the council is discussing is of interest to the entire court. And more.

"Why so many of you?" the queen asks.

There is much shrugging and scraping and few answers. They don't know. Or they're not telling.

They don't wish to discuss it with the queen.

She goes still, but her right hand brushes her skirts, and her left hides itself in one of the pleats. She lifts her chin, and I see the pulse at her throat, the vein blue against the whiteness of the skin there.

Fear rises in me like bile. The council hasn't been called to discuss the meeting with James of Scotland or the impending trip to France. The council has been called to discuss the queen. Father's voice rings in my memory. *Divorce*. The fear rises higher when I begin to wonder if perhaps Cromwell's questions weren't about Margaret.

They certainly weren't about me.

We were all lulled into a false sense of security. The soothing comfort of Cromwell's voice made us think nothing major was amiss. He was merely inquiring about some rumors. The king's assiduous cheer made us think the court had begun to find its balance on the sand—that perhaps normality had returned.

Nothing is normal.

The queen turns so quickly, she almost knocks me down. I don't even think she sees me as she brushes past to leave the room. But she grabs my arm and pulls me with her, muttering.

"Get my husband, Mary."

I freeze.

"Get my husband any way you can. I am going to the princess Elizabeth's rooms. He can find me there."

She lets go and walks away, the sea of courtiers undulating in her wake.

The vomitous fear knots in my stomach, and for the first time in my career at court, I don't do what the queen has asked of me.

I go to find Fitz.

As soon as the door is closed behind me, his lips are on mine, one hand beneath my hood, warm on my neck, the other on my back. I take a step to get closer to him, press my body to him. I want to hide in him. Hide all the knowledge and rumors and fears and just be.

But I can't.

I back up again, breaking contact. Put my hand on his chest, and my fingers contract against his heart. Wanting to hold it. Hold him.

Fitz's hands are still on my face, and he searches my eyes questioningly.

"The queen needs to speak with your father."

I say the words without thinking. Not *the king. Your father.*

Fitz blinks. It's not a flinch, but it's close.

"He's waiting for the report from the council," he says.

"I know. But she needs to see him. Now."

Fitz stills. Stares. I feel his heartbeat slow against my hand. I have to bite my lip to keep from kissing him again. Erasing all of it.

"I don't think I can do that. We are at a balance. A fragile one."

I see that Fitz loves the king as a son loves a father. He wants so much for that to be reciprocated.

"He loves you," I tell him.

"It doesn't matter," he says quickly. "What matters is his favor and good opinion. I need to stay on the right side of him. So I won't be sent to Scotland. So I can have you. Keep you."

"I want that, too." I want it so badly; the want is like a great, sucking hole in my chest.

"Then I can't do anything to upset the balance."

Fitz has always been the one to stand up for me. He cleared the way for me to step in front of my mother. To believe that I can come first. That maybe I *should* come first.

But I, too, am afraid to upset the balance. If we retain it, Fitz and I could be together.

Should I come first?

Never be afraid to follow your heart, the queen said.

"I have to believe we're meant to be together." I take his hand and run my finger along his knuckles. "That it *will* happen. Your father loves you. I believe that. You're his only son. But you're the only thing she's got right now." I look up at him. "She needs to talk to him, Fitz. Something is happening. And she has a right to be heard, too. Not just the council."

Fitz nods, straightens his doublet, and moves around me to open the door. He pauses, one hand on the latch, to kiss me quickly.

"I have a feeling this will not end well," he says.

"He needs to remember what love is," I say. "I have to believe that he loves her."

I have to believe that he loves Fitz, too.

Fitz looks sad.

"The king's love is not permanent, Mary. It's a struggle to hold on to it. I know from experience."

I can't speak. I try to swallow my fear, but it sticks.

Fitz presses his forehead to mine.

"My love, on the other hand, is immutable."

He kisses me again, long and slow. Our lips fit together perfectly.

As he strides his way back through the crowds to the Privy Chamber, I walk through empty rooms of the queen's apartments to the princess Elizabeth's lodgings. My footsteps echo on the floorboards and I can even hear my own breathing, it is so silent. Every step makes my stomach more hollow. The emptiness is more frightening than the most tightly packed crowd.

A maid lets me into the nursery, where the queen stands by the window, holding the baby. Elizabeth is two now—she'll be three in September—with hair the color of fire and eyes that take everything in. I always feel like she's judging my fashion sense, the absence of gold in my wardrobe.

"Mawy," she says.

I glance at the queen. A speech impediment isn't a good thing in a monarch.

"Your husband had a lisp as a child," the queen says, not looking up from where she's nuzzling Elizabeth. The movement reminds me so much of how Fitz just kissed me that I blush.

"Is he coming?" Her words are a whisper that barely stirs the hair at Elizabeth's temple.

"I think so. Fitz . . . Richmond has gone to fetch him."

"I knew you were a good choice."

I don't know what choice she means. To fetch the king. Or to marry Fitz. I nod anyway.

The sun blazes on the horizon, lighting up the queen's face and Elizabeth's hair. They look haloed—like the icons of the holy mother and child that adorn the chapel at Kenninghall. Serene.

The door behind me bangs open, shattering the peace and making the maid squeak.

"Madam, what is the meaning of this?" the king growls, throwing a look at me like a rain of fire.

It's not me he speaks to; it's the queen. His boots thump the floor like drumbeats. Or cannon fire. She doesn't flinch. She turns, the sun lighting Elizabeth's hair from behind. The queen gazes at her husband steadily.

Then she holds out Elizabeth to him, as if offering a gift. A plea.

He steps aside. Toward the window. The sun catches his hair, setting it alight just like Elizabeth's. The resemblance is breathtaking.

"Your daughter needs you," the queen says, cradling Elizabeth's head back on her shoulder. "More than the council."

The king's face softens for just a moment. Then he looks at his wife.

"I need more than a daughter," he says stonily.

"You always said that we had everything. When we were together." Her voice is steady. But I hear the meaning behind it. They are not together. She's trying to remind him. I don't know if it's love I see in her eyes, or the fight for survival.

"We don't have everything, madam." The king is unmoved. "And I don't believe we ever will."

"What is it that you need?" she asks. There is no pleading in her voice, only anger. Bitterness. I wish that I could stop her. Because the king is becoming more and more distant, just standing in front of her. But she cannot stop. "What is it you need so badly that I cannot give you?"

"A son. I don't have a son."

Fitz and I lock eyes, and I would do anything—give

everything—for him not to have heard. I wish I hadn't involved him in this. I wish we'd left for Scotland. That we were far away from these people who use love as a weapon and kinship as a bargaining tool.

"It's easy for you, isn't it?" the queen's voice hisses behind me. I can't look away from Fitz. I'm not going to abandon him, too. "You will always be heard. You will never have to face the consequences of your actions. You can easily leave them behind. Like a swallow flying over a lake. Ever moving, always dipping in, but never getting wet."

"You forget yourself."

The tone in the king's voice sends a sliver of ice through me. I can't move. I want to grab Fitz and take him far away.

"I am the queen of England," she says in a voice equally cold and brutal. "Like you, I wore the crown of Saint Edward at my coronation. I forget nothing."

Silence breaks over the room like a wave until Elizabeth starts to whimper. I look over my shoulder to see the queen holding the baby outstretched again.

The king does not hesitate.

He walks away.

"Neither do I."

The queen remains by the window, gently kissing Elizabeth's fingers. She has retreated somewhere within herself. Somewhere untouchable.

The king stops at the door and turns slowly until he is toe to toe with Fitz. At almost seventeen, Fitz is now nearly as tall as his father, but the king still seems to tower over him like a colossus. Fitz looks him in the eye and doesn't back down.

"*Never* do that again," the king says.

Fitz turns away—like he's been slapped.

43

Fitz is absolutely silent as we walk back through the empty chambers that surround the queen. He is half a pace ahead of me, his emotions enveloping him like a frigid shroud that I can't begin to penetrate.

We thread our way through knots and tangles of courtiers still waiting for the Privy Council. We pass through the Middle Court, now deep in shadow and smelling of a late spring frost, the sky above us turning from silk to velvet, deep and lightless.

I finally catch him. His hand is icy. And when I look up at him, his eyes cannot see me. He takes a deep breath, and the cold air makes him cough, the mist coiling about him like smoke.

"He doesn't care about me." Fitz's voice is bitter. Sullen, even. He sounds like a different person. Nothing like the confident boy who climbed into bed with me the night we were married. "I'm nothing to him. Worthless. He's ready to make Elizabeth worthless, too. That has to be what they're discussing. Divorce. The queen knows it. The court knows it. Divorce and bastardy. Then *he* will move on to the next victim."

"He's just going to pretend they were never married? On what grounds? She was never married before. She was a virgin when she came to the king's bed. She's done nothing *wrong*!"

"Right or wrong doesn't matter," Fitz says. "The only thing that matters is what people believe. He's ridding himself of her. So he can have a real heir. A real son."

"Are you upset because of Elizabeth?" I ask quietly. "Or because of you?"

"Me, Mary!" he shouts. "It's about me. I do everything he says, follow every rule, wait forever for what I want, and I only get it if he wants to give it. I want to live *my* life, not the one he's chosen for me."

"But you're his son."

"Didn't you hear him?" Fitz's voice breaks. "I'm not even that. He doesn't have a son."

I let him walk away. He crosses the courtyard and enters the next, his figure blending with the shadows.

44

L ATE THAT NIGHT, AFTER THE CANDLES HAVE BURNED DOWN and been replaced, the Privy Council adjourns and the crowds disperse.

The result of seventeen hours of discussion and deliberation?

The king's trip to Calais has been canceled. Nothing more.

And later, after the servants have gone to bed, and the candles have been snuffed, and even after the gossips have stopped spreading rumors, there is a knock at my bedroom door that is more like the scratch of a mouse.

I know it's him. I've stayed awake for him. I've sent my servants away, hoping he'll come to me.

But when I open the door, Hal is there, mussed and ruffled with dark shadows under his eyes. I draw my furred robe closer.

"Hal?" I ask. "What's wrong?"

"It's Fitz."

My ribs contract, and I have to put one numb hand on the doorframe to keep myself upright. "What is it? Is he all right?"

Heartache can make you sick; we all know this. They say Katherine of Aragon died of it.

"He's in my room," Hal says, and looks up at me. "He wants you."

Without another word or question, I put on my slippers and follow him. Through the frigid courtyards to the lodgings at the far end of the palace, where they run toward the orchards. The air smells of woodsmoke, and the stars overhead are like chips of frozen jewels.

Hal pauses at his door, one hand on the catch.

"He's alone."

"I know." I can't imagine how it would feel to lose my father. For it to be proven that I am nothing to him.

"I shouldn't let you in there."

I look at my brother. At the hesitation in his face. He thinks we're breaking the rules. He thinks Fitz *wants* me. He doesn't realize that Fitz *needs* me. We need each other.

"Please, Hal." I would get down on my knees if I have to.

"Keep him safe." Hal throws the catch and I realize he loves Fitz, too. Fitz may feel like he doesn't have a father, but surely he knows he has a brother.

I kiss Hal on the cheek before he opens the door and I slip through.

Fitz greets me with a kiss so deep and penetrating, I feel like we are one person instead of two. My hands are on his back and in his hair, and his are on my throat and beneath the collar of my robe. My heart thrums so loudly in my ears that I barely hear the latch click when Hal closes the door.

"Leave with me," Fitz whispers, his words bare and unfettered on my ear. "Let's leave here. Tonight." He kisses my collarbone, my shoulder, following the fur of my robe where it opens.

"Where will we go?" I ask, smoothing the hair at the nape of his neck so I can kiss him there. He shudders and straightens.

"France." He takes both of my hands in his and looks at me seriously. "I've always wanted to go back to France."

This isn't a game or a dream. He means to leave. Leave England. Leave the king. Leave tonight.

He wants me to go with him.

This is why Hal said, *Keep him safe.*

"For how long?" I ask. But I know the answer.

"We'd be together. With no one telling us what to do."

"We would never see our families again. Nor Madge, nor Margaret. Nor Hal."

"He'd come to visit us. You know he would."

"He'd be in danger." I step away and close my robe against the chill. "Everyone would think he was helping us plan to overthrow the king."

"Might not be such a bad idea."

"Stop, Fitz. Just stop."

I walk away from him. I have to. It's one thing to go against the king's wishes by consummating our marriage. Or to aid a lady of royal blood to marry without permission.

It's another thing entirely to plot treason.

"I can't bear to stay!"

I turn and look at him. His arms are stiff at his sides, hands in fists as tight as his expression.

"You *are* the king's son," I tell him. I walk back and put my hands on his arms, but they do not relax. "If you go to France and claim asylum everyone will assume you're planning a coup. That you have pretensions to the throne. Just like your grandfather."

The seventh King Henry lived for years in France until he had the funds and support needed to raise an army. He knocked the crown from Richard III's head and took his place.

"Our lives wouldn't be worth living," I say. "We'd have assassins and spies after us all the time. We would never be safe."

"So we stay? Imprisoned? Married, but unable to be together. In love, but kept apart. Lapdogs, kept for show, but always at the bottom of the pack."

I think of Urian, showing the other dogs who's in charge. And I want to leave. Escape. Believe in the dream of a palace in exile on the Loire.

I can't change the world, so I kiss him. Softly. Slowly. Like a lazy afternoon alone.

"Be with me, Mary," he whispers.

I remember what the queen said just a few hours ago. How what she fears most is regret for things she hasn't done. I press myself closer to him.

"I love you," I say, my words tangled in his kiss. I hold his face between my palms and force him to look at me. "I love you. *I* love you."

"Even if I'm nothing?"

I kiss his eyes closed so I don't see the despair so ripe in them.

"You are not nothing," I tell him. "To me, you are everything."

He slides his hands inside my robe and I wrap it around him. Every point where our bodies touch feels stung by fire. He strokes my back and presses one hand to my hip, nothing but my shift between his skin and mine.

I check back over my shoulder. The door is closed. He looks up, his eyes a little drunk. He lets me go and strides over to the door. Locks it without seeing who might be on the other side. Turns around and looks at me, a question in his eyes.

I nod.

Without speaking, he returns to me and slides the robe from my shoulders. I feel the chill of the air around me, but I am so warm, it cannot touch me. I move to unfasten his doublet, but he stops me. Steps back. And stares.

My back is to the fire, so he can see my shape silhouetted through my shift. I try to imagine what he sees. The curves where breast meets rib and the arc between rib and hip. I should be embarrassed. Nervous. Worry that I'm too buxom or that my belly is too round or my hips too flat.

But I'm not. Because beneath his gaze, I feel delicious.

"You are so beautiful," he says.

I look at him. Really look at him. Long limbed and broad chested, with the body of an athlete. Or—if I didn't know better—a dancer. The blue-gray eyes lined with thick lashes. The shock of red-gold hair lolling over the highly arched eyebrows. The freckle just at the corner of his mouth.

I stand on my tiptoes to kiss it.

"So are you."

I feel the corner of his mouth curl up beneath my lips just before he plunges his hands into my hair and he kisses me with such tenderness and force that I feel bruised.

Fitz lays me back on the great tester bed, the down pillowing beneath me. I marvel at the stroke of his skin on mine and the softness of his hands. At how we shed our clothes like the skins of snakes. At the way my body seems to know more than I ever guessed. Until a stripe of pain shoots through me and I freeze.

"Does it hurt?" Fitz stops moving. So still.

I remember what he told me. Long ago. Never to lie to him. Not even a little.

"Yes."

"Do you want to stop?"

I look into his eyes. Feel the heat of his skin against me. Thoughts come in a series of flashes like lightning strikes. Rules. Pain. Pregnancy. Parents.

But all I *feel* is Fitz. His body. His gaze. His love.

"No," I say. "Don't stop."

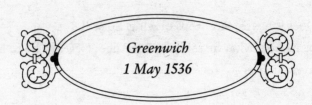

Greenwich
1 May 1536

45

I WAKE BEFORE DAWN WITH HIS ARM STILL AROUND ME. THE FIRE has gone out and the room is chilled. The counterpane slipped to the floor in the middle of the night. But I wake warmer than I ever have in my life.

I lie as still as possible. I barely dare to breathe. I want to hold this moment like a bubble captured in glass. I know I'll have to go soon. I can't be seen wandering the palace in nothing but my shift and robe. I've taken too many risks as it is.

"Let me show you the sunrise," Fitz whispers through a kiss on the back of my neck.

I turn to face him, rolling my body beneath his arm. His hand never leaves my skin.

"How did you know I was awake?"

His eyes are half closed and he murmurs lazily, "You stopped snoring."

I push him, and his hand drifts down to the crook of my hip, igniting little fires along the way.

"I don't snore." I can find no trace of offense or teasing in my voice.

"No, you're right," he says, closing his eyes fully and nestling closer, his hand sliding to the small of my back. "You purr."

Like a cat, I arch into him when he kisses me.

A noise outside the door stops us before we can take things any further. Fitz's eyes widen and I slip out from under his arm, pulling the counterpane around me.

"It's locked," he whispers.

"It's morning," I whisper back.

Hastily, I pull on my shift and wrap myself in the fur-lined robe. Compared to Fitz, it feels cold. He already has his breeches on, and is drawing a shirt over his head. I stroke his back once before it disappears, and he turns to give me a quick, tight kiss.

"It's May Day," he says. "They'll be preparing for the joust." His gaze still makes me feel luscious. But also conspicuous. I can't imagine the state of my hair.

"I don't know how we'll get you back to your room like that," he says, confirming my doubts.

"I didn't have time to dress last night," I say. "I was worried."

The day before comes back to him like a flood across his face and he frowns, but then quickly shakes his head.

"Today is something new," he says. "Things are going to change. I can feel it."

"They already have." *Joy* tastes like a plum—warm and freshly picked.

I unlock the door as quietly as I can. Hal sits just on the other side, his back against the wall and his forehead on his knees. He looks up.

"Mary," he says, and stands. "Come quickly." He glances once behind me, and I turn to see Fitz, his throat exposed by his open shirt.

"Jesus wept," Hal swears, without much force, and takes me by the hand. "I know a secret entrance. Through the maids' chamber. If we're very quiet, they'll never hear us. But you have to come with me *now*."

He looks more disheveled than I do, his doublet undone and his hair wild from running his hands through it. I feel a spasm of guilt for locking him out of his room all night.

"Hal," I say, "thank you."

"No, Mary," he says, "thank *you* for convincing him not to leave."

We don't speak again as he takes me behind his lodgings and into the garden, through a chill of near-frozen dew that wets our feet. The darkness has begun to fade, and just as we come to the wall that separates the garden from the river, a shaft of sunlight spills over it. I look up, and there on the thinnest of possible branches is the kingfisher.

It seems like an omen. A good one.

46

BY THE TIME I GET DRESSED, THE SUN IS HIGH AND THE REST OF the court is ahum with more than just the excitement of the joust. It comes in waves, like the throbbing of a bruise, the intensity escalating as everyone pushes out of the donjon and up to the tiltyard.

My entire body is alive with sensation. With the way my skirts brush my thighs and tangle around my ankles. The tightness of my bodice and the caress of my velvet hood on the back of my neck. I have to will myself not to look at Hal's lodgings as I pass by, knowing that the blotching of my skin will give me away.

"Everything is all askew," Madge says, catching up to me. "It's like everyone's talking, but no one's saying anything."

I remember what she said about trust, about telling her everything. I want so badly to express my euphoria, but when I open my mouth, I find I can't. I want to hold it close. Keep it sacred.

"The king and queen had an argument last night," I say instead.

I wonder if they once felt about each other as I do about Fitz. Like he and I are connected by some kind of invisible lute string, tuned to a perfect pitch. A vibration that runs through me like a hum.

If they did, what broke that string? Does all love disintegrate eventually? I can't imagine my parents ever loved each other.

"So what else is new?" Madge grumbles as we take our places in the stands.

The contenders in the joust are all the court favorites, including the queen's brother, George, and Madge's betrothed. We watch as Henry Norris rides up and down the lists, his horse skittish at the cheering of the crowds.

"I'm not sure I want to marry him, you know?" she says, tucking a wisp of hair behind her ear.

"Norris?" I crane my neck to look for Fitz, my fingers drumming the rail.

I don't know if he'll join the king after last night. Perhaps he'll come in search of me.

I suddenly wonder if he'll come at all.

He wouldn't leave without me. He wouldn't go to France on his own, never to see me again. We have a life to live together.

"He's kind of . . . old," Madge says.

"Norris?" I lean in to whisper to her. "So is the king."

"Yes," Madge says slowly. "But the king is *seductive*."

"The king is scary," I whisper back. "And dangerous."

"Exactly."

I watch the horse turn, one hoof skidding, and Norris compensating quickly by shifting his weight. His body moves naturally. He's leaner than the king, who no longer competes.

"Besides," Madge says, "I think Norris is in love with the queen."

Unlike the king. I'm reminded of Madge's analogy of the maypole. Frances is married to Hal, who is in love with Madge, who is betrothed to Henry Norris, who is in love with the queen. Or might be. All the men pretend to be—it's part of being at court. Even her brother flirts with her.

"We can't all be as lucky as you are," Madge says.

"That's exactly what Hal said."

"Being in love with me didn't stop him from impregnating his wife."

"You were the one who told me you don't have to love someone to go to bed with him," I say. I haven't talked to Madge about Hal before, but she has to understand. "You can't demand celibacy or monogamy from a person you can't love back."

"I wish I did," Madge says in a small voice. "It would be so much easier."

I put an arm around her shoulders. "And so much harder. He's married, and you soon will be. Maybe it's better this way."

"I just don't want to be with someone who is in love with someone else."

"Madge, you were with the king. And Thomas Wyatt. Both of them are in love with the queen."

"Not anymore," Madge says darkly as the crowd goes silent and the queen enters the stands. Alone.

Madge watches Norris calm his horse and slowly approach the queen's box. He bows to her, and nudges his horse into a little dip—kind of a cross between a bow and a curtsy. The crowd roars its approval and the queen smiles. But her face looks strained. Even from where I'm standing.

"You know what my *betrothed* said one day?" Madge says, her eyes narrowed. "In her rooms?"

"The men are always saying something."

The queen reaches into the top of her bodice and pulls out a yellow silk handkerchief. It flutters vividly in the breeze, catching the sunlight.

"Well, Norris said that he wasn't sure if he was going to marry me because he may be saving himself for someone else."

"And from whom did you hear this?" I ask. She couldn't have been there. Even Norris wouldn't be so indiscreet.

"I was behind the door," Madge says bitterly. "And then the queen says, 'I think that if anything ill were to happen to the king, you would look to have me.'"

"She never did!"

"And then she says, 'I would undo you if you tried.'"

This rings a bell.

"They've said this before, Madge. It's a personal joke between them. I think it goes back to something that happened long before she married the king."

"But that doesn't matter, does it? She shouldn't be saying that kind of thing."

No. She shouldn't. It sounds ominously like imagining the king's death.

Treason.

The queen ties her kerchief on the end of Norris's lance. She looks pale. As if she has aged a decade overnight. When she stands upright again, her mouth forms a brittle smile.

"Norris says she's worried. Worried that the king is looking for ways—for reasons—to divorce her. That that's why Cromwell was asking questions."

The argument last night. The endless Privy Council meeting. The king's declaration that he wants a son.

A cloud drifts over the sun, throwing us all into its shadow, and I shiver, part of me wishing I were on my way to France.

The trumpets blast and the king enters the stands, the crowds cheering. His face looks like a thunderstorm about to break. It carries clouds and demons, and I see every courtier turn away after bowing or curtsying. Avoiding a lightning strike.

He stands beside the queen. Doesn't touch her. Doesn't even acknowledge her. She is the only person in the stands to turn and watch him directly. She knows he can feel her gaze on his face. She knows that no one can remain steely forever.

But he does.

Fitz is behind him. He doesn't look at the king. Keeps his distance. He is thin and troubled, almost like a boy again. When he sees me, he smiles at the same time a shaft of sunlight pierces the clouds. And though we are separated, I feel as if his arms are around me.

I pay little attention to the horses and the crowds, to who wins and who falls. All I see is him.

But I know the joust does not go well.

George Boleyn can't seem to find his stride. Henry Norris lowers his lance too early and is almost disqualified.

The tournament is a disaster.

The bright moment comes when Norris manages to unseat his opponent. The crowd becomes a riot of color and noise as people shout and applaud, sleeves waving like flags. Norris unties the queen's kerchief from his lance and kisses it once. For luck.

Then everything goes silent.

I turn just in time to see the king thundering down the steps of the viewing platform. The sound reverberates across the tiltyard. He looks neither left nor right. Acknowledges no one. Most of the crowd is too stunned to bow before he reaches them, only managing it in his passing, so the crowds look like the wake left behind by a swift-sailing ship.

The queen stands alone, her hands gripping the rail in front of her. White in the pale spring sunshine.

"He didn't even speak to her," Madge says. "You might expect him not to speak to the others, but he didn't even speak to her. Not even to tell her he was leaving."

When the king has stridden away, the murmurs start, following behind him like the murmur of the wake.

"Begin, gentlemen!" the queen calls.

She sits, her back very straight. She watches only the men on the field. She doesn't reply when her ladies speak to her. She just watches. Unseeing.

Henry Norris fails miserably at the next tilt, and rides off the field defeated. Three men surround him as he dismounts. A pat on the back. A grip on the arm. Manly comfort. They disappear into the crowd.

Madge sighs. "He's gone off to sulk, I can guarantee you. When we return to the palace, he'll be nowhere to be found."

I put a hand on hers. "You do care about him, then."

Madge rolls her eyes and attempts a wicked grin. "Of course I do. I have to aspire to what you and Fitz have, even if he is in love with the queen."

The queen sits, still and impassive. Like the maypole around which all the ribbons of love and hope and desire tangle themselves.

Where the king once stood is an empty space. A hole waiting to be filled. And Fitz is in the shadows behind it.

47

Madge is right about Norris disappearing. He can't be found anywhere. Not his rooms, not the king's.

"Sulking," Madge says. And goes off in a sulk herself.

The king leaves for London before the post-tournament party—which is hardly a party at all—and when the queen retires early, I do, too. I send my servants away and cocoon myself in the counterpane and wait.

I know Fitz will come as surely as I know my own name.

He tries to quiet his footsteps as he crosses the room. I'm not sure why he doesn't want to wake me, because surely that's his intention. Surely, he intends to wake me. To climb into bed with me.

But he stops. I feel his gaze on the curve of my cheek, and the hair that has fallen back against my pillow. He must know I'm awake. He can hear me breathing. Or not breathing, because I'm holding my breath.

I move as silently as he has, and pull the heavy counterpane to the side. Silently, he climbs in beside me, turns me so my back is to him, and kisses me lightly on the shoulder. I fall asleep cocooned in *him*.

In the morning he is gone, the rain has started to mizzle,

and everyone looks drab and drawn. Few people are speaking, and when they do, it's in a whisper.

Someone suggests music, but Mark Smeaton can't be found. No one else seems willing to play. The king has left no word on his return, and the men seem a bit lost without his guidance.

They decide to blow off their nerves with a tennis match, and as the morning wears on, more and more people come to watch. Hal is beating someone roundly when I hear the queen swear quietly under her breath.

I glance at her, and she smiles.

"I should have bet on your brother," she says. "It might have changed my fortunes."

"At least you didn't bet against him," I tell her. "He has a way of discovering his opponent's weakest spots and exploiting them."

"He plays tennis like Cromwell plays politics."

My laugh sticks in my throat.

"I don't think for a moment that your brother will let his opponent win." She shrugs. "Just like Cromwell."

A man in the king's livery approaches.

"Your Majesty," he says to the queen, and bows so slightly as to be insulting. His face is blank, but his eyes bear judgment. "You are summoned by order of the king to present yourself to the Privy Council."

Everyone in the watching gallery shrinks back, as if from the plague. They stop flirting. Stop gossiping. The only sound is that of the tennis players trying to catch their breath.

The queen takes my hand and will not let me go. Her grip is like death—her fingers cold as ice.

The messenger looks at the queen, at me, at our hands entwined. He raises his head and looks her directly in the eye.

"Alone," he says.

I watch her walk away, her head held high, her neck elongated, her fingertips just brushing her skirts. I don't see her again until she returns to her rooms.

Under guard.

We eat dinner in silence. No music. No conversation. No men. Just her ladies. I miss Fitz as one would an absent limb. I almost miss the crowds.

The queen sits beneath the canopy of state, dressed in crimson velvet and cloth of gold. She takes small bites and eats little and then stares at her hands when the tablecloth is removed.

She isn't startled when my father enters, followed by Cromwell. And the captain of the king's guard. Father won't look at me.

But Cromwell smiles.

"Why are you here?" The queen breaks the glass-like silence.

"You are under arrest," Father says.

All the ladies gasp, but the queen shows no surprise when she looks up at him. Almost lazily. Like she doesn't really need to hear him. Like she doesn't need to respond.

Father raises his voice. "We are come by the king's command to conduct you to the Tower, there to abide at His Highness's pleasure."

"If it be His Majesty's *pleasure*," the queen says, fixing

Father with her penetrating gaze, "I am ready to obey."

"Father?" I turn to him, hoping he'll explain. But still he doesn't look at me. "What's the charge?"

"Hold your tongue, girl," he says.

"*Don't* do that." The queen stands and hisses in his face. "Don't say those words and don't call her that. I may be under arrest, sir, but I hope I still carry some authority. Your daughter deserves respect from you. She's worth more than that."

"Certainly worth more than others in this room," Father mutters. "You are under arrest for treason against the crown and the king's person."

I choke on a gasp and one of the other ladies titters, but the queen's absolute stillness brings us all back to silence.

Father reaches for her arm, and she twitches out of his grip. "I can walk on my own, thank you."

No one moves to rescue her, and she takes a deep breath and strides from the room. Her ladies peel away from her path like the skin from an apple. The men follow close behind as if they are hungry for the exposed flesh.

She is taken by barge to the Tower in full daylight. She isn't given time to change or pack or even say good-bye to her daughter.

We are left a court with no king and no queen. The immediate buzz of gossip sounds more like a roar. Half of the men leave immediately. Half of the queen's ladies claim they knew it was coming. That she tried to poison the king. That she supported a French invasion. That she seduced him with witchcraft.

The conflicting opinions only prove that we know

nothing. So everyone lapses into a silence so vast it is like being underwater.

Without the king, without the queen, we are not a court. We are like one of those globular, wraithlike sea creatures, fragile and transparent. No skin, no skeleton, held together by nothing but habit and hope.

I lie awake long into the night, but Fitz doesn't come. The king has reeled him back, brought him close. When I do fall asleep, I dream of the Tower, of dogs, and of the fall of bodies in the joust.

"Mary."

Madge startles me so much, I think I've awakened on the tiltyard itself.

"Mary, *wake up*," she whispers urgently. I look at her. Her hair is half stuffed into her hood, her eyes a little wild.

"They've arrested him."

"The king?" If they've arrested a queen, why not the king as well?

"No!" she hisses "Norris. My betrothed. Norris has been arrested."

"What for?" I ask.

"Adultery."

"But he's not even married." I pause. "Is he?"

"Mary, wake up! Norris has been arrested for adultery . . . with the queen."

Damn.

"Smeaton, too."

"The musician?" I almost laugh. "No one would believe

that. He's a commoner. He's *Flemish*. And such an ass."

"He confessed."

The laughter corks my throat and my stomach lurches, threatening to dislodge itself and my dinner as well.

"How do you know?" I whisper.

"Carradine. Norris's servant. He's been allowed to remain with Norris in the . . . in the Tower. He came out to get some things."

"And to find you." Even after all her disparaging remarks about Norris, she was still waiting.

"He said Smeaton was tortured. Racked. A knotted rope twisted around his head until his eyeballs nearly popped out."

I shudder. "I thought they didn't torture people anymore."

"Why else would he confess?"

"Did Norris?" I ask.

"They told her he did. But it was a lie. Carradine said that the king told Norris he would welcome him back if he confessed."

"And did he?"

"Stupid man," she says. "He said he would rather die a thousand deaths than confess to a crime he hadn't committed."

"Then surely, they will see the absurdity of it all. Any man would lie to save his own skin. None would lie to send themselves to prison."

"They could arrest anyone. They arrested *George Boleyn*."

"On what charge?"

"Adultery!"

My stomach heaves. "He's her brother." *He flirted with her. He kissed her in front of everyone.*

Madge nods. "Disgusting."

I clear my mind and sit up straight. "It didn't happen, Madge!" I reach over and shake her. "It's a lie! Do you understand?"

"How do we know?"

"Because it's just rumors. Rumors and lies." *It has to be.*

"Norris said he'd be next if she'd have him."

"Courtly banter, Madge!"

But the banter sounded like the queen was imagining the king's death. That's enough to put her on the scaffold right there.

"Smeaton said he aspired to love. . . ."

"And she rebuffed him!"

"I saw George Boleyn, Mary." She's hoarse now, the tears scraping at her throat but not appearing in her eyes. "I saw him come out of her bedchamber. Late one night."

"There are a thousand other explanations, Madge! He's her *brother.*"

She nods and looks up at the ceiling, her throat stretched tight as she swallows.

"Madge?" I ask. "You didn't tell anyone else this, did you?"

She looks at me again, and she is no longer behind her eyes. No longer Madge, but a ghost of her.

"Cromwell." Her voice is nothing but a whisper.

"You have to go back to him, Madge. You have to tell the truth."

"I *told* the truth! I told him what I saw. What I heard."

"Didn't you know it would be misinterpreted? Didn't you think at all?"

"All I was thinking of was *you*, Duchess!" she cries. "I couldn't tell them about that morning on the river or how you and Fitz look at each other or seeing you and Margaret leave Whitehall in a hired boat and how you didn't come back for hours, knowing that Fitz was in London. When Cromwell asked if anyone at court was being indiscreet, I told him what I knew."

My legs feel weak and my extremities tingle. I sink to the floor, a thick, cold sweat enveloping me. Everything the queen did was nothing but words. It was Margaret and I who acted. Who broke the rules. "It wasn't true."

"It doesn't matter what the truth is," Madge says harshly. "The only thing that matters is what *he* believes."

The king. Does he want to believe she's guilty?

Father said the king wants a divorce.

A quick one.

"Oh, Mary. What have I done?"

Madge sits beside me and we lean on each other, neither of us capable of carrying our own weight.

I think of all the rumors that have ever circulated. And I know that Madge is not the instigator of this tragedy. But she and I are both agents in it. Because I told Cromwell that everyone flirts.

Even the queen.

"No, Madge," I say. "What have *we* done?"

48

Guilt hangs like a demon from my heart. I can't shake it. I know the queen cannot be indicted because of my words alone. But I can think of no way to take them back.

There are more rumors than knowledge, more untruths than certainty. We hear that the queen made a deal with the devil, that she slept with half the men at court, that Lady Mary has been poisoned, that Jane Seymour is already pregnant.

I retreat to my room. To my sewing.

One white stitch after another.

If I embroider this sleeve, the rift will be mended.

If I can finish this hem, order will be restored.

If I just finish this stitch, the world will be put to rights.

They will realize their mistake.

She is the queen.

The king returns to Greenwich without her and locks himself in his rooms. The gossip is so thick and convoluted that I don't know who returns with him—if anyone. Some say Norris has returned. Others say Thomas Wyatt may be imprisoned.

The worst rumor is that Fitz is ill and cannot travel.

The absence of truth makes me feel sick, as if I had eaten too much sugar paste. I sit and I sew and I force myself to believe that I can stitch my life back together.

That night, in the silence of the re-formed court, I think I hear wailing coming from the king's rooms. Sobs.

I wonder if the king's grief is because he misses Queen Anne.

Or perhaps he is grieving his cuckolding.

I prick my finger, and a round spot of blood blooms on the linen. I watch as it spreads its corona through the fibers.

And I curse him.

Suddenly, I can't stop myself. I curse the Seymours and their bland, boring Jane. I curse my father for his ambition and my mother for being right: my marriage to a Tudor has brought me nothing but grief. I curse this ill-starred union when I could have had a nice, quiet marriage to a boring knight like Denny or Knollys.

"Or even Francis bloody Weston," I say, sucking my finger. "At least he can dance."

"Dancing isn't everything, Duchess."

At the sound of Fitz's voice, I want to collapse. Instead, I throw my sewing to the floor and run at him. He braces himself, one foot back. Ready for anything. Still, when I throw myself on him, he staggers against the door, a surprised cry escaping his mouth until I cover it with my own.

His face is drawn and he looks older. I feel the ache of eons in his limbs. I want to draw it out of him, stop the bleeding like I did with my finger. He lowers my feet back to the floor and breaks the kiss.

"I just came from the king's rooms."

I think of the sobbing I heard. What if it wasn't the king? What if it was Fitz?

"I went in to say good night," he continues. "He grabbed me. Hugged me. He started to cry."

Oh, God. He feels guilty. I feel a wave of relief wash through me.

"He said Queen Anne tried to poison me."

"What?" All hope vanishes, replaced by a stunned surprise.

"He says that's why I was ill at Christmas."

"That's ridiculous."

Fitz frowns. "I have yet to recover completely. My chest aches when I exert myself."

I feel the twinges of anger prickling at my fingers and in my chest. Fitz can't believe any of this. I open my mouth to argue. I want to shout. I remember my mother and change tactics.

"You exerted yourself without any ill effects the other night," I tease.

I want to kiss him when he blushes. But then he shakes his head.

"He says she tried to kill Mary, too. That Anne wanted all of his children dead so that hers would take the throne."

"You were never going to . . ."

His face hardens and I stop. He wanted to believe he might be king. He wanted more. He wanted to be able to expect as much as was expected of him.

"Every rumor has a grain of truth," he says.

The rumor that Fitz will be named as heir. The rumor that the queen is a poisoner.

"What did the king say exactly?"

Fitz turns away, staring at the gilded battens of the ceiling. "He said, 'Thank God you escaped the hands of that accursed whore.'"

I reel like I've been slapped. Like it's been said about me.

"You don't believe it. You can't."

We look at each other for a moment, both of us caught in thoughts of words and truth and belief.

"Let's go now."

I'm not sure I've said it until I see his reaction. Surprise. Pain.

"We can't. Now, more than ever, he wants me close. He won't let me leave his side. I'm surprised he didn't make me share his bed. I can't stay tonight. I barely got away to tell you."

"Maybe he does love you."

"I don't think it's love, Mary. I think it's survival."

His words echo the queen's so closely. She was talking about jealousy. About fighting for her place, her voice. And, it turns out, her life. Fitz is talking about something else.

"Survival of what?" I ask. "What does he need to protect?"

"The succession."

We look at each other steadily. The king is keeping Fitz close in order to protect the possibility of a Tudor heir. Lady Mary has been made illegitimate. Princess Elizabeth will be, too. With three bastard children, which one will take the throne?

The boy.

One day, you will be queen, my father said.

"I can use this," Fitz whispers fervently. "I'll be seventeen next month. I can ask for a place of our own. For Baynard's Castle. I have leverage. It's an opportunity."

It's an opportunity for us to be together. For him to prove himself. And if we make a baby—a boy—it will bring Fitz that much closer to the throne.

The guilt swings heavier. Gaining from someone else's collapse. Taking the queen's palace when she's dead. The word *sin* burns like vinegar.

"I don't think it's right," I say. "It seems disloyal. To her."

"You don't want to be with me." He says it flatly. His eyes have gone flat, too.

"I do." I want to shout the words, but they come out as a whisper.

"Just not enough." Fitz's jaw twitches. "You're just like me. Doing everything you're told. Doing everything because you think it's *right*. Really, you're a doll, being pushed and molded and set down in this situation or the next. A plaything. Waiting. Always waiting."

Everything he says needles holes in my heart, fraying them at the edges.

"Do you think the king or the Duke of Norfolk think that way?" Fitz's voice is raised, and the effort to quiet it strangles the words into a growl. "That they care what's right for everyone else? Do you think they try to be everything to everyone? No!"

He slams his fist on the wall and I flinch.

"They only do what's right for them. Fuck everyone else. The king doesn't wait for anything."

I don't realize I'm crying until a tear slides between my lips—salty and bleak. Fitz returns to me and raises his hands, palms out.

"Don't you see, Mary? I want this for us. So we can be what we're supposed to be."

Together? I don't have the strength to ask. *Or king and queen?*

"I don't *want* to wait." His voice is more harsh than I've ever heard it. "I've *been* waiting. I want this now. Because I love you."

"Is it love?" I finally croak. "Or is it mercenary?"

He takes my face in his hands and runs his thumbs along my cheekbones. My eyes never leave his. I see no cruelty there, but I can't stop the fear that curdles in my stomach. The fear that he might be just like his father. Willing to step on the downtrodden and ignore injustice in order to get what he wants.

He lowers his mouth to mine and kisses me roughly, his hands never leaving my face.

"It's love," he murmurs into my mouth, each word followed by a kiss. "Love. Love. Love."

I mimic his gesture, putting my hands on his face, and push him gently.

"Is it worth it?"

He drops his hands and steps away from me.

"I think it is."

I don't want to argue with him. I want everything to be perfect. I want us always to agree.

I just want to be in his arms.

But there is an arm's length between us when I say, "I'm not so sure."

"I am sure," he says. "I am more than sure. Because what if he decides that it doesn't suit him anymore for us to be married? What will happen then? We will no longer be married. And we will never see each other again."

"But we are married. We've consummated it."

"Against his wishes. And we have no proof."

The damnable bloodstained sheets. The signature at the bottom of the contract.

"But if we live together," he says, pleading, "there can be no argument."

"You can't take what isn't yours." The words rasp against my throat. "Don't be like him."

Fitz's head snaps back like I've punched him. In a way I have. I am just like my mother, lashing out in an argument. Striking the softest parts to provoke the most pain.

Fitz ends the argument just like my father always did.

By abandoning me to a cold, empty room.

49

I SURVIVE THE NEXT FEW DAYS BY CAUTERIZING ALL THE HOLES IN my heart. I don't see Fitz. Most of the men keep to the king's quarters. No one knows what to do with the women. Without a queen, we are not supposed to be here. Without a queen, women at court are unnecessary.

Jane Seymour is moved to Beddington Park in Surrey—to avoid scandal. The court grows ever more silent.

William Brereton is arrested.

"Brereton?" Madge hisses to me in the quiet of the queen's rooms. "He's the king's man. We never see him in here." She pauses, frowning. "He must be *fifty*." As if that is proof enough.

Then Francis Weston is taken to the Tower.

I remember how he looked at the queen. At the king. *Why should he be so lucky?* I remember the way his mustache rubbed my lip when he kissed me. I wonder if the queen had felt it, too. I shake the thought from my mind. Weston said he hoped he always knew when to stop.

Surely he knew when not to start.

Courtiers have begun to move. Gathering up their things in haste. Not sure where to go. What to do. Whom to support. Whom to speak to. So no one says a word.

The king moves to Hampton Court, and the men move with him. Including Fitz. The queen's ladies remain at Greenwich. With no one to serve.

On the eighth of May, Thomas Wyatt is arrested and taken to the Tower.

"What's to become of us?" Madge whispers. All the ladies are asking the same question.

"I assume we'll serve Jane Seymour next."

I can't believe Margaret said that.

"I won't." Madge is adamant.

"You will if you're told to," Margaret says, and turns to me. "And don't think you won't, Mary FitzRoy. If you want to stay married, you will go where you're sent."

Fitz asked. And I didn't go with him. Dread and doubt root me where I stand. The sour tang of *regret* burns the roof of my mouth.

"The duchess will stay married," Madge says, more assuredly than I feel. "The king was at her wedding."

"The king was at his own wedding, too," Margaret says. "But he will find a way to contradict that agreement. The accusations claim she's slept with these men for years. That she has thrown the entire line of succession into question."

"No one would ever believe Elizabeth is not the king's daughter," I say, remembering them both haloed in the window.

"Perhaps not," Margaret says. "But if they were never married, Elizabeth will be illegitimate, too."

"Rumors say the queen was married to Northumberland before she married the king," Madge says.

I gape at her. Henry Percy, Earl of Northumberland. Tall. Gaunt. Nervous. With hair like scrub and eyes like glass.

"Never." I can't imagine the two of them together.

"It would give him good reason to divorce her," Madge says. "That and the rumor that she carried on an affair with Thomas Wyatt at the same time."

"So why is Wyatt in the Tower and not Percy?" I ask, anger rising. "Why are any of them? The marriage can be annulled. Just like Queen Katherine's."

"I think the king learned from that experience," Margaret says quietly. "He doesn't want two queens in this country again. No matter how unpopular Anne Boleyn is."

I start to argue. *She isn't unpopular.* But the room goes silent when Cromwell enters. He sees the three of us together, and I'm afraid he thinks we're plotting. Colluding. Three witches brewing discord.

He approaches us and I get that same chilly feeling—that he is dangerous and yet also soothing. Like my father.

"Mary Shelton," he says. "You are to attend your mistress in the Tower."

I grab both of Madge's hands in mine and squeeze.

"Are you arresting me?" Madge's voice is barely audible.

Cromwell lays a hand over mine. It's warm, the pads of his fingers soft. Not the rough, chapped skin of a mercenary. The smooth, easy palm of a master secretary.

"I understand your concern," he says, and his voice is like the rush of a wave on a pebble beach. Throaty. "Your mistress and your betrothed and most of your sexual conquests face the block. You, my dear, do not."

This statement is not comforting. This man knows everything.

His hair is neat, his chin freshly-shaven. His nails are trimmed and he smells of rose water. He shows no ill effects of evil. Not like they say in the old wives' tales: that evil within is proven by deformities without.

Like Richard III, hunchbacked and with a withered arm.

Cromwell is whole. Clean. Almost trustworthy, despite his grizzled hair and pockmarked face.

Madge is squeezing my hand so hard, the blood has stopped running to my fingers.

"She says she trusts you," Cromwell continues. "And so do we."

Madge glances at me and licks her lips. I know why they trust her. I wonder if I'm the only one who sees the guilty conscience in her eyes.

"You are to attend her at her trial. And after."

After. He doesn't expect her to be acquitted.

"Please go and collect your things, Mistress Shelton. We will be taking you to the Tower tonight," he says, his voice velvety and comforting.

"You won't be there long," he adds. And smiles.

It is that smile that exposes his evil. I can see it like the hints of a face hidden behind a mask.

I stand to go with Madge. To help her pack. To give her

courage. To remind her to keep quiet. Cromwell stops me with a single raised finger.

"A moment, Your Grace. I wish to speak with you." He looks pointedly at Margaret, who has not risen. "In private."

As I watch the two of them leave, I feel more alone than I ever have.

"What do you want?"

"Your word."

"Just one?" My mother would have slapped me for that.

"You're needed to come to the trial."

I feel the blood drain from my face.

"No."

"I need you to repeat for me what you told me a few weeks ago."

I scramble to make sense of what he's saying.

"And what is that?" I ask. My voice barely wavers, but I know he hears it.

"That everyone at court flirts"—he pauses for effect—"even the queen."

I reach behind me for the arm of the chair by the fire. He steps forward, holding out a hand solicitously, but I'm afraid to touch him. Afraid that I will lose sight of who he really is if I do.

I use my own leverage to sit myself down.

"You want me to bear witness against the queen?" I ask.

"Against the men who are accused with her."

"And therefore against the queen." I will make him say it.

"You are not one of her ladies. You are not sworn to her service."

He's giving me loopholes. Free guilt.

"I would be sworn to tell the truth," I say.

"And so you will. You will be asked if you said this to me, and you will answer yes. It's simple. One word, and you will be done."

Uncannily simple.

"And if I refuse?"

He hesitates. Possibly the first time I've seen him do so. There is a flicker of uncertainty behind the mask. Then the smile returns.

"It may not go so well for you, Your Grace."

"And what can you do to me? I am the Duchess of Richmond."

"Perhaps not, Your Grace." He gazes at me steadily. "An unconsummated marriage is easily annulled."

Everyone keeps telling me this. Lady Mary. Father. Fitz. And now this man who is almost as powerful as the king. Is he willing to ruin my life if I don't ruin the queen's? I see in his eyes that he is. He is prepared to do anything.

I think of Fitz. Of his arms around me. Of his body next to mine. That I can be with him if I do this. That perhaps when this is over—when this is all over—we can finally be together. In our own house. Away from court. Away from the lies and deceit and men like Thomas Cromwell.

I think of the queen. Of the Tower of London with its thick, cold stone walls. Of its white tower rising above the Thames, and the guns facing southward, ready to fire when a traitor dies.

She is not a traitor.

"It's an easy choice, Your Grace," Cromwell says quietly. "Your past? Or your future? Which one, in the end, is more important?"

This isn't the difference between love and survival. This is about the survival of love. If I choose not to speak, I will lose my heart. My soul. My life.

If I choose the opposite, others will lose theirs.

One simple word. *Yes.* That's all it will take to save me. I can do what they say. Be what they want me to be. And be with Fitz.

Surely one word can't make that much difference.

Yes.

"No."

"So be it, Your Grace," Cromwell says, without a trace of comfort in his voice.

But he leaves without a smile.

15 May 1536

50

Four men are tried for adultery and treason. Norris, Weston, Smeaton, and William Brereton. Only Smeaton pleads guilty. But all are given the full sentence of hanging, drawing, and quartering.

The gossip is that she confessed.

The reality is that if *they* are guilty, then so is she.

The queen's household is dissolved and we are all cast adrift. Discharged from allegiance to their queen, the maids and ladies are free to go. Free to speak against her if it so pleases them—and Cromwell.

Margaret moves quietly to St. James's Palace, under the auspices of the king. Fitz moves to Whitehall.

Hal and I move into Father's rented lodgings on the Strand. Half the court is living on this street, waiting to hear the verdict. Waiting to testify. Waiting to pass judgment.

The night before Anne's trial, Hal writes. And drinks. His script is illegible, his eyes bloodshot; his hair stands in thick swirls from running his hands through it.

"You should sleep," I tell him. "Clear your head. You want to make a sound judgment."

Hal scowls and gulps his wine. "I don't want to make any

judgment, Sister. But I am a peer of the realm and compelled to be there by my king."

"You could say no."

Hal looks up at me. "No one says no to the king."

He leaves early for the Tower. For her trial and George Boleyn's. They are nobility, and therefore can expect a jury of peers. The streets are silent. Waiting.

The murmurs come in waves, long before Hal ever returns. Like the gentle lap of the river on a boat. I close my ears and wait for my brother.

Hoping.

Hal collapses by the fire when he comes. He can't stop rubbing his hands on his breeches. As if trying to remove blood that no one else can see.

"What happened?" I ask.

"It is treason for a queen to commit adultery," he says quietly. "It puts the succession under suspicion. Puts a pretender on the throne."

I hold my breath. I want him to say he doesn't believe it. That she never did such a thing.

"The attorney-general said she solicited them. All those men. Even her brother. That she'd promised to marry Norris. That she'd told George Boleyn the king couldn't . . . that he was impotent."

That's what Madge said.

"That she made fun of the way he dressed and the songs he writes." Hal barks a laugh. "That's probably what hurt him most."

He slumps against the wall.

"She was condemned before she even came into the room," he snarls, taking yet another goblet of wine to the window. "The damned ax should have pointed toward her as she entered. She knew she'd be found guilty.

"She denied every accusation, and then said she was willing to die. That we all die eventually. She was so calm. So reserved. But her fingers were dead white on the arms of her chair. Her voice only broke when she said she was sorry that others would die with her. She spoke so well."

I can hardly feel my lips when I speak. "What did you do?"

"As the youngest peer there, I had to vote first." He pours more wine. "We knew it was wrong and we did it anyway."

I hardly know what I'm doing as I stride across the room and push him. Wine slops from his goblet.

I wrench it from his hand and throw it across the room.

"You knew it was wrong! And you did it anyway?"

"I had no choice!"

He's trying to convince himself. But the doubt is scribbled all over his face.

"There's always choice, Hal." I push him again. It feels good. "You have a mind. A title. You have a responsibility!"

"I have a responsibility to *keep* my title," he growls.

"And that's more important than someone's life?"

"She was going to die, anyway. Whichever way I voted."

He won't look at me, so I push him again. He spins and grabs me by both arms, gripping me tightly as if pressing me back together.

"I will not fight with you, Mary," he says, his voice low and dark with pain. "But I will lock you up if you continue to assault me."

He means I'm acting like our mother. All aggression leaves me, but he doesn't let go.

"You say I should speak out," he says. "That I should stand up for what I think is right. But you never did, Mary. Throughout our childhood, you never once told Mother she was wrong. You did exactly as she said. Quietly and without argument."

I am tremulous and broken by any reference to my mother.

"That's exactly the kind of power the king has over all of us. The power to take what's most important and grind it into insignificance."

He finally lets me go and turns back to the window. "Father cried when he announced the verdict. Henry Percy fainted."

The Duke of Northumberland. The one rumored to have slept with the queen before she married.

"The audience. There must have been two thousand people watching. They didn't agree with us. The murmurs were deafening."

I heard them.

"What was the sentence?" I ask.

Hal looks up at me, blinded by haunted eyes and memories.

"She's to be executed by burning or beheading. At the king's pleasure."

The king's pleasure. Three years ago, he loved her enough to brave controversy and excommunication to be with her.

Today, his love is demonstrated by his choice for her manner of execution.

Hal and I don't speak again. We just watch while the fire dies in the hearth.

We hear later that the king celebrated, long into the night, on a brightly lit barge on the Thames. Jane Seymour at his side.

19 May 1536

51

FIVE MEN HAVE BEEN EXECUTED.

Mark Smeaton. Francis Weston. William Brereton. Henry Norris. And George Boleyn. The king took pity on them and they were executed by ax. It took three strokes to kill the queen's brother while the others watched. Hardly merciful.

Their heads are not impaled on pikes on London Bridge but instead are buried with them. Even the king wants no reminders of this treason.

Thomas Wyatt is left in the Bell Tower. Awaiting the king's pleasure.

The king's marriage to Anne Boleyn was annulled the same day the executions took place. She is now nothing but Marquess of Pembroke. Not crowned. No one. Not a queen, but a mistress. A whore.

No one asks the obvious question: If she was never married to him, how could she commit adultery?

Anne Boleyn's death is scheduled for Thursday, and all morning I sit. Watching my hands do nothing. Waiting for the roar of cannon on Tower Wharf. Or news of a pardon.

What comes is delay. The king in his great mercy and out of the vestiges of his love for her has requested an expert headsman from Calais. A man who can take a head off clean with a sword. Who never misses.

The night is unbearably long. Frightfully long. I don't sleep, but dream waking. Of going far away. To France. To Scotland. To the New World. Anywhere but here.

Here, all I can do is wait.

I imagine Anne in that Tower room. Having waited all day to die. And I imagine her facing the horde of spectators. All of them waiting for her death.

She needs someone in that crowd who doesn't wish her ill. Someone to wish her peace.

I pull myself out of bed and dress in my drabbest clothes. Brown kirtle, gray sleeves. A simple coif. I don't want to be recognized by anyone. I don't want to be another court voyeur.

The streets are teeming and smell of sweat and manure, fish and offal. The atmosphere is like a festival. Like Anne's coronation. Merchants are selling pies and wine. Priests yell themselves hoarse on the street corners. I hear men taking bets on how many swings the swordsman will require. A tune and snatches of lyrics catch my ear. That the king is a cuckold. That Anne was condemned by spite. That Jane Seymour is the next royal whore, and one who has screwed half the court already.

That almost makes me laugh.

Part of me hopes I'll never get to the Tower. That I'll somehow feel better just for trying, knowing that someone who loves her tried to be there when she dies. Someone who doesn't wish for her death, but wishes for her redemption.

The closer I get, the more I shiver and sweat. I am in the

shadow of the gate, the stink of the moat lapping at its base, when I hear a familiar voice.

I turn around and we lock eyes. For an instant, Fitz's face shows no recognition, then he shakes his head. Once. As if trying to get a shock of hair out of his face. I know what he means.

I reach for his arm and he shrinks away.

Only then do I see Hal behind him. Hal frowns at Fitz, then looks at me, and his face darkens with anger.

"This is no place for a girl," he says.

I turn and stride ahead of them. I am like Margaret walking the halls of Greenwich. I do not dodge around the knots of people. I do not slow my pace. I walk steadily, and a path clears. Each gap I see is there for me and me alone. I'm meant to be here.

I walk through the alley beneath the Bell Tower and into the belly of the Bloody Tower gate, vaulted like a crypt. The throng is packed more tightly here, and my progress slows almost to a standstill. I am shoulder to shoulder with merchants. Courtiers. City men.

Tower Green is even more crowded, and the sky presses down as heavily as the vault of the gate. Stinking bodies are packed up against one another, everyone striving for a better view. There must be a thousand people here. Just to watch someone die.

My breath comes in fugitive gasps and I suddenly—frantically—want to get away.

But the crowd pushes me forward and eddies up near the scaffold. Cromwell is there, close enough to catch the blood when it spills. He turns and sees me and I stop, the mob pulsing around me, my lungs utterly frozen in my chest. I feel Fitz's hand close around my upper arm, but I cannot look away from the king's master secretary. Not until Cromwell smiles.

Fitz is pressed up against my back. Like we were in bed. I can breathe again.

"Why are you here?" he growls in my ear.

"For her."

"You don't know what it's like. You have to leave now." He says the last word as a command. A duke, giving orders.

I turn to look at him. I can smell him. Taste him. I also taste the anger like bile rising in my throat.

"Why are *you* here?" I spit.

He flinches. "I am here at the king's command."

"You represent him," I press. "You're here for *him*."

I will make him say it.

"He's my father." He is adamant. His shoulders are still very straight and his head is held high.

But something inside him breaks. I hear it shatter. It's the only time I've heard him call the king his father. But what kind of father asks a boy to do such a thing?

Hal catches up to us and stands belligerently at Fitz's side.

"Make her go, Fitz," he says.

Like I'm not even here. Not a person. Like I'm a servant. Or worse. A wife.

"I will not leave." My voice carries more courage and conviction than I feel.

I see, suddenly, in Hal's face, a cross between Mother and

Father. The war that went on between them our entire lives. The one that always ended with a blow and a curse.

Because he can't hit me—won't hit me—he lands a thump on Fitz's shoulder.

"Now, Fitz!"

Fitz won't look at me. Won't look at either of us.

"It's not under my control."

"It's your responsibility!" Hal shouts. "*She's* your responsibility. As are every single one of her actions."

I step between them. Square up to Hal, pressed so close I can see the stubble on his chin.

"I am responsible for my own actions, *Your Grace*. I am no one's possession. I have a mind of my own."

"Then you are just like our *mother*," Hal snarls, and it would knock me to my knees if I had room to move.

Hal turns to Fitz. "I pity you, my friend. I've seen how this ends up. Make her do what you say now, or you will always regret it."

"I'm not my mother," I whisper, my breath coming in gasps. "I'm nothing like her."

Hal just turns and walks into the crowd that parts before the Earl of Surrey and swallows him back up again.

Fitz grabs my arm and pulls me away from the scaffold. He doesn't speak, his silence more condemning than anything he could say. He stands me directly behind a behemoth of a man dressed in faded leather breeches and a reeking leather jacket.

So I can't see. So she can't see me.

Then the crowd begins to move like the Thames against

the incoming tide. It shifts and turns and murmurs like an approaching wave as the yeomen of the guard march between the enormous towers of the Coldharbour Gate, followed by a tiny figure dressed in a long black robe and wide fur collar. She is accompanied by four women.

Four *girls*. Maids of honor brave enough to be there with her. Madge is the last. I can see, even at this great distance, that she's already weeping.

As they approach the black-draped scaffold, the crowd shifts again, suddenly surging forward. I'm pushed and drawn around the leather-clad giant, away from Fitz, sucked into the center of a crowd as if it's a whirlpool. I can't breathe. The darkness starts to close in from the sides. I feel Fitz grab for me once, and when I turn to reach for him, his face is stricken, as if he's losing me to the crowd.

Losing me to the sword.

Then I'm swallowed up and spit farther forward, surrounded by a gang of boys barely older than I am. Apprentices, already drunk.

I gasp a breath, wishing I had the space to put my head between my knees. I gasp again, and my vision begins to clear.

"I've never seen a witch die!" one of the lads cries gleefully to his mates. "Unless you count the Nun of Kent, but perhaps she really was holy. She predicted this, didn't she?

"I've seen monks die and men who didn't take the oath and those five scoundrels the other day." He is close enough to me that I can smell the rancid, sour stink of his breath. "But never a *queen*. Who'd a thought?"

He raises a wineskin and slops a little down his chin when he drinks. I try to move away, but the crowd is too tight. Pushing forward. I feel a knee against the back of my leg. An elbow on my upper arm. A shoulder behind my head. Breath on my neck.

I keep my eyes on the queen. She reaches the stairs and hesitates minutely, looking over her shoulder. I follow her line of sight back to the Tower wall, the Bell Tower, the scrap of sky beyond.

The queen wears a simple gable hood, the peaks and corners of it shading her face from the morning light. My heart seizes. She hardly looks like the Anne I knew, who dressed in bright colors and always wore a French hood.

She steps up onto the scaffold, exposing a crimson kirtle beneath her gown. The color of blood. The color of martyrdom.

I realize I'm holding my breath and try to let it out slowly, but can only suck it back in again with a gulp. And another. I can't get more than a mouthful of air into my lungs at a time.

Fitz was right. I shouldn't be here.

I try to turn. To walk away. I can't shift my weight without pressing against another body. Arms. Shoulders. Knees. Even the belly of the apprentice beside me. The codpiece of the man behind.

I look back up to see Anne addressing the crowd. Her words come on breaths of wind. "Judged to die. . . . Will of the king." She speaks steadily, scanning the crowd as she does so, her eyes lighting on every person there.

When she sees me, she bows her head. Takes a visible breath. Lifts her chin.

"I blame not my judges, nor any other manner of person."

My throat closes in on itself and I see Madge press her knuckles to her teeth. But Anne keeps her voice steady.

"Thus I take my leave of the world, and of you, and I heartily desire you all to pray for me."

The headsman kneels, asking for forgiveness. She touches his head once, absolving him. My heart squeezes to a stop.

The queen hands him a bag of gold.

Paying for her own execution.

She removes her hood, and a sheet of black hair cascades from it, around her shoulders and down her back. Madge brings her a coif and helps her tuck the hair up inside it and then remove the fur collar, revealing a low, square neckline that exposes her shoulders and a very slender neck.

Anne's hands tremble a little as she reaches up to untie the ribbon that circles it. Madge steps forward again, her face blank, her lower lip clenched white beneath her teeth. Together, they untie the knot and Anne lifts it away from her throat. The bauble hanging from the ribbon glows dully in the light coming from the cloud-clotted sky. It's a golden *A*, from which dangles a single pearl.

Anne looks back once more, to her lodgings, to the water gate, to the Bell Tower. Maybe hoping for someone to ride in at the last minute. Offer a reprieve. A pardon. She hands the necklace to Madge, whispers something in her ear, and lets go.

She bends to wrap her skirts around her ankles. Binding them.

"What's she doing?"

I don't realize I've asked it out loud until the apprentice beside me answers.

"The legs, they thrash when the head comes off. She doesn't want her skirts to come up and be *indecent*." He laughs.

I'm suddenly dizzy, my held breath no longer filling my lungs. My wobbly legs feel obsolete, like the very lightness of my head should keep me off the ground. The air before me starts to spark, and when I see her kneel, I turn.

High above the heads of others, three yards away, but completely unattainable, I see Fitz. He's scanning the crowd, not looking at the scaffold. He sees me and holds my gaze and we stare at each other, neither of us looking one way or the other, not to the crowd or the queen or the man with the sword. And finally a breath comes easy. My gasp is more like a sob.

Fitz tries to push toward me through the thickening crowd and I turn away. He'll never reach me. He cannot rescue me.

The crowd kneels and I sink to my knees. The queen kneels upright. There is no block. She lifts her left hand, holding the coif in place, her dark hair pulled back from her pale face, her gray lips moving. Praying. Her eyes open and scan the crowd. Dart once more upward. Toward the Tower walls. Toward the sky.

"Bring me the sword."

Anne turns her head, looking at the scaffold stairs. Looking for the approaching sword. She does not see the executioner remove it from a heap of straw behind her. Before she can turn back, he swings it over his head. Once—twice—to gain momentum. The blade gleams dully, reflecting the motley gray sky above it.

"Have pity on my soul!" she cries.

The sword slices the air with a sound that tears my heart and breath straight from my chest, and a fountain of blood follows. I hear a scream, a howl of agony. The cannons on the wharf go off before the head hits the straw, drowning everything. The ringing in my ears matches the death knell from the Tower chapel, St. Peter ad Vincula—"St. Peter in Chains."

There is blood. So. Much. Blood.

I glance over my shoulder. Fitz presses toward me, forcing his way through the still-kneeling crowd. A few grumble, but then look up to see his red hair. His arching eyebrows. His stormy gray eyes. And they peel away.

I am pulled to my feet and turned back to the scaffold by the press of people around me. My lungs are wrung empty and all I can hear is the shuffling roar of a thousand feet.

Then all goes silent. Because there in the dust of the scaffold, Anne's eyes look once more to the sky and her lips continue to pray.

The crowd surges backward, the apprentice beside me stuttering over his own prayers. I turn and stumble and reach for the only thing that can keep me upright. And Fitz is there to catch me.

52

I REMEMBER NOTHING ELSE. NOTHING OF THE JOURNEY BACK TO
the residence on the Strand. I don't see the streets or the people crowding them or the blue sky pinching its way between
the overhanging buildings. I don't notice the mud and muck
churning beneath our feet.

I don't even feel Fitz's hand on my arm.

I feel nothing.

Hours later, I see there's a little fire in the grate. I know I'm
sitting on a stool beside it. It's dark outside—and cold—but
there's a goblet of something warm and spicy-smelling in my
hand.

"Drink it."

It's Madge.

"How did you get here?" I ask. In my mind, she will forever
be on that scaffold.

Her face is tight. Pale. I shudder when I see a line of dark-
brown spots on the side of her neck. She catches me staring
and rubs. Hard.

"Her blood was everywhere," she whispers. "Her body lay
there for hours. There was no coffin. We didn't know what
to do."

She stares into the fire.

"They took everything," she mutters, rubbing her hands on her skirts. "Her jewels. Her clothes. In the end, we cleaned the body and wrapped it in a cloth. . . . We had to put her in an empty weapons chest. It was barely long enough for her body. We carried it to the chapel ourselves."

I swallow. My throat is too dry to speak. I lift the hippocras to my mouth. I am nauseated by the heady odor of it, but drink anyway. Sweet.

"Neither one of you should have been there."

The rest of the room swims into vision. Hal is here, sitting by the window. Glaring at me. Fitz is by the door. Like he's ready to bolt. He's thinner. Frailer.

We all are.

Hal stands.

"I *told* you, Mary." My name catches in his throat, and he turns away from me.

By the door, Fitz coughs. I can't look at him. I fear he will leave. That he agrees with Hal.

That I shouldn't have been there.

That I'm just like my mother.

That we will make each other miserable for the rest of our lives. Separate. Quarreling.

Falling out of love.

He's watching me. I wonder if he has been the entire time.

"You're right." Fitz's voice is quiet, but confident. A deep rumble edged in gold.

My throat fills with the horrible pounding of my heart.

"Mary shouldn't have been there." He looks around the room. "None of us should have been there. It should never have happened."

The room falls into silence.

"But given the situation," he continues, "it was the right thing to do. To be there for her. Not pick over her bones like buzzards."

We watch each other for a moment that lasts long enough for me to realize he's agreeing with me. He's willing to wait. Even if it costs us.

I stand to go to him, but Madge starts to cry. Her face withers and her shoulders shake with the effort of holding back sobs. When Hal reaches for her, she holds a hand out to stop him, covering her face with the other.

After an eternity, she reaches into the pocket at her waist.

"I don't know what to do with this."

She holds a worn black velvet ribbon. Hanging from the end of it, a golden *A* from which is suspended a single pearl. *A* for Anne.

I look away.

Madge grabs my sleeve.

"She told me to give it to Thomas Wyatt. I had to walk up all those stairs to the top of the Bell Tower. Around and around and around all the way to the top. But I went, Mary. I went for *her*."

No one can say her name now. The king has already hired workmen to spend night and day reglazing the windows, repainting the battens, chipping at stone. Removing every *A* in the entire kingdom, hoping no one will remember she existed.

"He wouldn't take it. He backed away from me. He looked positively wild—his hair every which way—and he hadn't shaved in a week, looked like. He had papers all over his little desk. Words everywhere."

I can picture it. The tiny room. The papers. The ink.

"He said he was afraid it would kill him if he took it. If he touched it."

Hal looks at the jewel as if it is a snake ready to strike.

"He wouldn't escape the scaffold if he did," he says. "It would be a sure sign that he'd loved her. Once."

"What do I do with it, Mary?" Madge pleads. "I can't keep it. I can't throw it away."

I reach out and touch the pearl, smooth and warm.

"We should give it to her daughter," I say. "Your mother would give it to her, wouldn't she?"

"My mother is on Lady Mary's side. Now that they're both illegitimate, I don't know what she'll do for poor little Elizabeth."

We hang our heads for a moment. Motherless bastard.

"So we wait until she grows up."

The jewel turns on its ribbon, the gold dull in the dim light cast by the fire. One *A* to remind Elizabeth who her mother was. Where she came from. That she's the daughter of a queen as well as a king.

Madge presses it into my palm, but I don't close my fingers around it. I want to refuse it. Drop it to the floor. But she lets it go, and it is all mine.

I want to throw it at her.

"Thank you," she says. "I knew you'd have an answer. You always do the right thing."

Madge walks to the door and I close my hand. The gold is warm. I shiver.

Fitz steps aside, and Madge pauses. Turns just a little, her head down, not speaking to any of us, but to the door.

"What will become of us?" she whispers.

No one can answer. Hal looks as if his heart is bleeding out through his sleeve. Fitz is watching me. We *could* have a home. Together. If he asked for it.

Madge runs one finger along the seam of the door.

Hal strides across the room to her. "I'll take you home."

"I don't have a home." She will not serve the new queen and can no longer serve the old one.

When Hal takes her elbow, she looks up at him. "Thank you," she says. When he puts one arm around her, drawing her to him, she lays her face on his chest and lets him guide her out the door.

Fitz doesn't close the door after them. We stand at opposite sides of the room. Waiting.

"I should go," he says finally.

I take a step to stop him and the dizziness returns, like I am again in the middle of the crowd. The room, the smell of despair, the darkness press in upon me.

"Stay with me." The blackness clings to the edges of my vision, and all I see is Fitz. He crosses the room in two strides and rescues me before I fall. Lifts me up and keeps me grounded. Kisses me so lightly and longingly that I feel our souls entwine.

"I will," he says, and I lift my chin in shock to look him in the eye. "One day. Not in your father's house."

My father wouldn't care. My father wants you in my bed.

"The king bade me return to Hampton Court with him tomorrow."

Fitz's eyes are almost feverish, his expression a war between anguish and the desire for his father's approval.

I recognize it perfectly. It's the one I wear around my mother.

I kiss him once. "If you can't stay, then come back. Please."

"I will."

My room is silent and empty when he's gone. I hear the servants next door. In the kitchen below. I hear shouts from the street outside. My room is like cotton stuffed in my ears. Hollow and noiseless.

And cold.

I go back to the fire, searching for the hippocras Madge gave me. My book sits next to it. In the rush and tumble of moving, I'd assumed it was still at the bottom of my cedar chest. Wrapped in my wedding bodice. But there it sits.

I turn through the pages until I come to a hand I don't recognize. The loops are dark with ink, the letters sharp-edged.

> *These bloody days have broken my heart.*
> *My lust, my youth did them depart,*
> *And blind desire of estate.*
> *Who hastes to climb seeks to revert.*

Of truth, circa Regna tonat.
Around thrones the thunder rolls.

Madge stayed in the Bell Tower long enough for Wyatt to copy this poem into my book. All those papers. All those words.

I hope he burned the rest.

Because these words are enough to show me he loved her. That he trusted us enough to keep it safe. No wonder he wouldn't take her jewel. He wasn't afraid it would condemn him. He was afraid his grief would kill him.

I open my hand, the *A* glowing dully in my palm.

These bloody days have broken my heart.

I fold myself over the fist that clutches the ribbon and gold and sob.

30 May 1536

53

THE KING DOES NOT MARRY JANE SEYMOUR IMMEDIATELY. A wedding so close on the heels of his former queen's execution might make people talk. Might make them think less of him. That he's rushing things. Being tactless.

That he wanted to get rid of his wife by any means possible in order to make way for another.

So he waits eleven days. To give us all time to forget.

Just as the evening begins to turn, and the streets below us melt into shadow, a knock comes downstairs and the servants rush about. It's like water falling on an anthill, causing panic and confusion.

"Please, Your Grace"—the new girl simpers into my room—"it is His Grace, Your Grace." She pauses, flustered. "It's His Grace the duke."

I let her flounder into silence.

"Which duke, Alice?"

She looks at me with wide-open eyes, terrified at the prospect of having to define which man has come to the door.

"Your husband, Your Grace," she blurts.

I stand so quickly, my embroidery falls to the floor. Fitz steps inside the doorway before Alice can even curtsy her way out of it. She's turned bright pink and seems completely unsure of where to go, or how to get by him. Graciously, he steps aside and lets her through.

"I'm not sure if it's your title or your features that fluster her so." I want desperately to touch his face. To kiss him. But he stands just inside the door.

"You look tired," I tell him.

He flashes a smile. "Thanks for the compliment."

A manservant leaves a jug of small ale, two mugs, and some bread and cheese before bowing his way out the door.

I cross the room as quickly as I can, and Fitz catches me. I want to find again that sense of near insanity—the feeling that he and I are all the world and we can scorch the very universe with a kiss.

But this kiss is sad and imbued with longing.

"I can't stand to be around him," he says, breaking the kiss and pulling me to his chest. The breath sounds thin in his lungs. "At Hampton Court, he had me dine beside him every night. Today he insisted I attend the wedding."

"How was it?"

"Quiet. Only a few people attended." He pauses. "Margaret carried Jane's train."

"Did she?" I pull away from him and go to pour the ale.

"The very picture of humility." I can taste his bitterness.

"She said she would serve Jane if she became queen."

Fitz strides over to me. "And you didn't tell her what you told me? You didn't take her to task for being mercenary?"

I look up at him. His eyes rest deep in their sockets.

"Perhaps she just doesn't care as much what I think."

"She's going to be made heir apparent." He turns away and takes a gulp of the ale, and it makes him cough.

"Margaret?"

"That's mercenary for you, isn't it? Waiting quietly while one daughter and then the next gets made illegitimate. None of the king's children will take the throne. His niece will."

"But Margaret . . ."

"Margaret what? Never wanted to be queen? How well did you really know her, Mary? Because it was always obvious to me. She's got more ambition in her than the rest of us put together."

"No." Margaret wasn't like that. "She's my friend. I know her better than that."

"When was the last time you spoke with her?"

Before these bloody days broke our hearts.

I sink down to the stool and bury my face in my skirts. It's as if we woke up from a nightmare into a different world entirely. I knew a Margaret who claimed the king would never control her. Who married my uncle in secrecy and against the king's wishes. Now there's a new Margaret, who quietly submits. The picture of humility.

There's a new Madge, who disappears without sound or trace.

There's a new Hal, who has an edge to him like a dagger waiting to be unsheathed.

And there's Fitz. Who is thin and drawn and frighteningly helpless, just as I was on our wedding day.

"I'm sorry," Fitz says, kneeling in front of me. "Forgive me, I don't know what I'm talking about."

"You do, though." I look up at him. "This spring has shattered us all. Broken us apart and left us lacking. Madge is gone. I don't even know where she is. Margaret has become someone I no longer know. Hal has . . . Hal has retreated into himself. He writes and follows orders and won't even speak to me anymore."

"He does more than that," Fitz says. "His wife is pregnant again."

"You see?" I cry. "He used to talk to me, Fitz. I used to have friends! People I could trust and talk to and . . . now I've got nothing."

Fitz puts his forehead on my knees. "You've got me," he murmurs into my skirts.

I look down at his head and stroke his hair. It's almost the color of firelight—red and gold and orange, and it flickers as my hand moves through it.

He doesn't lift his head when he speaks.

"The king is going to give me Baynard's."

We've talked about this. I don't want to again. "That's the queen's castle."

"I know."

He finally looks at me, and we gaze at each other for a long, slow moment, our previous argument as solid as a wall between us. If he takes Baynard's, will he be as mercenary as Margaret?

"I need a London residence," he says quietly. "I can't stay at court forever. I turn seventeen soon. *He* married at seventeen.

He can't turn us down for much longer. We could live there. Together."

I look at the man before me, with his long legs curled under him and his face raised to mine. He's so close to me I can see the dust clinging to the nap of his velvet doublet. Smell the fresh linen of his shirt collar.

There is no trace of venality in him.

"Mary, I didn't choose to marry you. It was decided before I even really knew what was happening. The way I remember it, Hal told me. I was twelve. He said we'd be brothers, and that seemed like the height of joy to me. It didn't matter who you were or what you were like. Hal would be family, and that was most important. Because he'd been like a brother to me all along."

I stay silent, knowing he's trying to say something else. Something that doesn't involve my brother. I feel a smile creeping up the corner of my mouth.

Fitz laughs.

"I sound ridiculous. And I'm saying it all wrong. It wasn't my choice. To marry you. It wasn't yours, either. But it was *right*. It *is* right."

He pulls me down off the stool and into his lap, his arms wrapped around me from behind. He rests his chin on my shoulder and murmurs into my ear. "I didn't ask for Baynard's, either. But it's been given."

His voice is a thrum I hear in my chest and my heart more than in my ears and my head.

"What if that's right, too?" he asks softly.

I turn my face to his. I feel squeezed by guilt, strung out by hope.

"I never got a chance to ask you," he says. "It seems like a choice you should have been given. To become a duchess. To be married to the son of a king."

He takes my face in his hands, his thumbs stroking my cheekbones.

"So I want to ask you, Mary," he whispers. "Will you marry me? Live with me? Baynard's isn't France, where no one can reach us. But it's a place where we can close the door on the outside world, and just be the two of us. Together."

Our parents cannot control us if we do not let them in.

I smile at him. "Just the two of us and all of our servants."

Fitz laughs, but thankfully doesn't let me go.

"Better than France, then," he says. "Because if we left England, we wouldn't be able to take many with us."

There are flakes of gold like a new-risen sun in his eyes.

Guilt still swings heavy on its pendulum within me, and I hope I can make the right choice. Do the right thing.

"I choose love," I tell him. "The ghost of Anne Boleyn may haunt the rooms and galleries of Baynard's, but she said—" Something catches in my throat. "She said she hoped my marriage would make me free."

"If we're together, we will be free," Fitz says, kissing me again. The longing is still there, but it is not the longing of grief. It is the longing for a future.

"You say everything is broken," he says. "But *we* aren't. We are not broken."

8 June 1536

54

"The Earl of Sussex is your new best friend," my father says by way of hello.

Robert Radclyffe is as old as the king and doesn't look as well for it. But today is the opening day of Parliament, so I assume my father is speaking metaphorically.

"He said, right in Privy Council," Father says, "that if all the king's children are illegitimate, the son ought to be first in line to the throne."

He pauses. Waiting for that information to sink in. I feel an echo of that surge of triumph I felt at my wedding. Making my father proud. Becoming something bigger than him. Better than my mother.

But ambition is what's broken my friendships. I won't let it break me, too.

"Jane Seymour will have a son," I say.

"That's not a given." My father approaches me. "Neither of his other wives have. There may be . . . reasons."

"I don't want to know."

"You must. Because you are the only person married to his only living son."

"His son is not the king. And probably never will be. Margaret is heir apparent."

"Margaret Douglas will never be queen, nor will any of her offspring."

"But how do you *know*?" My voice is shrill and I hate it. "How do you even know what will happen tomorrow, much less ten years from now? Or even one?"

"None of us knows what will happen tomorrow or next year or ten years from now." Father is so close I can taste the menace behind his words. He's looking down his nose at me. I've seen him stand this way with my mother.

"What we have to be," Father says carefully, his voice low and dangerous, "is prepared. For anything. A new act of succession has been proposed in Parliament. It will remove Mary and Elizabeth from the line to the throne. It will also give the king the right to name his heir. If Queen Jane doesn't give him a son—and soon—your husband could be next in line."

"I don't want to be queen."

I don't want to be anywhere near that throne or the thunder that rolls around it. I don't want Fitz to be, either. I want us to live our lives together in obscurity. Far from prying eyes and tongues desperate for gossip. Free.

"You say that today. But as you point out, things change in an instant. We must have everything in place for the ultimate eventualities. You, my dear, must be as good and as careful as you can be. The perfect picture of courtly grace. A princess. One so unlike his own daughters that he can't help but make you his."

"I don't want to be *his*." I lift my chin. "I want to be mine."

Father stops still, a frightening little tower of animosity.

"That's exactly what *she* used to say. 'I am my own, I belong to no one.'"

It's the first time anyone has mentioned Anne Boleyn. And he can't even say her name.

"I learned from the best."

For a moment, I think he really is going to hit me.

"Those are dangerous footsteps to follow, my dear." His face is so close to mine, I can see the pores of his skin, the tiny sprouts of beard that come late in the day.

"It is a path you set me on. You and she collaborated to get me here. She was my queen." She was my friend.

"Now you have another." Father steps away, as if wiping any tarnish of the former queen from his hands. As if it were that easy. "You will come to court in July."

"What if I don't want to?"

"I'm afraid you have no choice. You need to be seen. Before the king forgets his son is married. His memory only operates at his convenience. If you are at court, he will know you exist. Not to mention you will be closer to young FitzRoy's bed."

That is the only thing he could possibly say that might sway my decision. For my father, it is a business deal, something he can sign and seal, and then it happens. For me, it is more like hunger. My need to be with Fitz is so strong I might consider defying my own principles to achieve it.

"The new queen will need new ladies," Father says, and

pecks me on the cheek without touching me with his hands. "You will be nothing if you're not at court."

I am no more able to defy him outright than I am to defy my mother. Than Fitz is to defy the king. I cannot tell my father no.

I do not tell him yes.

But he leaves thinking that I have.

15 June 1536

55

I SPEND MY DAYS AVOIDING MY FATHER AS MUCH AS I CAN. HE'S waiting for the opportunity to insert me into Queen Jane's household. I am waiting for Fitz to come and tell me we have a place to live. Together.

Away from court.

It is late afternoon, and I'm sitting by a west-facing window, catching the angling light on my book. Reading the lists and poems and scribblings. Avoiding the verses written in by Thomas Wyatt.

There's a swift knock, and I have just time to stuff the book into my pocket before the door opens and Hal strides in. He is nineteen and a father and a poet in his own right. But I can still see the little boy in his eyes. The one I used to run to when my mother went into her rages.

"Hal!"

He pulls me into a swift hug. "We haven't much time," he says.

"For what?" I'm suddenly worried. A little twinge of terror. What can possibly happen next?

Hal smiles then. "It's a surprise."

He's ordered a litter to carry me and closes the heavy curtains so I can't see where we're going. I peek out between them, and start to feel nervous as we head southwest.

Toward Whitehall.

Toward the court.

I wonder if Hal would take Father's side in this argument. He always takes Father's side against Mother.

I close the curtains and my eyes until we stop and Hal flings the heavy velvet aside and I see a brick gatehouse, four stories tall, its narrow windows glittering in the setting sun. St. James's Palace.

"Fitz wanted to get you up at dawn," Hal says, helping me down. "But he hasn't been feeling well and slept late. He decided the sun*set* would be almost as beautiful as the sun*rise*."

Fitz's coat of arms hangs in the gatehouse, showing that he is in residence here. The lion of Richmond and the yale of Somerset and the arms of France and England crossed by a silver band, proclaiming his illegitimacy.

And his motto: *Duty binds me.*

This place is his and yet not his. He inhabits it, but doesn't own it. Just like his life.

An usher in blue-and-yellow livery escorts us through a courtyard into the relatively new palace. It used to be part of Eton College, but the king took it over, with an eye on the great park next to it. He walled up the park, tore down the buildings, and began to build his own. The presence chamber is a grand gallery, lined with windows and tapestries. The room is empty and cold, even in June, so I move to the fireplace to stay warm. Carved into the surround are emblems. Lover's knots, combining the letters H and A. Henry and Anne. An oversight in the king's campaign to erase all evidence of her.

I turn away.

The door opens again, and Madge enters, already talking. "So you have no idea what all this is about?"

"Madge!" I start to go to her but stop again when I see who stands behind her.

Margaret.

She is as still and as poised as ever. Her back straight, her neck elongated. She looks the part. Looks like royalty. She always has.

"Unfortunately, I couldn't get Thomas to join us for this expedition." Fitz enters from the other end of the room.

Hal laughs. "You should have seen the looks on their faces, Fitz."

Fitz's laugh grinds in his chest.

"Perhaps next time," he says. "I've ordered an outdoor feast in a fairy bower."

"You're getting fanciful in your old age, my friend." Hal locks his arm around Fitz's neck. Fitz widens his stance and puts his hands on Hal's chest to try to break free, but Hal wrestles him to the floor.

Easily.

We all stand for a stunned moment, until Hal pulls Fitz back up into an embrace.

"Happy birthday, Henry," Hal says.

"Birthday!" Madge cries. "No wonder this calls for a celebration."

I had forgotten the days. Or lost track of them. I slip between my husband and my brother and kiss Fitz quickly.

"I didn't get you a gift," I tell him.

"I'm giving you one," he replies, and looks at my friends one after another. "What's broken can almost always be mended."

He takes Margaret's hand and puts it over mine. "Be friends, ladies. Life's too short to be enemies with those you love."

With that, he turns and leaves the room. Margaret and I look at each other, still holding hands. She smiles tentatively.

"Friendship will always bind us," I say. "Even when we disagree."

She squeezes my hand. "I can't tell you how happy that makes me."

Fitz leads us through the guard chamber and out into a world sweet with sunshine. The wall that King Henry built around the park keeps the deer and game within it, while keeping the crowds and stench of London out. It's like a little Eden. Perfect and beautiful and cut off from the evils of the world. Fitz really has created a little fairy bower for us to feast in.

The table is covered with a damask cloth and set with gold and glass. The wine is like liquid rubies, and there are venison and strawberries and marzipan.

Madge steps between me and Margaret and grabs one of our hands in each of hers. "Your husband has given us the best gift," she says, swinging our arms. "Happy birthday, Fitz!" she calls, and lets go my hand to swing Margaret around and send her spinning.

Madge turns to me and grabs both of my hands. "It's a shame you love your husband, Duchess, because if you didn't, I certainly would." She whips me around into a dizzying whirl, the trees and sunlight blurring into flashes of light and shadow until I trip and tumble and she falls on top of me, giggling hysterically.

Hal grabs Madge around the middle to pull her off me, and both of them pause when she's on her feet, his hands still on her waist. I'm left on the ground, watching them watch each other.

Until Hal says, "I love you."

Madge takes a step back, and his hands drop to his sides. "I know." She helps me up and then turns back to him. "I just can't—" She swallows. "I can't stand any more heartbreak."

Hal presses his mouth into a line and nods. "I understand. I just had to tell you."

When Madge leans in to kiss his cheek, he closes his eyes and draws a long breath through his nose. Drawing her in. Tasting her.

And then he lets her go.

Madge turns swiftly and pounces on a piece of marzipan shaped like a rampant lion. "I declare we start this feast with the final course and work our way backward."

Margaret dips a strawberry in cream. "Why start with meat when there are sweeter things to be had?"

Hal pours the wine and begins regaling us with stories about Fitz when they lived together at Windsor.

"We had greater feasts than Priam's sons of Troy!" he cries.

> *"In active games of nimbleness and strength,*
> *Where we did strain, trailed by swarms of youth,*
> *Our tender limbs that yet shot up in length;*
> *The secret groves which oft we made resound*
> *Of pleasant plaint and of our ladies' praise—"*

"Ladies?" I ask, turning to Fitz, whose color has returned in a flash of red.

I am not jealous of some dalliance that Fitz had when he was thirteen, but of the ease with which my brother forms a verse. The words he conjures are sweeter than the marzipan that dissolves on my tongue.

"Perhaps that was later," Hal says, wrapping an arm around my waist and kissing me on the cheek.

> *"With dazed eyes oft, we by gleams of love*
> *have missed the ball and got sight of our dame."*

That tennis game. My first kiss. I look up to see Fitz staring at me. Laughing.

Madge smirks. "You're blotching, Duchess."

I wiggle away from Hal and go to Fitz. Press my body up against his and whisper in his ear, "You told him?"

"Only that I couldn't take my eyes off of you," he murmurs, and nuzzles me, sending tickly shivers down my neck.

"Perhaps we need to send these young lovers upstairs," Madge says, and she and Hal devolve into an exchange of bawdy remarks and sexual innuendoes that has them howling with laughter while Margaret tries to keep a straight face and fails.

"I still can't take my eyes off you," Fitz whispers. "Or my hands." His fingers slide along the curve of my waist. There is no need for distance. No need for pretense. We are just . . . together. The prying eyes of court and country are well outside the walls.

Fitz backs up and starts patting my skirts.

"What are you doing?" I laugh.

"There is something large and heavy on your person," he says, chuckling, and spreads his palms wide to stroke them down my sides—waist to hip to thigh. I laugh again, but want to grab him, kiss him, lose myself in him.

He finds my pocket and snakes a hand in before I can stop him, pulling out my book. He holds it gently, tracing the cover with his index finger.

I look at it with his eyes. It has begun to wear ragged at the corners, and a little bit of the spine has started to give.

"Your words," he says, smiling.

"And others'." I reach for it, but he holds it out of my grasp, turning to the first page. The list.

"'Poetry,'" he reads aloud. "'A nice ass. Power. Good kisser. Good dancer.'" He looks at me with a raised eyebrow. "What is this?"

"Just a list." I reach for it again.

"A list of what?" he asks, holding it high over his head, the other hand on the small of my back, pressing me close to him. He knows my bones turn to water when he touches me there.

"Things."

"What things?" he growls in my ear, and then kisses me and all my fight is gone.

Like a monkey, Madge leaps up and snatches the book out of his hand, laughing. "Your subtle charms won't work on me, Richmond," she says, waving it in his face.

Fitz reaches for it, but she swings it behind her—out of his reach.

And right into Hal's.

He opens it back up again, reading it while dancing away from Madge's fingers.

"'Not ugly, smelly, narcissistic, vain,'" he reads, and then stops, Madge crashing into him. "'Or married.'"

"It's a list of attributes," Madge says, snatching the book back. "Of what we were looking for in a man we'd fall in love with."

"I see," Hal says.

"I'm sure you noticed, I scratched *married* out."

They face each other for a moment, neither one willing to speak or look away.

Madge breaks the silence. "I'd put it back in again now." She hands the book to me.

"Do I meet the rest of your criteria?" Hal asks, adopting a

comic air. "Do you think I have a nice ass?" He turns, pretending to look.

"Your ass is poetry, Surrey," Fitz says, and slaps it.

Madge and I stare at each other, wide-eyed for a moment, and then she starts to laugh.

"My poetry is poetry," Hal grumbles.

"Then you must regale us with more," Margaret says, and seats herself at the table, plucking another strawberry from the bowl. Hal launches into another bit of verse and Madge rolls her eyes, but a little wickedness shows up in her smile when she steals Margaret's strawberry and drops onto the bench beside her.

Fitz pries the book from my hands and puts his arms around me so he can read and kiss me at the same time.

"'Charming, good-humored, quick-witted.'" He pauses. "'Must get along with friends.'"

Peals of laughter from the table startle us away from each other, and Fitz grins, pulling me close again. "I think I can do that."

He closes the book and gives it back to me.

"I don't have all these attributes," he says. "I can't dance, I am not a poet."

"Those don't matter."

"I have little ambition."

"That was Margaret's word."

"And my body isn't as healthy as it once was."

He's telling me something I don't want to know. So I kiss

him, hard. Searching for answers to the questions I'm afraid to ask. About his place in the succession, about his father, about Baynard's, about his illness.

I tell myself I'm imagining it when I put my arms around him and find fragility. The knobs of his spine. The sharpness of his jaw. His shoulder blades like wings beneath his doublet.

"Fitz—"

He buries his face in my neck and I raise my face to the sky just turning pink—all words forgotten.

Then he turns away, suppressing a cough until he can't hold it back and the force of it bends him in half.

Hal jumps up, but Fitz straightens and rasps a commanding, "No!"

He sounds like his father. And we are silent. Staring.

Fitz wipes his mouth on the back of his hand, his eyes bright with pain.

"No, Hal." His words come from deep within his throat, but his tone is softer.

He will not look at me.

He takes a breath and it doesn't catch, so he smiles.

"We still have much to celebrate." He reaches for my hand and leads me to the table. "A little of that wine, if you please, Surrey."

Hal sweeps a goblet off the table and pours the wine with a flourish before handing it to Fitz on bended knee.

We all laugh and sit. None of us talks about it. Or about

Margaret's position in the succession. Or love or parents or executed queens. We feast on rich food and one another's company until the sun is well and truly set and the stars appear overhead and the summer night washes us clean of everything but hope.

8 July 1536

56

THE STREETS ARE THICK WITH MARKET GOERS, BEGGARS, LAW-
yers, and animals of all descriptions. There is a three-legged
dog that sits outside on the Strand, waiting for a scrap or a
kick, content to take either one.

All I want is to leave. To get out of the city. I'd even go back
to Kenninghall with its devastating north winds whistling
hollowly in the scrub. At least it would blow away the stink and
the suffering.

But I can't leave Fitz. I won't leave Fitz.

Even though I'm not allowed anywhere near him. Father
doesn't want contagion to spread to the court. The king doesn't
want anyone to know his son is ill.

Late one morning, the dog howls and I hear a banging on
the door, a raucous thudding that can only mean bad news.
The voices are high-pitched and frenzied and I can't wait for
the news to come to me. I have to go meet it at the top of the
stairs.

Madge comes up without even reaching for the wall. Her
hair has been hastily tied beneath her hood, and feathers of
it fan her face, a single crease of worry marbling her forehead.

She pushes me back into my room and shuts the door behind her. "They've taken Margaret to the Tower."

I almost trip over the stool behind me.

"What for?" I ask.

Madge screams a short curse through clenched teeth. "I think you bloody well know what for."

I turn away from her, wanting to vomit into the fire. "How much do they know?"

"Enough to put our friend and her *husband* into the Tower under the accusation of treason."

I start to shake. Is there no end to the prey that can be caught in the net of that one word? *Treason* tastes of gunmetal and sulfur. Poisonous.

The king's ire is more potent than we imagined. In April, we might have predicted exile. A hefty fine. Social obliteration. We knew we risked his displeasure. We didn't know we risked our lives.

Now we know better.

"How can we get to them?" I ask, searching my room for slippers, cloak, money.

"My father commands a contingent of the Tower guards, and my brother is a porter there. I can get in."

"That's perfect, Madge." I open a little box to spill a handful of groats onto the fireside table, and on closing the lid, let my finger rest on the enameled kingfisher. Madge waits while I send up a silent prayer for him.

But when I turn, she shakes her head.

"What is it?" I ask. "We must make haste, Madge. Let her know we're here for her."

"I can't get you in."

"You just said your father could get us in. Your brother."

"I can get in, Mary. But I can't let you come with me."

"Why not? She's still related to the king. Surely she's allowed visitors!"

Madge twists her hands together. The knuckles turn white. When she looks up again, there is a film of tears in her eyes.

"They suspect you were privy to it," she whispers. "If they find out it's true and they decide to press charges, you could go to the Tower, too, for misprision."

I shudder; visions of the crowd at the scaffold at the queen's execution flutter at the corners of my memory. Would I be executed on Tower Green? Or dragged to Tyburn on a hurdle like the Carthusian monks?

I shake my head. Love? Or survival? Which is more important?

"I still have to see her. Support her. She's my friend."

"I won't let you." Madge moves to stand in the doorway. "It will only make things worse for both of you. For all of us."

"It's not fair!" I shout. Rage overwhelms me and I pick up the little casket and throw it across the room, knocking ink and papers off my desk. The box hits the wall with a resounding *crack*, and my heart breaks with it.

"Life isn't fair, Duchess," Madge warns.

I scream over her, a long, strangled noise that sends her back against the wall. "Love should set you free!" I cry, my throat raw. "It should be honored. Respected. It should be sacred, Madge."

Tears spring to my eyes. For Margaret, yes, but, shamefully, also for me. For Fitz. For Anne Boleyn.

Madge wraps her arms around me. "I'm sure Margaret will be all right. He won't harm his own blood."

I don't remind her that King Henry has already executed a cousin or two, including my grandfather, the Duke of Buckingham.

I hang my head. "But will he abandon his own blood?"

"You mean, will he just leave Margaret in the Tower until she dies?"

I nod. But I'm thinking of Fitz.

"I don't know what he will do to her. Word is that Thomas is going to face the scaffold."

"We have to get them out." I close my eyes and lay my fingertips over the lashes, brushing away the tears.

"We have to give them hope."

Madge's voice betrays that she feels anything but hope.

"How?"

"By letting her know that we care."

"Could your brother take her secret messages?" I ask, remembering my mother hiding notes in oranges sent to Katherine of Aragon.

"I wouldn't want to put him in that kind of danger."

I nod. I understand. I would do anything to keep Hal from

getting mixed up in any kind of treasonous activity. Then an idea blooms clear and fragrant in my mind.

"They can't object to you taking her a book, can they?"

Madge looks at me expectantly.

I find it under a slurry of shed paper. I trace the gold letters. M. F.

I hand it to Madge. "It's just poetry and scribblings," I say. "But we can write something in there. Something that can let her know she has allies."

Madge's eyes meet mine and there is something of the old mischief in hers. A delight in mystery and mayhem.

I turn the pages until I come to the list of men we'd be willing to kiss. Half of them are already dead. I pick up a thin-bladed knife from the desk and carefully cut the page out.

Madge watches all this with a thin-lipped smile.

"Who knew such girlish things could eventually imprison us?" she asks.

"Sometimes I think it's the very fact of being girls that imprisons us." I hand her the book. "We broke the rules. We made up our own minds. Now we have to face the consequences."

Madge slowly turns the pages of the book, but I can see that she's not reading. She's not even seeing the words.

"What if the only way she can save herself is to deny him?" she says. "Say she wasn't ever really married."

I feel as if I've had the breath knocked out of me. Margaret loves Thomas; I'm sure of it. As reserved as she is, she wouldn't face the king's wrath for anything less than that.

"She married him, Madge. I was there."

"Don't tell me that!" Madge pushes me. "I refuse to be the reason that both of you go to the scaffold!"

"You knew it already! You guessed. You can't have my trust and then say you won't be trustworthy."

"What if I can't help it?" she cries. "What if they ask a question and I answer and somehow they know? What if I think they're asking about something else? Like I did with the queen. It's my fault. . . ."

"It's not your fault, Madge. It's not anyone's fault. It just happened."

"Nothing just happens. There's no such thing as fate or destiny."

"Or love at first sight?" I ask, remembering what Margaret told me the day she married. *I've known I loved him since you introduced us.*

"None of it is real! There are only rumors and lies that seem like truth, and truths that have to be represented as lies."

What happened between me and Fitz feels more like fate. Yes, our fathers created the marriage. We didn't have to fall in love.

We just did.

"Love is real," I tell her. "Maybe not at first sight. But when it happens, it's real. That's truth."

The tears start to come. It can't all end like this. I wish that one way or another we could prove—even just to ourselves— that love matters more.

"You know better than that, Duchess," Madge says quietly. "It doesn't matter what the truth is. At best, she'll be exiled, like Mary Boleyn. At worst, she could be executed. She has to deny it. Deny love. Deny she was ever married."

"Then she is the king's prisoner," I whisper. "In more ways than one."

"Aren't we all?" Madge asks. "Prisoners of the king, prisoners of our parents, prisoners of circumstance? Maybe we should all be looking for freedom instead of love."

"Aren't they the same thing?" Isn't that what the queen wished for me three years ago when I married Fitz?

"Not for Margaret, Duchess. And some of us would rather be free than have our hearts broken."

Madge dodges around me and picks up a quill from my desk, dips it in ink, and sits down. She writes so quickly, her words are barely legible—a narrow, drawn-out scrawl.

The poem that emerges is full of truth:

> But mourn I may these very days
> That were appointed to be mine.

"Did you write this?" I ask, watching over her shoulder. Jealous of her rhythm and meter.

Madge shakes her head. "Just one of the things one picks up when one spends undue amounts of time with rascal poets."

She blots the ink and closes the book.

"I'll take this to her," she says. "It's just poetry and

scribblings, right? We've been passing secret messages to one another with it for years. And now they can."

"Margaret and Thomas?"

"Why not?" Madge says. "If they can remind themselves that they love each other now, perhaps it will be more bearable when she says she doesn't."

20 July 1536

57

I AM MADE A PRISONER IN MY OWN HOME.

They come to my door days after Madge's visit, and I am already so agitated by the waiting that I'm ready to tell them anything just so they will go away. But I am able to answer truthfully most of their questions.

"Did you know Lady Margaret was planning to marry without the king's permission?"

"No." *She told me on the way there. I knew nothing before that.*

"Do you know how long their attachment has been going on?"

"No." *Though I can guess.*

And so on. It is only when they ask if I know what date they married that I have to lie. I hope they don't notice my fingers shaking within the pleats of my skirts.

I am asked not to leave London—not that I would. Father asks that I not leave the house. He says they will follow me. They will take note of where I go and whom I visit. They will ask more questions.

I sit at home and I wait for news. Madge stopped coming when I told her I was being watched. She doesn't want anyone to make the connection between me and her and Margaret and the book. I don't blame her. Instead, she sends a different messenger every other day. Once, a little blond-haired waif of a boy with patchy hair and a missing thumb who befriended the three-legged dog. I gave him half the coin left in my coffer and wished him well.

I am not arrested, which consumes me with equal measures of guilt and relief. I feel the fingers of my father in the workings of it all. He cannot be seen to take my side, but I believe he does, all the same. Though he certainly doesn't show his face around my residence.

Parliament passes the Second Act of Succession without Fitz there to vote. Any child born of the king and Jane Seymour will inherit the throne. Barring that, the king is able to name his successor.

And anyone forming a relationship with someone of royal blood without the king's permission will be found guilty of treason. We knew that Margaret and Thomas would have to face the king's wrath. Now they will have to face the furious conviction of the law. There can be no escape but repudiation.

The king moves the court to Sittingbourne in Kent, on his way to Dover. Out of the City. Away from contagion.

Away from Fitz.

And the knock at the door this morning is not made by a waif or a fishwife or a yeoman of the guard on his way to the ale halls. It is Madge herself.

"Fitz is worse."

Damn the king's interrogators and my father. Damn the king himself.

I don't even put on a cloak or order a litter. My shoes turn a brownish gray before I reach the end of the Strand, and my skirts are heavy with the dust of the street and God-knows-what-else by the time I reach St. James's Palace.

The streets are quiet here. As if everyone in the vicinity is holding a breath. Waiting. Or mourning.

The usher in his livery does not move fast enough for me. I walk right on his heels, nearly tripping us both, through the guard chamber and into the presence gallery.

Fitz's chamberlain tries to block my progress. I can see to the end of the presence chamber. I have a long way to go before I reach my husband. The chamberlain watches me impassively and I wish that I had claws with which to shred him.

"I have to see him."

"I'm afraid he'll see no one."

"He will see me."

"He's with his doctors now."

"Good." I push past him. "They'll be able to answer my questions."

I am the Duchess of Richmond and Somerset.

No one can stop me.

The ushers at the end of the presence chamber think about it. I can see it in their faces, in the way they glance at one another and then to the chamberlain, who has not followed me. They're looking for permission. Their hesitation is all the welcome I need, and I walk between them like Margaret parting a crowd, through the privy chamber to a closed door guarded by an usher dressed in green and gold standing directly in front of it.

Tudor livery. One of the king's men.

"I demand to see my husband." This is not a wish. Not a request. I start to walk around him, but he doesn't move. Doesn't even acknowledge my superiority. He stares straight ahead, not looking at me, trying not to disobey any orders—mine or otherwise.

"I am to allow in no one but the doctors," he says.

"If the king should come, wishing to see his son, what would you say to him?" I ask. I draw myself up to my full height, which still barely reaches his chin.

"I would . . . of course I would let him in."

"Then you must let me in as well."

"Forgive me, Your Grace, but your request cannot supersede that of the duke."

I may be the highest female noble in the land—higher now even than Margaret Douglas, imprisoned in the Tower—but I am not as high as my husband. Certainly not as revered.

Then I hear him coughing.

It is so much worse than before. It is a sound that seems to carry on forever. Painful and unceasing and impossible to control.

I look back up into the usher's face. Catch his eye. And hold it.

"Please."

It is not an order. Not even a request. It's a plea.

The usher looks away again, but something flickers behind his eyes.

Another long, low, raucous cough erupts from the bedroom

behind him, and he glances at me once. I see the fear in his eyes now. It settles low in my own stomach, churning there.

"Please," I say again.

The usher steps to one side. Still staring across the expanse of the room. Pretending I don't exist and therefore he won't be disobeying orders.

I flick the latch of the door and ease it open.

The room beyond is dark—curtains pulled on all the windows. The fire is high and the warm, wet air of breath clings to me as I step inside. It is blisteringly hot, suffocatingly so. And the smell.

It isn't linen and healthy sweat.

It's the sweat of fear. The greasy stink of phlegm. The metallic redolence of blood.

The doctor at Fitz's bedside turns. He has blood on his hands. He's been trying to bleed the fever out of my husband, who lies gray and listless beneath a heavy velvet counterpane, one arm outstretched as if waiting for crucifixion.

My first thought is to run. To turn around and slip out the door before he sees me. Before I'm faced with his illness—with his *death*—in person.

My joints give way and I stumble. No one is there to keep me upright, so I end up on my knees like a supplicant. The noise turns Fitz's head, and behind the hallucinatory feverishness, I see fear. Real fear.

"No."

I barely hear the word uttered, but I see his lips move. They're cracked and dry and he licks them once before saying it again.

"No."

"Your Grace," the doctor begins, and takes a step toward me, his bowl and lancet clanking. Sloshing.

I stand on my own.

"Leave us," I say to the doctor. He wasn't given orders by Fitz to keep me out. He should listen to what I say. Or at least to the way I say it.

"Your Grace, the duke needs quiet. He wishes to be alone."

"And alone he will be. Please make it so."

The doctor hesitates. I can't look away from the wicked instrument lolling in the blood-filled bowl. He sees me staring and covers it with a cloth, then exits without further argument, closing the door behind him.

"Go away." The whisper doesn't sound like Fitz at all. "I don't want you to see me like this."

His hair is slicked back from his forehead, and I can see the bones of his skull stark beneath his skin. His eyes, wide and afraid, are sunken in the hollow sockets.

I swallow my own fear. My grief and my terror of sickness. I reach for his hands and don't let go when he flinches. I bend over and kiss him on the forehead, his terrified eyes on my face the entire time.

"No," I tell him. "I will not leave you."

He opens his mouth to argue, but I climb into the bed beside him and we lie like that, holding hands together, staring up into the vast darkness of the tester above us.

I listen to the wheezing of each breath as he struggles to fill his lungs. I feel the catch before he lets out the breath and wait a panicked beat of his heart before he drags in the next. With each one, I'm afraid that moment of silence will be his last.

Finally, I can't stand it anymore. I send my mind back to a time when the possibilities were endless. When Margaret was unmarried, and Hal and Madge were in love, and Fitz . . . Fitz was strong and upright and healthy and looked to live forever—when I was on the verge of falling in love with him.

"Look," I say, pointing with my free hand to the vast velvet expanse above us. "The stars. Can you see them? There they are, the three that make up Orion's belt."

Fitz rasps a laugh. "It's summer. Orion isn't visible."

"Oh, yes he is." I turn my head to look at him, his profile sharp and angled. "He's right there. You're just not looking hard enough."

Fitz licks his lips, but there's little he can do to alleviate the deep cracks in them. My heart lurches and I look back up. We are silent for a moment.

"I see it," he says. "And the blanket of the Milky Way."

"Soon we'll hear the kingfisher," I say. "Just you wait. The dawn will come."

I want him to fight this. For me. I want him to come out victorious and to meet me on the other side, where we can live in Baynard's Castle for the rest of our days, reveling in the joy of watching someone else ascend the throne.

I move closer to lay my head on his shoulder, wrap my free arm around him. And I think that maybe it's up to me. If I hold him tightly enough. Love him with the depth of the ocean and the brightness of the sun.

"I wish I could show you more. I regret so much." His eyes don't even see me, they are so focused on what we didn't have. "I wish we'd been allowed to do this then," he says. "I wish we'd been allowed to do this more."

"*Wish* is a word that tastes of sugar syrup. It is sweet and delicate, but ultimately has no substance."

Fitz smiles then and turns his eyes back to me.

"What about other words? How do they taste?"

I want so badly to kiss him. To make it end. To make us safe. But I know what wishes taste like.

"*Star* tastes like a good, rich, full-bodied wine."

"Why?"

"Because the sky around it is dark and mesmerizing but the star itself is as intoxicating as hope."

"What else?"

"Your name." My voice cracks a little. "Fitz. Your name tastes like an outdoor feast. One that begins with marzipan and ends with laughter."

He smiles and squeezes my hand. Then he turns his eyes back to the canopy above us.

"What about *king*?"

My husband will never be king. And I realize, watching his profile, that I never wanted him to be. I always wanted him to be Fitz. "The word *king* tastes like a fig—sweet and fine, with the subtle crunch of seeds."

He nods, but doesn't speak. I lay my palm on his cheek and turn his face to mine.

"It's a taste you have to be sure you want. Because within it you can find the bitterness of worms or the sting of a hornet that has burrowed its way inside." His eyes have almost lost their color. "It is not a word I'd wish on anyone I love."

"What does *love* taste like?"

I remember what Queen Anne told me the day we were married. That love tastes like strawberries. But fruit is seasonal—it doesn't last and it isn't filling.

I move my mouth closer to his ear. "Love tastes like bread," I tell him. "Warm and yeasty and fresh from the oven."

"But bread is so plain."

"Not plain," I assure him. "Simple. Uncomplicated. And absolutely necessary for survival."

I can feel the tears coming. They scratch at the back of my eyes. They clog my throat.

"When did you know you loved me?" Fitz asks.

I cast my mind back. Back to when he told me what love feels like. Back to my kiss with Weston that proved I felt *something*. Back to that aborted first kiss. And forward again.

"When you showed me the stars." Even before he kissed me.

"I knew from the moment I saw you enter the chapel on our wedding day. It was love at first sight."

I laugh. "There's no such thing. Besides, you'd seen me before that."

Laboriously, he lifts himself up.

"I'd seen you as a little girl. The scrawny little sister of my closest friend. But the day we got married, I saw you as the woman you are. Beautiful."

He kisses me lightly, his lips like paper, then rolls onto his back and closes his eyes.

I still feel like a little girl. Scrawny and terrified. And I cry. As silently as I can.

Fitz lifts his left hand, and touches the damp spot that's spreading on the sleeve of his shirt. Then feels my face, like a blind man, and clumsily wipes my tears. His skin feels like husks, scratchy and dry and empty of life already.

"I hope those aren't for me," he says through the rasp in his chest.

I shake my head. I can't answer.

"Because you can't rid yourself of me that easily. I plan to come back to haunt you."

His dry laugh turns into a cough that he stifles deep within his chest, his face turned to the curtains. When I sit up, I can see the pain distorting his features.

"You're not—"

"I am." Fitz turns back to me. "I'm dying, Mary."

The weight of my pain bends me over and I lay my forehead on his chest. He puts a hand on the back of my neck, smoothing aside the veil of my hood so he can touch the skin there. The other hand strokes my cheek, and I lift my face to look at him.

"You're beautiful," he says, and takes me back to the first

day we sat in bed together, surrounded by the men and ladies of the court, who laughed at our fumbling embarrassment.

"You don't think . . ." I can't say it. I can't even think it. I blink rapidly, but all the tears are gone, settling deep in my chest and swelling, like to drown me.

"What?" he asks quietly.

"Is it my fault?" The words come in a rush and then falter. "They didn't want us to consummate the marriage because the king was afraid it would make you ill. I . . . I threw myself at you. I made you . . ."

Fitz starts to cough, the rhythm of it shaking the entire bed. I sit up in terror, move to call the doctor. To run. But he grabs my wrist, and when I turn back, I see he's laughing.

With tears in his eyes.

"You didn't *make* me do anything. Sex can't kill anyone." He looks down at our hands clasped together, at his own sunken chest. "Well. Maybe it could kill me now." He pulls in a tired, ragged breath. "But . . . it's ridiculous. Something proven wrong over and over again. This? This is just . . . bad luck."

I trace the outline of his hand with my forefinger, and then the lines of his palm. I wish I could read there that he will live another forty years. But with the swelling of his joints, all the lines are shortened, and I'm not sure which is the life line, anyway. So I just trace them all.

Fitz closes his hand over mine.

"You believe me. Don't you?"

I nod. But I'm not sure I do. It seems that everyone who

broke the rules has had to pay for it somehow. Anne Boleyn tried to make herself heard. And was silenced for it. Margaret married a man she loved. And is in the Tower because of it. Madge broke every rule there was, trying to find love. And is all alone. And here I am, holding the hand of my dying husband. Trying to believe I didn't kill him.

"Don't tell my father." Fitz pulls himself up a little, still holding my hand. "Don't tell him anything."

"Why?" But I know the answer.

"Because he *will* blame you. He already blames her."

I pause.

"The queen?"

"Anne Boleyn. He thinks it's slow-acting poison." Fitz coughs another laugh. "My father can't stand the idea that sometimes things just happen. He has to have a cause. An adversary. Something to fight and beat down. The French. The Empire. The pope. The church." He pauses. "The Boleyns."

He squeezes my hand once.

"Don't let the next thing be you, Mary."

I nod and he lets me go, his hands falling limply to the counterpane, his head resting back against the pillows. He looks spent. His eyes turn to the drapes at the window. As if he can see through them to London beyond.

"He will not visit me."

"The king?"

"My father. Too afraid of contagion. Too afraid of death."

I cannot tell Fitz that the king has left the City. That his father has abandoned him as he lies here, dying. So for a long time, neither of us says anything. We watch imaginary stars spin across the velvet drapes, waiting for the dawn.

"He'll never know what I'm worth."

"I do." I want to shelter him. Protect him. Hide him from death and his father and everyone who expected so much from him, and left him to expect so little in return.

More than that, I want him to protect me.

Though I know he can't.

As if he knows what I'm thinking, he says, "What hurts most is leaving you." He adjusts his body, so we are touching each other, full-length—head to toe. "I will not haunt you as a ghost. But I will always be with you." He lays his hand on my chest, just above my heart. "I will take on your sadness, Mary. When you feel it lift, you'll know it's me."

My breath comes a tiny bit easier until I hear his stop. And start again.

I stay with him as his breathing settles, and each whistling, shallow breath is regular. I assume he's asleep, and don't move, for fear of waking him.

He must think I'm asleep, too, and that I won't hear him speak.

"I'm not ready," he whispers in the dark. "Please don't let me die alone."

But he does.

23 July 1536

58

THE WORD *DEATH* TASTES LIKE CLAY. COLD AND BARREN AND viscid, it leaves a gritty patina on the tongue and teeth.

Father comes when the sky outside is still deep gray, and the only thing that differentiates him from the rest of my room is the movement of his shadow. I know why he is there. I don't let him know that I'm awake.

I wait like a held breath, because until he says the words, I can believe it's not true.

Even after he says them—after he leaves me alone in the half-light—I don't remember exactly what he's said.

Because words no longer matter.

59

MUCH LATER, AFTER THE SKY HAS BRIGHTENED, THOUGH THE sun remains hidden, Hal comes to my door, haggard and shaken. He doesn't speak.

I can't bear to hear it, anyway.

Together, we sit in my room, silent. He writes until his fingers are stained and the paper piles up like leaves in autumn. All I can do is lay my head on my desk and watch him as the tears refuse to fall, leveed by the magnitude of my grief.

That is where Father finds us when he returns.

"The king did not take the news well."

The *king* didn't even see Fitz before he died. The king didn't send one word of love. The king may only be disappointed that he no longer has a son. I know nothing about the king's grief or the depth of it. All I know is that my own cannot be fathomed.

I stare at my father, my words caught somewhere below my grief, deep behind my breastbone.

Father doesn't seem to notice my silence. Or takes it as acceptance. He paces back and forth in the little room. I glance at Hal, whose head is still bent over his parchment.

"He has put me in charge of the funeral." Father's voice finally takes on a melancholy tone.

At least there's that. I imagine all the court at Westminster Abbey—all the dukes and earls and even Thomas Cromwell—their heads bowed over the Duke of Richmond and Somerset as Archbishop Cranmer speaks praise and sympathy.

"He suggests you go into mourning at Kenninghall."

The king suggests I go back to my childhood home. That I go back to childhood.

I finally find my voice. "After the funeral."

Father clears his throat.

"It won't be in London. I will arrange to have him buried quietly at Thetford. The king doesn't want it to be obvious."

I feel a creeping dread curl up my spine. Like Fitz's shadow is behind me, holding very still. Waiting for whatever remains of his father's absent love to manifest itself.

Father stops talking.

"Why?" I ask.

Father narrows his eyes at me. "I believe he wants it to be a secret."

"What?" My voice is sharper than I intended. "Fitz's death? Or his funeral?"

"Both."

Hal stands, knocking his pen and several pieces of paper to the floor, his expression slack and as white as the parchment in front of him.

The king wants no reminders of his son. He wants to erase Fitz as thoroughly as he did Anne Boleyn.

"The king wouldn't acknowledge him in life and now he wants his death obscured as well?" I hold on to the edge of my own table, knuckles showing white under my skin.

"You are getting dangerously shrill, girl." Not *Daughter.* Certainly not *my dear.*

"*He* wants to keep it a secret. *He* doesn't want commotion or pageantry for his son. *He* wants to pretend it never happened. That Fitz never happened."

"Mary . . ." Hal's tone is a warning. I look at him. His lips are gray and his eyes are rimmed with red, a smudge of ink beneath the left one.

I turn back to Father. "How will keeping it a secret help anything?"

"I believe he's hoping to announce that Queen Jane will give him an heir."

"I hope her womb is as impoverished as the king's heart."

The room is so still, even the dust motes stop dancing. Father doesn't move. Doesn't even breathe.

"That statement will not go any farther than this room."

Father's lips barely move; his words don't stir the air.

"You are no longer under your husband's control and are now my responsibility. You will not jeopardize my future by your injudicious words or actions. If I hear you say anything like that again, I will personally whip you."

He's never threatened me before. All his anger—all his violence—has always been directed toward my mother. I always thought it justifiable.

I look at Hal, but he is so submerged in the well of his own grief that he doesn't see me.

Father steps so close to me that I can feel the anger radiating off him in waves. "I will tell you the same thing I told the king's recalcitrant daughter. If you remain so in opposition to your monarch, I will beat your head against the wall until it is as soft as a baked apple. Don't think to defy me, girl. You are mine, now, and I will do with you what I like."

Hal turns away. Back to his writing. It seems to me that Father almost smiles.

My mind gropes for some kind of support. For the spirit Fitz promised would haunt me. But there is no rescue.

Father strides to the door and pauses without looking back. "Pack your things. It's time you went home."

Kenninghall
July 1536

60

My father's house is grand and cold. Its glaring stone front faces the dry scrub of the sandy heath. Miles of gorse and stunted pines, all obscured by the sandstorms that spin down from the north like a lacerating screen.

I feel so far removed from anything Fitz ever said or was, I hardly believe I knew him at all. It's as if the last three years have vanished, and I'm thirteen again, awkward and flat-chested and so bent in on myself I'm almost concave. Always looking inward and always finding myself lacking.

My mother is not here. Not physically.

But I feel her in the stones. They are as hard as she is. Unflinching, ever watching. Immovable.

Hal is here, closeted in a little room. He never comes out except to call for more wine. I worry that my grief is somehow less than his, because I can still function. I stand and sit and walk and eat. I cannot write. I don't know which is worse, because Hal seems to be disappearing, each word he writes shaving away a little of his soul.

His wife, Frances, has gone to visit her parents at their castle in Essex. I don't know if it's because she can't face his misery or because Hal asked her to go.

Jane Boleyn is here. She, too, is a widow. She, too, should be able to call upon her family—or her husband's—to take her in and meet her needs. But her father-in-law will not have her. Whether it's because he wants no taint of the traitors he raised, or because he blames her for George's death, I don't know. I can't ask.

I have my own grief.

Every morning, waking up is like struggling to the surface of a pond from deep within its depths. If I open my eyes before I reach it, I will drown.

However, it is the mornings I wake and don't remember that are the worst. Because then it hits me like a stone, and all I want is to sink back beneath the surface and stay there.

Father takes Fitz's body to Thetford Priory in the back of a wagon covered in straw. There is no string of mourners lined up behind it, just two men I don't know, dressed in green and unsmiling solemnity. Hal rides Fitz's favorite horse, bequeathed to him in his will with a saddle and velvet harness. His face is blank, waiting to be written on.

There are rumors that the king will close Thetford, as he has so many other monasteries. That he will seize the assets and turn the monks out on the roads of Norfolk. But my grandfather is buried here. And Fitz will be, too. Surely, the king has enough respect to leave them untouched. Surely, he can allow Fitz that much.

The stone floor of the chapel rings with the sound of Father's boots as he walks me toward the altar. It is cold and stark and I can hear the wind outside blowing the summer southward.

This bleak place is nothing like the chapel royal at Hampton Court. I do not wear pink. None of Fitz's family—his blood family—are here. Not his father or his mother or either of his half sisters.

I don't look at the lead-lined casket. I don't imagine what's inside. I don't hear what the prior says. I go through the motions of the ceremony, bowing when necessary, kneeling, genuflecting. Weeping. I hear no words of comfort. I see no symbols of everlasting life.

I leave him there. My husband. Imprisoned in lead and stone.

And I return to my own imprisonment.

Kenninghall
August 1536

61

ALL OF FITZ'S THINGS—HIS CLOTHES, FURNISHINGS, GILT, JEW-els, landholdings, everything—revert to the crown. The king gets it all, except for two silver spoons and one overlaid in gilt, rough around the edges and slightly bent. I get those. Three spoons for three years of marriage.

The heat of August settles over the fens, making everyone sluggish and irritable. Jane Boleyn keeps to her room. She has petitioned the king—through Cromwell—to claim her marriage jointure from her father-in-law. And to retain her title of Lady Rochford. As she is—plain Jane Boleyn—she has nothing. No money, no home, no prospects. All she can do is wait for an answer, hoping every letter that arrives will mean her salvation.

A flurry of messages comes for my father, causing Jane to rush from her rooms, only to turn back, disappointed. With every letter, my father's countenance grows darker and more frightening.

Or perhaps more frightened.

When a leash of greyhounds arrives, followed by a leash of merlins, Father throws the accompanying note to the floor with a growl that causes the poor dogs to cower in the corner.

He bellows at the servants to bring him paper and ink and sits down furiously to write.

Hal takes little notice. He is drowning in his own words in the corner. Cautiously, I pick up the note. The hand is not one I recognize, but the first sentence I see reads, *I am sorry for the great misfortune that has happened to you through the loss of the Duke of Richmond. . . .*

His loss.

"But I have lost everything." My voice sounds as if it has journeyed across a great distance.

Father turns, and when he speaks his tone is so cold the very room shivers with dread.

"And you think I have not?" he asks. "They say I shall be taken to the Tower."

Hal looks up sharply.

"Why?" I cannot feel my fingers or toes. Even my lips are numb. I can't lose my father as well. I will be left with less than nothing.

I will be left with my mother.

Father fixes me with a look of hostility I have never seen.

"Because of the funeral of *your* husband," he spits. "No." He stops and sneers at me. "Because of the funeral of the king's son."

"He was—"

"The king"—Father won't even let me speak—"who told me to keep it quiet, is now saying that the funeral wasn't done as befitted the king's son. That it wasn't done with enough pomp. That we didn't treat the bastard with the respect and solemnity that should be accorded to one so high and mighty."

Hal stands, and I can see he's reliving the funeral just as I am. It was quiet, yes. But we accorded Fitz more respect and solemnity than the court ever did.

"The king," Father continues, "who is mercurial at best, has now decided that his son deserved a funeral at Westminster. That he deserved a gilded carriage in the streets of London. That he deserved a princess and not the lowly daughter of a duke."

"Well, perhaps he should have thought of that earlier," I snap.

Father strides across the room to me so swiftly, I'm afraid he'll knock me down. He stands practically on my toes, and despite the fact that I want to step away—that I want to *run*—I stand my ground.

"You think you can criticize the king?" he says. "You think you are so worldly because you spent three years in the company of that *whore*? She taught you nothing but how to talk back. Now she is gone, and so is the child you married, and you are left alone. You were supposed to be my triumph and now you are worthless to me. Worthless."

My limbs have gone stiff with shock. This is my father, the one who always took my side against Mother. The one who told me I deserved to marry the king's son. The one who believed I could be a duchess.

A queen.

Hal, in his corner, does nothing.

Father looks at me as he would a horse. Weighing my

usefulness against the inconvenience of keeping me. I feel naked in front of him. Like he's trying to see all my secrets.

"Did you?" Father asks.

"Did I what?"

"Know him." Father steps so close to me that his breath tickles my ear. "Did you know him, Mary?"

I can't answer. I stare at the gold braid in front of me.

He grips my chin and raises it so I look him in the eye. "Did you consummate your marriage? Against the king's wishes?"

Yes.

He puts the flat of his hand on my belly, and something inside me snaps. Like the delicate pop of a bone tipping back into place. It brings with it just as much pain.

He is exactly like the king.

For him, my entire identity is fettered to my womb. And like Anne Boleyn, when that has proved worthless, I am only worthy of contempt.

"No."

What I did with Fitz is not for Father or the king to know. The night I spent with Fitz is mine. And his. It wasn't to fulfill a contract or to follow my father's orders. Love is what's important. Not the elevation or even the survival of the Howards.

Father steps away. "I thought not."

I do not look at Hal. And he doesn't contradict my lie.

Father walks across the room and throws open the heavy velvet drapes that shield me from the vivid sameness of the view outside the window.

"The king says the marriage is not valid," he says. "It was

not consummated, and therefore wasn't a real marriage at all."

My thoughts swim in the thick sea of grief and I stare out the window at the flat white sky above the gorse. It's what they all tried to tell me. Hal. Madge. Fitz. Even the king's daughter, Lady Mary. A marriage unconsummated is no marriage at all.

"Three years is a long time." It's almost like I'm not there, and he's talking to himself. "I could have married you off to any number of different men by now. Thomas Seymour, perhaps."

He rubs his chin while I try not to vomit.

"I will have to play this carefully."

He approaches me again and puts his hands on my shoulders, as he used to. When he said I would be the triumph of the family. Tears spring to my eyes unbidden. It's been so long since I was touched. Since someone cared.

Father has not yet said he agrees with the king. He will fight for me.

"I say that when I deserve to go to the Tower, then Tottenham shall turn French." He pats me once, as though all is mended.

He is thinking only of himself.

He cannot see me. He cannot see my shock or my grief.

Neither can Hal, who has gone back to his words.

I am invisible.

Squeezed breathless by a crowd of ghosts.

62

Father returns to court, and shortly afterward Jane Boleyn receives word that she is invited into the new queen's household.

I am almost jealous.

She will return to a place where women are not welcome and unmarried women are prey. To a place where her name is vilified either for being associated with a disgraced queen or for being the author of that disgrace.

At least she will not be alone.

"Why do you want to go back?" My voice is throaty. A croak, like that of the frogs down at the pond.

"Why?" Jane turns to me. "Because it's the only place to be. It is the only place."

She says this as if it makes sense. As if it will convince me. I wonder if it does.

The word *court* is like the shell of an egg. You don't know what it will taste like inside until you break it.

"I am nothing here," Jane finishes simply.

"You'll be nothing there."

Her gaze doesn't waver. Her eyes are odd. Golden like a lion's. Her deep-brown hair is streaked by the sun coming in from the window. The silver threads glitter like tinsel.

"At least I'll be there," she says. "At least I'll be useful."

"Useful?"

"I will serve the queen."

"You'll serve Jane Seymour. The woman who replaced your sister-in-law. Who replaced your *friend*. I thought the Boleyns stuck together."

She stands so quickly her stool clatters backward to the floor. The noise startles me, and I look up at her, fast approaching.

"There are no more Boleyns, or haven't you noticed?" she says. She's tiny, but she towers over me. "Just me and my father-in-law, who was disappointed in his children when they lived and even more so now they're dead. He certainly isn't sticking to anything but his own skin."

"So you will, too." I don't flinch or back down or shrink into myself. She can't scare me with her fury. I'm beyond caring.

"I *will* stick to my own skin," she says. She's shaking, but I can see it's not from anger anymore. It's from guilt. I can see it in her eyes.

"No one else will," she says. "Not Thomas Boleyn. Certainly not the Howards, who will cut you down as soon as look at you. So I have to make something of myself. The only thing I'm good for is service to a queen. I've already served two. What's one more? It's unlikely anyone will want to marry me."

I stand so I can look her in the eye. "After what you did to your last husband, I should think not."

She flinches, but doesn't shrink away. "It wasn't my fault."

"Wasn't your fault you sent him to the scaffold?"

"Wasn't my fault I told them," she whispers.

I remember telling Cromwell that everyone flirts—even the queen. Madge told him everything she knew, thinking she was saving me. I'd like to pretend it wasn't our fault, either.

I'm afraid it was.

"He wouldn't stop asking." Jane's voice is barely audible. "Always the same questions, a hundred different ways. Until they felt like beatings."

She pulls a rope of pearls out of the pocket at her waist and clicks them like rosary beads. "Cromwell knew everything. Everything I knew and more."

"But it wasn't true," I say emphatically.

"None of it was true," she says. "And all of it was true. She said those things. She told Norris that if anything happened to the king, he'd look to have her. She told Smeaton he wasn't good enough for her. She let Francis Weston believe he was in love with her."

"But she never slept with her brother, Jane. If you didn't tell Cromwell that, I don't know who did."

Jane is silent for a long while.

"Cromwell knew, somehow," she says. "He knew about an argument I had with Anne a long time ago. So long ago, I think it was even before the king's interest. I accused Anne of . . . of that. I accused her of having her brother in her room. I was so jealous. He loved her so much."

Jane stutters to an inaudible murmur. I step away from her in disgust.

"George Boleyn did not love his sister in that way," I tell her.

"I know that!" she screams. "But that doesn't change the fact that I thought it once. In some kind of insane jealousy. Someone overheard! Someone told Cromwell, and he wouldn't let it go. He asked and asked and asked and asked. He wouldn't stop asking until I told him what I'd said. That I had accused Anne of loving her brother and not wanting to marry anyone else. And then he stopped."

Jane stops, too. I almost don't hear her when she adds, "The silence was blissful. For a while."

"So now you want to go back to court and ruin someone else's life?"

"I will only do as I'm asked. I will serve the queen better than anyone. Because I won't be acting in my own interests, only hers."

"If you tell yourself that enough times, it might become true."

"The only thing I'm good for is service to someone else," Jane says. "It's the only thing any of us are good for, Mary. Women. A wife, a daughter, a servant. I cannot have thoughts or wishes of my own. I have nothing. I am nothing."

Is this all that is left for me? Loyal service to a queen I cannot respect in the court of a king I cannot tolerate?

When she turns to walk away, her back is straight. She looks nothing like that woman who has haunted the rooms and gardens of Kenninghall for these weeks. It's almost like she's proud to be nothing. To have made the choice to be nothing on her own, and to live only for someone else.

Or perhaps she did that before. She has been nothing but

George Boleyn's wife—Queen Anne's sister-in-law—for years. Defined by her association with others.

Like me.

The daughter of a duke.

The wife of a duke.

But nothing on my own.

"Jane," I call out, my voice once again cragged.

I reach into my pocket for the piece of ribbon and the little jewel, the golden *A* swinging from my fingers. I can think of no one better to give it to Princess Elizabeth. I hold it out to Jane, palm up.

"Take this."

"No." Jane steps back, a look of horror on her face, the pearls whispering beneath her fingers.

"Please."

"No." She shakes her head.

"She wanted it to go to her daughter." The lie tastes bitter, but it's the only way I can think to convince her. "Elizabeth may come to court."

Sooner than I will.

Jane stares at the jewel in my palm. I see her wavering.

"When she's ready," she says. There is a hunger in her voice. She wants it for herself. A Boleyn connection. Something to hold on to and crush with the pearls in her pocket.

"It's hers," I say, desperate for her to understand. "It's Elizabeth's now. It may be the only thing she'll ever have."

Like my ridiculous spoons. The ones that I keep beneath

my pillow so I can hold them when I sleep. The only tangible things I have to connect me to Fitz.

Jane nods, but she's not really listening. I let her take the jewel from my hand, watch as she examines the ribbon it hangs on. She strokes the single pearl straight on her palm.

I almost take it back. But her fingers snap closed over it as if she knows what I'm thinking.

"It will be delivered," she says. "She deserves to be remembered."

I think, as she leaves the room, *Don't we all?*

63

THE WORD *ALONE* CHANGES FLAVOR DAILY. IT IS HOLLOW WITH the absence of crowds. One day seasoned with the salt of grief, the next ripe with expectation.

Father is gone to court. Jane has followed him. Hal has gone to Norwich on Father's business.

But Madge enters Kenninghall like the surprising discovery of a single, succulent fruit long after harvest.

She sweeps into the room, her gown a pastiche of yellow and green and orange and blue. She looks like a mythical bird—a phoenix—come to grant me wishes. She hugs me until my tears are finally squeezed out of me.

"You got thin." Madge holds me at arm's length and looks me up and down, frowning. "Being alone doesn't suit you."

Not Madge, too.

"I refuse to go back to court." My voice is hard and bitter as a seed, and I will not look at her.

"I *was* going to say it's a lucky thing I came to visit and brought cake." Madge fists her hands onto her hips and stares me down.

"I'm sorry, Madge. Father is trying to get me to go serve Jane. Get married. He even suggested Thomas Seymour."

Madge puts a finger to her chin and raises her eyes to the ceiling—her classic thinking pose. "You could do worse," she says, and then grins at me. "But not much. That man is a scoundrel."

"You once thought he was handsome," I remind her, feeling a little of the ice around my heart melting.

"A handsome scoundrel, then," she modifies. "But not one I'd wish on my worst enemy, much less my closest friend."

We stand for a minute in the silence that surrounds her statement.

"How is Margaret?" I ask.

"The rumors are that they will both be condemned. She will have to deny him. Prove it was never consummated if she wants to save herself."

The irony that bubbles up in my throat tastes like week-old wine.

"I have to prove mine was." Everything hinges on the act of copulation. It's so unfair.

"Duchess." Madge takes a step toward me. "Mary. I'm so sorry about Fitz. I'm sorry about the queen and about everything. But mostly, I'm sorry about Fitz. I know how much you loved him."

I nod, unable to make my tongue and throat work past the tears that threaten.

"And I'm sorry . . ." She trails to a halt.

"Don't be." She doesn't need to continue.

"No," she says. "I'm sorry I was jealous."

I look up. She's staring at me so intently.

"I was jealous of what you had. Of all of it. Of your status and your family and your friendship with the queen. Mostly, I was jealous of what you had with Fitz."

"It doesn't matter now," I tell her. "Now, I've got nothing."

"No. That's not true. You had love. Real love."

"Had. Past tense."

"You haven't stopped loving him."

"No." It's choking me.

"I'm sorry, Duchess. I have to say this. I was so jealous of what you had with Fitz, I wanted some of it. I couldn't have your status, no matter whom I slept with. I couldn't have your family."

"You wouldn't want it," I mutter.

"I wanted the love you shared with Fitz."

I want to sink down to the floor. All of the things of mine that Madge wanted I no longer have.

"Stop," I whisper.

"I wanted to know what that felt like." Madge steps forward again and grabs my hands. "I'm so sorry for what I did."

I stare at her hands. I'm terrified to comprehend what she is saying. She keeps talking about Fitz. About her jealousy.

"What did you do?" I finally raise my eyes to hers.

"He didn't tell you?" Madge drops my hands and backs away. "I thought he told you everything."

"What happened?" I don't want to know.

"I went to his room at Greenwich," Madge whispers. "It was before May. Before . . . everything."

"Oh, God, Madge, what did you *do*?" I want to throttle her.

"I wanted him to look at me the way he looked at you! I wanted someone . . . I thought that maybe he could . . . I don't know what I thought." She takes a deep breath and looks me in the eye. Just like the queen used to when she was facing something difficult.

"I kissed him," she says.

"You didn't," I say. I say it as a statement of fact. I can't believe she would do anything like that to me. That he would let such a thing happen. I picture his mouth on hers and feel thoroughly ill.

And jealous. *I* want that memory.

"No, Mary," she says, her voice growing stronger, "*he* didn't. It was like kissing stone."

I almost laugh. I know exactly what that feels like.

"He sent me away," she continues. "I went to him a couple of days later and asked if he'd told you, and he said he hadn't. I begged him to tell you, Mary, because I couldn't. I felt so horrible about myself I couldn't even confess. He said he didn't want to break up our friendship over something so trivial. That's what he called it. Trivial."

"He never told me." I don't know how I feel about that. "He should have told me."

"I never wanted you to hate me. It wasn't about you."

"No, it was always about you, wasn't it? None of the rest of us matter. Not me, not Hal, not the queen. None of us."

Madge rocks back on her heels and looks down at her clasped hands. She says nothing.

"Well, now you've got one of your wishes, anyway, Madge

Shelton." I feel the anger bubbling up inside me like hot oil. Spattering and raising blisters. "You no longer have to show me any deference. I am just like you. I am plain Mary Howard. My husband is dead. I am no one. Nothing. Just like you."

Madge flinches. She takes every blow until the last one. Then she looks up at me, understanding dawning.

"What do you mean, you're just like me?"

"The king says that because we never consummated the marriage, the marriage never happened."

"No," she says, so forcefully that I blink. "That's not fair. The world deserves better than that, Mary. *Fitz* deserves better. You think you serve his memory well by just giving up?"

I shrug. I want to keep his memory, not serve it.

But Madge isn't finished.

"You're giving in. You're saying that everyone has always been right. Your mother for telling you you're nothing, your father for using you as a pawn, the king for never giving Fitz anything unless it served a purpose. He didn't even give him a decent *burial*."

I was a part of that. That was my father's doing.

"What can I do?" I ask. "He's the king." Even Fitz couldn't stand up to him.

"You can do what's right. That's what I've been most jealous about this whole time. That you do the right thing."

"I do what's expected."

"No!" Madge shakes me a little. "You're friendly and intelligent and literate and *good*. You remain loyal in the face of even

496

the worst betrayals. . . ." Madge chokes. "You have an opportunity. With your title and your jointure, you can be someone. Someone with a position and money. Someone on your own. Not dependent. Not a vassal." She pauses.

I finish for her. "Free."

The word rings like a bell and tastes like dawn.

64

Now that I've tasted the word, I find I want it. More than anything. Like love, freedom is intoxicating. And having it can only make me stronger.

Margaret should have been free to marry whom she liked. Madge and Hal should have been free to love each other. Queen Anne should have been free to speak without her words being twisted into treason. We all should have been.

Madge is right. I resolve to be free to make my own decisions. To control my own emotions.

Then my mother comes to visit.

My maid throws open the door to my room just after dawn with barely a whisper of a curtsy, the door banging against the wall and snapping back at her before she can stand straight. She trips forward, head bowed.

Mother elbows her way into my room, her skirts flapping around her like the wings of a great bird. My maid looks like she wants to sink *through* the floor, and I wish I could join her when she bobs out the door.

"Out," Mother says. At first, I think she's speaking to the maid, who left before dismissal. Then Mother reaches for my wrist and yanks me out from under the counterpane. "Now, miss. You are not a duchess to me, you're a little girl, and when I say to get out of bed: You. Get. Out."

My feet don't touch the ground before my elbows do, and Mother towers over me, glaring down as if someone has dropped a decomposing carcass on the floor at her feet.

"You're finished," she says, surveying the room, one lip curled. "I am here to get you back on your feet. That card has been played and you are no longer required to pretend to grieve."

It's not a pretense.

I cannot say the words. Mother has silenced me as effectively as the king silenced Anne Boleyn.

"Get up." Mother goes to my robing chamber and draws out a gown, bodice, and sleeves. "It does not do to mourn. It goes against the very will of God. You will not question him, will you? Succumbing to your grief only proves your weakness."

I rise from the floor and slowly pick up the heavy skirts she has laid out for me. I thought I had recovered from my grief. Enough to recover my sense of self. But the very presence of my mother has knocked it out of me.

She has knocked the taste of freedom from my lips.

"So you are back to nothing," she says. "Just like me."

Mother turns. Watching me. Looking at my body and all its imperfections. My round belly and stocky ankles and stubby fingers.

"My father was the Duke of Buckingham. Descended from Edward III. Son of the queen's sister." This is an old refrain. The line of the Staffords, ad infinitum.

She doesn't continue. Staffords, Beauforts, Nevilles. She doesn't mention our common ancestor with King Henry, John of Gaunt. Whose own illegitimate son was father of the first Duke of Somerset and King Henry's connection to the crown.

Instead, she presses her mouth into a line. "When I was fifteen, my father gave me to a man more than twice my age."

I had never thought of it before, but the difference in age between Madge and the king is almost the same as that between my father and my mother. He is old enough to be *her* father.

"I did as my father bade me. I did as my husband bade me. His first wife had been a princess. A daughter of Edward IV. And though she never gave him any children, I could never be her equal. I did everything he asked. I surrendered. My life. My title. My body in his bed."

I think about what Fitz and I had together. It didn't feel like surrender. It felt like consent. Like validation.

"I gave him children. An heir, which is more than that whore Anne Boleyn could ever do."

Anger starts to bubble low in my belly.

Mother levels her gaze at me. "More than you could do."

She turns me around and pulls so violently on the laces of my bodice that I cry out, the stiff buckram pressing my breasts flat against my ribs. I am a child again. Subject to her poisonous words and savage temper.

She pauses, her fingers caught up in the half-made knot behind my back. She leans in, her words raw against my ear.

"Did you fuck the little bastard?"

I wrench myself away from her, gasping a breath as my

bodice loosens, and stumble to my knees. I turn and shout up at her.

"I *loved* him!"

Mother freezes; animosity flows from her very pores and pools around her.

I scramble to my feet, almost as surprised as she is. I have never spoken back to my mother. But now that I have lost everything, I find I have nothing else to lose. My bid for freedom has to start somewhere.

"And he loved me. Which is more than I can say about you!"

Mother approaches me with the intensity of a caged lion, and I want to shrink from her. Slouch. Look away. Curl in on myself.

Instead, I force myself to stand upright, shoulders back, neck elongated. I keep my gaze on my mother's eyes as she draws back her hand, ready to strike. I don't flinch or move away.

She stops herself before her hand connects with my face. "Silly girl." She pats my cheek. Hard. "You think love will save you? It is the duty of a wife *and* a daughter to submit to ill-treatment. Imprisonment. That's what the king says."

"Fitz never treated me ill. Father—"

"Your father only ever acted in his own best interests, Mary. Not yours."

Father always took my side. Until it didn't suit him anymore.

"He will prostitute you to the next lordling who makes himself available," she continues. "He will parade you at court like fresh meat before a pack of dogs, claiming you are unsullied and eminently suitable. Or he will exile you to an empty prison."

As he did with her.

Suddenly I see her. Ruled by her father, her husband, her king. Ever warring with her jailers and rattling the bars of her prison while trying to lock me up as well. In fear and self-doubt and uncertainty. In believing I wasn't good enough.

It wasn't my mother who imprisoned me, but my father who imprisoned us both. By making us believe we couldn't function as individuals.

Perhaps my mother can't. Perhaps she needs her prison to define her.

"No, he won't, Mother," I tell her. "I have a key." One that is simple and true and bright as brass.

She narrows her eyes. Suspicious.

I press forward. "I don't accept your rules. I don't belong to you or to Father or to the king. I gave my heart to Fitz. But my mind and body are my own."

For an instant I see that other side of her. Helpless. Broken. She raises her chin to look down at me, that dangerous steel in her eyes. Her lips only tremble for a second before she presses them together in a flat line.

"Then I shall leave you to your father's mercy," she says. "Or lack of it. Your future is now your own."

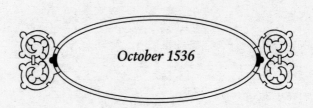

October 1536

65

WHEN FATHER AND HAL RETURN TO KENNINGHALL, I AM prepared.

My future is my own.

I have always been under my father's influence. Waiting for my brother's rescue. Bound by the rules of the king. Cowed by my mother's rage.

I have always done what was expected of me. Now it is time to raise my expectations.

Father comes in, puffed up with talk of war and rebellion in the north. He can prove his loyalty and strength by suppressing the Catholics in Yorkshire. Those who say they are on a Pilgrimage of Grace to protect their faith against our newly Protestant king.

Hal appears to be accompanying him under sufferance.

"Mary," Father says, "it's time to go back to court."

"There's nothing for me there." I hold my key tightly in my heart.

"There may be more for you there than you think." Father drinks down to the dregs of wine from a goblet handed to him as he walked in the door. He looks at me over the rim. "You're pretty enough."

"Pretty enough for what?"

"To entice the king."

Mother's words come back to me. *He will prostitute his only daughter.*

Hal won't even look at me. His eyes are so hollow, he is lost in them.

"He is a *father* to me," I say, "and no one can condone incest. Not even the head of the Church of England."

"If you were never married, he's not your father-in-law. He will either impregnate Jane Seymour or grow tired of her. And you will be there when he does."

"No."

The air seems to leave the room, replaced by a frigidity that is palpable against my skin.

"No?" Father's voice is calm and dry, backed by menace.

"I was married. Legally and lawfully."

"Not if the king says otherwise."

"I follow the laws of my heart."

"Your heart means nothing."

I stand firm. He cannot see the trembling of my knees beneath my skirts. He does not feel the bite of tears behind my eyes.

"The king says I was never married, but he is wrong. I remained faithful to my husband for three years. I listened to him, supported him. Through all the changes. I waited while his father decided whether he was worthy of inheritance. I sat with him through his illness and attended his funeral, which is more than his father ever did for him."

Father raises his hand so quickly I don't have time to flinch, but just before it connects with my cheek, Hal catches it. He and Father stare at each other for a long moment.

"I am your *father*, Mary," Father growls, pulling his hand from Hal's grip, but dropping it to his side. "The church tells you to honor and obey me. Me. Not some ghost of a child."

"He wasn't a child."

"You are a Howard."

"I am a FitzRoy. I am a duchess. I do not need a man to give me my identity, Father. I have my own."

"I will find another Howard girl," he says resentfully. "I will put *her* on the throne."

As if the throne ever really mattered.

"Then I pity her."

Father looks as if he's ready to make good on his threat to beat my head against the wall, but Hal steps between us, his back to me.

"Let me speak to Mary alone, Father."

"Talk some sense into her, Surrey."

Hal turns and takes me by the arm, his grip so tense it almost lifts me from the ground as we walk. I can do nothing but keep pace.

I can't even look at him.

When we are through the door and into the next chamber, he lets go and turns on me.

"Hal—" I start to say, but he puts a hand on each of my shoulders and sends me up against the wall with a quick, forceful shove.

"Do what he says, Mary. Or tell him the truth."

I can't control my body. My hands lift and fall back down again. My gaze won't settle. Not on the tapestries, or the wall, or the door, or the window, or my brother, who has never been angry enough to hurt me.

I take a deep breath. And steady my gaze upon his face.

It is not contorted with anger, but with grief.

"I can't," I tell him.

"Fitz is *gone*, Mary." He puts his hands on my shoulders again and I brace myself for another push. When he lowers his forehead to my shoulder, the weight of his sigh almost crushes me.

"He's gone," Hal whispers. "When are you going to give up this foolish quest to serve love instead of survival?"

"He's here." I put my palm on Hal's heart. "I am not on a foolish quest. I don't choose love *or* survival. I choose both."

"The only way to survive is to follow the king's wishes."

"The only way to survive is to follow my own heart," I reply. And I feel not only Fitz with me as my spirits lift, but Madge and Margaret as well. "I don't want to belong to the king," I continue. "Or be subject to Mother's will or Father's ambition."

I pause and wait for him to look me in the eye. "I don't want to be your responsibility."

"You're my sister."

"But you are not my keeper. I am not the daughter of a duke. Or the sister of an earl." My voice catches, and I hold on to him to steady myself. "I am no longer the wife of a duke."

I take a deep breath, remembering Queen Anne. I repeat what I told my father. "I am a duchess. If I am going to survive, I will not be owned. I refuse to be a doll or a piece of furniture, moved around and used and displayed but never cared for. I want to be me."

"You will have to stand up to the king." Hal sounds unsure.

"I'm ready." I lift my chin. "If he is. I will tell him exactly what I think of him and how he treats people."

Hal pales. "You once told me I am his subject and therefore subject to his command."

"Which is exactly why I want to retain my own sovereignty. I want to be able to rule myself."

"As much as you can."

"Father wants me to 'entice the king.'" I shudder. "I have no wish to get too close to that throne. By claiming my title—my freedom—I can maintain my distance from him."

"Then I shall do my best to help you do so." He turns very serious, and then very sad, all at once, in the space of a breath. "You will be a better duchess than our mother ever was. And possibly a better duchess than I will be a duke."

"The king just needs to know that we may be his subjects, but we are not all his pawns."

Hal bows his head and looks at his hands, clenched together in front of him.

"Perhaps we need to remember that, too," he says.

I put a hand on his. "The best way to do that is not to treat others as such," I tell him. He looks up at me. "Go back to

Frances after this, Hal. Bring her here and live with her. Get to know her. She's not just a thing, here to bear the future dukes of Norfolk—she's a person, too."

"She's not Madge."

"Fitz didn't fit all the things on my list, Hal. He couldn't dance. He wasn't a poet. But he had his own grace and rhythm. He had his own words. Love isn't making others into the people we imagine they should be. It's about letting people be themselves."

Hal looks at me sadly. "So I should allow you to do this. Defy Father. Defy the king."

"It's not up to you to allow me. That's the point."

He smiles. "Fitz said he couldn't control you."

"No, Hal. He said he *wouldn't*. There's a difference."

Silence surrounds us like a cloud of dust. Hal digs his toe into the rushes on the floor, stirring them as if they hold the secrets of the future.

"I'll talk to Father," he says finally.

"You don't have to."

"Just because you're not my *responsibility* doesn't mean I don't want to help."

He looks up at me and grins.

I throw my arms around him and pull him close. He is broad and solid and warm.

"I wish I were as strong as you," he says. "I wish I could defy the king and Father and not go north on this bloody crusade."

"Then do your best to make it as bloodless as possible," I tell him.

510

"You would have made a great queen."

I smile at him. "I never wanted to be."

"Which is exactly what would have made you great."

He looks at the door, behind which silence reigns. Father, waiting for a verdict. Waiting for my acquiescence. I have always taken his side. Done as he wishes.

"It may take time," Hal says. "For Father to agree. For us to convince the king."

I breathe in the emptiness of Kenninghall.

"I can wait."

"I will come back. And I will bring Frances with me."

"I'd like to get to know her."

Hal smiles. "So would I."

They leave early in the morning, before the sleepy autumn sun rises over gorse newly brittle with frost. I rise with them and wish them safe passage. The courtyard echoes with the cold loneliness beneath the blanket of the Milky Way. We are too far from water to hear or see the kingfisher, but just as the sun begins to rise, I hear the clear, joyous song of a wren. Simple. Common. Ordinary.

But not nothing.

Hal stops in the thick stone arch of the doorway and squints into the brightening northern sky.

"I have something for you," he says, putting his hands on my shoulders like Father used to.

He reaches into the leather bag that hangs from his shoulder and pulls out a book. It is plain, soft leather, and is not stamped with gold. But the pages are all blank.

"This is for your words," he says, and grins. "For *your* words, Mary."

"You are the poet," I tell him.

"It doesn't have to be poetry. It can be lists or memories or songs. There are no rules. They just have to be yours."

The leather feels warm, like it's alive.

"Thank you."

Hal strides away and swings himself onto his horse. Father doesn't look at me, but Hal waves—and winks—before they leave, accompanied by the drumbeats of hooves and the scattered stars of stones.

I climb the stairs to my room and sit at my desk at the open window. I dip my quill into the ink and open my book to the middle.

There are no rules.

Love.

Survival.

Truth.

Freedom.

I write my words. I savor them. They have taste and strength and memory and rhythm.

Outside my window, I see the morning star. And I watch it until it winks out in the light of dawn.

The world of the Tudor court is teeming with fascinating characters—executed queens and cunning politicians, rakish poets and scheming maids of honor. Why would I choose to write about the relatively obscure Mary FitzRoy? Why not Margaret Douglas (who got into trouble with the king more than once) or even Henry's own daughter Mary?

Two things about the Duchess of Richmond captured my imagination. The first was that she married at the age of fourteen. I remember being that age so well—I could hardly piece myself together in my own life, much less try to match it with someone else's. What could it possibly have been like to marry the king's son at fourteen?

The second reason Mary drew my attention was because she never remarried and spent years fighting to keep her jointure (the money owed to a widow by her husband's family) and title. In a world where women rarely spoke up for themselves and where a woman's worth was tied to her husband and children, this was decidedly unusual—even eccentric—behavior. What could have driven her to do this? Pride? Ambition? Obstinacy? Or did she really love Henry FitzRoy?

Marriage to Thomas Seymour was suggested more than once, and Mary stoutly refused. She finally was granted some of the Richmond lands by the king in 1539—almost three years after her husband's death. These lands provided a small income, but more importantly showed recognition of her status as a dowager duchess. She attended the reception of Henry's fourth wife, Anne of Cleves, when she arrived in England, but didn't return to court until Henry married Catherine Howard. When Cat fell, Mary returned to Kenninghall along with the disgraced Margaret Douglas, who was eventually welcomed back to court during Catherine Parr's tenure as queen. Mary continued to live quietly at her family home while the Howard family imploded around her. She outlived her husband, her brother, her father, and her father-in-law, but the exact date and even the year of her death went undocumented, though she was alluded to as the "late" Duchess of Richmond in January 1556.

Because Mary is a relatively unknown character, it was difficult to track her exact movements and actions during the time between her wedding and her widowhood. This makes the job of writing *fiction* both easier and harder to do. It is only a guess that Mary was at court for the entire three years Anne was consort. We know she carried Anne's train during her first mass as queen and Elizabeth's chrisom cloth at her christening. The historical record shows that Mary gave a gift of a gold tablet to the king in January 1534 and that she attended FitzRoy's funeral in 1536. But the sixteenth-century historian John Foxe said that Mary was "one of the chief and principal of [Anne's] waiting maids about her," which I took as license to keep my characters together as much as possible. And to make them friends.

We have very good evidence that Mary FitzRoy was closely associated with Margaret Douglas and Madge Shelton as well. The book Fitz gives to Mary is based on an actual volume called the Devonshire Manuscript, in which Mary, Madge, and Margaret wrote their own poetry and copied poems by Thomas Wyatt, Henry Howard, and Chaucer, among others. It is believed that the book was passed back and forth between Margaret and her husband, Thomas Howard, while they were imprisoned in the Tower. Though handwriting analysis shows that nineteen different people wrote in the Devonshire Manuscript, we know that it was originally owned by Mary because her initials are stamped on the cover. Some of the poems I quote in *Brazen* I've pulled directly from the manuscript itself, though I cite them out of the order in which they were probably written. I invented the lists and added a few notes to bring resonance to the story. I hope the actual authors of the manuscript forgive me my poetic license. They were the sixteenth-century equivalent of a literary "brat pack," and I love them for it.

Madge (or Mary) Shelton is one of the primary hands in the Devonshire Manuscript, writing adapted poems from Chaucer and even some verse that she probably composed herself. Historians disagree about who Madge actually was. Some say there were two Shelton sisters, Margaret and Mary. Some say they were the same person. I have done my best to create a believable composite and have kept her name as Madge to avoid undue confusion.

The gossipmongers claimed that Madge had an affair with Henry VIII sometime during 1535. Some historians suggest that her cousin, Anne Boleyn, put her up to it—to keep the affair in the family, so to speak. I chose not to believe that particular historical tidbit, based on Anne's wrathful outrage when she discovered Madge's "idle poesies" in a prayer book. It is not known who the "four young ladies" were who attended Anne at her trial and execution, but I thought my rendering of Madge would be a believable choice for one of them.

Margaret Douglas is an enigmatic historical character. She was obviously bright and well educated, having grown up in part with Henry's daughter Mary (who became Mary I). I think she must also have been a hopeless romantic, based on her disastrous affair with Mary FitzRoy's half uncle Thomas. It is not known if they were actually married or merely betrothed, but both were considered legally binding and in this instance, treasonous. Margaret again tested the king's wrath in 1541 when she engaged in a second affair with yet another Howard, Charles—brother to queen Catherine Howard. Her actions during Elizabeth's reign also imply that she had ambitions to the throne—if not for herself, then for her children. Ultimately, these were fulfilled when her grandson became James I.

Henry Howard is considered one of the great poets of Henry VIII's reign—along with Thomas Wyatt. Many accounts also describe him as hotheaded and ambitious, both traits that plagued the Howards for several generations. Henry Howard believed in the rigorous system of nobility and disparaged the "new men" of Henry VIII's reign, going so far as to come to blows with Edward Seymour (Jane's older brother), narrowly avoiding the punishment of having his right hand removed. But his behavior and his outspokenness made the king mistrustful of him (perhaps as mistrustful as Hal was of the king) and ultimately brought about his downfall. Ten years after the events in this book, Henry Howard reinstated the heraldic insignia of his executed grandfather, the Duke of Buckingham, to his own coat of arms. The king saw this as pretension to the throne and Hal was executed for treason in January of 1547. His father, the duke, would have been executed as well had the king not died first.

I wanted to write the story of a brother and sister who survived the trauma of their parents' animosity and forged a friendship because of it. But I can't avoid the fact that Hal endeavored to get his sister to marry Thomas Seymour in 1546 or that Mary spoke as a witness against her brother during his trial. Somewhere in those ten intervening years, their friendship was lost, but that is another story.

Hal's name has been linked to Madge's, though it's possible to believe that some of his greatest romantic poems were written for his wife, Frances.

In early 1531, Henry Howard and Henry FitzRoy both moved to Windsor Castle, where their friendship was established. The historical record only ever refers to them by full name or title, but I thought it reasonable to believe they gave each other nicknames. They traveled together to France in 1532 and lived with the sons of the French king before returning to England for Fitz's wedding. Hal went into deep mourning after Fitz's death, so I believe they had a profound, lifelong friendship. I've read that Fitz's marriage changed their relationship, but because neither boy was allowed to live with his wife, I can't imagine it changed that tremendously.

Some accounts call Fitz "haughty" and others insist that he "hated" Anne Boleyn. From the age of six, he was raised as the highest-ranking peer in the country after the king—believing in his own ability and given the means to make decisions as a landed magnate from a very young age. Perhaps this is why he didn't show the shyness and deference expected of one so young. But he was also raised in the company of tutors and grooms, not with his mother or father or half-siblings. His mother, once the king's mistress, married a knight and never returned to court. For his part, Henry VIII bestowed honors and responsibilities on his son, kept him close, and claimed to love him. But the king left London while Fitz was dying and didn't attend his paltry funeral. To me it seems that Henry's affections were always fickle at best.

FitzRoy did benefit from Anne Boleyn's death—receiving Baynard's Castle is one example—but despite the claims of some historians, I found no evidence that he wished her demise or believed she tried to poison him. Witnesses at Anne's execution said that the Duke of Richmond and the Duke of Suffolk were the only people who remained standing when Anne knelt before the headsman. I hope my reasons for keeping Fitz upright are believable.

I was unable to find any historical accounts of interactions between Fitz and Mary after their wedding day. They weren't allowed to cohabit because the king believed that sexual intercourse could be dangerously unhealthy before physical maturity (it was said that Katherine of Aragon's brother died from consummating his marriage at a young age). No allowances were made for Fitz and Mary to get to know each other, so could they have fallen in love? The Tudor court was a crowded and turbulent place, and Fitz was often there for holidays and matters of state, so I don't believe that they never saw each other or communicated. And anyone who has experienced a successful long-distance relationship can tell you that love truly does conquer all. There is no evidence that they fell in love—but then again, there is no evidence to the contrary.

I owe a huge debt of gratitude to Dr. Beverley A. Murphy's *Bastard Prince: Henry VIII's Lost Son*, the only book I could find devoted entirely to Fitz's life and legacy. For information on the Howard family, I relied heavily on Jessie Childs's *Henry VIII's Last Victim: The Life and Times of Henry Howard, Earl of Surrey* and *House of Treason* by Robert Hutchinson. My knowledge of Henry, Anne, and the Tudor court comes from the works of Julia Fox, Antonia Fraser, Kelly Hart, Claire Ridgway, David Starkey, Alison Weir, Josephine Wilkinson, and countless others.

I am forever indebted to Natalie Greuninger, coauthor with

Sarah Morris of *In the Footsteps of Anne Boleyn*, for answering my questions about the summer progress of 1535. According to her extensive research, the interaction between Mary and her mother probably didn't happen that summer (despite one historian's claim that it did), but I chose to keep that scene there because it's an integral part of the novel.

History and story are two different things and the challenge of combining the two is one of the reasons I love writing historical fiction. Facts are the skeleton without which the body of the novel can't stand up. Fiction is the muscle and breath. *Brazen* is based on historical accounts of real people and their actual lives, intensified through the invented narrative, and colored by my own romantic sensibilities. It is my hope that, by putting them all together and dressing them up in details and dialogue, I have created believable, relatable characters who will live with you, dear reader, as powerfully as they have lived with me, despite their imperfections. And perhaps inspire you to discover more.

We cannot possibly know who these people really were or anything about their private thoughts, emotions, and interactions. What I love best about writing historical fiction is that I can put myself in those uncomfortable shoes and imagine.

Acknowledgments

This book would not be in your hands today without the care, dedication, and support of the following people.

My editor, Kendra Levin, read my first draft that was almost, but not quite, entirely *un*like a book and handed it back to me to try again with these words of encouragement: "You can do it." Thank you, Kendra, for not letting me throw it away and start over.

My agent, Catherine Drayton, believed I had three books about Henry VIII's court in me, and continued to do so, even when I wasn't so sure.

The combined forces of Penguin Young Readers Group and InkWell Management make me feel I have the best team an author could wish for behind my book. All my thanks to Ken Wright, Joanna Cardenas, Marisa Russell, Lindsay Boggs, Kate Renner, Theresa Evangelista, Janet Pascal, Kathryn Hinds, Lisa Vanterpool, Charlie Olsen, Nathaniel Jacks, Lyndsey Blessing, and many, many more.

The YA Muses alternately fortified and consoled me

throughout the writing of this book. Thank you Bret Ballou, Donna Cooner, Veronica Rossi, and Talia Vance for your insight, your inspiration, and your love of good story. But especially, thank you for your friendship. Many thanks as well to A. C. Gaughen for reading early and to J. Anderson Coats for advising well.

My family has championed my creative endeavors from the very beginning. I wouldn't be the person I am today without Judy Longshore, my mother, who is (thankfully) nothing like Mary's. My dad's love of great literature reinforced my love of words, and my sister Martha's dedication to the craft prompted me to try fiction. I am a writer because of them.

Gary, Freddie, and Charlie—thank you for accepting late dinners, dusty windowsills, and my absences from ski trips. Thank you even *more* for celebrating the journey from first page to launch party with me, every step of the way.

And, as always, thank *you*, for reading.